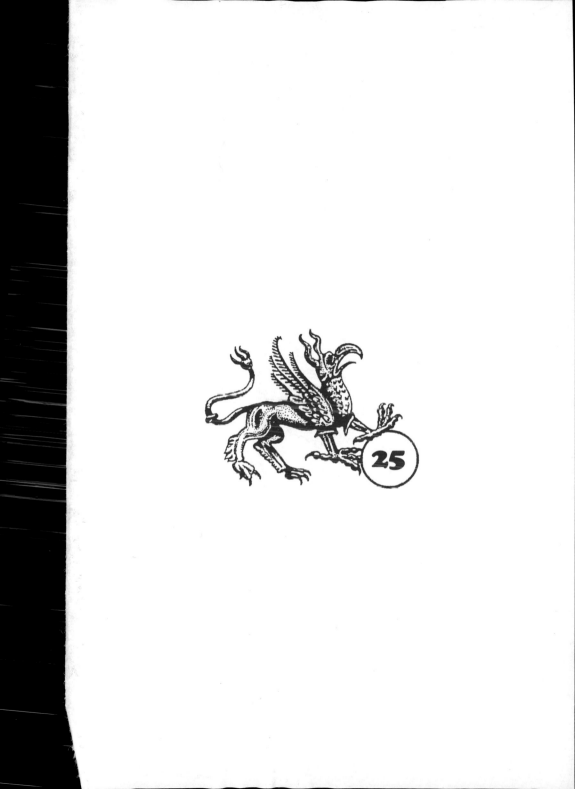

25

The Silver GRYPHON

EDITED BY
GARY TURNER & MARTY HALPERN

GOLDEN GRYPHON PRESS • 2003

Copyright © 2003 by Gary Turner

LIBRARY OF CONGRESS CATALOGING–IN–PUBLICATION DATA:
The silver gryphon / edited by Gary Turner & Marty Halpern. — 1st ed.
    p.   cm.
    ISBN 1-930846-15-0 (alk. paper)
       1. Science fiction, American.   2. Fantasy fiction, American.
    I. Turner, Gary, 1955–   II. Halpern, Marty, 1950–
PS648.S3 S46 2003
813'.087608—dc21   2002015481

First Edition.

Contents

For Jim . . .

Foreword:
The Silver Anniversary

*W*HAT MAKES A STORY ENGAGING AND ENTER-
taining? Is it one in which the author has portrayed a
vibrant and living storyline, one that the reader can visualize and
experience? Or perhaps the delight that arises from the work of a
clever wordsmith, who dazzles and bemuses with his style? Or
cutting humor, where sacred perceptions are torn asunder and
revealed to be mere fluff? Or fabulous fantasy or hard science
fiction or mystery or horror. . . .

Humor and pathos, optimism and despair, light and dark. This
anthology, unlike most, does not have a common theme or particular focus—rather, in celebration of Golden Gryphon Press's
twenty-fifth book, we asked those who contributed to the first
twenty-four to write a story that best defines _them_ as a writer. Given
such a criterion, it hardly surprises that the stories are varied.

Some authors do not limit themselves to a single genre, but
jump genres at whim, and with a wild and wacky flair. Only Neal
Barrett, Jr., could pen a story about disguised alien bovines picking
up astrophysicists at a science convention, and have the central
scientist named Bobby Lee Spock. Richard A. Lupoff satirizes the
Election of 2000, and in his world, George W. Bush and Al Gore
are named co-presidents, which results in the fall of American
democracy.

Many of these writers have established niches from which they
provide thought-provoking and horrifying tales. Michael Bishop,

using his customary skill at literary SF, spins the sad and violent tale of a dead Vietnam War soldier who won't die, and continues to lay down his undead life to help others. Raconteur Joe R. Lansdale tells of a man who lives high on the hog as a firehouse dog, but then has to deal with doggie retirement—what do people do with old, unwanted dogs?

Alternate history and fantasy have been, and will without a doubt continue to be, fertile sources of fiction. Historian R. Garcia y Robertson takes us on an adventure involving a Scottish mercenary fighting for the Tartars, a blonde, blue-eyed English harem girl carrying the Persian heir, vessels that fly, rocs, lust, love—were only History 101 so enjoyable to read! Warren Rochelle stays closer to home: his Twentieth Century portrays a struggle between magical and normal humans, with the associated hate, fear, and distrust of anyone being "different."

Since H. G. Wells wrote *The Time Machine* in 1895, time travel stories have become a subgenre in their own right. Philosopher George Zebrowski plumbs the question of what to do when you are thrust two and a half years into the past. How do you reclaim your life as you wait for the past to catch up with the present? Geoffrey A. Landis mixes humor with geekyness, with greed, and with murder to highlight a peril of time travel between parallel universes.

In what can only be called a weird tale, Andy Duncan combines his literary style with folk tales and his Southern heritage in a very strange tale of courtship on a ghost trolley car.

While Walt Disney, in his 1964 World's Fair exposition, thought that "It's a great big beautiful tomorrow," many see the future as not automatically being better, and to some the future is downright bleak. In the future Earth of James Patrick Kelly, a homeless misfit attempts her best to stem the disppearance of humankind—one psychopathic woman against aliens and almost everyone else. The future envisioned by Richard Paul Russo is even bleaker, with the distance between the "haves" and "have-nots" impossibly wide— the planet is poisoned, poverty abounds, and the rich don't care as long as they have what they want and can do as they wish. Yet there are sparks of hope embedded in both of these stories.

Imperfections in the human condition are also explored. Lucius Shepard uses the setting of a Central American river barge to demonstrate how each man—and woman—is an island. Howard Waldrop takes a movie star, seen by millions in the cinema yet now forgotten and alone in a nursing home, and walks us though his last decade of life.

All stories are autobiographical to some extent, and one of the most difficult stories to write is of a loved one dying, the aftermath and associated memories. Jeffrey Ford tackles this in such a manner that it seems to be familiar to anyone who has walked this path, but with his own special flair.

Who else could pen a tale of a woman escaping the rat race, finding peace, and then having to fight again to retain what she has, better than Kristine Kathryn Rusch?

Paul Di Filippo frequently explores the conflict between men and women and technology, and in this story he pits the inventor of the next-generation worldwide web against a vindictive classmate. Will the latter destroy all that the former created, and bring civilization crashing down as well?

In the "worlds" that these writers have previously created, some are revisited herein. Kage Baker gives us another "Company" adventure, with two familiar immortal cyborgs on a mission to gold-rush-era San Francisco. Kevin J. Anderson returns to the timeline prospectors of Alternitech, with an agent who has a personal vendetta that she pursues through multiple alternate universes. Robert Reed treats us to another *Marrow* adventure, involving one of the oldest living beings in the universe.

Sometimes the future, while basically good, can be sad and strange, as Ian Watson dramatizes in his tale of elder lovers, one of whom is banished to an alternate universe for their "crime" of fornication over forty.

For those of you familiar with some of these writers' other works, we hope that reading their stories in this anthology will be like reacquainting yourself with some old friends—sitting and chatting for a spell on the porch on a nice spring afternoon, or in the drawing room as you serve herbal tea, or merlot, or even break out a few cold ones. For others we hope these stories engender new friendships and acquaintances—writers you'll want to remain in touch with, to look up again and again.

Whether by old friends or new friends, these tales provide readers with a smorgasbord of writing styles, tone, and content—a diverse spectrum of short fiction from some of today's best writers. Read their stories, and hear their voices.

Gary Turner and Marty Halpern
September 2002

The Silver Gryphon

Mother

James Patrick Kelly

*L*ES TRIED NOT TO THINK ABOUT THE BABY. IT'D
had that swampy cough for two days. Now its temperature was
a hundred and one. Was that dangerous? She didn't know. Probably
have to bring it to a doctor or maybe even a hospital. She stood on
the pedals as her cart climbed Deacon Parker Road. Wouldn't be
cheap. Have to temp somewhere to pay the bill. Cost her two days,
maybe more, assuming anyone would hire a boo living out of a cart.

She hated the baby.

Birth Control said the baby's name was Gary. The people there
were as smothery as the ones on the moon. Should be her decision
what to call the son of a bitch. When she had a baby of her own,
Gary was the last thing she'd name it. Les would call her baby
Shithead Bleeding Motherfucker before she'd call it Gary. She
knew it was probably points off that she couldn't think of the baby
by its Birth Control name. When she took it to the doctor, she'd
have to say its name. A mother didn't call her kid *it* or *the baby*. She
wondered whether the judge at Birth Control would certify her fit
to mother, if he knew how Les felt about this one. She'd heard they
could see inside your head now. Just like the aliens.

Gary, she thought. Poor little Gary.

If she didn't pedal fast enough, little flying bugs would catch up
to her cart. Didn't bite, but they buzzed into her eyes and up her
nose. She kept batting at them. They were too stupid to live. On the

3

moon, there weren't any bugs. But she wasn't on the moon and she could never go back. Not knowing what she knew. The aliens had seen to that. Les's mother had figured them out, so they killed her and sent Les down. Made her mad, how stupid people were. The aliens said they had come to help but what they really wanted was to wipe everyone out. First they'd take care of the women. Which meant the end of men too—not that Les would miss *them* much. Then the only ones left would be little girly snips that owed everything to the fucking aliens.

That's why she had to have babies of her own. Lots of babies.

It was a warm spring afternoon. If she pulled the cowling down to protect herself from the little flying bugs, she'd start to sweat from pedaling. Sky was blue and cloudless and she could see the moon making a mocking silver face at her. Knees didn't hurt that much. Getting used to Earth gravity. She pedaled faster because she was still in Massachusetts. Would be at least another week before she got to Portsmouth, especially if she stopped for the baby. She'd be twenty-eight years old on May third. Maybe her father, who she had never met, would give her a birthday present. *Hi, Dad, I'm home from the moon. How about a nice fat cash card?* She wouldn't have to get married then. She could stay on the road. Nobody understood that Les loved her cart. She *liked* being a boo.

If she were married, they'd let her have her babies. Sure, just like that. Bonus points for being married. But they couldn't make her sleep with men if she didn't want to. Or with aliens. Or dogs. No, they couldn't make her live in a house or work a steady job or bathe more than once a week, like a good fucking clem. It was the law. If she wanted to have a baby or two or ten, all she had to do was take care of the Birth Control's baby. Finish their training to be certified a mother. She had it all figured out.

Except she could hear the baby crying. Hear it even though it was in the trunk, smothered in the sleeping bag. "Shut up," she muttered, and squeezed the handlebars until her knuckles went white. For ten more minutes she pedaled, telling herself the little asshole would go back to sleep. Its yelping made her squirrelly. Finally she pulled over and opened the trunk.

She took a bottle of formula from the crate and shook it warm. For a while, she couldn't find the mouth peripheral. It had slid under her mother's ashes. She untangled the cord and snapped it to the baby's I/O port. Opened the baby.

For a change it stopped crying when it saw her. The fever hadn't gone up, but it hadn't gone down either. Its eyes were shiny. Of course, the poop light was blinking. She had to change the little shitbag before she could feed it. She peeled a nap off the roll, leaned out of the trunk and stuffed it into the mouth. The baby gave Les a noseful of stink as the mouth processed the nap. Shreds drifted to the ground like paper snow. The pix showed babyshit that was runny and as green as pond scum.

Les stretched a nipple onto the bottle of formula and stuck the bottle into the mouth. The mouth began to process it with moist sucking sounds. She held it there, leaning out of the trunk while the spent formula dribbled onto the ground. Most parents fed their Birth Control babies over a sink or a toilet. Mother Nature was Les's toilet.

Back in February, Les had tried holding a cup under the mouth to catch the formula. She knew mouths put some nastiness into spent formula to keep parents from reusing it. A Birth Control baby was supposed to cost what a real baby cost. Part of the training. But Les had been too hungry to care. Stuff tasted like liquid cardboard, but that was all right. Filled her belly and she'd kept it down. But it gave her nightmares for two days. The kind of nightmare where the aliens cut her nipples off and her jaw clenched so hard that her teeth shattered as she slid down razor wire. Ever since, she had let what came out of the mouth alone. She had *that* all figured out.

Formula was about two dollars for a two hundred milliliter self-warming bottle. The baby needed three a day. Four if it spat out the oatmeal, which it better never do again. That was forty-two dollars a week. Naps were another eleven a week. She had just eighty-seven dollars and thirty-seven cents left on her cash card. She was at least a week away from Portsmouth. *Her* lunch would be a belly full of water and a slice of spun cheese.

When the baby finished eating, Les unplugged the mouth. The baby just lolled on its screen, paying no attention to her. They said she was supposed to talk to it, but she never knew what to say.

"Go back to sleep, you dumb little fuck."

The pallid glow of the pix reminded her of when she hid in her mother's locker on the moon for two days. Took that long for the squirrelly men to find her. Took a minute for them to tell her about the accident.

She put everything away and climbed back onto the saddle of the cart. Changed the pix in the center of the steering wheel from Newsmelt to a map. Les loved maps. They made her feel free, like she had escaped all the traps the aliens had set. Sometimes at night she would fall into her maps for hours, plotting a course for the next day. So many ways to go. She would've lived in a map if she could. She wouldn't have minded being flat. According to the map genie, she was at the intersection of Deacon Parker Road and Route 10, which GPSed to N 42º 40.587' W 72º 29.761'. If she didn't cross the Connecticut River soon, she'd have to go all the way north to Brattleboro, Vermont. She had told the genie to keep her off big roads and away from cities, but that was too long a detour. So she figured she had to cross in Northfield. There were two choices, the Route 10 Bridge and the Schell Bridge. She decided on the Schell Bridge because it was named after someone. To get to it, she'd have to pass by places called Hell's Kitchen and Satan's Kingdom. Maybe the devil would invite her to dinner.

A stupid little flying bug bounced off her ear.

She never saw the devil. Talked to a cop instead. Came up behind her on Route 142 and just hung on her tail at fifteen kilometers an hour. Maybe they didn't see many boos this far up in Massachusetts. Clems thought all boos were the same. Thought they were lazy. Thought they were anti-social. A lot of clems thought they were crazy. But Les wasn't breaking any laws, that she knew of. The gun wasn't loaded. Didn't even own ammunition.

She pulled over, slid off the saddle and walked back toward the cop. He let his car roll to a stop. It was an electric, quiet as the inside of Mom's locker. Said *Town of Mount Hermon, Massachusetts* on the door.

Cop lowered his window. "Afternoon, ma'am."

"You know, I used to live on the moon." Les pointed. "The Mare Nubium, right at the bottom of its mouth there."

"That so?" Cop didn't look.

"We don't have police on the moon. You know why?"

Cop waited.

"Because the moon kills you her own self if you break her rules."

Cop squinted at her, as if she had feathers coming out of her nose.

"Look," she said, "I've got everything I own in this cart. Take us about ten minutes to sort through. You want to see?"

Cop shrugged. "No, ma'am."

Les was relieved. Didn't want to be explaining about the baby. "Then why are you following me?"

"You're one of those boos we heard of. You don't live anywhere."

I'm a boo, she thought, and you're the mudhugging clem of all time. "I'm traveling," she said. "That's all."

"Where are you going, ma'am?"

"I'm hoping for Northfield tonight. Portsmouth, New Hampshire, eventually. I've got family there."

"That so?" Cop made no move to write her up. Acted as if he had nothing better to do than sit and chat with her. Only he didn't have anything to say.

"Tell you what I'm going to do." She pictured the map. "In a little while, I take a right onto River Road. I follow it to the end and take a left onto Caldwell. I stay on Caldwell until I get to East Northfield Road, where I take a right. In two tenths of a mile, I cross over the Schell Bridge and I'm in Northfield. That make any sense to you?"

Cop leaned out the window. "I bet you met some of those aliens up there on the moon."

"A few." She couldn't tell what he wanted her to say.

"Did they stink?"

The little bugs had caught up to her again. "They had a smell, sure." She waved some toward the cop.

"I've heard that." He pulled his head back into the car like a turtle. "Do you ever get lonely," cop said, "pedaling that thing around all by yourself?"

Les got that crinkle in the back of her neck but she didn't want to do anything bad. Not until she was finished with the baby. "No." She gave him a shriveled little laugh. "I'm my own company."

"I'll bet you are." Cop wasn't smiling.

"It's getting buggy," she said. "I've got to go."

Les didn't look back and he didn't stop her. She swung onto the saddle and started pedaling the cart. Spotted him in the rearview. He was following as if nothing had happened. Probably had his hand between his legs. Les turned herself into a pedaling machine. There was steel in her calves. She flew down the road. Nothing like homicidal rage to add a couple of klicks an hour. They always did this to her, men and their fucking attitudes. Fucking her over. She imagined the sound he'd make if she shoved his stumpy fingers between her spokes. His dick too, only there probably wasn't enough of it. All of a sudden he's interested in aliens? He didn't know shit. Les knew. They were smart, the aliens, and clems like the cop were bone stupid. Sure, the aliens shared some of their tech and said all the right things about not fucking with human culture. Except they were offering immortality to pre-pubescent girls only. So when all the little girls got snipped, there would be no one to have the babies. How hard was that to figure out?

Cop bastard followed her all the way to the river.

There were no women doctors in Northfield. At least, none that the search genie could find. Twelve hundred clems living in a town that could house three thousand. No wonder there weren't any woman doctors. Les was in no mood to put herself in another man's power. Except the goddamn baby's temperature was one hundred and two. She zoomed on his face. Spots on both cheeks, the color of the blush on a peach.

Les was still a little sticky from escaping the cop. Parked in front of the clinic on Woodruff Way. The doctor had better be in or something bad was going to happen. Maybe she'd go looking for ammunition. It was a sweet gun she'd hidden next to the wheel well. Ruger AP11 recoil-operated autoloader. Les hurled the sleeping bag against the side of the cart and grabbed the baby.

The receptionist made her wait almost an hour because she wouldn't fill out any forms. Les told her she didn't have to. It was the law. All Les had to do was give her ID number. She had it all figured out. The receptionist didn't like that. But then Les didn't like the receptionist. A cancer of a woman with an overdose of blonde hair. Les didn't like having an ID number, either. What she wanted was to be invisible to the computers. The aliens could see into computers. She had figured that one out too. In other countries, ordinary folks could be invisible. Brazil. Egypt. Uzbekistan. But not in the U S of A. Here you had to be a boo. Live on the road. Fine with Les.

Finally they let her into Dr. Majumdar's office. On one wall was a collection of old clocks. They tocked and clacked and whirred insults at her. She was wasting his time, they said. They said he had diplomas from the University of Wisconsin and the Medical School of Tufts University. Busy man. A clem, with a house and a dishwasher and a queen-sized bed. A pixwall behind his desk showed a home vid of India. A little girl wandered through empty stone temples. Whoever had shot her had a nervous eye. Not a book in the room.

"Ms. Isenberg?" The doctor blanked his desktop pix. Rose from his chair. "What seems to be the problem?" He was too busy to come around the desk to greet her.

It wasn't that Les didn't like the way men looked. She did. She just didn't want to sleep with them. This one was easy on the eye. Slim with the posture of an oak. Good cheek bones, handsome in a dark way. Bonus points for the gray hair at the temples. She'd need sperm someday, when they certified her to have her babies. Sure, she'd probably get it from the Birth Control bank. But Doctor Majumdar had genes worth passing on. She pictured herself milking the spew out of him like a cow. She smiled, catching it in a silver cup.

"It's poor little Gary." She leaned across the desk to hand him the baby. "He's sick."

He took the baby from her but did not open it. There was a greasy smudge on the outside. Chain oil, maybe. Maybe a fried chicken fingerprint. Dr. Majumdar pulled a tissue from the desk drawer and wiped the baby's cover. Dropped the tissue into a woven basket. Les should have scrubbed the baby down with ammonia. Points off for sure. He sat, opened the baby and studied its welcome screen.

Les sat opposite him but couldn't keep still. Her nerves sang.

He tapped through various screens, checking records, making choices. Even though his face showed nothing, he was judging her. She could tell. The baby coughed up green mud. Then it cried. The tinny speakers made its voice squeak like a bad bearing.

"Ms. Isenberg," said Dr. Majumdar, "the minimum daily requirements for a child this age are at least three meals of at least four hundred calories . . ."

"He ate this morning, a whole bowl of oatmeal."

". . . with an interval of not more than eight hours between daytime meals."

"We've been on the road all day."

"Even so. And he needs liquids at regular intervals. Juice. Milk. Water. Does he cry a lot?"

"Some." Wasn't about to tell him that it cried all the time.

He glanced up at her. "Why have you applied for a parenting permit, Ms. Isenberg?"

"Nobody's having babies anymore." The nerves in her leg were singing so loud that her left foot tapped. "I'm different."

"It won't be easy in your circumstances."

"Nothing is easy."

"I'm sure." He nodded and closed the baby. "I've entered a record of this visit in your baby's medical file. Gary has Selkirk's pneumonia. Don't worry, we've caught it in plenty of time. You may have heard that Selkirk's is caused by a new strain of pneumococcus that is resistant to first generation antibiotics. I'm afraid I have to prescribe Difloxcid, one of the oxazolidinones."

"You're afraid?"

"It's very expensive, about thirty dollars a day. He'll need to take it for ten days."

Three hundred dollars. Two days lost, maybe more. The back of her neck crinkled. She pictured herself bashing Dr. Majumdar's head in with the baby. That would get her on Newsmelt for sure. Top of the welcome screen. He knew she didn't have insurance. Insurance puts you into too many databases. Wasn't fair. The baby was a fucking simulation. Nothing about it was real, except the time and money it took her to take care of it. Then she realized what was happening. The aliens were trying to blow her up. If she didn't pass the training then Birth Control would never let her have babies of her own. The cop and the doctor and the Birth Control judge, all of them in on it. She had it all figured out now.

"Can I ask you a question, Doctor?"

He frowned. "I suppose."

"What do you think the aliens are up to?"

"I beg your pardon?"

"Take that little girl there." She pointed at the pix behind the desk. "Let me guess—your daughter is an only child?"

He turned around to look at the pix. The little girl was sitting at the edge of a swimming pool, dangling her legs in the water. Behind her was a white building with a lot of domed towers.

"Ms. Isenberg. . . ."

"Suppose she wants to get snipped? Live forever? What if all the little girls in the world get snipped?"

"It won't happen." He faced her again. "Less than five percent choose. . . ."

"It was two percent back when I was on the moon. And the birth rate was way down even before the aliens came."

He raised his hand to stop her. "You were on the moon?"

She leaned across the desk and slapped his hand down. "It's poison, Doctor. The aliens slipped us slow-acting poison." She saw the shadow of fear on his face. She could tell he was not often afraid.

"You can't be from the moon. They quarantined everyone after the accident at Tycho."

"Wasn't an accident. They've been waving lies at you, Doctor, and you're too scared to do anything but salute. The aliens know exactly what kind of humans they want living here and it isn't us. Which is why you need me. I just want to bring life into the world. So why make me jump through hoops?"

"It's hard work being a parent." He made a twitchy pass over the desktop and all the pixes lit up. "Not everyone can do it."

"So my babies will be a little wild. At least, I'm going to have babies. Your little girlie snip sure as hell isn't." She guessed he had called for help. That was all right. Slapping him had smoothed the crinkle. Nothing bad had to happen just yet. Dr. Majumdar wasn't the real problem. He was just a man. "Be careful, Doctor." Les tucked the baby under her arm. "Your clocks are ticking."

She shot out of her chair, deliberately knocking it over. He jumped. That made her feel better about the visit. It helped that clems were scared of her. She kicked the overturned chair out of her way. All right, then. She'd get the baby its fucking medicine. Finish her training and then make the Birth Control judge let her have her babies. Girl babies, who would grow up to hate aliens and men. What her mother would have wanted.

Les was the only one now who could save the world. She had it all figured out.

Present from the Past
Jeffrey Ford

*A*FTER MY MOTHER FINALLY QUIT DRINKING, SHE entered a brief epoch of peace in her life. Gone were the paranoia, the accusations, the belittlements, the bitter rage of judgment, her look of fear. For twenty years, nearly every day a lost weekend, she had been possessed by the dark amber ghast of gag-sweet Taylor Cream Sherry. Living with her back then had been like living with a vampire whose bite drained but never conferred immortality. What eventually brought about my mother's unexpected exorcism, I can now only guess, but when she resurfaced she was quiet and ready to laugh. She was watching and listening.

One day in the spring of her new self, she asked my father to go out and buy lumber for her. She told him that she wanted to do some woodcarving. My father purchased the planks she requested along with chisels, rasps, and other necessary tools. She set about her task, working on the picnic table beneath the cherry tree in the backyard, laying the boards flat and gouging away at them. She told me over the phone that her subject was the stations of the cross —Christ's fourteen-part journey to his own crucifixion. Each of the planks would bear a different tableau.

"When I'm done with the boards, I'm going to have your father make them into a bus stop with a little bench attached inside," she said.

"Yeah, what are you going to do with it?" I asked.

"Sit in it and drink my coffee in the evening."

A couple months later, Lynn and the boys and I drove to Long Island to visit my parents. From the kitchen window, I saw the bus stop assembled beneath the giant oak at the back of their property. That evening, while Lynn took our two boys for a walk down to the school field, I sat with my mother inside her creation. We smoked and drank coffee, while my father sat facing us in a lawn chair.

The small structure had a slanted roof and its walls were painted the same redwood stain as the picnic table. The hand-carved figures that lined the inside were more crudely rendered than I had imagined they would be. They had no faces, just ovals, dug out and painted white. However, the folds of Christ's flowing garments were more detailed, as was the grain of the cross and the Roman soldiers' armor and helmets. In painting them, she had used very bright colors—a sunflower yellow, a neon lime, a sky blue, a hot pink— that appeared resilient against the redwood stain. I had to duck slightly to fit inside and the bench only held room for two.

"You should have been here the day we finished putting that thing together," said my father. "A couple of weekends ago. It was a bright day but the wind was really blowing strong. Branches had come down in town. I finished nailing the roof and stood it upright in the middle of the yard. We stepped back to look at it, and then this enormous gust of wind came, got under it, and lifted it about ten feet in the air." My father's eyes were wide behind his glasses and he was looking up, his hands apart in front of him, one holding his coffee, one a cigarette. "Remarkable," he said.

My mother was staring off toward the clothesline, smiling. "It landed here," she said.

"Right on this spot," said my father, "so I anchored it down."

"That's some wind," I said.

"It was a strong wind," said my father. He took a drag of his cigarette. "This thing's nothing but a big wooden envelope and the wood is pretty thin. But it still surprised the shit out of me when it happened."

Throughout the remainder of that spring, my mother wrote a film script on the old manual typewriter in the room she called her office at the back of the house. In June she bought a used super eight camera and some film. By early July she had learned how to use it and began casting parts for her production.

"It's about a bullfighter," she said. She had called to see if I wanted a part. "It's got a Spanish theme."

I was unable to make the trip the Saturday of the filming, and didn't get to see the finished movie until September. We all sat in the dining room on the braided rug, facing a movie screen my father had found at the curb somewhere on trash day. Of course, with a super eight camera, it was a silent film, but it was in color. For background music, my mother had taken the opening from the Motown hit, "I Heard It Through the Grapevine," and somehow created an endless audio tape loop of just those jaunty, slightly sinister, first bars.

The film was shot right outside the backdoor of my parents' house on Pine Avenue, and nearly every family member had a part. Along the wall where the garage extends was hung a hand-painted backdrop of hundreds of faces in a stadium. Onto the screen walked Don Diego, portrayed by my portly brother, Jim, wearing a matador's costume, and a penciled-in twirl of a mustache. Each of my brothers-in-law played one end of the bull. After the great Don Diego slew the bull in the arena, he went to the fortuneteller—my grandmother Nan—first glimpsed through a blazing fire. She wore a mantilla, a black shawl, and laughed wickedly. As she read the tarot deck for the bullfighter, she turned over the Death card. This caused Don Diego to lose all self-confidence, and a rival matador —my sister, Dolores, dressed as a man—vied for the top spot in the arena and for the heart of Don Diego's mistress—my sister-in-law Patty—who clenched a long stemmed rose between her teeth. My brother's oldest boy played a wooden religious statue that came to life; my father did a turn on the dance floor, wearing a gaucho hat with dingle balls; the bull returned from the dead for one last duel in the sun; and Don Diego regained his courage in the melodramatically protracted moment of his death just before the film ran out and slapped the projector.

That evening, on the very barbecue grill that held the fortuneteller's veiling flame, my father created his meal of a hundred meats—sausage, steak, chicken, hamburgers, and hot dogs. We all stood, sons and daughters, spouses and grandchildren, in the cool September twilight, holding grease-smeared paper plates, assiduously chewing. Nan sat in her lawn swing, smiling, a glass of wine tipped in her wobbly grip, threatening to spill. My mother played "Until the Real Thing Comes Along" on her guitar, and my father told stories about Kentucky, when he was stationed at Fort Knox, especially of the crumbling mansion that held a library.

"The place had four floors of bookshelves," he said. "And the librarians were these two ancient sisters, both blind, who knew where every book was."

*   *   *

One night after dinner, in November of the same year, my mother had a difficult time catching her breath. She admitted to my father that she had been experiencing this for a month or two but never quite as bad. He immediately called an ambulance. At the hospital, they found a tumor like a tree branch growing up out of her lungs and blocking her breathing passage. After the operation to remove the tumor, my mother began a series of chemotherapy and radiation treatments. The prognosis, however, was terminal. The initial treatments almost killed her, but she managed to survive them and fight back for nearly two years.

Throughout this new struggle, I visited as often as I could, but I lived quite a distance away in South Jersey. Lynn and I both worked and we had the two young boys to look after. So I called my mother on the phone every day. Sometimes she didn't have much to say while other days we would talk for over an hour. She often told me how tired she was and, occasionally, she told me her dreams, unsettling scenarios like the one in which she walked with the spirits up Pine Avenue in the rain. For a brief period of a couple months, she fumed with anger, trying to pick fights with me over everything from politics to parenting. I managed to "keep it light," as my father would say.

During one of her frequent stays in the hospital, well after it was obvious she wasn't going to make it, I went to visit her. It was the middle of the day, and the ward she was on was particularly quiet. She was sleeping when I arrived, so I sat down in the chair next to her bed. For a long time I stared out the window, watching the breeze in the leaves of the birches that lined the bay road. At the end of that road was a dock where I had once kept my clam boat years earlier before I had gone to college. I remembered the flats across the bay, the red-winged blackbirds, the cattails, and the sun on the water.

When I turned back toward her, she was awake and quietly watching me. She looked very frail. I took her hand, and she told me, "I'm not afraid of dying." We sat in silence for quite a while. Then I told her everything I could remember about my days clamming on the Great South Bay. She lay there smiling as I recounted those days, all of it except the one about the Trentino boy who had drowned scratch-raking in the flats. He had stepped in a sink hole, gotten stuck, and then the weather had turned bad, the tide had come up. My mother knew that story, though, and when I returned to silence I wondered if, by my omission, I had caused her to remember it.

"You remind me of your father right now," she said.

There were instances when I found myself detached from my emotions and could almost marvel at the complexity of her disease, as if the slow-motion process of her organic demise might offer some elusive truth. This variety of cancer, *oat cell* it was called, usually spreads from the lungs to the brain. The brain feels nothing, though. Once in the brain the cancer does its work painlessly, methodically shutting down the controls of the vital organs. What amazed me was that it was slow to scramble my mother's reasoning. She was conscious and could talk with some effort for quite a while.

My father brought her home, and set up her hospital bed in the back room that had once been her office, where she wrote her stories and painted. She was weak and slept much of the time, but when awake, propped up on pillows and accepting visitors, she exuded a strange contentment. She laughed a good deal and her silence drew honesty from those who came to see her. But the aperture of clarity through which she communicated closed a little more each week, until finally she could only take your hand and mumble a phrase that made no sense. One afternoon while I was there she told my sister, Mary, "You're bad at bad," and on the same occasion told us both, "Chihuahua Mexicawa."

I saw much more of my brother and sisters during those months than I had in a long time. Jim was a year older than me, married, and had three boys. He lived only two towns away from our parents and was very close to our father, having followed in his footsteps and become a machinist. Our lives had gone in different directions, and we hadn't talked much in the intervening years since I had left home. While we conducted ourselves on the deathwatch, he spoke a great deal, in a very self-assured manner. These utterances were more proclamations than any attempt to really communicate.

One evening when we were all at the house during one of our weekend visits, I reached a point where the sight of my mother wasting away in that hospital bed, in that cramped room, became too much for me. I stepped away and went outside, around the corner of the house, to stand by the chimney where the irises always grew in spring. It was dark enough, so I took out a joint and lit up as surreptitiously as possible. Just as I was taking a big hit, Jim came around the corner. He saw me and stopped.

He shook his head and quietly laughed. "What the hell are you doing?"

"Catching a buzz."

Then he stepped up close to me, put his arm around my shoulders and hugged me. It lasted only seconds, and I was startled.

"I'm going out for some beer," he said. "Let's sit at the picnic table tonight and have a few."

"Okay," I said, and we did. In the shadow of the cherry tree, moonlight slipping through, he interweaved tales of personal success at work with smatterings of his fundamentalist, Lutheran dogma. His church had him interpreting the Book of Nehemiah. I nodded and drank one beer after another.

My sister Mary was six years younger than me. She was also married and had two boys. They lived in Brooklyn. Mary could easily cry or laugh at any situation, and often did both within a matter of seconds of one another. Both she and her husband, Jerry, were artists. He was into realism, creating very fine line drawings, whereas Mary made huge abstract paintings, amalgamations of colors that had never before met each other on canvas. Later, Mary's creativity changed direction; the last time I visited their place, setting all about the house were writhing amorphous lumps formed from chicken wire and papier-mâché.

My father was so dedicated to the care of our mother that he wouldn't eat properly. When we would take him out to the local diner to make him eat, Jerry would stay at the house with the children—seven boys in all. He and the boys would play a game of wiffle ball in the backyard. If the boys got too raucous, Jerry would threaten, "If you don't calm down, I'm going to have to have another beer." By the time we'd arrive home from dinner, Jerry would be crocked, passed out in the living room lounger, and the boys would be sitting quietly watching a video.

In the last days before my father was forced to return my mother to the hospital, a mouse was spotted in the house, and I had a dream that it was a projection of my mother's will, allowing her buried consciousness to dart around and overhear our conversations. One night I felt the little creature run the entire length of my body while I was sleeping on the couch. When I told Mary about my theory, she neither laughed nor cried, but merely nodded her head, and in earnest said, "Maybe."

Dolores, the youngest of us siblings, was only a few years out of college, but she faced this family challenge head-on, and, more than any of us save my father, actually took on the grim practical tasks. She dealt with the nurses who came to the house in the morning and at night, making sure they turned our mother often to prevent bedsores. When the nurses failed to show, Dolores took over their tasks. She was always there, always making sure mother had her drinking water. Perhaps it was Dolores's degree in philosophy that gave her the strength, though I doubt it.

One night, after the boys were bedded down in their sleeping bags and most of the grownups had also gone to bed, Dolores stood in the kitchen, hip propped against the drain board (my mother's drinking spot from the old days), and leaning toward me across the narrow room, whispered:

"This nurse down the hall with the white nail polish and frizzed hair," she said, pointing with her finger close to her body, "she's a trip. Real trailer trash, but a good nurse. She knows what she's doing." Dolores spoke so low then I had to turn my head to catch her words. "She told me she saw *the coffee*."

"She saw 'the coffee'?" I said.

"She told me that when people are very close to dying, they vomit up this brown grainy stuff that is known as *the coffee*. She said she saw the coffee."

"Man," I said, and grimaced.

Dolores just shook her head, which then gave way to silent laughter. Her attempts to suppress her giddiness made me laugh too. When we regained control, she wiped her eyes and said, in a normal voice, "Could you possibly . . . ?"—one of my mother's stock phrases from the days of wine and no roses.

Below the surface of this forced, seemingly amiable family reunion, there were secret tensions swirling. Mary's husband got fed up with my brother's decrees. When Jerry refused to carry out an order, Jim quietly offered to break his arm. Dolores was mad at Lynn, my wife, because, as a nurse, Lynn felt the care that my mother was receiving in the hometown hospital wasn't the best. But no one wanted to hear it, especially Dolores, who had been working hard with what she had been handed. There were recriminations, judgements, clashes of style, that lived only until they were voiced to my father, who crushed them one by one, like ants in the kitchen, with a single word, "Bullshit." I, of course, laid low, my specialty perfected in childhood.

After she had returned to the hospital for the last time, my mother soon fell into a coma that lasted for weeks. When I would think of her there, I always envisioned her room filled with bright sunlight and a view of the trees along the bay road. I never thought of her in the dark. To preserve this image, I never went to visit her during those final days. Dolores would call and complain to me that the nurses ignored our mother. "I'm afraid she'll die of thirst," she said. But I continued to make up excuses why I couldn't drive up to Long Island. No matter what I told him, my father always said, "Don't worry. I'll tell you if anything changes."

Then, in the middle of a particularly beautiful spring day, I took the boys out in the double stroller and we walked through the park and around the lakes. On our journey, passing through a small tract of woods, we came across a woman in a long raincoat and a man with a bow, and a quiver of arrows strapped to his back. He looked a little like actor Charles Bronson. A target with a bull's-eye was set up against a tree no more than four feet from where the guy stood. While the woman smoked a cigarette and watched, he shot arrows into the target. I said hello to them as we passed, and the man turned and made an angry face at us. The weirdness of the people and the presence of the bow frightened me, and I picked up the pace.

"What the hell was that all about?" I said, once we were out of the woods.

"Robin Hood," said Jack, the older of my two boys.

After we arrived back home and I was letting us into the house, the phone started ringing. It was Jim. "Mom's gone," he said, and in that instant I pictured inside her mind, like a chamber in a deep cave, a candle going out.

On the afternoon of the wake, the immediate family was allowed a private viewing time before the other mourners arrived. My brother and sisters and I went with my father. We stepped into the parlor, made claustrophobic with floral wallpaper and dim light. I could only look at my mother for a second or two at a time. She was a frowning void in a turquoise dress to me. My father turned away and stepped to the back of the parlor. Facing the wall, he let out a sound I have never heard another person make. It was something like the cry of an animal. His shoulders moved slightly then and I could tell he was weeping. I wanted to approach him, but I could almost see an impenetrable aura around him that I knew I would never be able to pass through. A few minutes later, he dried his eyes and turned around to face the casket once again.

Through the entirety of my mother's illness, I had never seen him show any emotion. Whatever needed to be done, he did. He always kept it light with my mother and never complained. Trying to continue at his job, taking care of her at home, the sleepless hours the nights the nurses failed to come, had physically depleted him. He forgot to eat regularly and grew so thin we started referring to him as Gandhi. There were times when he was absolutely zombielike, stooped over, haggard, but he continued to function.

When my brother and I were very young, our father took us out in the bay in an aluminum rowboat. He rowed way out by Captree Bridge. The water started to get choppy and the wavelets were slapping the prow, sending water onto us. Only minutes passed before the wind started to howl and the weather really got nasty. He manned the oars—I can see the sleeves of his shirt rolled up over his biceps—and started rowing like a machine. There was never a look of concern on his face, even though we were heading against the wind. He held a lit cigarette in the corner of his mouth, and rowed steadily with great determination until we reached the shore three quarters of an hour later. When we landed, he said, "That was a little hairy." No matter how many short jabs to the head he had sustained through my mother's illness, no matter how many body shots or pummelings in the corner, I knew that relentless oarsman was at work inside of him, pulling for shore.

At the beginning of my mother's final decline, before any of us could know just how bad it was going to get, I found my father, at two in the morning, down in the basement—his new smoking lounge. Sitting in his bathrobe on a folding chair, beneath a bare bulb, surrounded by the chaos of Christmas decorations, Mary's abstract paintings, mildewed books, and broken furniture, he pointed upstairs with the two fingers holding the burning cigarette and said to me, "I have to do this right."

Throughout the days of the wake, strange occurrences were reported in my parents' house. The television would turn itself on and off at will. This I personally witnessed, sitting in the living room around midnight drinking a beer. I was nowhere near the remote, and the television came on with a loud buzz to show a field of static snow. There were also strange knocking sounds in the walls, phone calls with only silence at the other end of the line, sudden cold breezes that blew down the hall, and photographs brushed off the wall.

These uncanny events brought to mind a student, an older Chinese woman, I had taught in a composition course a few years earlier. Mrs. Fan had written a paper about her husband's death, in which she revealed why it was important, on each night for a month following the death of a loved one, to stand at the table when dinner was served and moan loudly for a few minutes. This kept the loved one's spirit centered, so as it awaited passage to the next world, the spirit would not become confused and wander off on this earth to become a frustrated ghost.

The wake made me realize that it was so named because all one wanted to do was *wake* from it. Nothing I had ever experienced had been so much like a dream. Minutes became hours in the presence of the dead. In that flower-choked room, like a vault at the bottom of the ocean, people I had not seen or thought of in years approached me from every direction. I shook hands with guys I had lost track of in junior high school, relatives from Oklahoma I had met once when I was three. I could have sworn some of the older folks I chatted with had died years back. Mary and I began calling the two viewings each day the matinee and the evening show.

The morning of the burial a small service was held at the funeral home before the casket was taken to the church for "critical mass," as my father called it. At the gathering in the wake parlor, people were invited to share remembrances of my mother, read poems, and so on. My father had asked me to read a Tennyson poem he and my mother were fond of, "Crossing the Bar." I agreed even though it didn't seem like a very good choice to me. As I took the little red book in my hands and stepped up in front of the mourners, I was thinking instead of lines from Tennyson's "In Memoriam"—"Time a maniac scattering dust, Life a fury slinging flame." I suddenly became aware that I was two lines into "Crossing the Bar." Something inside me gave way, like a flywheel snapping, and I put the book down on the table in front of me, excused myself, and left the room.

The next thing I knew I was outside the funeral home, and Lynn was standing in front of me. The day was cool and beautiful.

"I couldn't do it," I said.

"I know," she said, "that's okay. Do you feel all right?"

I lit a cigarette and shook my head. "Lame."

"Don't worry," she said, "your brother jumped up, grabbed the book, and finished the reading."

We both laughed, but I had a brief memory flash of being sick as a child, dizzy and weak, calling to my mother from the top of the stairs. I started to pass out, and the last thing I saw was Jim charging up the steps to catch me as I fell forward.

Lynn asked me if I wanted to go back inside.

I flicked the butt away. She took my hand and we returned to the parlor.

The church was a vaulting rib cage of wooden beams, frozen saints subtly winking in the stained-glass light of Christ's stations, dolorous music, and incense-laden intonations mixed with muffled groans and sniffles. In all, a blur to me, save for the heft of the casket on the way out to the hearse. It was only then, when we slid my mother's shiny canoe into the back of the car, that my senses returned.

Lynn and I and our two boys rode in a limo along with my parents' neighbors from across the street, Dan and Lily Curdmeyer. Old Dan was blotto, eyes red, hands quivering, reeking of VO; when the car took a sharp turn, he'd lean way over. Each time, Lily straightened him up nonchalantly, while recounting, in her brogue, stories of her adventures with Nan and my mother. The cemetery was some distance out on Long Island, the trip was slow, and the car hot as hell. Without warning, my son, Jack, puked on the black leather seat. Dan's eyes widened for a moment, he burped, and Lily merely said, "The poor darlin'."

A high chainlink fence surrounded the cemetery. A few hundred yards down the road from the entrance stood an abandoned strip joint whose sign still clearly read *Inn of a Thousand Eyes*. The grounds of the cemetery were vast green lawns rolling into the distance, here and there sprouting rows of gravestones. The procession of cars wound through the place and then stopped a quarter of a mile inside the gate at a spot where tree-lined roads intersected.

Cemetery employees—men and women dressed in black uniforms, like tuxedos—herded us about, and at one point had our entire immediate family, and then the extended family, line up. A woman carrying a huge armful of yellow roses walked down the line and distributed a flower to each of us. When our turn came, we were to walk forward and toss our flower onto the casket, which hovered, as if by magic, over the open grave.

Jack, who was feeling better then, held my hand as we moved up in line. He pulled at my jacket and I looked down. He was pointing at my flower.

"Pink," he said.

I nodded to him. He moved his arm slowly so that it scanned the other mourners in our line. Then I realized what he was trying to tell me. The rose I had been given, from the dozens that had been distributed, was the sole pink one.

"We win," he whispered.

I put my finger to my lips and gave his hand a squeeze.

Following the funeral, there was a party back at the house on Pine Avenue. I spent the afternoon hanging out in the backyard, eating potato salad, drinking beer, and talking to cousins I hadn't seen in years. Charlie, who was studying Chinese herbal medicine, told me how to make a hallucinogen from crushing and boiling locust shells. Dylan described to me the plot of Whitley Strieber's alien abduction book, *Communion*. My uncle Darrel, who sold insurance and worked part time as a Walt Whitman impersonator, raked his fingers through his great gray beard and lectured me about quitting smoking. Eventually, everybody but my sisters went home. My father had disappeared into his room and had fallen asleep fully clothed on the bed. Dolores offered to wake him before Lynn and I and the kids left for South Jersey, but I told her not to.

Two days later, I called my father to see how he was getting along. He told me that the night of the funeral he woke up with a splitting headache, so he went down into the basement to have a cigarette.

"There's a good idea," I said.

"It didn't help. The pain was really bad, I could hardly see. I went upstairs, found the Tylenol and took about half a bottle of them."

"Jeez."

"I know. It seemed like a good idea at the time," he said. "But it made me feel dizzy, so I decided to go out in my car and drive around with the window open."

"Hey, why not?" I said.

"I felt like I was going to pass out, so I pulled the car over and parked. *Then* I passed out."

"How long were you out for?"

"Not long, a couple of minutes maybe. I realized I hadn't eaten in about three days, so I drove to the all-night deli and bought a half pound of turkey breast."

"How was the driving?" I asked.

"A little wobbly."

"You're insane," I said.

"I ate that turkey like a sideshow geek," he said, "right in front of the store."

"Did anybody see you?"

"Who gives a shit? I stumbled to the car, got back in, and drove home."

"What then?"

"I went to bed and woke up the next morning."

"You're lucky," I said.

"Yeah, sure, but wait a second . . . By morning I was feeling fine. I made a pot of coffee and took a cup outside and sat on the back stoop. It was a nice day. I was just sitting there, thinking, when suddenly I heard this loud cracking sound. I thought maybe the neighbor behind us was working on his house. A few minutes passed, and then I heard it again, only louder. That time I saw some twigs and crap fall out of the oak tree in the back. I looked closer and noticed it was swaying slightly. And then there came a sound of splintering wood and a crack so loud I jumped! I watched that giant oak tree break nine-tenths of the way to its base and just fall. It crushed the tool shed, blasted apart your mother's bus stop thing, and sheared off one side of the cherry tree."

"What do you think happened? That's a lot of tree."

"Must have died," he said.

"What, termites?" I asked.

"No. I'm sure it died of a broken heart."

A few days later Dolores phoned in her report.

"Did you hear about the tree?" she asked.

"Yeah," I said.

"Dad went out and bought this set of four gas-powered chain saws. One of them will even cut through metal, and he said he could break out of a bank vault with it. He's busy taking the tree apart. That's all he does. He's cutting it up into these perfect little wheels, each about five inches in length and then cutting them each into four wedges."

"He told me it died of a broken heart," I told her.

"You should see the inside of it," she said. "I was there the other day. I'm telling you, it's riddled with the most amazing little tunnels. They run all throughout the tree. It's like lace inside. Like a work of art."

"What's that all about?" I asked.

"How do I know? At least he's got something to keep himself busy."

I called my father every couple days for a while, and then he told me not to call him so often because he didn't have that much to say. He promised me that we would talk every Sunday morning. During our weekly conversation about two months after the tree came down, he told me he had finished cutting it up. All he needed to do now was pull the root out of the ground, and he wanted me to come to Long Island the next weekend and help him if I could.

"That root's probably huge," I said. "How are we going to get it out of there?"

"It's been dead for a while. We'll dig down around it and cut the roots with the saws. If I can get to the taproot, we can get it out.

Your brother has a chain. Once the bole is free, we're going to hook it up to the back of his truck with the chain and pull it out."

"Sounds half-assed," I said. "I'm in."

When I arrived at his house early the next Saturday morning, I let myself in. He was sitting in the dining room with the lights out, drinking a cup of coffee and smoking a cigarette. All of the curtains and drapes were shut tight; the place needed to be vacuumed and dusted. The lawn mower was in pieces on the kitchen floor.

"Are you on the lam, or something?" I asked him, opening the living room drapes.

He gave a brief snort. "Welcome to my world."

"Are you ready to give me a hernia?" I asked him.

"Jim's out there already, digging. Go ahead out, I'll be right there."

My brother showed me the stacked wedges of tree, the neatly bundled branches. "He puts only a few yards of it out a week, so the trash guy doesn't get pissed."

"How's the root?" I asked.

He shook his head and rolled his eyes. "A ball buster. I told him we should just pour gasoline on the damn thing and burn it out. But no, we can't burn it. Why? Who the hell knows?"

My father came out then and we set to work. I hadn't worked that hard since the hay. It took all morning and well into the afternoon to move the huge tangled knot of wood enough to where my father could get under it with one of his saws. He climbed down into this trench we had dug around it, while Jim and I worked on the other side and pulled back on the loosened bole.

"Make sure you're cutting root and not leg," said Jim, just before my father got the saw going.

Through the saw's smoke and the flying wood chips, we saw my father's face. He had his teeth gritted and his eyes and hair were wild. It was like he was battling a monster. Jim and I looked at each other and started laughing so hard I could barely hold on.

The weight of the bole nearly pulled the bumper off my brother's truck, but we managed to get it out of the hole. It sat in the middle of the backyard like some weird brain sculpture, wooden tentacles twisting together and reaching out. As twilight started to come on, we pulled up some lawn chairs around it. Jim went inside and brought out a twelve-pack of beer. We were all dirty and sweating. My father smoked. I tried to think of something to say but couldn't. We all just sat there.

When it was barely light enough to see, my father leaned

forward in his chair. "What's that?" he said, and pointed at the gnarled behemoth.

"Where?" I said.

He got up and walked over to it. "There's something in here." Turning sideways, he stuck his arm into its tangled center. A few seconds passed while he worked to free whatever it was. Then he pulled out a small wrapped parcel. Walking back to where we sat, he handed it to Jim.

"What's that?" said my father.

Jim pulled away the outer layers of rotted string and tattered wax paper. When he had torn through to what lay beneath the wrappings, he said, "Holy shit, I think I know what this is." He sloughed off the brown dry husk, and tossed the object to me. As it landed in my lap, I could see that it was an old black-and-white composition book, a little damp, slightly mildewed, but still intact. I opened the cover and a water bug rolled out onto the ground. The writing on the first page, in the errant script of a child, had been rendered in pencil.

While my father and brother set to making a fire in the barbecue, I sat in the gathering dusk, scanning my own forgotten words. Then night rose up around me, and with its first exhalation, the blue lines, the red margin, the backwards b's, the dotless i's, all vanished and that book became a clear window into the past. Staring hard through the thin, impenetrable boundary, I saw myself as a spindle-limbed, crewcut boy in blue pajama bottoms, creeping quietly down the shadowed stairs after midnight. I passed my mother sleeping on the couch, past the open, empty bottle on the kitchen counter, whose scent was ipecac and cotton candy, and let myself out the backdoor into the star-filled, cricket heat. Under my arm was my journal, wrapped in wax paper and string, bound three times to protect the truth. I made my way over wet grass, beneath the lowering cherry tree, to the base of the oak where big roots erupted from underground and formed the opening of a small cave. There, I knelt, and thrust my words deep into the dark unknown.

The Door Gunner
Michael Bishop

SERGEANT PENNINGTON

D. G. REEKS OF DECAY. HE SWEATS FROM HIS greasy pores the belly-turning stench of a corpse in the sun.

I always cringe to see D. G. in the door of a Huey slipping down into the rotor-whipped elephant grass to yank me and my fellow Lurps out of the field, but I gulp back my disgust and didi like a sonuvabitch to reach the chopper and somersault inside. No Lurp has ever died on one of D. G.'s extractions, and sitting in his keen over-ripeness all the way back to camp has it all over lying facedown in a wedge of triple-canopy jungle giving off that stink yourself.

D. G. does his job. He, his crew chiefs, and the pilot he rides with—different chiefs at different times, but the same pilot—always get you home. The chiefs defer to his uncanny sense of which door *he* needs to man. Granted, you hate to see him empty-eyed and lean under an olive-drab helmet, LOVE BONG JOE stenciled on it in Day-Glo orange, cause he flat-out spooks you. But you also rejoice, for it means you and your buddies will live. You'll return to Indian Country—to befuddle Charlie or to lay him waste—and D. G., no matter who he partners with, is the only blessed chopper guard who *guarantees* that return. Your survival depends on the rank, ugly dude.

Our whirlybird dips and stitches over the sultry countryside.

27

Inside it, you can eyeball D. G. all you want. He never leaves his pocket, a skinny guy with his boots swallowing his legs like hungry mudcats from the muck of Perfume River. He seldom glances at the jittery fucks he's just helped save, but peers down with a knife-slit mouth at the seesawing earth, nursing a contempt that's hard to tell from boredom. The nametag on his fatigues says EXLEY.

What else would it say? SLAUGHTER? SKELTON? DeFUNK?

"Thanks, D. G.," says Carlson, our radioman. "God bless your stinkin hide." He has to yell—over the rotors, over the *pop-pop-pop* of gunfire—but everybody hears him, and D. G. grins a big grin. Rather than talk, he lets flow a storm of deadness from every cut and pore—so that even in our flying wind tunnel the stink of his mortality settles on us six Lurps and the Huey's crew chief like river fog.

"Christ!" Greene cries. "Cut us some slack."

"Instead of the cheese," Fearless says.

Without looking at us, D. G. takes off his helmet—what's he need a helmet for, anyway?—and sweeps his straw-colored bangs aside with a meaty gray hand. Above and to the left of his nose, a third eye appears. It doesn't engage us, either. It's a bullet hole, not an organ of sight, and it gives D. G. the wigged-out serenity of a Buddha on drugs. It also gives him . . . immunity.

The Huey banks. D. G.'s stench intensifies, then dissolves. I look at Carlson, Greene, Fearless, Stonecroft, and Rodriguez. D. G. has saved our asses. He'll keep us safe until we land at Camp Eagle and he wanders off to monitor incoming NVA rockets while the guys and I retreat to Lurpland to debrief and bend our elbows.

Once he's got you home, you probably won't see D. G. again until, out in the boonies, you sprawl in dire peril of extinction, his third eye triangulating and his aura of crazy defunctitude spinning its magic.

D. G. frets and calms us, disgusts and amazes us. Greene calls him a fucking zombie, often to his blank gray mug, but everyone else calls him D. G., as if saying any syllable of his name—of either Joe or Exley—would hoodoo the whole company. As if reminding him of his past as a breathing, eating, eliminating, lovemaking human animal would revoke the miracle of his inhuman hanging-on.

CORPORAL FEARING

D. G. and I had zilch in common but Georgia and the goddamned war. I mean, I prowl the Beyond with the Lurps, he flew door gun-

ner on the slicks *whop-whopping* in to tractor us out. I dig Cream
and Iron Butterfly, he got off on Johnny Cash. I'm a lapsed Savan-
nah-bred Catholic, he was a practicing Valdosta-reared Baptist. I
smash Carling cans—tin, not aluminum—on my forehead, he
stacked them up like pyramids. I have a nose like a champion blue-
tick, and he—nowadays, anyway—has the aroma of a goat and no
clue how high he stinks.

Don't get me wrong. D. G. pulls his weight as a gunner. But
back in camp—thank God, Shiva, or the Great Cosmic Maw—he
shuffles around like a hundred-year-old hobo. If he veers your way,
you cross the duckboard to keep from having to nod, much less
brush his shoulder.

Some numbnuts call him Lurch or Herman Munster, but not to
his face. That goes for me, too, Chet "Fearless" Fearing, top point
walker in the Lurp brotherhood, K-bar none. Close up, the death
smell pouring off D. G. floods your senses. You gag or retch. You
scurry away to keep from shaming yourself. On his last mission
before his DEROS (designated return from overseas), you see, the
poor guy took a sniper's bullet to the forehead and slumped backward into his Huey, dead.

By that time, over months of boonie-humping, I'd served a full
tour in the Lurps and reupped for another, and I'd *earned* my
nickname. (I can scarcely remember my cherry days when Old
Foul Dudes like Pennington and Roquemore called me Tremble-
und-Fearing: "Hey, Tremble-und-Fearing, get your ass over here!"
Nobody uses that handle for me anymore, though. Everybody
knows better.)

But when I saw D. G. walking in full combat gear the day after
Mr. Stickl flew him back to Camp Eagle dead, I nearly let go a stink
as putrid as any that'll ever blow from him. I clutched my belly and
bent over like a cooze with the cramps. I thought I'd hitchhiked the
black-light arrow around the bend. I even considered talking to the
RC chaplain, Captain Urbanec, about my spiritual condition.

But, hey, Camp Eagle teems with smells—diesel fuel burning
shit in rusty metal drums, damp canvas steaming, mangoes and
bananas rotting in a rocketed supply truck. And as a Lurp, you get
the deep tropical funk of a hootchful of dudes in sweat-soaked
cammies—crotch rot, jungle foot, camouflage grease, halazone-
tablet halitosis, spent fear, the lingering stench of our dreams in the
Cong-haunted Beyond.

But D. G. coming at you after buying it in Mr. Stickl's chopper
—damn, he's a marching one-man graveyard. And *I*—action-

baptized Fearless—I step into somebody's tent, cover my nose with a bandanna, and pray that he'll shuffle on by. He has the run—the gimpy walk—of the camp. Who's going to grab the sloppy scruff of his neck and tell him to park his zombie self in a body bag?

Yesterday, I decided that maybe *I* have to.

MIKE LAMONICA, UPI

I met the whacked-out door gunner *before* his apotheosis into a Vietnam legend. In my opinion, a bogus Vietnam legend.

No one hates the press like arrogant command-grade officers, who accuse you of sabotaging the war effort if you mention a short-age of *shower soap*. But enlisted men and field-grade officers, guys who'll pass you their flak jackets in a firefight, also like to test your mettle.

I fly into Phu Bai on a C–130 out of Cam Ranh Bay. An Afro-sporting sergeant named Stonecroft, a Lurp from J Company, tells me I need to write a story about Sp4. Joe Exley, a dead helicopter gunner still flying missions. Obviously, the flimflam-the-media machinery of the Army's biggest pranksters has cranked into high gear.

"I aint kidding," Stonecroft says, steering our jeep along a road between rice paddies. "D. G.'s dead but too dumb to lie down."

"You must think I just washed up on China Beach." (That too-dumb-to-lie-down line has kept the chuckleheads chuckling since World War II.)

"I aint bullshitting you. You should interview him. Buy me a cold one and I'll take you to him."

The smells of decaying fish and sun-warmed water mingle with the rank aromas drifting toward us from Camp Eagle.

About a year ago, I saw Exley in a chopper in action over a village suspected of harboring Viet Cong officers and supplies. He trained hellfire from his M–60 into the thatched roofs and along a road over which some peasants and half-naked children fled. Most of these people fell under his barrage. Then the Huey swung about so that Exley could chatter out the *coup de grâce*.

Afterward, in a plywood canteen near the helicopter pads, I talked to him. "It's hard to tell the good guys from the bad over here, but, still, how can you shoot women and kids?"

Exley took a sip of beer. "Easy—you just don't lead em so much." Then he told me about shoving VC collaborators out of choppers after they'd refused to cooperate with allied interrogators. In fact, in this way, he'd posted at least three or four dinks to their well-deserved demises. Later, I filed his "you-just-don't-lead-em-so-much" remark in an article about the aimless barbarism of some of our operations, without attributing it to Exley by name, and it gained notoriety throughout all the U. S. forces in Vietnam.

Now, Luther "Panther Eyes" Stonecroft wants me to sit down with Exley again, on the dubious assertion that he has kept on serving his country *as a dead man*. So I let Stonecroft deliver me to him. The product of shameless Grand Guignol makeup, Exley squats in a test-fire pit near the perimeter. We have to meet outside, Panther Eyes says, because only a few can abide D. G. indoors —usually just the Lurps whom he's flown in to rescue. (His stench, they understand, somehow prevents theirs.)

At twilight, I hunker five or six feet from Exley, hating myself for surrendering to all this hocus-pocus. He declines to brush away the flies landing on his face and arms. He ignores them, even when they crawl into his mouth or over his filmy eyes. Yoga, I tell myself. A mental discipline that will reward him big-time when his ruse suckers me and I declare it authentic in print—Exley's payback for my splashing around his offhand brag about his marksmanship.

"You hung your fatigues downwind from a dead water buffalo," I say. "You used a grease stick to get your skin that bloodless gray. You had a friend paint the hole on your forehead."

"Put your finger in it," Exley says. His voice has a breathy husk. If I moved a few feet off, I couldn't hear it. His invitation doesn't tempt me, though. It has accused me, subtly, of impiety.

Exley pushes his bangs aside. Flies lift and circle—heavily, as if sated. "Put your finger in it." I walk toward him, feeling tipsy, almost sick. I touch my finger to the edge of his "wound." Exley grunts, a wordless *Put your finger in the hole.* I obey.

"Deeper," he says.

I insert my finger to the second knuckle, reaching a psychic barrier that stops my probing. Exley's mismatched eyes make him look like a big human gecko. I pull my finger out and back away until I've escaped the pit and the awe-creating dispassion of his stare.

CAPTAIN DICKMAN

Shortly after noon, Sp4. Exley barges into my paymaster's Quonset. Corporal Leslie and my other brave clerk-typist call my name and retreat into the road. I stride to the inner doorway and cover my nose with my arm. I don't bolt, though. I ask D. G. what he wants. When he speaks, his voice seems to work in reverse from yours or mine. His sentences don't come out backwards, but he sucks in rather than expels air to make sounds. He tells me he wants his pay, and his voice vacuums some of the stink that he's brought in with him back into the loose sack of his body. I lower my arm and study him with honest-to-God perplexity.

I didn't like him before. I don't like him now. Usually, the least strac guys in the 101st show up as Lurps, but D. G. outdoes them all. From the start he dressed like a pirate. He got away with it because he could shoot and never quavered in the air. That's what Major Burke says, who swears D. G. had a banner in his hootch—DOOR GUNNERS DO IT FOR FUN—and target cutouts of Charlie on the wall. The cutouts had overlapping bullet holes in their hearts.

D. G. returned from his last official mission dead. Graves Registration wrote him up, Personnel recorded it, and his name went to MACV. Then the bastard got up and put himself back on duty. He's become Chief Warrant Officer Stickl's favorite door gunner. Stickl doesn't care who else you assign to him as a gunner, so long as the pair includes D. G. Stickl has ferried so many otherwise doomed Lurps home, dusting them off in the hairiest of circumstances, that you can't deny him his gunner of choice. So Major Burke, Stickl's CO, gave him D. G., and Stickl's rate of pickups without death or injury, always pretty good before, has soared.

I changed paperwork listing D. G. as KIA (Killed In Action) to indicate a mix-up in the field. Major Burke told me to send his pay to a southeast Georgia nursing facility caring for D. G.'s mother. She was a paraplegic, the only surviving member of a nasty car wreck during his training at Fort Benning. A dead man, even one still on duty, would surely rather keep his coma-ridden mama alive than squander his pay on useless food and drink, Major Burke said.

Lots of Lurps talk back. But so will jerks in other units if they've seen combat and lived to tell of it. If you're a desk jockey, only the threat of a stretch in Long Binh jail can keep their attitudes in check. But what incentive does a walking corpse have to respect you? He's already suffered worse than what you or the Code of Military Justice can mete out. A dead GI has shuffled off not only his mortal coil but the whole ever-shaking chain of command.

"D. G., what do you want your pay for?"

"For doing my duty," he says in his painful in-gulping way. "For saving the sorry asses of J Company cowboys over and over again."

"What do you plan to *do* with it? You don't eat, booze, read, or buy new clothes anymore."

Lizard-faced, he stares at me. "What would be the point?"

"Exactly. Don't you want your pay to keep going to your mother's life-support maintenance?"

D. G. says nothing.

"Nobody here's swindling you," I tell him. "You're dead, D. G., but Uncle Sam keeps paying you through me." I spread my arms, but hurriedly drop them. What if he stepped forward and tried to hug me?

D. G. looks at me as if he's just pushed a dead half-track across ten hectares of Indian Country. He sucks in air. He puts a moist gray hand on Corporal Leslie's desk and growls that he doesn't give a fuck what happens to his mama—she's luckier than some he knows of. If I can't see the justice in giving him all his pay, maybe my better angel—he *says* "better angel"—could spring for an allowance.

"Allowance? What do you mean, allowance?"

"Put your wallet on the desk." His hand makes a greasy print on the blotter when he pounds it, hard. "Now, Dickhead!"

"Dick*man*," I say. "*Captain* Dickman to you, soldier."

"Now!" He pounds harder.

I fear that a part of his hand—its heel or a finger—may fly off. I lay my wallet on the desk. He cracks it open and seizes some scrip, two twenty-dollar bills, and a creased photo of my wife Patti.

"Leave that," I say.

"No." The air conditioning feels really cold. "Make up what I've taken out of my next nursing-home payment."

"All right. But what if they try to evict your mother? What if—?"

"What if she *dies*?" D. G. says. "I don't know, Dickhead. I hope she can, all the goddamned way." And he leaves, thank God.

After that visit, I send him money every other week or so by Corporal Leslie, who eventually files a 1049 requesting transfer to a combat unit.

D. G.'s mother dies—all the way, I suppose—but I don't halt his payouts to her nursing home until its director notifies us. Morons who pun on my name warrant nothing but contempt. As for D. G., may he soon die his longed-for second death.

MISS BU'Ó'UM

He comes to Hue by himself, walking. Most GIs arrive together in a jeep, settle on a price with Madame Vinh, and then come in to pick their girls and take them to rooms. It's good money and sometimes fun. Lucky girls get GIs with quick triggers, guys who finish in three minutes, with no time to reload. They've got other bars to visit, fistfights to start, and maybe prawns to cook on the beach near Phu Bai. What we do for money, though, is better than scrubbing clothes on a rock.

No other girl wants this GI, no matter what he pays. He has a crooked face and a smell like he rolled on a dead dog cooking in the sun. He looks dead, or very tired, a sort of grown-up orphan. I feel sorry for him, but not sorry enough, at first, to lead his skinny body to my room.

Madame Vinh says to him, "If you bathe in sea and come back smelling better, my girls will like you more."

He laughs at her in his rough queer voice. He shows U. S. scrip and brand-new dollars.

Madame Vinh shakes her head, protecting every girl in the old brick building where we keep house. She does not budge on this. Some girls have *fathers* who would sell them faster than Madame Vinh.

"For one hour's talk and nothing more." The ugly GI waves his money.

Madame Vinh stands before him in a purple *ao dai*, like a brave mouse defying a hungry bear.

"I'll take him," I say. "For one hour's talk and nothing more."

To the other girls' great surprise, the skinny fella and I retreat to my chamber. I dip my handkerchief in perfume—just one drop—and hold it beside my nose, not like a mountain bandit but like a highbred Saigon lady in a smart café. There's no need to smell him up close, but no need to hurt his feelings, either. A well-trained courtesan has delicacy, which I learnt from watching overseas movies, *not* from listening to women talk at Madame Vinh's. So I wait.

Sitting on my bed, he doesn't make hungry eyes. He doesn't talk. Maybe he will grab me like a bread stick and crack my spine. I hold my handkerchief down to see him better and ask him what he likes to talk about.

When he still doesn't speak, I say, "Why do you *only* want to talk? Were you shot? Do you have bad combat stress?"

"Something like that."

I wait. I wait a scary, long time.

Finally he says, "There's an island where my government sends men who are too sick to return to the States—an island in the South China Sea. The soldiers who go there have Black Syphilis."

"Do *you* have this sickness?"

"No. I'm one very clean dead boy, Miss."

Black Syphilis—I can hardly say it—sounds bad, worse than leprosy or cancer or maybe even leprosy-and-cancer together.

"You ever heard of such a place?" His voice sounds like a cello, played deep and wrong in a bad Hollywood movie. My room feels empty of living air.

I say, "This island comes from GIs' heads, only. It does not exist. GIs like to scare other GIs. It's a game you play. But if you are VD-free—I don't sleep with sick fellas—stop worrying and have some fun." Maybe I should do it. This Exley man has no rhythm and very bad blues. He needs no-stress boom-boom with Miss Bu'ó'um. "My name," I say, "means butterfly." This news often leads to happy talk or cuddles. "My name comes from—"

He interrupts, "I need to find that island."

"Why?"

"It sounds like a cross between Tahiti and hell. The dead belong in hell."

"Not if they die sanctified," I say.

"My God, a Catholic gook B-girl. I didn't die sanctified. I died with blasphemy on my lips and my M–60 rockin n rollin. I *belong* in hell, hopefully one with a beach."

I think of how a great-uncle on my mother's side of our family drove to Saigon a few years ago, poured gasoline on his body, and set himself afire to protest the repressive Diems. "Maybe Vietnam is such a place."

Small lights jump in my visitor's eyes. "Minus the gooks and grunts, it'd be a helluva country, Vietnam. Scratch that—it'd be *paradise.*"

"You feeling better? You like some fun now?" I hear traffic in the streets, jeep doors slamming, and gruff American voices in the parlor.

He stands. "I'd only seed you with death. Six months from now, you'd bear one stillborn freak that looked like you and another just like me." His swallowing laughter makes another fat hole in my air.

I hold my perfumed handkerchief to my face. Standing, he rolls his back from one wall to the next, leaving damp spots on the plaster. He shows me his bullet hole. Says that he has wasted my time. Throws scrip and money on my cot, and, by accident, a picture of a pale woman with short yellow hair. Her hair clings to her face like wings. I pick up the photo.

"Your sweetheart?"

"My wife. I shouldn't be here. I'm breaking my vows."

"She'll forgive you," I say. " '*If you can't be with the one you love, love the one you're with.*' Wise GI saying."

Wise GI saying does its work. Match flares jump again in his eyes, and he comes to me almost dancing. I turn the photo over on my cot. I veil my mouth and nose with the handkerchief. He clutches my arms with his damp hands and touches his lips to my forehead. I feel faint, but not from the fancies of a woman in a love story by Stendhal or Tolstoy.

The door to my room bangs open. The GI named Chet Fearing, who thinks he loves me, barges in. "Take your filthy hands off her, D. G.!" He grabs Exley just as Exley grabbed me. Then he flings Exley into the hall. The door gunner shrugs his loose shoulders and stares back in with flat, dead eyes.

"You have no business entertaining this man," Corporal Chet says.

"You think I have no business 'entertaining' anyone but you. If I listen to you, I starve."

He shakes his head. "No time to jaw, Miss Bu'ó'um." He goes out and grabs the stink-heavy GI, to drive him back to Camp Eagle.

"Don't forget your wife." I stick the photo of the yellow-haired woman into the hall and shake it at him.

Corporal Chet takes it and examines it closely. "I didn't know you were married, D. G." He slips the picture into the other's shirt pocket. Then he tugs on this man's arm and pulls him to the stairs.

After they leave, I go down to an alley and throw up on the cobbles. I throw up a spoonful of black stuff, only. Then I dab my lips with my handkerchief and go back into the parlor to wait for evening.

CORPORAL FEARING

When I shove D. G. into the jeep with Cockroach Greene and Panther Eyes Stonecroft, they pile out. They say they'll catch a ride back to camp with somebody else. I call them pussies and make that jeep jump out of Hue like a racehorse from a starting gate. I came to see Miss Bu'ó'um, but finding D. G. with her, even if they were dressed and upright, gave me the kick in the pants I needed to tell D. G. to stop hanging on, to haul his carcass to Graves Registration and lie down in one of those aluminum coffins that MACV sends our dead home in. Then he'll rest in peace back in Valdosta with his mama and the other putrefying Exleys.

"Why would somebody still walking lie down in a coffin?" D. G. asks from the jeep's shotgun seat.

"I don't know. Maybe if you stopped walking and got in a box, you'd fuckin die the whole fuckin way."

D. G. thinks about this. "Maybe." He sings like Chuck Berry with laryngitis: *"I've got de walkin pneumonia and de boogie-woogie flu."*

We ride. D. G. takes this chick's photo out of his pocket and holds it up like Chaplain Urbanec elevating the host. I remember that, after one super-hairy extraction, D. G. told Mr. Stickl that he'd never had a steady girl, but he thought his singleness a blessing. Otherwise, he might not risk as much as he did, and a few more Lurps might die as he huddled in his pocket trying to save his manhood for the Girl Back Home. As a bachelor, though, he could pop out and blast away at the jungle like a who-gives-a-shit wild man.

Then it hits me. "You don't have a wife. You're a fuckin free agent. So *whose* picture is that, anyway?"

"Patti Dickman's." D. G. turns the photo so that I can see it. "Unhappy spouse of Captain Edgar Dickman."

"Unhappy? Why's that?"

"Cuz Edgar's dick, man, is so small he uses it for a phonograph needle."

This tickles me, but also puts me in an odd funk about the state of D. G.'s soul. He could go to hell. Why do I care? I don't even *believe* in hell, anymore. And, hey, maybe D. G. showed up at Madame Vinh's planning not just to diddle Miss Bu'ớm but to steal her affections. I almost stop the jeep and plug him with every bullet in the clip of my .45.

Would I go to hell for murdering—*intending* to murder—a GI that a VC sniper has already fatally shot? This question ignites my brain like a brand setting a hornet's nest afire.

"Watch what you're doing," D. G. says. "You want to kill us both?" He presses the photo of Patti Dickman to his forehead. It sticks like a decal.

Sunlight sparkles on the rice paddies on either side of the raised road. I get the jeep back into its center and tell D. G. I'm taking him to Chaplain Urbanec. The sky pilot will urge him to "let go and let God." He'll tell D. G. that his obnoxious hanging-on has to end, and end soon.

"Spoken like a real self-doubting papist," D. G. says.

Shots sing out across the paddies. A bullet *pings* off one fender. I duck, spin the wheel, and stomp the gas to keep D. G. and me in our current separate states of being and nonbeing. Maybe D. G. laughs. From reflex, he fires his own sidearm out into the gook-infested paddies . . .

CHAPLAIN URBANEC

A Lurp everybody else calls Fearless and I call Chester drags the door gunner, Exley, into the plywood building that Major Burke allotted us for religious services and God talk.

Six men are sitting with me in a semicircle discussing grace, the uselessness of REMFs (rear-echelon motherfuckers), and other issues. Three of them beat it even before Exley's corpse starts to befoul the already funky atmosphere. With fingers like sausages, he peels a small photograph from his forehead and sticks it in his pocket. Only Sergeant Pennington, Mike Lamonica, the helicopter pilot Mr. Stickl, and I remain to greet the newcomers, who don't apologize for interrupting us. Instead, Chester says I must give last rites to Exley and send him to Cam Ranh Bay for shipment home, in an aluminum box.

"I can't give extreme unction to a dead man, Chester. The Church reserves that sacrament for persons in imminent peril of dying."

Everyone looks at Exley. Candlelight pools in and ebbs from all the men's eye sockets and cheek hollows.

"I'll be right back," Pennington says, and ducks outside. Our cramped sanctuary fills with the smells of sweat and corruption. Pennington ducks back in and sets joss sticks burning in three glass ashtrays. Their counter-fragrance doesn't work well—often it's a veil for pot parties – but the men in my chapel don't seem to mind. The nearness of a sky pilot to a walking corpse fascinates them.

"Doesn't the Church call extreme unction the 'anointing of the sick'?" Chester asks me.

"Some priests may. I'm more comfortable with the old term."

"But 'anointing of the sick' aint wrong?"

"No."

"Well, have you ever seen anybody sicker than a walking dead man?"

"Good question," Lamonica says. "I'd bet his breath wouldn't fog a mirror. And two of the three Mortis Brothers have laid claim to his body."

"Mortis Brothers?" Chester says. "Who're they? Undertakers?"

Lamonica says he meant *algor, rigor,* and *livor mortis.* "You get algor mortis when body temp falls to that of your environment. Livor mortis occurs when blood pools in the extremities and internal organs."

Exley lifts his gangly arms like a horror-movie ghoul. "Rigor mortis aint got me." Lifting his arms proves the point. Against all physiological logic, his skeletal muscles have still not rigidified. "Yet," he adds. Pennington and Chester, both allegedly heroic Lurps, shrink back. I lower Exley's arms and walk him to a chair. "I'm an amphibian," he states, sitting down. "I patrol the border-land between life and death. More than half my body's in twilight."

Mr. Stickl says, "I'm an amphibian too, D. G."

Exley, who flies with Mr. Stickl more than with any other pilot, turns his head. "How you figure?" His eyes, which usually resemble smudged thumbprints, spark with curiosity.

"The Army appointed me a warrant officer. I fall somewhere between a noncom and a bona fide officer. No one calls me 'Lieu-tenant' or 'Major,' but no one calls me 'Corporal' or 'Sergeant,' either. Everyone calls me 'Mister.' I exist somewhere between the enlisted and the commissioned ranks. My borderland takes its boundaries from my technical specialty, flying helicopters."

Finally, Chester slaps his knee. "Wow. Who'd've ever figured that zombies and warrant officers have so much in common?"

Mr. Stickl flushes in the reddening candlelight. "I only meant that, in a real way, D. G. and I are neither one thing or the other. We hang between states that everyone else sees as normal. So the larger world views us as freaks."

"D. G.'s got it all over you in the freak department," Chester says.

Pennington, a Lurp team leader who I must keep reminding myself is only twenty-two, says, "Hey, D. G., can you like *commune* with the dead? I mean, get on a radio frequency with people who've bought it? Hear them break squelch from the *real* Beyond?"

Before Exley can answer Pennington's question, Chester asks him if two Lurps who went missing in action five months ago—Road-Dog and Fahey—escaped, or were captured, or died.

Exley closes his eyes, subjects their names to a disturbing psychic calculus, and quietly says, "Dead—they're both dead."

For a moment the door gunner floats before me as a meaty superimposition on the raw bones of my faith, a ghost of flesh atop a ghost of notions, a make-believe Christ in a makeshift chapel, but Pennington pierces my fugue by approaching him.

"And who's dead, D. G.?" he asks. "Who else besides Fahey and Road-Dog and Yielding and Portress?"

"Amelia Earhart," Exley replies. "I regret to inform you that Amelia Earhart is dead. And your mother, six years past. And Fear-less's kid brother Charles, a decade gone, and Mr. Lamonica's sister-in-law, chronic ileitis, last January, and both your folks, Chaplain, not to mention a favorite aunt, of cancer, and a pretty childhood cousin struck down at twelve by scarlet fever.

"Fearless isn't so fearless, really. He misses Chaz, and a nun, Sister Filomena, who told him he wasn't a wuss, despite what Cray O'Conley said. The sister struggled with recurrent stomach cysts and many surgeries—" Exley takes a startling in-sucking breath "—until she bought the window box because she couldn't afford the farm, all when Fearless was fourteen and just Chet to everyone who cared. Chet's nigh on to dead, too, along with—"

Chester says, "Shut up, you lousy zombie."

But Exley has already stopped. He interrupts himself with a gesture, pulling the photo that was plastered to his brow out of his pocket and lifting it into the candle scatter so that everyone can see it. "And Captain Dickman's wife, Patti," he says. "Dead. Dead at noon today, Topeka, Kansas, time. Shot in the face—this face—by her little boy, with a pistol from the headboard of her and Edgar's king-size bed. To sort of quote Petronius, 'She's gone to join the great majority.'"

No one speaks until Lamonica says, "I'll check that out," and escapes into the night. Pennington sits down. Chester slams the wall with his fist. I ask Exley, "What about Captain Dickman and their little boy?"

But *they* belong to the living, the distressed minority, and Exley can say nothing about them. Because I need to visit Captain Dickman, I seize Exley by the forearm—an unnatural act—and pull him from the bunker.

Lights flash from the westward mountains, either lightning or North Vietnamese rockets. The air tastes like a broth of thin sewage and battery acid.

"You can't keep doing what you've just done," I tell Exley. "Maybe *you'd* better join your people, too." (God forgive me for this impertinence.)

He slaps my hand aside and blunders away: a sober drunk, a self-conscious ape, a walking whited wall.

CAPTAIN DICKMAN

Oh my God, no!

SERGEANT PENNINGTON

Rockets strike beyond the revetments shielding our copters. Among the Hueys and Cobras, huge azalea-like explosions bloom and fade.

Rotors, struts, drive shafts, and cowlings shoot up into the darkness
—then, like crazy compass needles or tornado-flung sheets of tin,
whirl away.

Camp Eagle, an anthill brutally kicked, swarms under the barrage. Without my helmet, I run for the revetments carrying no
weapon but a .45. Other men scurry, too, in the compounds and
out on the perimeter. Cannon cockers in the arty rev up to answer
the incoming 122mm rounds with our own deafening 155mm
guns. Viet Cong sappers have breached our defenses, and, as I run,
dodgy silhouettes slide through the elephant grass, a satchel
charge bursts in an ammo bunker, and fireworks tumble, kaleidoscope jewels in a high smoky mirror.

My every bruising footfall triggers the syllable of a prayer: *Dear
/ God, / don't / let / me / die, / I / vow / to / do / bet- / ter, / I'll / love /
you / like / a / natch / 'l- / born / son. / A- / men, / a- / men, / a- / men.*

Chaos boiling at the gates, fire dropping from heaven, my future
rushing toward me like a racetrack wall. A gook teenager pops up
beyond the glinting surf of razor wire on our island shore and trains
his AK–47 on the pupil of my eye. He wants me dead the way the
parent of a murder victim wants to rip the death house switch. My
.45 and my prayer won't help, so I turn sideways—to reduce the
size of the bullet pattern that will choreograph my final midnight
boogaloo and to await the perforations that will part me forever
from the dance.

Then D. G. steps in, shielding me and blasting away in gleeful
mirthless fury with a Colt Commando. Bullets snap from his
fatigues like bees or buttons, pieces of body meat whirling away as
earlier two helicopters had fragmented. But he doesn't fall or even
stagger; and the teenage gook vanishes, engulfed by razor-wire surf
and drowned in a brassy horizontal rain.

A C–47—*Puff the Magic Dragon*—circles the treacherous outer
barrens, its 7.62 Gatlings saturating the grass with death. Tracers
crammed with willie-peter dust—white-phosphorus powder—link
their airborne points of origin to the enemy dead with incandescent
hyphens. Stitches of relentless silver from a vengeful flying sewing
machine.

"Ted," breathes D. G., turning around, "you okay?"

I'm fine, but the door gunner looks like a monstrous rag doll
plucked to tatters by unseen beaks. He looks like hell, a zombie
denizen of the empire of war. But he doesn't bleed, he's past that,
and when my knees buckle, he catches me with one hand, rescuing
me again from extinction. I black out anyway . . .

MR. STICKL

Before he flew with me, back before a sniper picked him off, D. G. saved me, too. I was choking on a piece of stewed python that a J Company Lurp had cooked behind his hootch and slipped into my chow. D. G. grabbed me with finger-linked hands and yanked them from my belly to my backbone. I expelled that gob of python like a howitzer shell. Everyone in the mess hurrahed except Major Burke, who had to duck the projectile.

"Jesus, Pierre-Claude, you almost put my eye out!"

I gripped a table and reclaimed my poise. As my name suggests, I am of French-Canadian extraction. Once I felt adrift, even if purposely so, among so many blue-collar Anglo, Afro-American, and Hispanic soldiers. Although I grew up in Washington State, I took my primary helicopter training at Fort Wolters, Texas, and my advanced training at Fort Rucker, Alabama. In these places I acclimated myself not only to the sweltering heat, but also to the skin colors, actions, and mores of the local populations. I can work with anyone, even if they call me Frog, if they recognize my expertise as a pilot and pay me in the coin of respect.

Anyway, the morning after we repulsed the VC attack, Major Burke finds me in the 101st Airborne Division's plywood chapel. Mike Lamonica and I stand on one side of the refrigerator-crate altar on which D. G. sprawls like a sacrificial animal or the guest of honor at a memorial visitation. A candle flickers at each of D. G.'s shoulders, as does a third candle just below his mud-caked boots. He has clasped his hands on his stomach, and his dead eyes cut slowly from side to side, first at me and Lamonica, and then across the altar at Chaplain Urbanec and Sergeant Ted Pennington.

"Fly him to Cam Ranh Bay, Pierre-Claude," Major Burke orders me. "Get him out of here, double-damned-quick." He exits the chapel before Urbanec, Pennington, or Lamonica can intercede on D. G.'s behalf. A dead fellow twice killed plays horrible systemic havoc with morale. Major Burke thinks he should have exiled the gunner after his *first* fatal wound.

Pennington nods at D. G. and backs out rotating his hat like a bashful suitor. Urbanec nears the altar, mumbling in Latin. He places the Eucharist on D. G.'s swollen tongue. Then he dips a Q-tip in the communion wine and swabs D. G.'s lips with the intinctured cotton.

"Christ has paid your fare," Urbanec says in English. "Now you may leave Camp Eagle."

"Take me to the Island of Black Syphilis," D. G. says. "Maybe the poor schnooks there will tolerate me."

"Anywhere you want, D. G.," I answer.

Lamonica begs to go, too. The trip promises him a scoop of major proportions, for no reporter has yet set foot on this fabled island of quarantine.

By noon I have my chopper, the *Hue Home*, tanked with two hundred gallons of fuel, my cyclic stick in hand, and my helmet down over my earphones. With the UPI guy in the copilot's chair, I finish my instrument check.

D. G. rides in the cargo bay with Captain Edgar Dickman, whom Major Burke has granted compassionate leave—to find a shrink at Tan Son Nhut and then to fly to Topeka for his wife's funeral. The major foisted Dickman off on us assuming that I would run an ass-and-trash mission (men and equipment) to the Saigon area. But I'm not 'coptering to Tan Son Nhut or any other inland air base, and I've let Lamonica come because I need a writer to record for all you death-destined mortals the secrets of your mythic posthumous journey.

Which is why I fly east over the imperial capital and out to sea rather than south. If depression hasn't entirely incapacitated him, Dickman must wonder why the luminous green of water rather than the broccoli-top green of trees billows beneath the *Hue Home*. In his clueless despair I can almost imagine him leaping from one unguarded door or the other hoping for oblivion or bliss.

On the other hand, maybe not. Before Lamonica and I climbed aboard, he was poring over his wife's bent photo, which D. G. had just returned to him. Maybe studying it will fully engage him until we arrive at the immense pelagic cave and its sentinel spires of karst.

Lamonica speaks into his helmet mike: "How far off is this notorious island of syphilitics?"

"Too far for anyone to get there without me," I tell him.

Even his sunglasses' mirrored lenses can't conceal his foreboding. The crawling shadow of the *Hue Home* on the green-marbled endpaper parchment of the sea heightens his dread, just as does the empty loping expanse across which my chopper ferries him and his fellows. We will fly for hours.

Actually, the metal body of a helicopter doesn't fly at all. The disk that the rotor blades create—a streaming halo blur—suspends the fuselage in the air by the mast and carries it along like the gondola of a hot-air balloon. If you cut the gondola's tethers, it falls away from the balloon. If the Huey's mast breaks, or if a hairline crack in a blade-root lamination splits and widens, or if the Jesus nut securing the entire mast assemblage fails, the Huey also drops.

No wonder Lamonica fidgets. No wonder most chopper pilots check every control twice and continually pray. In fact, I am the only such pilot who has *no* fear of dying or its uncertain aftermath.

"Tell me something reassuring." Lamonica laughs nervously.

"Chief Seattle once said, *'There is no death, only a change of worlds.'*"

But Lamonica isn't reassured. D. G. prowls his thoughts. The imaginary Island of Black Syphilis beguiles him. The fear of falling like a cut-loose gondola nibbles at his focus. But I will show him vastly more wonderful terrors . . .

CAPTAIN DICKMAN

I can't credit that Eddie blew her face away. I touch Patti's photo to my lips. The *thwup-thwup* of the rotors mimics the maddening churning of my thoughts. Why did she leave her pistol unsecured? What must Eddie have felt when Mommy's head burst into red, red shrapnel? What must he feel now? Has Patti's sister made it down from Detroit to care for him? Should God strike me dead for training my wife to shoot when I learned my next assignment would carry me to war? Why has Mr. Stickl kicked his bird out over the water when the crow would fly an inland southerly route?

"What's going on?" I shout at D. G. Not long ago he took up his door-gunner post behind the buttinsky journalist impersonating a copilot. He points his M–60 at the dancing sea sparkles.

D. G. shouts something unintelligible, and I realize that Patti has joined him in death—but a paralytic form denying her speech or movement. Why should this lanky sack of shit guarding me *from the ocean* get to talk and move when Patti no longer does? At least D. G.'s gradual dehydration and the flight of the chopper keep his stench from overwhelming me.

But I *am* overwhelmed. The pitch and flow of my memories refuse to come under control. I see Patti laughing—stripping off her clothes—receiving me—squeezing Eddie skull-first from her body—holding a living pink mummy that is partly me in her ghost-white arms—spooning orange glop into his monkey face—tying a pair of powder-blue sneakers—running beside a squat blond pygmy toward a lake outside Topeka—throwing bread to the rude Canadian geese—gazing at a surface that sparkles exactly like the South China Sea.

D. G. stands over me with one hand on the bulkhead. His face has slipped since he came into my office, deranged into a gooey and leatherlike mask. One dead eye has finally gone blind. Only the wood smoke and jungle muck soaking his fatigues give off any smell anymore. He's retreated that far from life, a slow withdrawal even from the processes of decay. "Dickman!" he cries. "Dickman, get your head out of your ass!" He uses my name like a curse. Why? I helped keep his sick mother alive, and for many long minutes I've looked upon his hideous mug without flinching.

"Patti's been in touch," D. G. says, tapping his temple with a palsied finger. "She wants to see you."

"Not funny, D. G."

"She wants to see you."

"Fuck you."

"Same to you. But whatever you think of me, Mr. Stickl will carry you to her—straight ahead and down."

This revelation scares me. It's probably a lie. (Who can read the dead?) My hate and fear ooze out even more rankly than D. G.'s. To save myself, to save *him*, I press my back harder against the bulkhead.

"You oughta love me like a son, Dickman. Eddie and I have lots in common—we murder civilians for no good reason."

I should at least tongue-lash the son of a bitch tormenting me, but I don't. My hand opens. The photo on my palm has pleats. My fingers rip the photo in two, and I eat the strips, one at a time. The tastes of stale developing fluid and tender flesh mingle in my head.

D. G. grunts and returns to the door pocket behind Lamonica.

MIKE LAMONICA, UPI

South China Sea, approx. 14.00 N, 110.25 E—The sea off the coast of Vietnam has no remarkable attributes. In its endless calm, it appears to lack both frenzy and secrets. If a chopper had to ditch out here, you half-believe that it would settle easily and float. But your pilot, Warrant Officer Pierre-Claude Stickl, 27, of Bellingham, Wash., has already told you otherwise.

Disquiet invades your heart. Does Mr. Stickl foresee setting down on an island or an aircraft carrier? Will he turn inland before you run out of fuel? You would ask, but his demeanor no longer invites direct inquiry. What if he plans to die and to take you and his other two riders with him?

One of these men, Sp4. Joseph K. Exley, 20, of Valdosta, Ga., has supposedly died already. Except for talking and walking, his skin tone and his expression support this allegation. Does his presence aboard Mr. Stickl's helicopter foretell a bad end for the entire flight?

The other man in the cargo section, Capt. Edgar Dickman, 31, of Topeka, Kan., appears grief-stricken. His son, Edgar, Jr., 8, killed the boy's mother, Patti R. Dickman, 32, with a pistol he found in his parents' bedroom. The police have ruled the shooting an accident.

An hour passes, and then two, and part of a third. Out your right-hand window, the sun edges nearer the horizon, and only a rare sighting of a freighter or a fishing boat convinces you of the reality of your noisy aerial voyage.

Finally, an open range of karst towers appears—so many towers that you can't count them. Each spire is an island or part of a barricade of spires across an island, and each island glows pink or rose or soapstone green. The sunset bronzing the tin mirror of the sea invests the whole group with a disturbing glamour.

"The Chain of Erebus," Mr. Stickl says. "Or the Spires of the Dragon Forbearant. They go on for miles."

"Must we go with them?" you dare to ask. "Or is there someplace we can land?"

"Look at them." Mr. Stickl nods. "Do you see even one you'd like me to set my skids on?"

The ever-widening bowl of unroofed stalagmites is an archipelago of spears, an ocean-bound tiger pit. "No," you say. "Not one."

But what options other than ditching exist? Have you traveled to this deep-sea fairyland to die? Are you the only sane person aboard the *Hue Home?* Will you preserve your sanity once the sky has gone dark and the engine begins to cough?

You fly on, dropping to the level of the tallest spires, which pivot about you in apparent slow motion. Below most of their pinnacles cling shrubs, and a few tiny basket boats or sampans navigate the puzzle-piece coves and inlets.

"Who comes all the way out here to fish?" you ask Mr. Stickl.

"The hungry. The heroic. They already lack so much that even forfeiting their lives doesn't scare them."

The Spires of the Dragon Forbearant wheel about, pushing ahead like trees in a spell-taken petrified wood. A wide plain of seawater streams toward an immense cave between these spires, an island so smooth and black that it looks like a basalt hunchback on the sea's prostrate body. The hole in this hump is of Olympian size.

Mr. Stickl targets this entrance. To keep from wresting the controls from him, and to hold yourself in your own skin, you grab your knees. Mr. Stickl heads into this ebony flume to nowhere, and you can't imagine returning. (Astronauts approaching the funnel of a black hole might experience a like sense of exhilaration and terror, but who else would understand?)

Soon the all-obliterating roar of the sea renders the *thwacking* of the disk rotors inaudible, and the palate of the cavern darkens above you as the South China sky and the limestone outcroppings of the archipelago vanish behind.

Erebus East—Either the unrelenting roar of water inside the throat of hell stops impinging on your senses, or, three hundred yards inside the grotto, a silence akin to total Mammoth Cave darkness arises. The silence and the darkness grow in twain until they are one indistinguishable substance.

"Doesn't this cave have stalactites or bends in it?" you ask Mr. Stickl.

"Plenty. But chill, okay? I've done this before, and my training included flying by instruments wearing a hood and blind landings on foggy nights at airfields I'd never seen before."

"This feels different to me."

Mr. Stickl barks a laugh. "Really? Well, if it has your gut agitated, keep a tight asshole and your eyes on the lighted dials."

You obey because you must, for the only light available in Erebus East, as the *Hue Home* tracks inward at speed and down by small increments, issues from radiant dial faces and needles. You amaze yourself by continually thwarting the impulse to scream.

"Tell me again why we're doing this."

"Dickman has to meet briefly with his bride, and Exley—Exley's long overdue for check-in and processing."

The blackness outside never lightens or perceptibly marbles. It persists, as does the silence that earlier twinned with it. You can hear your heartbeat, but not the 'copter's engine, and you wonder if Mr. Stickl has already landed his machine atop a mesa or if it has become a boat pitching downstream to Tartarus.

When motes of glancing brightness begin popping into view, you understand that neither of these guesses applies. The *Hue Home* continues to fly, Mr. Stickl to pilot you above the flood, and the flashbulb-bright motes whirling toward you to tumble past like a snow of exotic moths.

These moths—for they *are* moths, of a kind—never strike the windscreen, but eddy up and over you, or out and around. Their wingspans measure from a half-inch to nearly six, and their antennae look like every bristly thing from tiny ferns to intricate fish bones.

The moths somersault dreamily, their wings showing orange and melon green, cherry and ivory, or zebra hide and crumpled tinfoil. Their change from human spirits to cavern-flying moths has spun them from such materials as acetate, vinyl, enamel, fur, and precious metals, but their bodies weigh no more than milkweed fluff.

"Those things really don't move much," Mr. Stickl says. "They hover in this grotto while we putt-putt through."

The lepidopteran blizzard abates. The moths thin out to a few flickering points, like the universe at its outskirts, and Mr. Stickl must again use his instrument training to navigate. The darkness grows no darker even when, in your profound anxiety, you close your eyes.

Lights do appear again, but well below the *Hue Home*. They blaze at intervals similar to those among the Spires of the Dragon Forbearant. Mr. Stickl takes you lower, almost to the height of these strange torches. Cruising forward, you recognize each one as a humanoid form burning, burning, burning—with the inextinguishable passion of a bodhisattva.

These spectral figures induce a familiar horror. Aboveground in Saigon, Danang, Quinhon, and Hue, you've seen them before—Buddhist holy men immolating themselves to protest the policies of the South Vietnamese regime. Most such suicides ceased with the fall of Ngo Dinh Diem, whose sister-in-law, Madame Nhu, once said, "*Let them burn, and we shall clap our hands.*" But here, in numbers surpassing belief, they blaze without letup or apology.

Mr. Stickl says, "They remind me of Thich Quang Duc, the seventy-three-year-old monk from Hue who had an associate douse him with gasoline in Saigon in June 1963 and then struck a match. Over time, thirty more monks followed suit, but the sentinels down here must have burned from time immemorial."

"Why?" you blurt, but Mr. Stickl merely shrugs.

In our passing rotor wash, the Thich Quang Duc sentinels weirdly reconfigure, shimmering and smoking not on spires but on five-sided stones at the tops of elaborate karst pagodas. You can't see to the bottoms of these shrines or to the floor of the grotto, but the burning figures themselves seem to range to infinity.

You shut your eyes again, and the drifting bubble in your gut suggests that Mr. Stickl has spurred the *Hue Home* a few hundred

feet upward. You retreat into the self-beguiling safety of a deliberate
autism. Your journey goes on and on.

"Look," Mr. Stickl eventually says.

You obey. The domain of human bonfires has given way to a
shiny surface of basalt or pitch as wide as the Tonkin Gulf. On it
float thousands of flat-topped vessels with the design of ancient
barges but the dimensions of aircraft carriers. The *Hue Home* drops
toward the point vessel, from which all the others range out to the
rear in a series of interlocking diamonds.

"Will we land?" you ask. Even though you've wanted to land
since entering this submarine world, the prospect of actually doing
so frightens you. You seriously consider losing consciousness.

"That's a roger," Mr. Stickl says.

The *Hue Home* descends toward the point barge (as much an
island as a ship), and you abruptly hear rotors again, continuously
thwacking. This vessel and all the others in the armada boast
pagodas for masts, and in the pagodas' windows hang gleaming
human-skull lanterns. They flash on and off, as if signaling.

Meanwhile, pajama-clad golden wraiths glide over the deck of
the barge without touching it. Clearly, they man the vessel. Now,
though, they flit toward the *Hue Home* expectantly, as they would
for approaching aircraft.

CAPTAIN DICKMAN

Mr. Stickl cuts the rotors. D. G. drags me up from my seat by my
shirt and over to the door. Here, he lowers me out onto a surface
like black burlap over wood chips, all smelling powerfully of an
acrid resin. The cold here bites into my bone marrow. D. G.
doesn't jump out with me, and who can blame the son of a bitch?
Why crawl into the deepfreeze when you can squat in the lettuce
crisper? Above the gunwales of this huge ship, mother-of-pearl panels block our view of the other vessels—a thousand or more—in
this end-time fleet.

A dozen childish ghosts—the spirits of annoying urchins in
Saigon or Rio or even Topeka, their lower bodies trailing off into
mist—pluck at my sleeve and guide me away from the chopper
toward a cemetery of upturned aluminum coffins. All across the
black-burlap deck, battered coffins stand on end like tombstones,
but the one nearest me has an aura about it, and I start bawling
even before I get there. Its lid falls forward at my feet with a dull
whump, releasing a stink like sulfur and raw acacia, and I raise my
hands as if a mugger has stuck a pistol into my ribs.

The coffin doesn't contain Patti, but a three-quarter-length photograph of her in the Topeka morgue. This photo hangs from a hook in the coffin and twists slowly from front to back, revealing my dead naked wife from the rear as well as face-on—a souvenir and an insult at the same time. All the ghostly urchins whirl into and out of her coffin, spinning her glued-together likeness and plucking at my khaki sleeve or trousers as they unceremoniously depart.

I know that inside other coffins hang photos of others of the recent dead—Lurps, grunts, helicopter pilots, artillery gunners, nurses, officers, South Vietnamese soldiers, Viet Cong, North Vietnamese regulars, and civilians of every hue and stripe. If I walked among them, I'd find Fahey, Portress, Road-Dog, and Yielding, among dozens of others. But I can't leave Patti's photo.

The bullet hole in her forehead reminds me of D. G.'s, just as the gray of her flesh in the color photo reminds me of D. G.'s gray skin tones. Surely, I think, she is no longer here. Her crossing has transformed her.

Cobalt-blue moths with indigo eyespots on their wings circle a lantern in a nearby pagoda, and their circling gives me a frail hope. D. G. calls me back to the chopper, but I can't get behind that notion. Instead, I pick up the coffin lid. A wispy child returns and spins maddeningly about me. I haul the lid toward Patti's coffin and swing it into place with me inside.

I've trapped the urchin, too. The cold ices my blood, and the frost twinkling about me reminds me too late that an unhappy circumstance changed Eddie, Jr., into yet another orphan, but one who really matters. In our upright trap, ice replaces everything in me that formerly moved . . .

MIKE LAMONICA, UPI

En route to Tartarus—During this layover, you jump out of the chopper's cockpit and climb into the cargo bay with Exley, who says that Dickman has "literally sealed his fate." Mr. Stickl must agree, for he engages the rotors and lifts you from that bleak chthonic deck with scarcely any warning.

"What now?" you shout at Exley, perplexed.

"Transfiguration!" Exley shouts back.

"We don't have enough gas!"

Exley gives you a dry-snipe glare, unimpressed by your bourgeois rationality and concern. The *Hue Home* strays farther into the reaches of nightmare, insensible to the cold and immune to the calculus of fuel loss. The armada of black barges beneath you extends in a web of diamonds to another inner horizon—which, after an epoch of silent traveling, you pass.

"Where the hell are we going?"

"Tartarus." Exley shrugs, and his whole decaying upper body seems to slump inside his shirt. "The Dragon's Maw."

Beyond the last edge of the final level of Erebus, water spills into a silver-purple maelstrom the size of Australia. Maybe you are under that island continent. Maybe you have shot along a synapse crackling with the vision of your most potent dread.

In any case, the *Hue Home* drops toward this whirlpool, and you lock your teeth against the impact that must result. The shouts and counter-shouts of this nether portal pack your skull with gunpowder and compressed metal springs.

Exley totters across the vibrating cargo bay to your seat and puts his hands on the bulkhead to brace himself. You feel like a midge in the halo of spray at the top of Angel Falls. Exley leans in and yells, "Push me out!"

You gape at him like someone lobotomized.

"*Push me out, Lamonica!*"

You can't. You won't. The demand violates your self-concept as a respecter of life. But Exley doesn't care. He argues that denying the dead baptism into the covenant of total extinction hardly qualifies you as a priest of integrity.

"You *have* to push me, Lamonica."

"Jump," you say. "Just jump."

"If you make me jump, I'll take you with me."

The argument goes on. How do you know that consenting to push him won't evolve into an opportunity for him to defenestrate you? Because, he retorts, he wouldn't require your permission to fling you overboard, he'd simply do it. On the other hand, *being pushed* will reconnect him to his pre-Vietnam self, the lost young man whom the war has so terribly debased. The logic of this explanation sidesteps your understanding, but finally you accede to it.

Hugging, you and Exley waltz to the door, to the dizzying panorama of the great silver-purple whirlpool. With a strenuous shove, you expel him from the *Hue Home*, then catch yourself on the doorframe, panting, and goggle into the abyss as Exley plunges lazily, belly-down, toward it.

Soon, he spreads his arms and rolls to his back. His legs bend under him at the hinge of his knees, as if his mud-caked boots were soled with iron. He falls for a long time, dwindling.

Mr. Stickl holds the chopper in a hover above Exley. The deep purple maw of the Dragon incandesces, fringing Exley in light, and the bullet hole in his brow emits a beam of stinging white toward the *Hue Home*. This taut umbilical links him and your machine all the way down.

When Exley's body has dwindled to a point no bigger than the width of the beam itself, you hurl his M–60 into the pit after him. The chopper shudders, tilts, and plummets after him.

You grab a strap on the bulkhead and cling to it like a bull rider, but the skilled Mr. Stickl has lost control and his machine catapults you across the nonstick metal floor, smiting you slam-bang-silly . . .

CORPORAL FEARING

Like in Job, where it says, "*And only I am escaped alone to tell thee*," only the UPI guy came back from Mr. Stickl's last mission, which division intelligence believes ended in a crack-up or shoot-down out to sea. Lamonica, though, has gone nuts. In the stories he pounds out in the Danang infirmary, he claims Mr. Stickl flew him, D. G., and Dickman to a secret well of hell, west of Vietnam, as if Vietnam itself doesn't qualify as a smoky annex of that everlasting rubbish heap.

Apparently some gooks in a sampan fished Lamonica out of the water and rowed him to Danang, where the medics treated him as if he were a shell-shocked Lurp. The best of care. Hot and cold slumming nurses. A typewriter from supply. Three squares a day. And time enough to churn out addle-brained fairytales. We pass his dispatches around the Lurp compound, even give readings of them. Or we *did*, until Pennington collected the carbons and ordered us to stop.

"Out of respect to D. G., if to nobody else," he said. "I mean, how many times did that ugly stud save your bacon?"

And how many times do you want to thank a dead man for keeping you out of his personal territory? Not that many, especially if he puts a rush on your in-town honey. Hailing from South Georgia bought D. G. some slack with me, sure, but he yanked the rope between us taut more times than I care to remember. He yanked it with his soppy country music, his hard-shell upbringing, his revolt against that raising, and his putrid and peevesome hanging on. All that shit gets old early. Anyway, I'm not sorry I told D. G. to lie down at fuckin last, or that Urbanec stuck a flea to that effect in D. G.'s waxy ear canals. I mean, my God, he wasn't ever a Lurp like Panther Eyes, Cockroach, Carlson, and me, and the dead belong to the dead.

MISS BU'Ó'UM

Sergeant Pennington comes to visit. I like this man. The war has not turned him into a bum or a bragger. After we lie together, he talks about his wife and daughters and the men in his platoon. He has *two* families, one far away, one here. He never says his men's names or talks of what they do, but some have made boom-boom here in Madame Vinh's. Their duties, I think, turn their dreams into scary midnight movies. I surprise the sergeant by asking what has happened to the ugly stink-heavy GI who wanted to visit the Island of Black Syphilis.

Pennington gets his wallet from his pants, pulls a picture from it, and gives it to me. In its front part, six soldiers with painted faces squat before a cloudy helicopter. (The machine has a furry outline and bursts of light all over.) The men, not quite smiling, hold weapons. Pennington points at the helicopter's door, where the ugly GI stares out over the heads of the other soldiers. It's a bad picture, the whites, blacks, and silvers all melting together.

"A man in my platoon took this before these six men went on patrol," my visitor says. "But before he did, a guy with a chopper unit borrowed the camera and snapped a shot of Mr. Stickl's chopper just before a rescue mission with his favorite door gunner, Joe Exley."

"I don't understand," I say.

"You've seen this happen before—it's a double exposure. The only recognizable face in the earlier shot belongs to D. G. That same day a VC sniper shot him dead, or mostly dead. And the only recognizable faces in the second image belong to the only two men who died on *their* patrol."

In serious curiosity I ask, "So what does this mean?"

"I don't know." Pennington rubs his forehead, using his fist like a sleepy little boy rubbing his eyes. "Maybe that it's a bad idea to have your picture taken before going out on a mission."

"The other men in the exposures didn't die," I tell him. "So that cannot be what these cloudy images mean."

"Maybe not. Maybe they're meaningless."

I return the weird photo to the sorrowful sergeant. "Of course not," I say. "They mean for you, don't they? Even for me they have meaning." But he does not really seem to be listening.

I pause to think.

After a time I remember something that I read in French in Catholic school, long before I came to work for Madame Vinh.

" '*Don't wait for the Last Judgment,*'" I tell the sergeant. " '*It takes place every day.*'"

The sergeant looks surprised and then confused. Then he frowns, tears the weird snapshot in two and throws the pieces on the floor. One part faces down, the other faces up, and the black-and-silver image of the door gunner seems to watch us from a distance impossible to bridge.

A Night on the Barbary Coast

Kage Baker

J'D BEEN WALKING FOR FIVE DAYS, LOOKING FOR
Mendoza. The year was 1850.

Actually, *walking* doesn't really describe traveling through that
damned vertical wilderness in which she lived. I'd crawled uphill
on hands and knees, which is no fun when you're dressed as a Fran-
ciscan friar, with sandals and beads and the whole nine yards of
brown burlap robe. I'd slid downhill, which is no fun either, especially when the robe rides up in back. I'd waded across freezing
cold creeks and followed thready little trails through ferns, across
forest floors in permanent darkness under towering redwoods. I'm
talking *gloom*. One day the poets will fall in love with Big Sur, and
after them the hippies, but if vampires ever discover the place
they'll go nuts over it.

Mendoza isn't a vampire, though she is an immortal being with
a lot of problems, most of which she blames on me.

I'm an immortal being with a lot of problems, too. Like father,
like daughter.

After most of a week, I finally came out on a patch of level
ground about three thousand feet up. I was standing there looking
down on clouds floating above the Pacific Ocean, and feeling kind
of funny in the pit of my stomach as a result—and suddenly saw the
Company-issue processing credenza to my left, nicely camou-
flaged. I'd found Mendoza's camp at last.

There was her bivvy tent, all right, and a table with a camp stove, and five pots with baby trees growing in them. Everything but the trees had a dusty, abandoned look.

Cripes, I thought to myself, how long since she's been here? I looked around uneasily, wondering if I ought to yoo-hoo or something, and that was when I noticed her signal coming from . . . *Up?* I craned back my head.

An oak tree rose from the mountain face behind me, huge and branching wide, and high up there among the boughs Mendoza leaned. She gazed out at the sea; but with such a look of ecstatic vacancy in her eyes, I guessed she was seeing something a lot farther away than that earthly horizon.

I cleared my throat.

The vacant look went away fast, and there was something inhuman in the sharp way her head swung around.

"Hi, honey," I said. She looked down and her eyes focussed on me. She has black eyes, like mine, only mine are jolly and twinkly and bright. Hers are like flint. Always been that way, even when she was a little girl.

"What the hell are you doing here, Joseph?" she said at last.

"I missed you too, baby," I said. "Want to come down? We need to talk."

Muttering, she descended through the branches.

"Nice trees," I remarked. "Got any coffee?"

"I can make some," she said. I kept my mouth shut as she poked around in her half-empty rations locker, and I still kept it shut when she hauled out her bone-dry water jug and stared at it in a bewildered kind of way before remembering where the nearest stream was, and I didn't even remark on the fact that she had goddamn *moss* in her hair, though what I really wanted to yell at the top of my lungs was: *How can you live like this?*

No, I played it smart. Pretty soon we were sitting at either end of a fallen log, sipping our respective mugs of coffee, just like family.

"Mm, good java," I lied.

"What do you want?" she said.

"Okay, kid, I'll tell you," I said. "The Company is sending me up to San Francisco on a job. I need a field botanist, and I had my pick of anybody in the area, so I decided on you."

I braced myself for an explosion, because sometimes Mendoza's a little touchy about surprises. But she was silent for a moment, with that bewildered expression again, and I just knew she was accessing her chronometer because she'd forgotten what year this was.

"San Francisco, huh?" she said. "But I went through Yerba Buena a century ago, Joseph. I did a complete survey of all the endemics. Specimens, DNA codes, the works. Believe me, there wasn't anything to interest Dr. Zeus."

"Well, there might be now," I said. "And that's all you need to know until we get there."

She sighed. "So it's like that?"

"It's like that. But, hey, we'll have a great time! There's a lot more up there now than fog and sand dunes."

"I'll say there is," she said grimly. "I just accessed the historical record for October 1850. There's a cholera epidemic going on. There's chronic arson. The streets are half quicksand. You really take me to some swell places, don't you?"

"How long has it been since you ate dinner in a restaurant?" I coaxed. She started to say something sarcastic in reply, looked down at whatever was floating in the bottom of her coffee, and shuddered.

"See? It'll be a nice change of scenery," I told her, as she tossed the dregs over her shoulder. I tossed out my coffee too, in a simpatico gesture. "The Road to Frisco! A fun-filled musical romp! Two wacky cyborgs plus one secret mission equals laughs galore!"

"Oh, shut up," she told me, but rose to strike camp.

It took us longer to get down out of the mountains than I would have liked, because Mendoza insisted on bringing her five potted trees, which were some kind of endangered species, so we had to carry them all the way to the closest Company receiving terminal in Monterey, by which time I was ready to drop the damn things down any convenient cliff. But away they went to some Company botanical garden, and after requisitioning equipment and horses, we finally set off for San Francisco.

I guess if we had been any other two people, we'd have chatted about bygone times as we rode along. It's never safe to drag up old memories with Mendoza, though. We didn't talk much, all the way up El Camino Real, through the forests and across the scrubby hills. It wasn't until we'd left San Jose and were picking our way along the shore of the back bay, all black ooze and oyster shells, that Mendoza looked across at me and said:

"We're carrying a lot of lab equipment with us. I wonder why?"

I just shrugged.

"Whatever the Company's sending us after, they want it analyzed on the spot," she said thoughtfully. "So possibly they're not sure that it's really what they want. But they need to find out."

"Could be."

"And your only field expert is being kept on a need-to-know basis, which means it's something important," she continued. "And they're sending *you*, even though you're still working undercover in the Church, being Father Rubio or whoever. Aren't you?"

"I am."

"You look even more like Mephistopheles than usual in that robe, did I ever tell you that? Anyway—why would the Company send a friar into a town full of gold miners, gamblers and prostitutes?" Mendoza speculated. "You'll stick out like a sore thumb. And where does botany fit in?"

"I guess we'll see, huh?"

She glared at me sidelong and grumbled to herself a while, but that was okay. I had her interested in the job, at least. She was losing that thousand-year-stare that worried me so much.

I wasn't worrying about the job at all.

We could smell San Francisco miles before we got there. It wasn't the ordinary mortal aroma of a boomtown without adequate sanitation, even one in the grip of cholera. San Francisco smelled like smoke, with a reek that went right up your nose and drilled into your sinuses.

It smelled this way because it had been destroyed by fire four times already, most recently only a month ago, though you wouldn't know it to look at the place. Obscenely expensive real estate where tents and shanties had stood was already filling up with brand-new frame buildings. Hammers pounded day and night along Clay, along Montgomery and Kearney and Washington. All the raw new wood was festooned with red, white and blue bunting, and hastily improvised Stars and Stripes flew everywhere. California had only just learned it had been admitted to the Union, and was still celebrating.

The bay was black with ships, but those closest to the shore were never going to sea again—their crews had deserted and the ships were already enclosed by wharves, filling in on all sides. Windows and doors had been cut in their hulls as they were converted to shops and taverns.

Way back in the sand hills, poor old Mission Dolores—built of adobe blocks by a people whose world hadn't changed in millennia, on a settlement plan first designed by officials of the Roman Empire—looked down on the crazy new world in wonderment. Mendoza and I stared too, from where we'd reined in our horses near Rincon Hill.

"So this is an American city," said Mendoza.

"Manifest Destiny in action," I agreed, watching her. Mendoza had never liked being around mortals much. How was she going to handle a modern city, after a century and a half of wilderness? But she just set her mouth and urged her horse forward, and I was proud of her.

For all the stink of disaster, the place was *alive*. People were out and running about, doing business. There were hotels and taverns; there were groceries and bakeries and candy stores. Lightermen worked the water between those ships that hadn't yet been absorbed into the city, bringing in men bound for the gold fields or crates of goods for the merchants. I heard six languages spoken before we'd crossed Clay Street. Anything could be bought or sold here, including a meal prepared by a Parisian chef. The air hummed with hunger, and enthusiasm, and a kind of rapacious innocence.

I grinned. America looked like fun.

We found a hotel on the big central wharf, and unloaded our baggage into two narrow rooms whose windows looked into the rigging of a landlocked ship. Mendoza stared around at the bare plank walls.

"This is Oregon spruce," she announced. "You can still smell the forest! I'll bet this was alive and growing a month ago."

"Probably," I agreed, rummaging in my trunk. I found what I was looking for and unrolled it to see how it had survived the trip.

"What's that?"

"A subterfuge." I held the drawing up. "A beautiful gift for his Holiness the Pope! The artist's conception, anyway."

"A huge ugly crucifix?" Mendoza looked pained.

"*And* a matching rosary, baby. All to be specially crafted out of gold and (this is the important part) gold-bearing quartz from sunny California, U.S.A., so the Holy Father will know he's got faithful fans out here!"

"That's disgusting. Are you serious?"

"Of course I'm not serious, but we don't want the mortals to know that," I said, rolling up the drawing and sticking it in a carpetbag full of money. "You stay here and set up the lab, okay? I've got to go find some jewelers."

There were a lot of jewelers in San Francisco. Successful guys coming back from the Sacramento sometimes liked to commemorate their luck by having gold nuggets set in watch fobs, or stickpins, or brooches for sweethearts back east. Gold-bearing quartz, cut and polished, was also popular, and much classier looking.

Hiram Gainsborg, on the corner of Ohio and Broadway, had

some of what I needed; so did Joseph Schwartz at Harrison and Broadway, although J. C. Russ on the corner of Harrison and Sixth had more. But I also paid a visit to Baldwin & Co. on Clay at the Plaza, and to J. H. Bradford on Kearney, and just to play it safe I went over to Dupont and Clay to see the firm of Moffat & Co., Assayers and Bankers.

So I was one pooped little friar, carrying one big heavy carpetbag, by the time I trudged back to our hotel as evening shadows descended. I'd been followed for three blocks by a Sydney ex-convict, whose intent was robbery and possible murder; but I managed to ditch him by ducking into a saloon, exiting out the back and across the deck of the landlocked *Niantic*, and cutting through another saloon where I paused just long enough to order an oyster loaf and a pail of steam beer.

I'd lost him for good by the time I thumped on Mendoza's door with the carpetbag.

"Hey, honeybunch, I got dinner!"

She opened the door right away, jittery as hell. "Don't shout, for God's sake!"

"Sorry." I went in and set down the carpetbag gratefully. "I don't think the mortals are sleeping yet. It's early."

"There are three of them on this floor, and seventeen downstairs," she said, wringing her hands. "It's been a while since I've been around so many of them. I'd forgotten how loud their hearts are, Joseph. I can hear them beating."

"Aw, you'll get used to it in no time," I said. I held up the takeout. "Look! Oyster loaf and beer!"

She looked impatient, and then her eyes widened as she caught the scent of the fresh-baked sourdough loaf and the butter and the garlic and the little fried oysters . . .

"Oh, gosh," she said weakly.

So we had another nice companionable moment, sitting at the table where she'd set up the testing equipment, drinking from opposite sides of the beer pail. I lit a lamp and pulled the different paper-wrapped parcels from my carpetbag, one by one.

"What're those?" Mendoza inquired with her mouth full.

"Samples of gold-bearing quartz," I explained. "From six different places. I wrote the name of each place on the package in pencil, see? And your job is to test each sample. You're going to look for a blue-green lichen growing in the crevices with the gold."

She swallowed and shook her head, blank-faced.

"You need a microbiologist for this kind of job, Joseph, surely. Plants that primitive aren't my strong suit."

"The closest microbiologist was in Seattle," I explained. "And Agrippanilla's a pain to work with. Besides, you can handle this! Remember the Black Elysium grape? The mutant saccharomyces or whatever it was? You won yourself a field commendation on that one. This'll be easy!"

Mendoza looked pleased, but did her best to conceal it. "I'll bet your mission budget just wouldn't stretch to shipping qualified personnel down here, eh? That's the Company. Okay; I'll get started right after dinner."

"You can wait until morning," I said.

"Naah." She had a gulp of the beer. "Sleep is for sissies."

So after we ate I retired, and far into the hours of the night I could still see lamplight shining from her room, bright stripes through the plank wall every time I turned over. I knew why she was working so late.

It's not hard to sleep in a house full of mortals, if you tune out the sounds they make. Sometimes, though, just on the edge of sleep, you find yourself listening for one heartbeat that ought to be there, and it isn't. Then you wake up with a start, and remember things you don't want to remember.

I opened my eyes and sunlight smacked me in the face, glittering off the bay through my open door. Mendoza was sitting on the edge of my bed, sipping from her canteen. I grunted, grimaced and sat unsteadily.

"Coffee," I croaked. She looked smug and held up her canteen.

"There's a saloon on the corner. The nice mortal sold me a whole pot of coffee for five dollars. Want some?"

"Sure." I held out my hand. "So . . . you didn't mind going down to the saloon by yourself? There are some nasty mortals in this town, kid."

"The famous Sydney Ducks? Yes, I'm aware of that." She was quietly gleeful about something. "I've lived in the Ventana for years, Joseph, dodging mountain lions! *Individual* nasty mortals don't frighten me anymore. Go ahead, try the coffee."

I sipped it cautiously. It was great. We may have been in America (famous for lousy coffee) now, but San Francisco was already *San Francisco*.

Mendoza cleared her throat and said, "I found your blue-green lichen. It was growing on the sample from Hiram Gainsborg's. The stuff looks like Stilton cheese. What is it, Joseph?"

"Something the Company wants," I said, gulping down half the coffee.

"I'll bet it does," she said, giving me that sidelong look again. "I've been sitting here, watching you drool and snore, amusing myself by accessing scientific journals on bioremediant research. Your lichen's a toxiphage, Joseph. It's perfectly happy feeding on arsenic and antimony compounds found in conjunction with gold. It breaks them down. I suspect that it could make a lot of money for anyone in the business of cleaning up industrial pollution."

"That's a really good guess, Mendoza," I said, handing back the coffee and swinging my legs over the side of the bed. I found my sandals and pulled them on.

"Isn't it?" She watched me grubbing around in my trunk for my shaving kit. "Yes, for God's sake, shave. You look like one of Torquemada's henchmen, with those blue jowls. So Dr. Zeus is doing something altruistic! In its usual corporate-profit way, of course. I don't understand why this has to be classified, but I'm impressed."

"Uh-huh." I swabbed soap on my face.

"You seem to be in an awful hurry."

"Do I?" I scraped whiskers from my cheek.

"I wonder what you're in a hurry to do?" Mendoza said. "Probably hotfoot it back to Hiram Gainsborg's, to see if he has any more of what he sold you."

"Maybe, baby."

"Can I go along?"

"Nope."

"I'm not sitting in my room all day, watching lichen grow in petri dishes," she said. "Is it okay if I go sightseeing?"

I looked at her in the mirror, disconcerted. "Sweetheart, this is a rough town. Those guys from Australia are devils, and some of the Yankees—"

"I pity the mortal who approaches me with criminal intent," she said, smiling in a chilly kind of way. "I'll just ride out to the Golden Gate. How can I get into trouble? Ghirardelli's won't be there for another two years, right?"

I walked Mendoza down to the stable anyway, and saw her safely off before hotfooting it over to Hiram Gainsborg's, as she suspected.

Mr. Gainsborg kept a loaded rifle behind his shop counter. I came in through his door so fast he had the rifle out and trained on me pronto, before he saw it was me.

"Apologies, Father Rubio," he said, lowering the barrel. "Back again, are you? You're in some hurry, sir." He had a white chin beard, wore a waistcoat of red and white striped silk, and gave me the disconcerting feeling I was talking to Uncle Sam.

"I was pursued by importuning persons of low moral fiber," I said.

"That a fact?" Mr. Gainsborg pursed his lips. "Well, what about that quartz you bought yesterday? Your brother friars think it'll do?"

"Yes, my son, they found it suitable," I said. "In fact, the color and quality are so magnificent, so superior to any other we have seen, that we all agreed only *you* were worthy of this important commission for the Holy Father." I laid the drawing of the crucifix down on his counter. He smiled.

"Well, sir, I'm glad to hear that. I reckon I can bring the job in at a thousand dollars pretty well." He fixed me with a hard clear eye, waiting to see if I'd flinch, but I just hauled my purse out and grinned at him.

"Price is no object to Holy Mother Church," I said. "Shall we say, half the payment in advance?"

I counted out Chilean gold dollars while he watched, sucking his teeth, and I went on:

"In fact, we were thinking of having rosaries made up as a gift for the whole College of Cardinals. Assuming, of course, that you have enough of that *particular* beautiful vein of quartz. Do you know where it was mined?"

"Don't know, sir, and that's a fact," he told me. "Miner brought in a sackful a week ago. He reckoned he could get more for it at a jeweler's because of the funny color. There's more'n enough of it in my back room to make your beads, I bet."

"Splendid," I said. "But do you recall the miner's name, in case we do need to obtain more?"

"Ayeh." Mr. Gainsborg picked up a dollar and inspected it. "Isaiah Stuckey, that was the fellow's name. Didn't say where his claim was, though. They don't tell, as a general rule."

"Understandable. Do you know where I might find the man?"

"No, sir, don't know that. He didn't have a red cent until I paid for the quartz, I can tell you; so I reckon the next place he went was a hotel." Mr. Gainsborg looked disdainful. "Unless he went straight for the El Dorado or a whorehouse, begging your pardon. Depends on how long he'd been in the mountains, don't it?"

I sighed and shook my head. "This is a city of temptation, I am afraid. Can you describe him for me?"

Mr. Gainsborg considered. "Well, sir, he had a beard."

*   *   *

Great. I was looking for a man with a beard in a city full of bearded men. At least I had a name.

So I spent the rest of that day trudging from hotel to boarding house to tent, asking if anybody there had seen Isaiah Stuckey. Half the people I asked snickered and said, "No, why?" and waited for a punch line. The other half also replied in the negative, and then asked my advice on matters spiritual. I heard confessions from seventeen prostitutes, five drunks and a transvestite before the sun sank behind Knob Hill, but I didn't find Isaiah Stuckey.

By twilight, I had worked my way out to the landlocked ships along what would one day be Battery and Sansome Streets, though right now they were just so many rickety piers and catwalks over the harbor mud. I teetered up the gangplank of one place that declared itself the MAGNOLIA HOTEL, by means of a sign painted on a bedsheet hung over the bow. A grumpy-looking guy was swabbing the deck.

"We don't rent to no goddamn greasers here," he informed me. "Even if you is a priest."

"Well, now, my son, Christ be my witness I've not come about taking rooms," I said in the thickest Dublin accent I could manage, "Allow me to introduce myself! Father Ignatius Costello. I'm after searching for a poor soul whose family's in sore need of him, and him lost in the gold fields this twelvemonth. Do you rent many rooms to miners, lad?"

"Sure we do," muttered the guy, embarrassed. "What's his name?"

"Isaiah Stuckey, or so his dear old mother said," I replied.

"Him!" The guy looked up, righteously indignant now. He pointed with his mop at a vast expanse of puke on the deck. "That's your Ike Stuckey's work, by God!"

I recoiled. "He's never got the cholera?"

"No, sir, just paralytic drunk. You ought to smell his damn *room*, after he lay in there most of a week! Boss had me fetch him out, plastered or not, on account of he ain't paid no rent in three days. I got him this far and he heaved up all over my clean floor! Then, I wish I may be struck down dead if he don't sober up instant and run down them planks like a racehorse! Boss got a shot off at him, but he kept a-running. Last we saw he was halfway to Kearney Street."

"Oh, dear," I said. "I don't suppose you'd have any idea where he was intending to go, my son?"

"No, I don't," said the guy, plunging his mop in its pail and getting back to work. "But if you run too, you can maybe catch the son of a—" he wavered, glancing up at my ecclesiastical presence, "—gun. He ain't been gone but ten minutes."

I took his advice, and hurried off through the twilight. There actually was a certain funk lingering in the air, a trail of unwashed-Stuckey molecules, that any bloodhound could have picked up without much effort—not that it would have enjoyed the experience—and incidentally any cyborg with augmented senses could follow too.

So I was slapping along in my sandals, hot on Stuckey's trail, when I ran into Mendoza at the corner.

"Hey, Joseph!" She waved at me cheerily. "You'll never guess what I found!"

"Some plant, right?"

"And how! It's a form of *Lupinus* with—"

"That's fascinating, doll, and I mean that sincerely, but right now I could really use a lift." I jumped and swung up into the saddle behind her, only to find myself sitting on something damp. "What the hell—"

"That's my *Lupinus*. I dug up the whole plant and wrapped the root ball in a piece of my petticoat until I can transplant it into a pot. If you've squashed it, I'll wring your neck," she told me.

"No, it's okay," I said. "Look, could we just canter up the street that way? I'm chasing somebody and I don't want to lose him."

She grumbled, but dug her heels into the horse's sides and we sped off, though we didn't go very far very fast because the street went straight uphill.

"It wouldn't have taken us ten minutes to go back and drop my *Lupinus* at the hotel, you know," Mendoza said. "It's a really rare subspecies, possibly a mutant form. It appears to produce photoreactive porphyrins."

"Honey, I haven't got ten minutes," I said, wrootching my butt away from the damn thing. "Wait! Turn left here!" Stuckey's trail angled away down Kearney toward Portsmouth Square, so Mendoza yanked the horse's head around and we leaned into the turn. I peered around Mendoza, trying to spot any bearded guy staggering and wheezing along. Unfortunately, the street was full of staggering bearded guys, all of them converging on Portsmouth Square.

We found out why when we got there.

Portsmouth Square was just a sandy vacant lot, but there were wire baskets full of pitch and redwood chips burning atop poles at its four corners, and bright-lit board and batten buildings lined three sides of it. The fourth side was just shops and one adobe house, like a row of respectable spinsters frowning down on their neighbors, but the rest of the place blazed like happy Gomorrah.

"Holy smoke," said Mendoza, reining up. "I'm not going in there, Joseph."

"It's just mortals having a good time," I said. Painted up on false fronts, garish as any Old West fantasy, were names like The Mazourka, Parker House, The Varsouvienne, La Souciedad, Dennison's Exchange, The Arcade. All of them were torchlit and proudly decked in red, white and blue, so the general effect was of Hell on the Fourth of July.

"It's brothels and gambling dens," said Mendoza.

"It's theaters, too," I said defensively, pointing at the upstairs windows of the Jenny Lind.

"And saloons. What do you want here?"

"A guy named Isaiah Stuckey," I said, leaning forward. His scent was harder to pick out now, but . . . over *there* . . . "He's the miner who found our quartz. I need to talk to him. Come on, we're blocking traffic! Let's try that one. The El Dorado."

Mendoza gritted her teeth but rode forward, and as we neared the El Dorado the scent trail grew stronger.

"He's in here," I said, sliding down from the saddle. "Come on!"

"I'll wait outside, thank you."

"You want to wait here by yourself, or you want to enter a nice civilized casino in the company of a priest?" I asked her.

She looked around wildly at the happy throng of mortals. "Damn you anyway," she said, and dismounted. We went into the El Dorado.

Maybe I shouldn't have used the words *nice civilized casino*. It was a big square place with bare board walls, and the floor sloped downhill from the entrance, because it was just propped up on pilings over the ash-heaps and was already sagging. Wind whistled through the planks, and there is no night air so cold as in San Francisco. It gusted into the stark booths, curtained off with thumbtacked muslin, along one wall where the whores were working. It was shantytown squalor no Hollywood set designer would dream of depicting.

But the El Dorado had all the other trappings of an Old West saloon, with as much rococo finery as could be nailed on or propped against the plank walls. There were gilt-framed paintings of balloony nude women. There was a grand mirrored bar at one end, cut glass glittering under the oil lamps. Upon the dais a full orchestra played, good and loud, and here again the Stars and Stripes were draped, swagged and rosetted in full glory.

At the gambling tables were croupiers and dealers in black suits, every one of them a gaunt Doc Holliday clone presiding over monte, or faro, or diana, or chuck-a-luck, or plain poker. A sideboard featured free food for the high rollers, and a lot of ragged men—momentary millionaires in blue jeans, back from the gold fields for the winter—were helping themselves to pie and cold beef. At the tables, their sacks of gold dust or piles of nuggets sat unattended, as safe as anything else in this town.

I wished I wasn't dressed as a friar. This was the kind of spot a cyborg with the ability to count cards could earn himself some money to offset operating expenses. I might have given it a try anyway, but beside me Mendoza was hyperventilating, so I just shook my head and focused on my quarry.

Isaiah Stuckey was in here somewhere. At the buffet table? No . . .

At the bar? No . . . Christ, there must have been thirty guys wearing blue jeans and faded red calico shirts in here, and they all stank like bachelors. Was that him? The beefy guy looking around furtively?

"Okay, Mendoza," I said, "if you were a miner who'd just recovered consciousness after a drinking binge, stone broke—where would you go?"

"I'd go bathe myself," said Mendoza, wrinkling her nose. "But a mortal would probably try to get more money. So he'd come in here, I guess. Of course, you can only win money in a game of chance if you already have money to bet—"

"STOP, THIEF!" roared somebody, and I saw the furtive guy sprinting through the crowd with a sack of gold dust in his fist. The croupiers had risen as one, and from the recesses of their immaculate clothing produced an awesome amount of weaponry. Isaiah Stuckey—boy, could I smell him *now!*—crashed through a back window, pursued closely by bullets and bowie knives.

I said something you don't often hear a priest say and grabbed Mendoza's arm. "Come on! We have to find him before they do!"

We ran outside, where a crowd had gathered around Mendoza's horse.

"Get away from that!" Mendoza yelled. I pushed around her and gaped at what met my eyes. The sorry-looking bush bound behind Mendoza's saddle was . . . glowing in the dark, like a faded neon rose. It was also shaking back and forth, but that was because a couple of mortals were trying to pull it loose.

They were a miner, so drunk he was swaying, and a hooker only slightly less drunk, who was holding the miner up by his belt with one hand and doing her best to yank the mutant *Lupinus* free with the other.

"I *said* leave it alone!" Mendoza shoved me aside to get at the hooker.

"But I'm gettin' married," explained the hooker, in as much of a voice as whiskey and tobacco had left her. "An' I oughter have me a buncha roses to get married holding on to. 'Cause I ain't never been married before and I oughter have me a buncha roses."

"That is not a bunch of roses, you stupid cow, that's a rare photoreactive porphyrin-producing variant *Lupinus* specimen," Mendoza said, and I backed off at the look in her eyes and so did every sober man there, but the hooker blinked.

"Don't you use that kinda language to me," she screamed, and attempted to claw Mendoza's eyes out. Mendoza ducked and rose with a roundhouse left to the chin that knocked poor Sally Faye, or whoever she was, back on her ass, and her semiconscious fiancé went down with her.

All the menfolk present, with the exception of me, drew back eagerly to give the ladies room. I jumped forward and got Mendoza's arm again.

"My very beloved daughters in Christ, is this any way to behave?" I cried, because Mendoza, with murder in her eye, was pulling a gardening trowel out of her saddlebag. Subvocally I transmitted, *Are you nuts? We've got to go after Isaiah Stuckey!*

Snarling, Mendoza swung herself back into the saddle. I had to scramble to get up there too, hitching my robe in a fairly undignified way, which got boffo laughs from the grinning onlookers before we galloped off into the night.

"Go down to Montgomery Street!" I said. "He probably came out there!"

"If one of the bullets didn't get him," said Mendoza, but she urged the horse down Clay and made a fast left onto Montgomery. Halfway along the block we slowed to a canter and I leaned out, trying to pick up the scent trail again.

"Yes!" I punched the air and nearly fell off the horse. Mendoza grabbed my hood, hauling me back up straight behind her.

"Why the hell is it so important you talk to this mortal?" she demanded.

"Head north! His trail goes back toward Washington Street," I said. "Like I said, babe, he sold that quartz to Gainsborg."

"But we already know it tested positive for your lichen," said Mendoza.

At the next intersection we paused as I sniffed the air, and then pointed forward. "He went thataway! Let's go. We want to know where he got the stuff, don't we?"

"Do we?" Mendoza kicked the horse again—I was only grateful the Company hadn't issued her spurs—and we rode on toward Jackson. "Why should we particularly need to know where the quartz was mined, Joseph? I've cultured the lichen successfully. There'll be plenty for the Company labs."

"Of course," I said, concentrating on Isaiah Stuckey's scent. "Keep going, will you? I think he's heading back toward Pacific Street."

"Unless the Company has some other reason for wanting to know where the quartz deposit is," said Mendoza, as we came up on Pacific.

I sat up in the saddle, closing my eyes to concentrate on the scent. There was his earlier track, but . . . yes . . . he was heading uphill again. "Make another left, babe. What were you just saying?"

"What I was *about* to say was, I wonder if the Company wants to be sure nobody else finds this very valuable deposit of quartz?" said Mendoza, as the horse snorted and laid its ears back; it wasn't about to gallop up Pacific. It proceeded at a grudging walk.

"Gee, Mendoza, why would Dr. Zeus worry about something like exclusive patent rights on the most valuable bioremediant substance imaginable?" I said.

She was silent a moment, but I could feel the slow burn building.

"You mean," she said, "that the Company plans to destroy the original source of the lichen?"

"Did I say that, honey?"

"Just so nobody else will discover it before Dr. Zeus puts it on the market, in the twenty-fourth century?"

"Do you see Mr. Stuckey up there anyplace?" I rose in the saddle to study the sheer incline of Pacific Street.

Mendoza said something amazingly profane in sixteenth-century Galician, but at least she didn't push me off the horse. When she had run out of breath, she gulped air and said:

"Just *once* in my eternal life I'd like to know I was actually helping to save the world, like we were all promised, instead of making a lot of technocrats up in the future obscenely rich."

"I'd like it too, honest," I said.

"Don't you *honest* me! You're a damned Facilitator, aren't you? You've got no more moral sense than a jackal!"

"I resent that!" I edged back from her sharp shoulder blades, and the glow-in-the-dark mutant *Lupinus* squelched unpleasantly under my behind. "And anyway, what's so great about being a Preserver? You could have been a Facilitator like me, you know that, kid? You had what it took. Instead, you've spent your whole immortal life running around after freaking *bushes!*"

"A Facilitator like you? Better I should have died in that dungeon in Santiago!"

"I saved your LIFE, and this is the thanks I get?"

"And as for freaking bushes, Mr. Big Shot Facilitator, it might interest you to know that certain rare porphyrins have serious commercial value in the data storage industry—"

"So, who's making the technocrats rich now, huh?" I demanded. "And have you ever stopped to consider that maybe the damn plants wouldn't *be* so rare if Botanist drones like you weren't digging them up all the time?"

"For your information, that specimen was growing on land that'll be paved over in ten years," Mendoza said coldly. "And if you call me a drone again, you're going to go bouncing all the way down this hill with the print of my boot on your backside."

The horse kept walking, and San Francisco Bay fell ever further below us. Finally, stupidly, I said:

"Okay, we've covered all the other bases on mutual recrimination. Aren't you going to accuse me of killing the only man you ever loved?"

She jerked as though I'd shot her, and turned round to regard me with blazing eyes.

"You didn't kill him," she said, in a very quiet voice. "You just let him die."

She turned away, and of course then I wanted to put my arms around her and tell her I was sorry. If I did that, though, I'd probably spend the next few months in a regeneration tank, growing back my arms.

So I just looked up at the neighborhood we had entered without noticing, and that was when I really felt my blood run cold.

"Uh—we're in Sydney-Town," I said.

Mendoza looked up. "Oh-oh."

There weren't any flags or bunting here. There weren't any torches. And you would never, *ever* see a place like this in any Hollywood western. Neither John Wayne nor Gabby Hayes ever went anywhere near the likes of Sydney-Town.

It perched on its ledge at the top of Pacific Street and rotted. On the left side was one long row of leaning shacks; on the right side was another. I could glimpse dim lights through windows and doorways, and heard fiddle music scraping away, a half-dozen folk tunes from the British Isles, played in an eerie discord. The smell of the place was unbelievable, breathing out foul through dark doorways where darker figures leaned. Above the various dives, names were chalked that would have been quaint and reassuring anywhere else: The Noggin of Ale. The Tam O'Shanter. The Jolly Waterman. The Bird in Hand.

Some of the dark figures leaned out and bid us "G'deevnin'," and without raising their voices too much let us know about the house specialties. At the Boar's Head, a woman was making love to a pig in the back room; did we want to see? At the Goat and Compass, there was a man who'd eat or drink anything, absolutely *any-thing*, mate, for a few cents, and he hadn't had a bath in ten years. Did we want to give him a go? At the Magpie, a girl was lying on a mattress in the back, so drunk she'd never wake before morning, no matter what anyone did to her. Were we interested? And other dark figures were moving along in the shadows, watching us.

Portsmouth Square satisfied simple appetites like hunger and thirst, greed, the need to get laid or to shoot at total strangers. Sydney-Town, on the other hand, catered to specialized tastes.

It was nothing I hadn't seen before, but I'd worked in Old Rome at her worst, and Byzantium too. Mendoza, though, shrank back against me as we rode.

She had a white, stunned look I'd seen only twice before. The first was when she was four years old, and the Inquisitors had held her up to the barred window to see what could happen if she didn't confess she was a Jew. More than fear or horror, it was *astonishment* that life was like this.

The other time she'd looked like that was when I let her mortal lover die.

I leaned forward and spoke close to her ear. "Baby, I'm going to get down and follow the trail on foot. You ride on, okay? I'll meet you at the hotel."

I slid down from the saddle fast, smacked the horse hard on its rump, and watched as the luminous mutant whatever-it-was bobbed away through the dark, shining feebly. Then I marched forward, looking as dangerous as I could in the damn friar's habit, following Isaiah Stuckey's scent line.

He was sweating heavily, now, easy to track even here. Sooner or later, the mortal was going to have to stop, to set down that sack of gold dust and wipe his face and breathe. He surely wasn't dumb enough to venture into one of these places . . .

His trail took an abrupt turn, straight across the threshold of the very next dive. I sighed, looking up at the sign. This establishment was The Fierce Grizzly. Behind me, the five guys who were lurking paused too. I shrugged and went in.

Inside the place was small, dark, and smelled like a zoo. I scanned the room. Bingo! There was Isaiah Stuckey, a gin punch in his hand and a smile on his flushed face, just settling down to a friendly crap game with a couple of serial rapists and an axe murderer. I could reach him in five steps. I had taken two when a hand descended on my shoulder.

"Naow, mate, you ain't saving no souls in 'ere," said a big thug. "You clear off, or sit down and watch the exhibition, eh?"

I wondered how hard I'd have to swing to knock him cold, but then a couple of torches flared alight at one end of the room. The stage curtain, nothing more than a dirty blanket swaying and jerking in the torchlight, was flung aside.

I saw a grizzly bear, muzzled and chained. Behind her, a guy I assumed to be her trainer, grinned at the audience. The act started.

In twenty thousand years I thought I'd seen everything, but I guess I hadn't.

My jaw dropped, as did the jaws of most of the other patrons who weren't regulars there. They couldn't take their eyes off what was happening on the stage, which made things pretty easy for the pickpockets working the room.

But only for a moment.

Maybe that night the bear decided she'd finally had enough, and summoned some self-esteem. Maybe the chains had reached the last stages of metal fatigue. Anyway, there was a sudden *ping*, like a bell cracking, and the bear got her front paws free.

About twenty guys, including me, tried to get out through the front door at the same moment. When I picked myself out of the gutter, I looked up to see Isaiah Stuckey running like mad again, further up Pacific Street.

"Hey! Wait!" I shouted; but no Californian slows down when a grizzly is loose. Cursing, I rose and scrambled after him, yanking up my robe to clear my legs. I could hear him gasping like a steam engine as I began to close the gap between us. Suddenly, he went down.

I skidded to a halt beside him and fell to my knees. Stuckey was flat on his face, not moving. I turned him over and he flopped like a side of meat, staring sightless up at the clear cold stars.

Massive aortic aneurysm. Dead as a doornail.

"NO!" I howled, ripping his shirt open and pounding on his chest, though I knew nothing was going to bring him back "Don't you go and die on me, you mortal son of a bitch! Stupid *jackass*—"

Black shadows had begun to slip from the nearest doorways, eager to begin corpse robbing; but they halted, taken aback I guess by the sight of a priest screaming abuse at the deceased. I glared at them, remembered who I was supposed to be, and made a grudging sign of the cross over the late Isaiah Stuckey.

There was a clatter of hoofbeats. Mendoza's horse came galloping back downhill.

"Are you okay?" Mendoza leaned from the saddle. "Oh, hell, is that him?"

"The late Isaiah Stuckey," I said bitterly. "He had a heart attack."

"I'm not surprised, with all that running uphill," said Mendoza. "This place really needs those cable cars, doesn't it?"

"You said it, kiddo." I got to my feet. "Let's get out of here."

Mendoza frowned, gazing at the dead man. "Wait a minute. That's Catskill Ike!"

"Cute name," I said, clambering up into the saddle behind her. "You knew the guy?"

"No, I just monitored him in case he started any fires. He's been prospecting on Villa Creek for the last six months."

"Well, so what?"

"So I know where he found your quartz deposit," said Mendoza. "It wasn't mined up the Sacramento at all, Joseph."

"It's in Big *Sur*?" I demanded. She just nodded.

At that moment, the grizzly shoved her way out into the street, and it seemed like a good idea to leave fast.

"Don't take it too badly," said Mendoza a little while later, when we were riding back toward our hotel. "You got what the Company sent you after, didn't you? I'll bet there'll be Security Techs blasting away at Villa Creek before I get home."

"I guess so," I said glumly. She snickered.

"And look at the wonderful quality time we got to spend

together! And the Pope will get his fancy crucifix. Or was that part just a scam?"

"No, the Company really is bribing the Pope to do something," I said. "But you don't—"

"Need to know, of course. That's okay. I got a great meal out of this trip, at least."

"Hey, are you hungry? We can still take in some of the restaurants, kid," I said.

Mendoza thought about that. The night wind came gusting up from the city below us, where somebody at the Poulet d'Or was mincing onions for a *sauce piperade*, and somebody else was grilling steaks. We heard the *pop* of a wine cork all the way up where we were on Powell Street . . .

"Sounds like a great idea," she said. She briefly accessed her chronometer. "As long as you can swear we'll be out of here by 1906," she added.

"Trust me," I said happily. "No problem!"

"Trust you?" she exclaimed, and spat. I could tell she didn't mean it, though.

We rode on down the hill.

The American Monarchy
Richard A. Lupoff
[with a lift of the Lupoff lid to William Tenn]

*H*ALF AWAKE AND IN A PRETTY PLEASANT MOOD, Kam Meehan was drinking kona coffee and listening to a Schubert concerto in his surfer shop in Pu'unene Village when the limousine pulled up and the men in the black hats and mirror shades climbed out. They wore identical midnight-blue suits, white shirts, and plain ties. They entered Kam's shop, removed their mirror shades, and glanced around suspiciously. Their eyes said nothing.

The newcomers could have been clones, if human cloning had been legal. In fact there were subtle differences among them. One was a trifle taller than his companions, one a trifle older than the others, and so on. Even so, they looked as alike as the proverbial peas in a pod. Finally the man in charge—the one, that is, presumably in charge—presented himself at the counter.

Kam lowered his steaming cup onto the polished surface of split bamboo, turned down the Schubert on the Bose speakers, and asked the chief visitor if he could help him. The man was hardly dressed the way Kam's customers usually dressed. No flowered shirt. No khaki shorts or sneakers. This guy looked like something out of a late night movie that would come over the dish out on Kam's lanai.

"Is this shop secure?" the man asked.

Kam laughed. "Sure is. Hardly even leaks when it rains."

75

"That isn't what I meant," the man said.

Kam shrugged. "You need a good board? Some swim fins? Spear gun? Sunscreen?"

The man shook his head. "Take a look at this, please, Mr. Meehan." He reached inside his jacket and pulled out a leather wallet. He flipped it open and showed Kam a badge.

"Very nice," said Kam. "What about a few aloha shirts? I've got some beauties. One for you, one for each of your friends, show the folks back on the mainland where you've been."

The man gestured to one of his companions, who approached the counter. He laid an attaché case on the smooth surface. Kam noticed that it was connected by a polished chain to a handcuff, which in turn circled the man's wrist.

The first visitor slipped his wallet back inside his jacket, reached into a trousers pocket and pulled out a set of keys. He unlocked the lid of the attaché case without unlocking the handcuff that held it to his assistant's wrist. He opened the attaché case and withdrew a sealed manila envelope. He slit the seal, pulled a slim sheaf of papers from the envelope, and laid them on the counter in front of Kam.

"Please," the man said, nodding indicatively toward the papers.

Kam looked at the top sheet, picked up his steaming cup and sipped. "Would you like some coffee?" he asked the visitor. "On the house."

The man shook his head. "Thank you, no. Would you please read the documents?"

Kam lowered his cup, picked up the papers, studied the top sheet briefly, riffled through the other pages and laid them back on the counter. He said, "When it comes right down to it I'm not much for reading. Now if you want some really good board wax—"

"Please," said the visitor.

"Pair of swim fins? Latest in scuba gear?"

Outside Kam's shop the black limousine glittered in the intense Pacific sunlight. A couple more men in dark suits had remained with the vehicle. Waves of shimmering overheated air rose from the hood and tonneau roof. There was nothing particularly noteworthy about the limousine. It was a late model, looked as if the bodywork was armored and the thick glass bulletproof, and—well, come to think of it, one other thing was a little bit odd. There was no manufacturer's nameplate, no *Lincoln* spelled out in shiny metallic script, no Cadillac crest, no old-fashioned Chrysler escutcheon. The limousine was just—black. Even its windows were tinted to near opacity.

The visitor poked a finger at the sheaf of papers. His forehead furrowed in earnest concentration. "Please, sir. I urge you."

"Can't you just tell me?" Kam asked.

The visitor pursed his lips. He closed his eyes, raised his hand and rubbed them, thumb against one eyelid, forefinger against the other. He held his breath briefly. Then he exhaled, nodded once, and said, "Mr. Meehan, I am here to ask you to undertake a very important mission on behalf of your nation."

"Really." Kam frowned slightly. It was a facial expression which he rarely used, and it was barely discernible at that. But the corners of his mouth dipped slightly and a shallow crease appeared between his eyebrows, then disappeared again.

"And just what country is that?" he asked.

The man in black looked startled. "The United States of America," he replied, a note suggestive of religious devotion in his voice.

"Say," Kam responded querulously, "you boys aren't from the IRS, are you? Because I filed for my extension. I filled out the form, anyway. I'm pretty sure I mailed it in. I have to find my records, that's all, I've never been much for keeping records, but then I'll catch up on my paperwork."

"Sir," the chief visitor said, "we are not from the IRS."

Kam looked doubtful.

"Really, sir," the man reassured him.

Kam looked beyond the palm trees, beyond Waiehu Beach, at the glittering swells of Kahului Bay. "Okay," he sighed. "I guess you won't go away until you've had your say, so you might as well go ahead." He nodded, then added, "You sure you wouldn't like a cup of coffee? Handful of macadamia nuts? They're delicious. Any of you fellas?" he asked the other men in dark suits.

They all shook their heads, no.

"Well, let's have it," Kam said wearily to the chief suit.

The dark-haired woman in the little black dress sipped at her martini, lowered the glass to the rich, dark mahogany and shook her head. Her hair swung slightly, then settled perfectly back into place. Through glittering lenses held in chic golden wire rims she studied the rim of her glass, relieved to see that no telltale stain had transferred from her lips.

She had an amazing memory which she had cultivated from childhood. In high school she was famed for her ability to ignore a teacher, or seem to ignore a teacher, only to feed back a lecture verbatim. In college she was known for her ability not merely to remember a hundred or a thousand facts once she'd turned them up for a research paper, but for her ability to correlate them into a meaningful pattern.

Now she was re-creating her interview with an Associate Justice of the Supreme Court of the United States.

"I could tell she was upset all during our conference," Cheryl quoted the Justice. "Her eyes were red and she kept sniffing. At first I thought she had an allergy until we took a break and she asked me to go to the ladies' room with her."

The interviewer's name was Cheryl Sanders, or at least that was the name by which she was known in the trade which she had conquered. This is exactly what she said:

The Justice removed her horn-rimmed spectacles and polished them with a wisp of linen. When she had put them back on she resumed. "As soon as we got there she collapsed in tears. I'd never seen anything like it. Sandra Day O'Connor wouldn't cry if she saw her firstborn flattened by a steamroller and here she was bawling like an infant. I put my arms around her and told her to cry until she was ready to stop, and then she could tell me what was the matter."

She reached for her glass of iced tea and took a sip. That seemed to be her style. Give a little, pause a little, give a little more.

Okay. I waited for her to continue. It isn't often that a young reporter gets an opportunity to interview an Associate Justice of the Supreme Court of the United States, one on one, no holds barred, and I wasn't going to blow my chance by pushing her too hard, or too fast. I studied my notebook. I carried it mainly as a prop, so the Justice would believe I was legitimate. Hellfire and brimstone, I had my questions lined up like ducks in a row, I could have done the interview bare naked and empty handed, but I knew the note-book made the subject feel better. Besides, by mutual consent the interview was being recorded. Justice Ginsberg wanted to make sure she wasn't misquoted and even though I knew I'd get every word straight, my editor insisted that I cover my ass. If you'll pardon my Hawai'ian.

The Justice resumed, "When she finally calmed down a little Sandra said, 'I can't go on like this. It's just too much. I can't sleep nights, I get up and watch the news on television and it only gets worse. I can't—I have to come clean.'

"I said, 'Just tell me, dear. I'll keep your secret if that's what you're worried about.' But she just shook her head and said that wasn't the problem, she'd have to tell the truth to the whole Court."

Justice Ginsberg pursed her lips. You always think of Supreme Court Justices as sitting behind a bench wearing their black robes but of course we weren't in the Court and Justice Ginsberg was wearing an aloha shirt with giant toucans all over it and khaki shorts and a pair of white tennis sneakers. We were sitting on her lanai looking out over the harbor. Palm trees swaying in the trade winds and the sun sparkling off the emerald surface of the Pacific looked more like a travel poster than the scene outside her house.

"'Do you want to tell me first?' I asked. She shook her head, no. 'It's just that there was so much pressure, I know I should have resisted and I did in the beginning. But Barbara kept coming at me, and Jim Baker, and of course Clarence. I can't stand that man! And Jeb called me, and that horrible Harris woman, and even George Senior. He kept out of it for a while but then he telephoned me, and I even had a call from Nancy Reagan. Can you believe it, the poor woman, suffering so, trying to care for her Ronnie, but she picked up the phone and called me too, and I finally couldn't hold out anymore, I gave in and voted their way and—and—well, you know what happened.'

"'Of course I know what happened. It was dreadful, but it's behind us now,' I told her. But Sandra said, 'No, it isn't. I can't sleep. I can't eat. I'm a nervous wreck, and it's all because of what happened.'

"She took my hands and said, 'Can I recuse myself *ex post facto*, do you think? Do you think Bill would let me? If I told the truth, told everything?'

"'Maybe you should just talk to him,' I suggested, but she said she'd rather tell the whole Court at one time, so we went back into the conference room and took our places. Bill Rehnquist was studying an application for a writ in one of those crazy-vicious Justice Department cases but he looked up at us with that owlish expression of his and nodded. There was an awful silence so I finally said, 'Sandra has something to tell us all.'

"Bill nodded to her and everybody just waited, and she told her story, how she knew she was doing the wrong thing but she couldn't stand the pressure any longer, and so she voted the way she did and that settled the election, and that settled the Presidency, of course."

Justice Ginsberg got up and went to the kitchen. She brought back a plate of *petit fours* and I took one, more to be polite than because I really wanted it. Before I popped the little mango cake in my mouth I asked her how the other Justices reacted to Justice O'Connor's outburst.

She shook her head, "I can't tell you about our deliberations. But I can tell you there was resistance to doing anything at all. The election was over, the Administration was in office, we'd just have to wait until the next election came around, but Sandra said that wouldn't do. She'd taken courage from Madame Le Gougne and—"

I didn't want to interrupt, but Justice Ginsberg must have seen a puzzled look in my eyes. She said, "I didn't know who Madame Le Gougne was either. Sandra told us she was Marie-Reine Le Gougne, the French ice skating judge at the 2002 Winter Olympics. There were nine judges and everyone knew that the Canadians had won the competition, but the other judges were split, four to four, for political reasons. Marie-Reine would cast the deciding vote. She knew what the right thing was, but she was under so much pressure, she voted for the Russians instead of the Canadians."

The mango cake was delicious. I washed it down with some iced tea. "Yes, I remember," I told Justice Ginsberg. "I didn't pay much attention to the Olympics, I hadn't taken note of the judges' names, but I remember the incident. Just one more Olympic scandal. I don't write for the sports page but everybody was talking about it for a while."

"Yes." Justice Ginsberg smiled. "And do you remember the solution?"

"They gave the gold medal to the Canadians after all."

"But they didn't take it away from the Russians. They just decided that there would be two gold medals for the pairs skating event. It was Madame Le Gougne's courage that inspired Sandra, and it was the decision of the International Olympic Committee that inspired the Court's ruling."

A bright yellow seaplane swooped out of the perfect sky and dropped toward the sparkling water of the harbor. I certainly didn't miss Washington with its stifling summers and its bitter winters. Just another day in Paradise!

I said, "So the two-President solution was based on the Olympic medal tactic."

Justice Ginsberg nodded.

"But neither the Russians nor the Canadians were happy about that. The Russians felt that they'd won the gold, fair and square. Or maybe not so fair and square, but they felt that they'd won it and now the prize was only half theirs. And the Canadians felt that *they* deserved the prize, and even though they got a gold medal they felt it was tainted," I recalled.

"That's right," the Justice said. "And they were both right. But it defused a dangerous situation and both sides could live with the solution, which is the best that anyone could have hoped for. If they'd simply let the Russians keep the medal there would have been a very ugly international incident, and if they'd taken it away and given it to the Canadians instead they might have restarted the Cold War all in one fell swoop. Instead, they gave both a way to save face and claim victory."

"And that's how we wound up with two Presidents, George Bush and Al Gore." No Supreme Court Justice had ever revealed that much of the Court's reasoning before now. I had a great story and I was going to run with it for all it was worth!

"There were reports of squabbles in the White House," I said, "who would get to sleep in the Official Residence, who would have to settle for the Lincoln Bedroom, and that chalk line down the middle of the Oval Office." I wondered what Justice Ginsberg would have to say about that.

"It was a good thing that Laura and Tipper got along. They treated their husbands like two overgrown boys and made them keep the peace. Can you imagine a fistfight between two Co-Presidents in front of a foreign dignitary and a row of cameras? Unthinkable! Thank heaven for the ladies."

"There were more problems, though, weren't there, Madame Justice? It worked out for the Olympics but things kept getting more complicated for the government."

"Yes." She looked wistful for a moment, gazing out at the lovely setting, but then she smiled. "The Olympic Committee didn't have to worry about getting through the next three years. And they didn't have to worry about the Vice Presidency."

That was right, of course. Once Al Gore was sworn in as Co-President—I can still hear the grinding sound as Chief Justice Rehnquist gritted his teeth when he administered the Oath of Office—the first thing Co-President Gore did was demand that Joe Lieberman be sworn in as Co-Vice President. And of course he was right on that score.

Once Lieberman became Vice President he had to give up his Senate seat, and that provoked a new crisis. Things kept on getting messier and messier. I remember the day he took office as Co-Vice President, and Trent Lott demanding a new vote on the organization of the Senate.

It had been divided right down the middle, fifty Republicans and fifty Democrats, but with a Republican Vice President to cast tiebreaker votes, the Republicans ran the Senate. For a while. Then Jim Jeffords of Vermont declared as an Independent and the Democrats took over, fifty to forty-nine. And he was willing to vote with the Dems if he had to, to keep things in order. But now with Lieberman's seat vacant it would be tied again and the Vice President would get to cast the tie-breaker, but there were two Vice Presidents and depending on who was presiding on a given day the parties had to take turns running the show.

Of course the Governor of Connecticut would soon appoint a new Senator to take Joe Lieberman's seat, but before that could happen there came the day that the two Vice Presidents got their calendars mixed up. There was some confusion over a holiday or a recess or, well, it never did get fully sorted out, but when the Senate next convened both Vice Presidents showed up, ready to preside.

Laura Bush and Tipper Gore had kept their husbands from fighting in the Oval Office, but Lynne Cheney and Hadassah Lieberman weren't in the Senate Chamber to keep their husbands at peace, and the result was a tussle over the gavel. Lieberman was a wiry little guy with good reflexes and he managed to grab it first but Cheney was a big outdoorsman from Wyoming when he wasn't busy being an oil cowboy in Texas, and he was able to wrestle the gavel away from Lieberman.

But Lieberman was wily and feisty as all get-out and he reached into the pitcher of ice water that they used to keep on the rostrum for the comfort of long-winded Senators. He grabbed an ice cube and shoved it down Cheney's shirt collar. Cheney was so surprised he relaxed his grip on the gavel and Lieberman snatched it out of his hand and scampered off the rostrum and up the aisle, making a passage between the Republicans and the Democrats like Moses parting the Red Sea for the Children of Israel.

Cheney let out a roar and jumped off the rostrum and took off after Lieberman like a bear chasing a fox. That was when Cheney's pacemaker gave out. Nobody ever knew what caused it, but a lot of us in the press corps think it was somebody in the media gallery trying out a new model cell phone, but I'm not going to say who that might have been because it's never been proved.

Cheney hit the floor like a sack of Longhorn feed and didn't move.

That left the United States with one Republican President and one Democratic President but only one Vice President. And he was a Democrat.

George Bush wasn't going to stand for that. Cheney wasn't even cold when Bush announced that he was going to nominate a new Co-Vice President.

Co-President Al Gore objected. He argued that the Twenty-fifth Amendment said that the President should name the new Vice President when the Vice Presidency was vacant, and since the Vice Presidency wasn't vacant, there was no reason to name a new Vice President. Gore had been criticized in some quarters for not fighting hard enough over the dubious Presidential election of 2000 and it looked as if he was making up for that now.

Further, the Democratic National Committee demanded, even if the new arrangement of Co-Presidents and Co-Vice Presidents required that the vacancy be filled, the new Vice President should be chosen by agreement between the Co-Presidents.

The whole thing seemed headed for disaster. Pundits argued that Presidential decisions were too important and often too urgent to be shared by two people. The country needed one President and only one.

But a committee of historians pointed out that the Roman Republic at its height had been ruled by two Consuls. And later, after it became an Empire, it was eventually divided into Eastern and Western halves, with two Emperors, one sitting in Rome and the other in Byzantium. Besides, the old slogan of "One Leader" had been part of Hitler's program in Germany and even after all these years there were enough people who remembered their history to shudder when the phrase was revived. Remember Tom Lantos of California carrying on in the House? You get a Holocaust survivor in the Congress, he's going to be a living history lesson as well as everybody's conscience.

A popular Ex-President suggested that the two Presidents have separate capitols, perhaps one in Key West, Florida, and one in Bremerton, Washington, so as to keep them as far apart as possible.

That seemed like a pretty good plan but it left the question of the vacant Co-Vice Presidency unresolved. In fairness I have to say that most people felt it was only fair, since we had Republican and Democratic Co-Presidents and a Democratic Vice President, the second Vice Presidency should be filled by a Republican and he should be chosen by Co-President George W. Bush.

Okay.

Co-President Bush decided to take the bull by the horns and

simply send a name to the Senate, and battle it out in court if the Democrats objected. After all, it was the Supreme Court had made him President. They wouldn't abandon him now.

The name he sent to the Senate as his nominee for Vice President was that of Attorney General John Ashcroft, the former Senator from Missouri who had run for reelection in 2000 and been defeated by a corpse.

With Vice President Lieberman presiding, the Senate opened confirmation hearings on the qualifications of Co-Vice President-Designate John Ashcroft. The nomination was turned over to the Judiciary Committee, Attorney General Ashcroft showed up to testify, and the fur began to fly.

I won't go into all the nasty details, I'm sure you remember them all too well. If you don't remember, I'm wasting my time talking to you. And I'll have a refill on the martini while we're at it, bartender. All this talk is giving me a dry throat.

Anyway, the government was in a state of complete turmoil.

The first person to suggest the royal solution may have been a columnist for the *Oakland Tribune*, a pretty good California daily but not exactly what you would call a newspaper with major national presence. I mean, it was no *New York Times* or *Washington Post* or *Wall Street Journal*. Hey, it wasn't even *Larry King Live*. The columnist apparently had his tongue in his cheek when he made the suggestion, and nobody paid much attention. I'm sure a few of the paper's faithful readers got a chuckle out of it, but outside of the *Trib's* circulation area it passed without notice.

But as the crisis in Washington deepened some reader sent a letter to the editor that ran in the paper. That provoked a few more, which led to an op-ed piece, then an above-the-fold editorial. That led to responses from the *San Francisco Chronicle* and *Examiner* and the *San Jose Mercury-News*.

One thing led to another. The local radio talk shows got involved, then the local TV newscasters. The *Los Angeles Times* started covering the story. It was treated as a silly season story like UFO sightings and kids trying out stunts to try and crack the Guinness book, but then some of the East Coast papers, in fact, exactly the ones that had ignored the story at first, jumped on the bandwagon and Congressmembers started making speeches about it.

How could the United States change from a federal republic to a monarchy, and who would be king?

A California congresswoman known for her strong feminist convictions demanded to know why there had to be a king anyway, why not a queen?

Then there was the Washington, DC British Society, an organization of Americans who traced their roots to the United Kingdom and expressed an ongoing nostalgia for the period prior to July 4, 1776, and what they called The Big Mistake. The Society adopted a resolution calling upon Congress to invite the ruling Queen of the United Kingdom of England, Scotland, and Wales, Defender of the Faith and Yadda Yadda and so forth, to welcome her troublesome former colonies back into the Britannic fold.

Not to be outdone by the British Society, existing groups with their roots in other nations laid their own respective claims. More groups sprang into being, *ad hoc*.

Of course there weren't that many kingdoms left in the world. Thailand, Sweden, the Netherlands, Spain, Denmark, Belgium, and Norway got into the act. It was suggested that either the Grand Duchy of Luxembourg or the Principality of Monaco might send somebody over to accept the American crown, but nothing came of that. The Sultan of Brunei allegedly placed a phone call to the Oval Office, but a three-way conference call involving the Sultan and both Co-Presidents failed to reach agreement.

The Emperor of Japan, the argument was advanced, could trump all the others, being an emperor rather than a king, sultan, or duke, but it was given out that Japan needed the United States too badly as a market to make it part of the Empire and lose it as an export destination.

Rumors flew that the King of Saudi Arabia had been short-listed by certain oil interests in the United States, but that he was vetoed behind the scenes by the powerful Israeli lobby in Washington.

Any number of Pretenders started clamoring for recognition, squabbling among themselves in the hope of gaining a new throne in place of the ones their ancestors had been summarily tossed off. These included would-be royals from Italy, Greece, Bulgaria, Romania, Albania, France, and Mexico. Several claimants to the title of Kaiser of Germany and King of Prussia, and that of Tsar of all the Russias presented themselves to the pubic media and attempted to gain recognition at the State Department in Washington, but were denied their wishes.

L'Osservatore Romano floated a trial balloon in the name of the Holy Father, but back in the USA the Southern Baptist Convention went ballistic and that put the kibosh on that plan. Then the Chairman of the Federal Reserve Board suggested that the job should be auctioned off. Bill Gates and Donald Trump could bid, and maybe Warren Buffet, and whoever won could not only grab himself a nifty crown, he'd pay off the national debt, or at least chop a fat chunk out of it, while he was at it. But Gates, Trump, and Buffet issued a joint statement saying they were too busy to get involved, and good luck America and settle your own problems. George Steinbrenner did put in a bid but he was too disgusting even for Federal work.

One self-styled Pharaoh said he wanted to move the capitol to Las Vegas and set up headquarters in the glitzy fake pyramid there, but the gambling interests vetoed that. Would have been fun, though, don't you think?

Yes, I would love another martini. And some macadamia nuts, if you don't mind.

The World Government Alliance offered their own solution to the crisis. They proposed that the United States cease to function as a nation and cede its sovereignty to the United Nations. Once the USA had done this, the WGA suggested, other nations would follow suit, a World Government would come into being, and perfect and eternal peace would follow.

The New Sons of the Glorious Confederacy and National League of Home Artillerists, from their headquarters in the back room of a coin-operated laundry establishment in an unnamed Southern State, issued a manifesto agreeing with the first half of the WGA's plan, that of the dissolution of the United States Government. However, rather than becoming directly subject to the United Nations, the Several States would use their newly regained sovereignty to go their separate and respective ways, henceforth and forever after.

One Constitutional historian appearing on a television talk show created a stir by pointing out that the Continental Congress had offered George Washington a crown shortly after the successful conclusion of the American Revolution. The Father of His Country had turned down the offer, choosing instead to accept the Presidency some years later, after the Constitution was ratified.

"General Washington turned down the offer," the historian told his host, "but the Congress never formally withdrew it. He could change his mind," the expert suggested. He was wearing a striped button-down shirt, a polka dot patterned bow tie, and a rumpled plaid suit coat. Since he was sitting behind a news desk as he spoke, it was impossible to tell what kind of trousers he was wearing, or footgear, if any.

"Isn't George Washington dead?" the host asked. He was a snappy dresser himself, widely noted for his ownership of the largest suspenders wardrobe in the known universe. Tonight he was wearing a bright red pair, with alternating pictures of little green and gray aliens on them.

There was a moment of uncomfortable silence. Then the Constitutional historian said, "I suppose he is."

"Is what?" asked the host, recovering from an apparent senior moment.

"Dead."

The host said, "Oh."

There was another moment of silence. Then the historian said, "Oh, oh, I see what you're driving at. Sure. George Washington is dead, all right. But if he actually had become king, then his descendants would have been inheriting the throne for all these years. The current King Washington would be, well, whoever was in the most direct line of succession. I guess he, or she, depending on the rules of the monarchy, could still claim the crown."

At once telephones began to ring at the network headquarters, at television stations and newspaper offices throughout the country, and of course in the nation's capital. Turned out there were no fewer than 23,981 Washingtons and otherwise named collateral Washington descendants in the country, and fully ninety per cent of them wanted to become King or Queen of America. One Washington, a self-described androgyne, offered to become both.

It's a tribute to America's diversity that the claimants included members of every identifiable ethnic group including several recognized tribes of Native Americans, a number of recent immigrants, the members of a religious commune living near Mount Shasta in the great Pacific Northwest who claimed to be able to channel, collectively, the identity and persona of the original George Washington, and an elderly widow surviving on Social Security checks mailed to her in Sonora, Mexico, who claimed that her aged and quarrelsome Chihuahua bitch was the current avatar of Martha Washington. George had risen to a higher plane of existence, the widow explained, and was waiting there for Martha to join him, but Martha had chosen to remain on the mortal plane for several additional cycles of reincarnation as an act of compassion for all living things.

All of this was getting nowhere, the state of world affairs was not merely muddled but perilous, and the United States was politically paralyzed.

Cheryl Sanders lowered her glass to the polished mahogany bar and slid carefully off the leatherette barstool. She held onto the bar for a moment, steadying herself on her stiletto heels. Even in this informal environment, there were some elegant watering holes and Cheryl favored them.

Her companion reached a hand for Cheryl's elbow. "Okay? You okay?"

Cheryl managed a small smile and an even smaller nod. "Where's the fucking loo?" she demanded of no one in particular.

The bartender nodded toward a discreetly marked alcove and Cheryl's companion, unbidden, guided her carefully toward its darkened entryway. He waited for her, a worried expression on his face, but she did finally emerge looking none the worse for wear.

"Where was I?" the newswoman asked.

"I think you were just wrapping up a lecture on Constitutional law." Cheryl's companion took her by the elbow. "I think you could use a breath of fresh air."

Cheryl's brow furrowed.

"Are you—" her companion started to ask, but she interrupted.

" 'm okay, 'm okay." She hiccuped and for a moment it looked as if something a lot more disastrous than a hiccup was in the offing, but she returned to her normal color or at least a rough approximation thereof and permitted herself to be guided out of the establishment.

The tropical night was like something out of an old Alice Faye movie. All that was missing was John Payne in a white dinner jacket and maybe a ukulele soundtrack.

"No way," Kam told his visitor. "Not a chance. I'm too happy the way I am. I don't want any part of it."

Outside the shop customers kept arriving, eager to buy bobblehead dolls of hula dancers and straw hats with beer can attachments, and the dark-suited men from the black limousine kept turning them away.

Kam growled. To the chief man-in-a-dark-suit he complained, "Look, your guys are ruining my business. Those folks are my poi-and-guava juice. Bad enough to lose tourists, but you drive away my regulars, I'm in the surf without a boogie-board."

"We'll make it up to you," the head visitor said. He was starting to sound impatient. "I don't think you understand what you're being asked to do, Mr. Meehan."

Kam cast an eye longingly at the amplifier nearby. The Schubert had long since ended, replaced by a seldom-performed Bach solo violin sonata.

"Okay," he voiced wearily, "tell me once more exactly what you want me to do and why you think I should do it."

"We want you to become King of Hawai'i and Emperor of the United States."

"And the why part?"

"Because we need a monarch, Mr. Meehan. The country is at a complete standstill. The economy is grinding to a halt. There is an unbreakable political logjam. Our nation's prestige and influence on the world stage are nil. We're a laughing stock in every chancery from Whitehall to the Forbidden City. You are in a direct line of descent from King Kamehameha. You are of royal blood. If you'll just accept this job, sir, you will be doing an immeasurable service to us all."

Kam shook his head. "You guys are amazing. You came over here a hundred, hundred twenty-five years ago. Everything was going swell. You messed it, wrecked our country, tried to wipe out our culture, stole our land, and finally gobbled us up completely. And now you're in the soup and you want us to rescue you."

He reached over and turned up the Bach. Over the music he said, "Nope."

The man in the dark suit surprised him then. He uttered a loud sob. His shoulders shook and teardrops began to roll down his cheeks.

Kam reached across the split-bamboo counter and put a hand on the visitor's shoulder. The visitor looked up at him — the visitor was of normal height but Kam was taller by several inches — and shrugged as if to say, "Please, please help me."

With a loud exhalation Kam said, "Maybe I can do something for you."

The visitor looked at him imploringly.

"Come on, then."

Kam managed to circle the end of the counter without removing his hand from the visitor's shoulder. With a free hand the visitor snatched up the papers that he'd laid on the counter. Kam Meehan marched the dark-suited man to the door. He turned back and said to the other dark-suited men, "Just watch the place for me, fellas."

Then he propelled his visitor ahead of him, out of the shop.

"Where are we going?" the visitor asked. "We'll take the limo." He flashed a hand signal.

Kam said, "Don't be silly. We're going to my sister's house right over here on Liloliho Street. Don't tell me you can't walk that far."

They made a strange procession, Kam Meehan in his casual

togs, the visitor in his dark suit, the visitor's entourage of clones trailing in their wake flashing suspicious looks in every direction as they strolled across rough island grass and climbed the steps to the shaded terrace of a small house.

"Lily," Kam called.

The door swung open to reveal a woman who looked very much like Kam Meehan. Behind her two girls, by appearance aged six and five, were playing dress-up. The six-year-old wore a paper crown colored gold and red with crayons, a large bougainvillea blossom in her hair, an oversized Marvin the Martian beach towel for a cape and a wooden ladle for a scepter. The five-year-old wore a vest, linen shorts, and a University of Hawai'i baseball cap turned sideways. With one hand she held the end of the Marvin the Martian towel; in the other, a plastic Star Wars light saber.

To the man in the dark suit Kam said, "My sister, Lily." To the woman he said, "This is—actually, I never got his name." He looked questioningly at the visitor.

"A pleasure." He shook hands with Kam's sister.

Kam said, "We need to talk, Lily. Let's go inside."

Lily paused to shoo the two girls outside. "Hinny, Mara, now you girls play and don't get into trouble. Ice cream if you're good."

Hinny, the older girl, said, "Yes, Mama."

Mara, the younger, echoed her sister.

The adults settled in the living room. Lily looked questioningly at her brother and the man in the dark suit.

The visitor got as far as "Miz Meehan," then Lily cut him off, "Kalani. My name is Kalani."

Now it was the visitor's turn to look puzzled. "Kalani Meehan?"

"No, Lily Kalani."

"I see." The visitor fumbled for his papers and laid them on a low table in front of the woman.

Kam said, "This fella wants me to become King of Hawai'i and Emperor of the United States of America."

Lily laughed out loud. "Right, and I'll be the Queen of the May."

The visitor said, "This is serious, Miz Mee—er, Kalani."

Lily heaved herself to her feet, made her way to the kitchen, and sorted through the kipple in a miscellany drawer until she found a pair of reading glasses. She padded back to the couch and lowered herself onto it. She carefully hooked the glasses behind her ears, accepted the papers from the stranger and read them.

Then she laid them back on the table and said, "Not me. Not a chance."

"Your full name is—?" The stranger nodded encouragingly.

"Lily Kalani."

The stranger turned in his seat.

"Kam Meehan," Kam said.

The stranger studied his papers as if he hadn't read them over a score of times. "I believe your proper names are slightly different. According to our records they are Kamehameha and Liliuokalani. You are descended from the great Kamehameha and the brilliant, tragic Liliuokalani. One or the other of you must accept the crown. We need you. I—"

The stranger squirmed in his seat. He actually ran his finger around the inside of his shirt collar, a move he must have picked up from Rodney Dangerfield. "I am empowered to offer whatever inducements are required."

Lily and Kam exchanged glances, then excused themselves from the room. When they returned, Lily spoke while Kam stood nodding agreement.

"Kam won't take it and neither will I. But the girls love to play. Hinny's full name is Hine-Nui-Te-Po. Mara is Marawa. If we have to do this, it has to be on our terms."

The visitor waited.

Lily ticked off the items on her fingers:

"Capitol moves to Maui."

The visitor nodded.

"The girls get to play Queen and Princess until they're old enough to learn that it's for real. In the meanwhile, it's all a game to them."

The visitor raised his eyebrows.

"That won't work for you?" Lily asked.

"Bu—but—a game, Miz Kalani? These are world affairs."

"They take it seriously in Washington?"

"Certainly!"

"Better play it like a game."

The visitor groaned, then nodded.

"And we keep our house. And the girls go to kindergarten and first grade with their friends, just like now."

The visitor jerked as if he'd been punched in the face. "Miz Kalani! The security!"

"You'll handle it, I have confidence in you. Take it or leave it. Just tell me which it will be and get going. I have to make lunch for my girls."

The visitor got up and turned toward the door.

"I'll walk you back to your car," Kam Meehan offered. "I've lost most of the morning's business. I have to make some money whether you do or not."

"Okay," said the stranger. "Tell you what, I'd really like to bring home a Hawai'ian shirt. Flowers and tikis and hula girls. The more outrageous the better."

"I can accommodate you," Kam said.

"And one for my wife," the stranger added.

"Gotcha."

"We have five kids," the stranger said.

"Wow!" said Kam. "We'll take care of 'em."

Cheryl Sanders leaned against her Alfa-Romeo Spyder, fumbling in her purse for her keys. Her vision was a little bit out of focus and her head was feeling fuzzy but she could drive herself back to her hotel, she was pretty sure of that.

She felt a hand on her wrist and turned. It was the bartender. With a deft motion he lifted the keys from her hand. Before she could say anything he slipped her car keys into his pocket.

"I'll get you a cab, Miss. Don't worry. We'll get you back to your hotel safely. You just sleep it off and when you come downstairs in the morning you'll find your keys waiting at the desk."

He whistled and a cab appeared from somewhere. "Which hotel, Miss?" the bartender asked.

Cheryl told him.

He put her into the back seat, walked around the cab and leaned in the driver's window. Cheryl saw the bartender nod toward her, hand the driver her car keys, and reach for his own pocket.

He pulled out a roll of bills. Cheryl could see him peel an orange bill and a blue one off the roll. She watched as he handed the bills with their portraits of the ancient King Kamehameha and Queen Liliuokalani to the cab driver.

Cheryl leaned her head against the back of the seat and closed her eyes. She dozed comfortably all the way back to her hotel, where the driver wakened her gently and sent her upstairs in the care of a solicitous concierge.

An Innocent Presumption
Kevin J. Anderson

A FREAK ACCIDENT. NEVER HAPPEN AGAIN IN A million years.

Rain slicked the pavement like a black mirror, reflecting the amber lights of the tow truck and the squad car's scarlet and blue flashers. A Toyota SUV had stalled high on the span of the Oakland Bay Bridge, angled so that it disrupted two lanes of traffic. Cars slowed across the bridge, crawling forward like a slow but belligerent garden slug.

A cop stood in the cold drizzle, waving his arms and fruitlessly directing traffic while a tow truck backed up, aligning itself to remove the offending SUV. Its warning beeps sounded like high childish screams.

A placid-looking older man in a blue Mercury eased forward to change lanes and bypass the obstacle. The cop held up one hand and waved with the other. The blue Mercury lurched forward while cars in the adjacent lane struggled to stop.

The driver behind him accelerated, then hit the brakes. The car skidded forward on the slick road and crunched into the rear of the Mercury. With the impact, the older man's trunk popped open.

Disgusted, the cop walked forward, holding out both hands to stop traffic. The driver of the rear car rolled down his window to yell curses.

In the Mercury, the older man opened his door and stood

staring—dazed, determined—at the bridge railing high above the gunmetal-gray water.

The frowning cop saw the young woman's bloody body in the Mercury's trunk. Two deep and brutal slashes across her face, her cheeks sliced open to expose white teeth. Both eyes ruined by the blade. Her throat cut all the way to the windpipe and spine.

The cop yanked out his service revolver, holding it in a stance he had often practiced at the firing range but had never used in the line of duty. The old man froze before he could make a run for the edge of the bridge. The drizzle continued, but everything else had fallen silent, a snapshot tableau.

After two years and seven victims, intensive manhunts and giant budgets from crack crime-solving agencies, "Slasher X" was caught because of an insignificant fender-bender, a mere coincidence.

Another day on the job exploring alternate timelines.

Heather Rheims shouldered her pack, looking like a non-descript student. She wore a loose flannel shirt and comfortable jeans, a look that was in style in virtually every parallel universe. Timeline prospectors had to be unobtrusive, finish their tasks without drawing attention to themselves, then slip back through the portal to the central complex of Alternitech.

With her long rusty-brown hair and large gray-blue eyes, she passed as a typical college sophomore. Only her sharp gaze and hard expression revealed that she had scars and concerns beyond looking for parties at the student union or picking up guys in her poly-sci class.

Now, inside the main control room, portal frames gleamed in the too-white light. The room was always frigid, overly air-conditioned to pamper the dimensional-access equipment. A fellow timeline prospector, a tall crewcut blond who looked as if he belonged in an ROTC recruiting office, approached her. Rod's normally stony face was a mixture of sympathy and victory. "Hey, I hear they caught the bastard last night."

Heather's lips formed a grim line. She took a moment before answering to make sure her voice was steady. "Better late than never, I guess. Although if they'd caught him after victim number three instead of number seven, then I could still go biking on the headlands with my sister."

Rod squeezed her shoulder, then turned away as the tech supervisor called his name and prepared the portal for his day's assignment.

Heather said, "Still looking for novel leukemia treatments?"

"No, just novels." Rod gave a foolish smile. "Maybe Mario Puzo's sequel to *The Godfather*, or another historical epic by James Clavell. Maybe I'll find a universe where Stephen King never did retire." He went over to the dimensional doorway as the air shimmered and crackled with a smell of ozone.

Alternitech explorers like Heather sidestepped into parallel universes nearly identical with the modern world but with subtle differences: timelines where the Beatles had not broken up, where James Dean had a long and successful film career, where scientific researchers had achieved useful medical or technological breakthroughs that, for whatever reason, had been stymied in this world. A timeline prospector's job was to identify these differences and bring them back home, where Alternitech would sell them to the highest bidder.

"Oh, Ms. Rheims?" called the tech supervisor in his thick British accent. "If you would grace us with your presence, we are ready for you."

With the news of Slasher X in all the papers, the tech supervisor didn't give Heather his usual deprecating smirk about her "embarrassing" current quest; since her patron paid a generous fee for Heather's skills, Alternitech allowed him his eccentricities and loosened some of their rules for her work.

"Money-Is-No-Object" Feldman was obsessed with the John F. Kennedy assassination. For over a month now he had sent Heather on expeditions into parallel universes in order to secure evidence that proved or disproved the old conspiracy theory.

Now she shouldered her backpack, taking several deep breaths to prepare herself. She exhaled all the air, then stepped forward into the ripple—

—Without moving, she found herself in another universe that seemed identical to her own. She had three hours here, enough time to ransack the archives in the university library.

The city maps were similar in every timeline, with only the most minor deviations of street names. She knew exactly how to get to the UC San Francisco library or, failing that, the city's main downtown branch. For her purposes, all she needed was a microfilm archive or public access computer with newspapers dating back to 1963. Despite each universe's differences, the Windows Operating System seemed ubiquitous across timelines.

The routine was familiar by now. Heather even had her favorite carrel picked out. Occasionally she had found greater evidence for a conspiracy, various shooters other than Lee Harvey Oswald; in some timelines, no assassin had ever been caught or even accused. In others, no crusader or conspiracy theorist like Jim Garrison had even raised the possibility, and Kennedy's murder went quietly into the history books as the work of a single madman.

"Money-Is-No-Object" Feldman was delighted with each nuance, each deviation, although so far the clues added up to nothing more tantalizing than the blurry photos often used to "prove" the existence of Bigfoot or the Loch Ness monster.

In this timeline, though, Heather felt a thrill as she discovered a significant change in history: This universe's Kennedy had survived the shooting, living out his term in office paralyzed from the waist down. After the assassination attempt, however, he had no longer been a fiery leader, and his presidency was remembered as basically ineffective. No shooter had ever been caught.

She followed the history threads, surprised at how easily the timeline's broad strokes had shifted back to her version of "normal." Heather used her hand scanner to copy the documentation. Feldman would be ecstatic.

Since she had a little time remaining before she needed to find her way back to the Alternitech portal, she glanced at current events. When she stumbled on the headline of the morning edition of the *San Francisco Chronicle*, Heather sat frozen in disbelief, as she read, and reread, each word:

"Slasher X Claims Eighth Victim."

Then, of course, she knew exactly what she had to do.

Parallel line after parallel line. Feldman's enthusiasm did not diminish as Heather continued to retrieve tantalizing nuggets that maintained the eccentric millionaire's funding. But she had another mission too. She no longer cared about the razzing from the tech supervisor or the other timeline prospectors who didn't consider her "tabloid work" to be worthy of Alternitech's potential.

Now, Heather was saving lives, innocent people just like her sister Janni.

In each new parallel universe, her first action was to check the newspapers, then make an anonymous phone call to tip off the police. The story was always the same: Her own parallel universe was the only one in which a bad-luck traffic accident had exposed the serial killer's identity.

When she delivered her bombshell of information, the detectives were sometimes skeptical, sometimes angry, other times mercifully grateful for any lead. Since the killer had been caught in her own timeline, Heather had followed the details of the case, and she could offer enough veracity to convince the investigating homicide detectives that she wasn't a crank.

She understood, for instance, that Slasher X—an older retired man with the unusual name of Eric Keric—used a fat black marker to draw an X on the faces of his victims before commencing the bloodier work. Keric slit the throats first so that the victims didn't struggle, and his thick carving knife could make precise strokes along the dark line he had marked, crossing out their faces. Many nightmares ago, Heather had been called in to identify Janni's mutilated body—her face gashed with the deadly X, her throat cut. . . .

After a while, Heather stopped even checking the reports before she made her anonymous calls. She simply tipped off the police to Eric Keric and let the professionals handle it from there. It was so easy to be a good citizen, to get her revenge for Janni . . . and to make sure that Slasher X paid the price for his terrible crimes. She began to feel like a hit-and-run crusader for justice, almost like Jim Garrison's tireless attempts to track down JFK's killers.

In her work for Feldman, she also came back in triumph to Alternitech. At last, she found a parallel line where Lee Harvey Oswald had lived long enough after being shot by Jack Ruby to blurt out a confession. With his dying breath, Oswald had fingered a man named Francis Tarryall, a shitty Dallas businessman with ties to Cuba and the Soviet Union. He'd been in trouble with the law many times but had managed to hire the best lawyers, to get evidence dismissed. But after Oswald's accusation, Tarryall's trial was swift and the outcome sure. Tarryall never confessed, but the investigations by that universe's Warren Commission yielded seemingly incontrovertible evidence.

Heather copied several months of news stories so Feldman could study the aftermath.

She was rushed toward the end because her usual call to the police had taken an excessive amount of time. The detective—not one of the familiar names usually assigned to the Slasher X case—asked too many questions, wanted to know about the killer's victims, pumped her for even the most obvious details.

Frustrated, she insisted that he check out Eric Keric, even divulging the old man's address, which she had memorized. The fact that the detective knew Keric's name and where he lived was a good sign. Perhaps the police had already been following him. . . .

Rushed and exhilarated with her new Oswald discovery,

Heather hurried back to meet the Alternitech portal. She promised herself a nice restaurant meal to celebrate a productive and satisfying day.

Alternitech prospectors rarely returned to the same parallel universe, but Mr. Feldman offered a substantial bonus. He had discovered, with great relief, that Heather hadn't obtained the full story about Francis Tarryall. His quest could continue.

She'd copied later articles without reading them, and one of her last wire-service transcripts cast extreme doubts on Oswald's dying confession. Other evidence came to light that Tarryall and Oswald had been very personal enemies, their philosophies close enough that minor differences led to shouting matches and hatreds. Some of the Warren Commission's conclusions had begun to unravel . . . but Heather had not obtained the rest of the story.

She supposed that her patron wanted to seize any possibility that the conspiracy hadn't actually been solved. In his subconscious at least, Feldman perhaps needed something to hold onto. Her last mission had apparently given him the answer, but now he hoped she could cast doubt once again.

Heather stepped through the portal, backpack and equipment slung on her shoulder, and went right to work. The answer was obvious as soon as she scrolled through newspapers a few months farther ahead in time. Francis Tarryall was proven innocent, much of the evidence found to be false or misleading, Oswald's confession dismissed as a dying man's last vendetta with no relevance to the JFK assassination.

As she copied the articles, she recalled that this was the parallel reality where she had spent so much time arguing with the skeptical detective about Slasher X. Heather flipped through recent newspapers in the library, looking for headlines proclaiming that the killer had been caught, that innocent victims had been saved. She could take credit for the justice, but she alone would know it. This was her quest . . . just like Feldman's.

But she found no headline, no story whatsoever, no mention of Eric Keric or his arrest. The detective had ignored her! She couldn't believe it.

With a fluttery dread, she flipped past several months and found no banner stories announcing the serial murders. Heather brushed her rusty-brown hair behind her ear, blinking in puzzlement. It didn't seem possible that Slasher X had managed to hide all of his victims, that people like poor Janni were simply written off as missing persons, runaways, unexplained disappearances . . . maybe even alien abductions.

What if, in this alternate timeline, Eric Keric himself didn't exist?

Breathing quickly, hoping that that was the answer, she pawed through the residential phone book. In her own universe, Keric did not have an unlisted number. She found him right where she expected his name to be. The address listed was the same.

The bastard hadn't been caught. She had called the police, given her information—but the idiot detective had apparently done nothing, and the killer remained on the loose.

She looked at her watch. Still more than an hour left, since she had been so quick to get the answers Feldman needed.

Indignant, Heather thought about calling the detective again, demanding to know why he hadn't acted on her information. But she would not be coming back to this parallel universe, and if she didn't make sure that Slasher X was caught, then all his later victims would be on her conscience.

She could go to the address herself. She had never faced her sister's killer, never even seen the madman. Eric Keric had no idea who Heather Rheims was, despite the fact that she had turned him in timeline after timeline.

She made up her mind in an instant, even though this was probably a very bad decision; she had visions of playing a role in a real-life horror movie. But Alternitech would sweep her away in an hour, no matter what happened. After all, Eric Keric had no reason to suspect her, or even recognize her. Heather decided to take the risk.

The murderer's house was repulsively charming and quaint. Neat bluechip junipers lined the walkway up to his little cottage. Flower boxes held green succulents and brown perennials that had died back for winter. Heather thought of the wicked crone's gingerbread house from the story of "Hansel and Gretel."

The front door was painted a slate gray with white trim. Obviously the old sociopath took time between killings to keep his house immaculate. She drew a deep breath and glanced at her watch again before knocking on the door. Only half an hour remained before the Alternitech portal would return. In her jacket pocket she clasped a can of pepper spray. She always carried it in her backpack but she'd never needed to use it.

Eric Keric had never seen her before in his life. She convinced herself she had nothing to worry about. Heather hoped that she looked like a newspaper salesperson or some other door-to-door annoyance. Then she rang the bell.

The old round-faced man pulled back the curtains beside the door and stared at her for an instant, then ducked away. Keric opened the door, and Heather stepped forward, tense and ready to lure him into a brief but incriminating conversation.

But his hand struck quickly like a rattlesnake, snatching her long rusty-brown hair. "I'm not taking any more of this!" He yanked her head toward him. "And I've certainly had enough of *you*."

Before she could fumble the pepper spray out of her pocket, he swung the baseball bat that he kept beside the door, striking her a harsh sharp blow on the side of the head. Heather didn't even have time to cry out. . . .

Pain hammered through the grogginess. She had been stunned into twilight for only a few minutes, but Eric Keric had had enough time to drag her into the kitchen and thrust her into a metal chair beside the dinette table. He had lashed her elbows and wrists with two rubbery bonds—*extension cords*, she realized as she fought her way back to full awareness. Her ears rang, and bright colors swam at the fringes of her vision.

Keric dragged a thin wooden easel across the linoleum floor, standing it in front of her. He was dressed in a checked shirt, partly unbuttoned so she could see his low-necked undershirt and wiry gray chest hair. His sleeves were rolled up on his forearms as if he was ready to get down to work.

The smells and appliances in his kitchen, speckled Formica countertops and stainless-steel sink, were the trappings she had come to associate with kindly grandfathers, but Eric Keric seemed anything but paternal as he glared at her with both fear and anger in his eyes. He pulled the easel in front of her, and Heather lifted her throbbing head to look at it.

"I don't know who you are," the old man growled, "or why you keep tormenting me. What have I done to you?"

She tried to make words, but only a groaning sound came from her slack mouth and thick tongue. The ringing in her ears grew louder. He pulled up the white cover sheet on the easel's large sketchpad, and Heather was astonished to see an accurate, painstakingly rendered pencil and charcoal sketch of her own face. Keric straightened the easel so that she was forced to look at herself. She wondered if she might be hallucinating.

"You . . . killed my sister," Heather finally blurted.

The old man scowled at her. "I didn't kill anyone—no matter what you keep saying, no matter what the police accuse me of." Heather couldn't figure out what he was talking about. "You are an evil, spiteful woman. I know you won't tell me who hired you, or who is responsible for this conspiracy, but you've succeeded in ruining my life—if that was your purpose."

He drew a deep breath, and his eyes flickered shut as if he were composing himself, then he squared his shoulders. "But I cannot change other people. I must change myself. I must take control of my life."

He turned away from her as if he couldn't bear to look at Heather's face. She knew she'd been stunned for only a few minutes at best. He couldn't possibly have drawn such an exquisite portrait in that amount of time.

"The police have come to my house five times, twice with search warrants. They ransacked my private possessions, everything I own, but they found nothing, won't even tell me what they think I've done or what they're looking for."

Then he pointed an accusing finger at her. Heather was so frightened she tried to squirm away. The chair screeched with her movement, but she could not break free of the extension cords.

"Because of your harassment, I've lost my job. It wasn't much, but I worked hard at it. They had no reason to fire me." Keric paced the kitchen floor, and his face had a pathetically desperate plea written across it. "Don't you think every day isn't enough of a struggle? I walk on the edge, but I have the strength. I know how to deal with this burden. . . ."

His voice became a low growl, and his eyes lit up. "But *you* keep piling more and more stress. You're *trying* to drive me over the edge. You want to push me into some violent action. I don't know what you have to gain by making me go . . . mad."

He clenched his fists but then squeezed his eyes shut again, breathing deeply as if reciting a silent mantra to himself. "But I won't let you. You don't have the power. My life is under my control. You cannot force me to break the law or to hurt anyone."

He withdrew a fat black marker from his pocket and wrenched off the plastic cap with a squeak. She could smell the ink's pungent sour fumes, and her heart skipped a beat. Slasher X always scribbled his indelible mark on the faces of his victims before he cut with the heavy knife.

"You have no power over me," he said, and turned.

With a brutal swift stroke and then a backwards slash, he made a black accusing mark across the picture he had drawn, crossing out her face, obliterating the sketched eyes as if he had eliminated her.

"There," he said, satisfied. "You can no longer bother me."

Keric tore the picture off the easel and carried it, fluttering in his hands, over to a wooden closet door beside the refrigerator. On the back of the door, skewered on a long nail, hung a stack of sketches. Now, Keric stabbed Heather's portrait on top of the others, faces of men and woman, all of them X-ed out.

"Like all those others, you simply don't matter to me anymore."

Her thoughts spun with what he had said. Could it be true that in this parallel timeline Eric Keric had never become Slasher X? That he had found a way to divert his murderous rage and take it out symbolically on his sketches rather than using a knife? She felt sick.

And if this particular incarnation of Eric Keric also had deep psychological problems but retained his sanity by the thinnest of threads . . . then by making anonymous phone calls accusing him of crimes, had she driven the old man closer toward an edge he had so far managed to avoid?

He went behind her, and Heather was afraid he would strike her, cut her throat. But then she felt the extension cords tug at her elbows and wrists—and Heather found herself freed.

The old man tossed the cords onto the linoleum floor. "Go. Get out of here. You are erased from my life."

Heather stood, disoriented, still feeling the concussion. She looked at the old man, but couldn't say a word. Too many conflicting ideas clamored in her mind.

Bolting like a frightened rabbit, she ran for the front door. She had only a few moments before the Alternitech portal would appear. Keric stepped after her, not in pursuit, but eager to seal the door tight behind her. She looked over her shoulder. "I'm . . . sorry. I made an assumption, perhaps a wrong one."

She yanked open the door—and startled herself. She stood facing a carbon copy of Heather Rheims, another *her*. But this one held a handgun, drawn and ready to fire.

Heather's first absurd thought was that this version of herself had come more sensibly prepared than with a pocket can of pepper spray, though smuggling a handgun would have been tricky. She recovered and figured it out first. "Of course. There have to be Alternitechs in parallel timelines."

"Yes, and we both had the same idea," the other Heather said. "Did you kill him?"

Then Eric Keric stepped up, crestfallen and anguished. "Why won't you leave me alone?"

The other Heather's lip curled, and she swung up the handgun. She said accusingly to Heather, "Why did you let him live?"

"Because he . . . isn't guilty," she said. "Did you look for the headlines in this universe? Did you see any mention of Slasher X? Did the police react strangely when you called to turn him in?"

The alternate young woman kept the pistol aimed at Keric, but her expression wavered.

"This guy might be a brutal killer in most of the parallel universes we've visited, but not here. Oh, he's got plenty of mental problems, but so far he has managed to deal with them. He hasn't hurt anybody."

"That's ridiculous," said her counterpart.

"I know . . . but it's still true."

Keric looked back and forth between the identical young women, resigned instead of surprised. Heather realized that an endless succession of parallel versions of herself had come here to accuse him.

"This one doesn't kill people," Heather insisted. "He just draws pictures."

"How can I accept that?" said her alternate. "I need to do something for Janni. This was my only chance for revenge. How can I let that go?"

"Would I lie to you?" Heather looked at her with a deeply sincere expression. And then the other part of the puzzle slammed into place with thunderous force. "And in this timeline, Janni must still be alive."

Before she could continue the argument, before she could hope to see her sister again, the Alternitech portal shimmered in the air, tracking her. Heather looked at her counterpart, who wore a startled expression on her face probably identical to her own.

But she couldn't stay. The portal beckoned. She knew she was not likely to come back to this parallel universe . . . and she had squandered her time here. Heather had no choice but to return, without seeing Janni again.

But perhaps her counterpart would use her time for something more beneficial than useless revenge.

When she returned, blinking and disoriented, Heather stepped out of the portal into the Alternitech control room. Quickly, the tech supervisor and two security men came up to surround her. Heather didn't know what had gone wrong, why they were so intent on intercepting her.

"Ms. Rheims," said the tech supervisor, "kindly hand over all of your documentation on the John F. Kennedy assassination. Your investigation is now terminated, your information forfeit."

Heather shrugged off her backpack, her mind spinning in another direction. She hadn't even thought about Feldman and his obsessive quest. "What's wrong?" She removed all her scans and copies about the frame-up of Francis Tarryall, how the JFK conspiracy remained unresolved. "I found some interesting information, but—"

"Mr. Feldman apparently deceived us and has cost Alternitech a great deal of money. He defaulted on his last several payments, and we've just discovered that he's bankrupt."

"Bankrupt? Money-Is-No-Object Feldman has no money?" She tried to wrap her mind around that shift in reality.

With his sarcastic British reserve, the tech supervisor looked at her. "Mr. Feldman insists it's a conspiracy designed to prevent him from discovering the truth about the JFK murder."

Heather felt numb. Somewhere, in another universe, an alternate Heather Rheims was again accusing an alternate—innocent— Eric Keric of unspeakable crimes. Or maybe she was embracing a confused but warm-hearted Janni.

Swallowing hard, she stepped away from the portal. Now she could hope for a reassignment exploring parallel universes for a more legitimate purpose, finding medical cures, scientific discoveries, even artistic works. Heather's vigilante streak made her a poor dispenser of justice. She would no longer solve crimes, not personal ones or political ones. The truth wasn't always clear-cut, even in her own timeline.

Instead, she would remember Janni, keep the fond memories, maybe do some good things in her honor. She was alive, somewhere.

That was a truth Heather could hold on to.

Why Then Ile Fit You

Howard Waldrop

ONE OF THE ONES I CAN SEE TOLD ME IT IS already the year 1951. Good Gracious!

I believe one of the other ones told me it was 1950, last year, when they took me out to act in *David and Bathsheba*.

I can't keep them straight anymore, the years or the people floating in and out of here—they come, they go, the ones I can see and the ones no one can.

It had been good to see Hoey again on that quasi-Biblical set—we had not acted together since he was Lestrade and I Moriarty—No, no, it was the *other* one, the one in Washington, where I wasn't Moriarty—how long ago was that? It must be years and years. The time goes by—I never know whether it has been a day, two minutes, or five years since something occurred.

They even tell me I was in a film two years ago—a musical with Gene Kelly and Judy Garland. I have absolutely no memory of that. Upon my soul, I do not.

You see, my agent comes to get me—I'm sure he has checked with the staff and doctors, and has probably even talked to me, but I do not remember that, either—and he takes me to the studios, and I act, and there are various pleasantries, and then I find myself back here in what I have come to refer to as Shady Bedlam Manors, though I am sure the name is something quainter, more reassuring.

105

Others here call it The Home for Old and Bewildered Actors. . . .

I have just noticed an insect—some beetle or one of the true bugs—which probably flew in when the wide back doors were open during visiting hours. It seems to like the very-well-designed bedside lamp on the somnoe—it is crawling in an endless pattern over the rim of the shade, down inside, across the far side, reappearing at exactly the same place above the rim each time.

I shall time its circumnavigation of the lampshade. Perhaps this will give me a clue to . . . something or other.

Appropriately enough, my clock has stopped. I give a small laugh, and think that it has been a long time since I've done *that.*

Still the insect appears, disappears, reappears, so time does go on. . . .

I must have been doing something naughty, or non-U, and been seen, for I find myself lightly restrained to my bed.

I must have told them about the insect, or it found its way out of the Magellanic voyaging of its luciferian world, for now it is gone.

And I am reminded of poor Dwight Frye. How long now? There we were, in my fitter years, making *Dead Men Walk* in the middle of the war. I am playing, if I remember right, a vampire whose one goal in life is to suck all the blood out of his twin brother—also me—a Goody-Two-Shoes. And then there's Dwight, doing his usual, as Jewish-Americans say, schtick, giving it his all, like always. And then there he is, lying dead of a heart attack, at little more than half my age.

How many deformed and demented human wrecks did he play in his time? Twenty? Thirty? In the movies, and more on stage. The fellow was a fine actor. Yet there we both were on Poverty Row, bugging our eyes out like Mantan Moreland . . .

It was as nothing that each of us had Shakespeare, Shaw, Galsworthy in our pasts, great and enduring roles. There we were in films which barely lasted as long in theaters as it takes to dress for dinner at a country-house weekend . . .

And now, Dwight dead and me here.

Someone I couldn't see must have been here. My restraints are gone. There is a new clock on the bedside table. It seems to be working very well.

There is also a swelling in my left arm—a sure sign one I can't see has given me an injection, while the others are invisibly ransacking my room, looking for money or sweets. Or watching me. Jove knows what.

One can never be sure whether they are there or not.

I often wonder if it were for my eyes that I was cast as all those crazy doctors, Moriarty, small-town Torquemadas? It was a small trick—letting the face go soft but keeping the eyes hard, flinty, moist. An old Victorian rep thing—I learned it from older heavies and villains when I was playing leads in my much younger days. Then came the films, and I worked in them. And one reviewer had said: "He enters the movie. His eyeballs come on the screen before the rest of his head does."

I *never* forgot that review.

I had a very nice letter from dear old Jimmie Whale yesterday. He says he will come out of retirement—what, ten, twelve years now? —and direct a film again, but only if I appear in it.

I call my agent. Then I am asking one of the male nurses if he thinks I am well enough to do a movie again, when one of the invisible ones comes in, makes me do a bad thing, I think, and then jabs me in the arm with the kind of needle they always had me fooling with at Monogram and PRC, the kind that is really used to extract blood from cattle and horses for serum. . . .

This morning, free of the bands again, I write Jimmie a courteous note, thanking him for the offer but telling him I really don't feel up to it. I do not know if he is really trying to come out of his self-imposed exile only a few miles from here, or is just being kind to me, or if I am favoring him with a negative reply, that he expects, so he won't have to go through with all the bother and nonsense.

Out here, in what others call Tinseltown, one can never be sure who is doing a favor for whom.

I just don't want to embarrass myself, or Jimmie, if there were a movie and I were in it.

Dear old Marjorie Main. Now playing Ma—what? Some utensil. Ladle? Pot? Kettle—yes, Kettle! She could always outact almost anyone she was onscreen with. Now that she has the security of a series, she can pick and choose her other roles, and can perhaps slow down.

Dear Eve Arden. I can now listen to her on the radio, in the teacher-part, Constance Brooks.

Dear old—Ah! What's the use. If I keep going on like this I shall begin to sound like Dear Old Boris Karloff. One thing is sure—he and Lugosi will be doing this stuff forever, dropping in harness like Dwight. Only, fittingly and not nearly so young. . . .

I must have been asleep in my chair, in my dressing gown, reading Cedric Hardwicke's book.

There was a touch on my arm.

I opened my eyes.

"George," he said.

"Jimmie!" I said, dropping the book to the floor, reaching for it.

He retrieved it, putting it on my reading table, carefully placing the bookmark in it before closing it.

Except for a few wrinkle-lines, and the fact that his hair was now pure white, he hadn't changed a bit in more than a decade. (I've not had more than a fringe of hair at the back of my head since my late thirties. . . .)

"Jimmie, old fellow! What brings you here?"

"Well, George," he said, "the movie might be on again, and I've come to ask you once more to be in it. I absolutely won't, can't do it without you."

"It's very nice of you to ask, Jimmie, but—look about you. Does this seem to be the lodging of a *working* actor? Scripts everywhere, bad food boiling in a pot, unpaid bills stacked up? No. This is very much the room of an *ex*-actor."

"You know as well as I, George, that it's like the sound of the bell to an old firehorse out to pasture—the right role comes along, you can smell it like a fire, miles away. I'm surprised you hadn't written me in the last few weeks, scenting the script."

"Of course, that's the line *every* producer or director uses on *every* old bunged-up actor," I said. "I believe I heard Beerbohm-Tree used it on Mrs. Patrick Campbell herself, a couple of years before he *himself* quit producing and started teaching."

"No, George. This time it's a real role. I promise you, you won't have to eat a rat, or anything. You get to act. An actor's dream!"

"But not, I'm sure, alas, *actor-proof*," I said.

"At least tell me you'll look at the script if I send it," he said, smiling earnestly. "When I first asked you, two years ago, it wasn't quite ready. Now it is."

"Oh, Jimmie. I'm truly flattered. But I'm so rusty."

Jimmie put his hand on my shoulder. "I absolutely can't do this without you, George. It will be bad enough coming back to *all that*. I really don't want to do this if you don't."

"Oh, Jimmie," I said. I believed him. "Ask Karloff. I don't think he's taken a day off since 1931, and that was a world away. You and he did so well together, every time out . . ."

"Karloff isn't right for the part, George," he said quietly. "No matter how well he and I got on and helped each other, he would have to tie himself in a knot—no doubt he'd find some way to do it—but why do that, when it's your role in the first place? Something you can do as naturally as . . . as reading Sir Cedric's book there?"

"I'm just too old and too . . . too confused to do a film just now. You're seeing me at my best, my very best. I haven't felt so good in, oh, days and days. And those, Jimmie, are becoming more and more infrequently. Good days, I mean."

He laughed. "I believe you're having Fear of Success, George."

That broke much of the tension. I called down for tea to be brought up. (Wrong time of day, I know: Jimmie used to have real tea at four on his sets for all the expatriate Brits—Karloff, Lanchester, himself, anyone else vaguely British or colonial—and there were lots of us in the old days.)

We talked, then, about those old days and compatriots. He caught me up on such gossip as he had; after awhile I showed him around the place, feeling quite the squire. He paused in the walk to talk with another old, old actor, who'd been in *Journey's End*, when Jimmie had come over to direct it in New York before coming out here to film it in 1930. It was very nice of Jimmie to do that; the man was much older than I, and had been in this place long before I got here.

Before he left, Jimmie, of course, asked me to reconsider one more time, and I of course declined.

That night I had a dream. In the dream, I was asleep. People kept waking me up and giving me Academy Awards. I kept telling them to get out and let me sleep. Every time I got back to sleep, another person came in and gave me another one. I had more than Walter Brennan, more than some scene designers, more than costumers, more than anyone. And all I really wanted was sleep.

When I awoke in the morning, I was surprised to find that the room wasn't full of gold statuettes. Same old room; same bedside stand, same chairs and tables. No Academy Awards.

I was out of sorts all that day and the next.

*   *   *

The only trouble with this place, fine though it is, is that they think I'm crazy. Don't they know it's not me, but the ones I can't see, *they* can't see, that are doing things to me? I don't know if they—the Unkind Ones—are truly invisible, or whether they just move so fast the human eye cannot take them in. I have suggested to the doctors they set up some—is it undercranked or overcranked?—time-lapse cameras to test this latter hypothesis.

I have been reading a book of famous last lines, dying words of the famous, notorious, and not-so-either. Such as that of the condemned man who stepped onto a rickety scaffold and asked the sheriff, "Is it safe?" Or the last words of Arthur Flegenheimer, that is, Dutch Schultz, which was more than four thousand words long spoken in a raving 104° delirium, which ended with the words "French Canadian Bean Soup."

I shall try to exercise enough restraint that my last ones should not be something like "bibble-bibble-bibble. . . ."

One of the new nurses, named I think Bettina, brought my paper in this morning.

"Mr. Zucco," she said. "They asked me to tell you that Mr. Whale passed away yesterday."

I could tell that she was upset. I reached out and patted her hand.

"There, there," I said. "I'm sure it was time for him to go, and I'm sure it was for the best."

She left. Whale. Whale? Where have I heard that name before? Possibly an old, *old* timer.

I shall have to ask Jimmie next time I see him if he knew any-one named Whale. Strange name, that.

One of the Unkind Ones is here: but this one I can *see*. It is not one of the people I can usually see—but I know that she is one of the ones usually invisible. She looks somewhat like Aquanetta from the Paula the Ape Woman movies. (If it were her, I could make her laugh. I could do that, like I used to do, with the woman who played Pauline Dupree, by simply saying; "Rondo Hatton: Why the long face?")

But it is not her. I know, because she has with her the longest, largest hypodermic syringe imaginable. It is grotesquely huge. In her other hand is a cotton swab, smelling of alcohol.

Inside the glass barrel of the syringe is a green liquid filled with dancing, moving sparks of light. She is not here to take, but to give. She leans close. Her breath is sweet.

"The Russians," she says warmly, tenderly, "have put up a satellite."

She swabs my bared arm.

"It's called *Sputnik*," she says, and plunges the giant needle in.

This must be something akin to what a heroin or cocaine or opium addict feels—this sense of bliss and happiness, well-being and, and —of knowing and understanding Everything!

It was like those movies I was in—all the potions, the brain-and-spinal-fluids, the suspended-animation gasses they always had me mucking about with!

Of course! Of course I see it all now. So sharp and clear! The needle is just a metaphor for the transcendent power of

What's Up, Tiger Lily?
Paul Di Filippo

1
Duck Soup

*T*HE FIRST INDICATION BASH APPLEBROOK RE-
ceived that all was not right with his world happened over
breakfast on the morning of Tuesday, June 25, 2029.

The newspaper he was reading turned into a movie screen.

Bash was instantly jerked out of his fascination with the current
headline (MERCOSUR FREETER MAKES SPINTRONICS
BREAKTHRU!). His jagged reaction caused some Metanomics
Plus nutrishake to spill from his cup onto the tabletop, where it was
quickly absorbed.

Looking at the clock on the wall—a display made of redacted
fish scales whose mutable refractiveness substituted for ancient
LEDs—as if to reassure himself that he hadn't been thrown entirely
out of the time stream, Bash sought to gain some perspective on this
alarming occurrence.

In itself, this transformation of his newspaper boded no ill. Such
things happened millions of times daily around the globe, thanks to
proteopape. And since Bash himself was the much-lauded, well-
rewarded inventor of proteopape, he was positively the last person
in the world to be astounded by the medium's capacity for change.

There was only one problem.

Bash had not instructed his newspaper to swap functions.

This impulsive, inexplicable toggling by his highly reliable newspaper scared Bash very much. Proteopape simply did not do such things. Eleven years ago, Bash had first engineered the substance with innumerable safeguards, backups and firewalls specifically intended to prevent just such herky-jerky transitions. In all the time since, out of billions of uses, there had been no recorded instances of proteopape malfunctioning. Even when sustaining up to seventy-five-percent damage, proteopape continued to maintain functionality. (Beyond such limits, proteopape would just shut down altogether.) The miracle material that had transformed so much of the twenty-first century's media landscape simply did not crash.

And if proteopape were suddenly to develop a glitch—Well, imagining the immense and catastrophic repercussions from any flaws in the ubiquitous material raised shivers with the magnitude of tsunamis along Bash's spine.

Having assimilated the very possibility that his fabled invention could behave in unpredictable ways, Bash gave his newspaper a shake, hoping to expunge this anomaly by the most primitive of engineering tactics. But the newspaper stubbornly continued to function as a movie screen, so Bash focused for clues on the actual movie being displayed across his ex-newspaper.

This particular sheet of proteopape on which Bash had been reading his newspaper measured approximately two feet by three feet. Possessing the stiffness and texture of heavy-bond dumb-paper, yet not quite as rigid as parchment, this sheet of proteopape had been folded in half vertically, producing four different faces, two outer and two inner. A bit old-fashioned, Bash preferred to read his newspaper on multiple pages, allowing him to refer backwards if he wished simply by eyeballing a previous face of his newspaper. Of course, upon finishing with the fourth page of the paper, Bash simply turned back to the front, where the fifth page was now automatically displayed, with pages six, seven and eight following.

But now every page revealed only the same movie, a quartet of active images. Bash turned the newspaper upside down, hoping to erase the unrequested show, but the inscribed sensors in the newspaper merely registered the new orientation and flipped the movie upright again.

Bash recognized the leering face of Groucho Marx, one of his father's favorite actors. Groucho wore some kind of ridiculous military uniform. *Duck Soup*, then. Now Margaret Dumont entered the scene, all dowager-haughty. But although the actions of the actors were canonically familiar, the conversation that followed bore no resemblance to any extant Hollywood script.

"So," said Groucho, in his familiar intonations which the MEMS speakers of the proteopape reproduced with high fidelity, "the little lady who wants to waste her mind and talents on artsy-fartsy stuff finally deigns to show up. Well, I'm afraid I've lost all interest in whatever crap you wanted me to watch."

"Okay, granted, I'm a little late," replied Dumont fruitily. "But you did promise after the Woodies that you'd come with me to hang out with my pals."

As this warped yet still meaningful dialogue from his personal life began to resonate with Bash, he started to feel queasy. He laid the newspaper nearly flat on the breakfast table, right atop his plate of auk eggs and fried plantains with mango syrup, and as the crease separating the half-pages disappeared, the movie redrew itself to fill the whole expanse of one side.

Groucho struck a mocking pose, one hand cradling his chin, the other with cigar poised at his brow. "Well, a self-important louse like me can't be bothered with that bunch of crazy amateur *artistes* you hang out with. Such crazy ideas! So I've decided to abandon you and return to my cloistered sterile existence."

"Hit the road, then, you jerk! But I'll have the last laugh! You just wait and see!"

With that parting sally, Dumont and Marx vanished from Bash's newspaper. But the words and images that comprised Bash's regular morning blue-toothed installment of *The Boston Globe* did not reappear. The sheet of proteopape remained a frustrating virginal white, unresponsive to any commands Bash gave it.

After his frustrated attempts to regain control of the newspaper, Bash gave up, reluctantly conceding that this sheet of proteopape was dead. He slumped back in his chair with a nervous sigh, admitting to himself that the origin of this sabotage was all too evident.

Why, oh why had he ever agreed to a date with Dagny Winsome?

2

The Big Chill

York and Adelaide Applebrook had gone bust in the big dotcom crash that had inaugurated the twenty-first century. Their entrepreneurial venture—into which they had sunk their own lifesavings and millions of dollars more from various friends, relatives and venture capitalists—had consisted of a website devoted to the marketing of Japanese poetry. Behind the tasteful interactive facade of *Haiku Howdy!* had been nothing more than a bank of public domain images—Oriental landscapes, for the most part—and a simplistic poetry generator. The visitor to *Haiku Howdy!* would input a selection of nouns and adjectives that the software would form into a haiku. Matched with an appropriate image, the poem could be e-mailed to a designated recipient. Initially offered as a free service, the site was projected to go to pay-per-use status in a year or two, with estimated revenues of ten million dollars a year.

This rudimentary site and whimsical service represented the grand sum of the Applebrooks' inspiration and marketing plan.

The fact that at the height of their "success," in the year 1999, they named their newborn son Basho, after the famous master of haiku, was just one more token of their supreme confidence in their scheme.

When *Haiku Howdy!* collapsed after sixteen months of existence, having burned through millions and millions of dollars of OPM, the Applebrooks had cause to rethink their lifestyle and goals. They moved from Seattle to the less pricey rural environs of Medford, Oregon, and purchased a small pear orchard with some leftover funds they had secretly squirreled away from the screamingly burned investors. They took a vow then and there to have nothing further to do with any hypothetical future digital utopia, making a back-to-the-land commitment similar to that made by many burnt-out hippies a generation prior.

Surely the repentant, simple-living Applebrooks never reckoned that their only child, young Basho, would grow up to revolutionize, unify and dominate the essential ways in which digital information was disseminated across all media.

But from his earliest years Bash exhibited a fascination with computers and their contents. Perhaps his prenatal immersion in the heady dotcom world had imprinted him with the romance of bytes and bauds. In any case, Bash's native talents (which were considerable; he tested off the high end of several scales) were, from the first, bent toward a career in information technologies.

Bash zipped through public schools, skipping several grades, and enrolled at MIT at age fifteen. Socially, Basho Applebrook felt awkward amidst the sophisticated elders of his generation. But in the classroom and labs he excelled. During his senior year on campus he encountered his most important success in the field of moletronics, the science of manipulating addressable molecules, when he managed to produce the first fully functional sheet of proteo-pape.

Alone late one night in a lab, Bash dipped a standard blank sheet of high quality dumb-paper into a special bath where it absorbed a tailored mix of dopant molecules. (This bath was the four hundred and thirteenth reformulation of his original recipe.) Removing the paper, Bash placed it in a second tub of liquid. This tub featured a lattice of STM tweezers obedient to computer control. Bash sent a large file into the tub's controllers, and, gripping hold of each doped molecule with invisible force pincers, the device laid down intricate circuitry templates into the very molecules of the paper.

Junctions bloomed, MEMS proliferated. Memory, processors, sensors, a GPS unit, solar cells, rechargeable batteries, speakers, pixels, a camera and wireless modem: all arrayed themselves invisibly and microscopically throughout the sheet of paper.

Removing the paper from its complexifying wash, Bash was pleased to see on its glistening face a hi-res image. Depicted was a small pond with a frog by its edge, and the following haiku by Bash's namesake:

> *Old pond*
> *Frog jumps in*
> *Splash!*

Bash tapped a control square in the corner of the display, and the image became animated, with the frog carrying out the poem's instructions in an endless loop, with appropriate soundtrack.

Bash's smile, observed by no one, lit up the rafters.

Thus was born "protean paper," or, as a web-journalist (nowadays remembered for nothing else but this coinage) later dubbed it, "proteopape."

Bash's miraculous process added merely hundredths of a cent to each piece of paper processed. For this token price, one ended up with a sheet of proteopape that possessed magnitudes more processing power than an old-line supercomputer.

In effect, Bash had created flexible, weightless computers practically too cheap to sell.

But the difference between "practically" and "absolutely" meant a lot, across millions of units.

I^2—the age of Immanent Information—was about to commence.

A visit to the same canny lawyer who had helped his parents survive bankruptcy nearly twenty years earlier insured that Bash's invention was securely patented. Anyone who wanted to employ Bash's process would have to license it from him, for a considerable annual fee.

At this point, the nineteen-year-old Bash went public.

By the time he was twenty-one, he was the richest man in the world.

But he had still never even ventured out on a date with any member of the opposite sex who was not his cousin Cora on his mother's side.

3
The Breakfast Club

Dagny Winsome resembled no one so much as a pale blonde Olive Oyl. Affecting retro eyeglasses in place of the universal redactive surgery to correct her nearsightedness, Dagny exhibited a somato-type that evoked thoughts of broomsticks, birches, baguettes and, given her predilection for striped shirts, barber poles. But her lack of curvature belied a certain popularity with males, attributable to her quick wit, wild impulsiveness and gleeful subversiveness. Her long pale hair framed a face that could segue from calm innocence to irate impatience to quirky amusement in the span of a short conversation. Dagny's four years at MIT had been marked by participation in a score of famous hacks, including the overnight building of a two-thirds mockup of the Space Shuttle *George W. Bush* resting in a simulated crash in the middle of Massachusetts Avenue.

Bash stood in awe of Dagny from the minute he became aware of her and her rep. A year ahead of Bash and several years senior in age, yet sharing his major, Dagny had seemed the unapproachable apex of sophistication and, yes, feminine allure. Often he had dreamed of speaking to her, even asking her on a date. But he had never summoned up the requisite courage.

Dagny graduated, and Bash's senior year was overtaken by the heady proteopape madness. For the next decade he had heard not a word of her postcollege career. Despite some desultory networking throughout the IT community, Bash had been unable to learn any information concerning her. Apparently she had not employed her degree in any conventional manner.

So in Bash's heart, Dagny Winsome gradually became a faded yet still nostalgia-provoking ghost.

Until the day just two weeks ago, on June 11, when she turned up on his doorstep.

Women were not in the habit of showing up at the front

entrance of Bash's home. For one thing, Bash lived in seclusion in a fairly well-secured mansion in the exclusive town of Lincoln, Massachusetts. Although no live guards or trained animals patrolled the grounds of his homestead, the fenced estate boasted elaborate cybernetic barriers wired both to nonlethal antipersonnel devices and to various agencies who were primed to respond at a moment's notice to any intrusion. Bash was not particularly paranoid, but as the world's richest individual he was naturally the focus of many supplicants, and he cherished his privacy.

Also, Bash did not experience a steady flow of female callers since he remained as awkward with women as he had been at nineteen. Although not technically a virgin any longer at age thirty, he still failed to deeply comprehend the rituals of human courtship and mating. Sometimes he felt that the shortened form of his name stood for "Bashful" rather than "Basho."

Naturally, then, Bash was startled to hear his doorbell ring early one morning. He approached the front door tentatively. A curling sheet of proteopape carelessly thumbtacked to the inner door conveyed an image of the front step transmitted from a second sheet of proteopape hanging outside and synched to the inner one. (When weather degraded the outside sheet of proteopape to uselessness, Bash would simply hang a new page.)

Imagine Bash's surprise to witness Dagny Winsome standing impatiently before his front door. After a short flummoxed moment, Bash threw wide the door.

"Dag—Dagny? But how—?"

Ten years onward from graduation, Dagny Winsome retained her collegiate looks and informality. She wore one of her trademark horizontally striped shirts, red and black. Her clunky eyeglasses incorporated enough plastic to form a car bumper. Her long near-platinum hair had been pulled back and secured by a jeweled crab, one of the fashionable ornamental redactors that metabolized human sweat and dead skin cells. Black jeans and a pair of Neet-Feets completed her outfit.

Dagny said with some irritation, "Well, aren't you going to invite your old fellow alumna inside?"

"But how did you get past my security?"

Dagny snorted. "You call that gimcrack setup a security system? I had it hacked while my car was still five miles outside of town. And I only drove from Boston."

Bash made a mental note to install some hardware and software upgrades. But he could not, upon reflection, manufacture any ire against either his deficient cyberwards or Dagny herself. He was pleased to see her.

"Uh, sorry about my manners. Sure, come on in. I was just having breakfast. Want something?"

Dagny stepped briskly inside. "Green tea and a poppy-seed muffin, some Canadian bacon on the side."

Bash reviewed the contents of his large freezer. "Uh, can do."

Seated in the kitchen, sipping their drinks while bacon microwaved, neither one spoke for some time. Dagny focused a dubious look on the decorative strip of proteopape wallpaper running around the upper quarter of the kitchen walls. A living frieze, the accent strip displayed a constantly shifting video of this year's *Sports Illustrated* swimsuit models, at play in the Sino-Hindu space station, *Maohatma*. Embarrassed, Bash decided that to change the contents now would only accentuate the original bachelor's choice, so he fussed with the microwave while admiring Dagny out the corner of his eye.

Serving his guest her muffin and bacon, Bash was taken aback by her sudden confrontational question.

"So, how long are you going to vegetate here like some kind of anaerobe?"

Bash dropped into his seat. "Huh? What do you mean?"

Dagny waved a braceleted arm to sweep in the whole house. "Just look around. You've fashioned yourself a perfect little womb here. First you go and drop the biggest conceptual bombshell into the information society that the world has ever seen. Intelligent paper! Then you crawl into a hole with all your riches and pull the hole in after yourself."

"That's ridiculous. I—I'm still engaged with the world. Why, just last year I filed five patents—"

"All piddling little refinements on proteopape. Face it, you're just dicking around with bells and whistles now. You've lost your edge. You don't really care about the biz or its potential to change the world anymore."

Bash tried to consider Dagny's accusations objectively. His life was still full of interests and passions, wasn't it? He ran a big A-life colony that had kicked some butt in the annual Conway Wars; he composed songs on his full-body SymphonySuit, and downloads from his music website had hit an all-time high last week (53); and he was the biggest pear-orchard owner in Oregon's Rogue River Valley (the holding corporation was run by York and Adelaide). Didn't all those hobbies and several others speak to his continuing

involvement in the world at large? Yet suddenly Bash was unsure of
his own worth and meaning. Did his life really look trivial to an out-
sider?

Irked by these novel sensations, Bash sought to counterattack.
"What about you? I don't see where you've been exactly burning up
the I^2 landscape. How have you been improving the world since
school?"

Dagny was unflustered. "You never would have heard of anything I've done, even though I've got quite a rep in my field."

"And what field is that?"

"The art world. After graduation, I realized my heart just wasn't
in the theoretical, R & D side of I^2. I was more interested in the
creative, out-of-the-box uses the street had for stuff like proteopape
than in any kind of engineering. I wanted to use nifty new tools to
express myself, not make them so others could. So I split to the
West Coast in '17, and I've been mostly there ever since. Oh, I
travel a lot—the usual swirly emergent nodes like Austin, Prague,
Havana, Hong Kong, Helsinki, Bangor. But generally you can find
me working at home in LA."

The list of exciting cities dazzled Bash more than he expected it
to, and he realized that for all his immense wealth he had truly
been leading a cloistered existence.

"What brings you to stuffy old Boston then?"

"The Woodies. It's an awards ceremony for one of the things I
do, and it's being held here this year. A local group, the Hubster
Dubsters, is sponsoring the affair. It's kind of a joke, but I have to be
there if I want to front as a player. So I figured, Bash lives out that
way. What if I look him up and invite him to come along."

"But why?"

Dagny fixed Bash with an earnest gaze. "I won't pretend you
meant anything to me at MIT, Bash. But I knew who you were, boy
genius and all. And when you invented proteopape—well, I was
kinda proud to have known you even a little bit. Proteopape is a real
wizard wheeze, you know. It tumbled a lot of tipping points, sent
some real change waves through the world. I admire you for that.
So I guess what I'm saying is I'd like to map your *gedankenspace*,
and maybe help wake you up a little bit."

Bash considered this speech for a short time.

"You were proud of me?"

Dagny grinned. "Do porn stars have sex?"

Bash blushed. "So, when is this awards thing?"

4
Valley of the Dolls

Some years back, Kenmore Square had been turned into a *woonerf*. The Dutch term meant literally "living yard," and referred to the practice of converting urban streets from vehicular to pedestrian usage. The formerly confusing nexus of several Boston avenues beneath the famed Citgo sign (now a giant sheet of laminated proteopape, like all modern billboards and exterior signage) had been transformed into a pleasant public venue carpeted with high-foot-traffic-sustaining redactive grasses and mosses and crisscrossed by flagstone paths.

On this early evening of June 12, the temperature registered typical for Neo-Venusian New England, a balmy ninety-two-degrees Fahrenheit. The Square was crowded with strolling shoppers, picnickers, café patrons, club and moviegoers. Children squealed as they played on the public squishy sculptures and under the spray of intricately dancing cyber-fountains. Patrolling autonomes— creeping, hopping and stalking, their patternizing optics and tanglefoot projectors and beanbag-gun snouts and spray-nozzles of liquid banana peel swivelling according to odd self-grown heuristics —maintained vigilance against any possible disrupters of the peace. A lone cop mounted on his compact StreetCamel added a layer of human oversight (the random manure dumps were a small price to pay for this layer of protection).

Bash and Dagny had parked her fuel-cell-powered Argentinian rental, a 2027 Gaucho, several blocks away. They entered the Square now on foot from the south, via Newbury Street, engaged in earnest conversation.

"Mutability, Bash! Mutability rules! We're all Buddhists now, acknowledging change as paramount. Nothing fixed or solid, no hierarchies of originals and copies, nothing stable from one minute to the next. Every variant equally privileged. That's what proteopape's all about! Media and content are one. Can't you see it? Your invention undermined all the old paradigms. First editions, signed canvases, original film negatives—Those terms mean nothing anymore, and our art should reflect that."

Bash struggled to counter Dagny's passionate, illogical and scary assertions. (Carried to its extreme, her philosophy led to a world of complete isotropic chaos, Bash felt.) But the novelty of arguing face-to-face with a living interlocutor had him slightly flustered. "I just can't buy all that, Dag. Proteopape is just a means of transmission and display. The contents and value of what's being displayed don't change just because the surface they're displayed on might show something different the next minute. Look, suppose I used this store window here to display some paintings, changing the paintings by hand every ten seconds. That would be a very slow analog representation of what proteopape does. Would the canvases I chose to exhibit be suddenly deracinated or transformed by this treatment? I don't think so."

"Your analogy sucks! The canvases are still physical objects in your instance. But anything on proteopape has been digitized and rendered virtual. Once that happens, all the old standards collapse."

Their seemingly irresolvable argument had brought them to the door of their destination: a club with a proteopape display in an acid-yellow neon font naming it the Antiquarium. The display kept changing sinuously from letters into some kind of sea serpent and back. A long line of patrons awaited entrance.

A tall bald guy walking up and down the line was handing out small proteopape broadsides for some product or service or exhibition. Those in the queue who accepted the advertisements either folded the pages and tucked them into their pockets, or crumpled them up and threw them to the turf, where the little screens continued to flash a twisted mosaic of information. Bash remembered the first time he had seen someone so carelessly discard his invention, and how he had winced. But he had quickly become reconciled to the thoughtless disposal of so much cheap processing power, and aside from the littering aspect, the common action no longer bothered him.

Dagny turned to Bash and gripped both his hands in a surprisingly touching show of sincerity. "Let's drop all this futile talk. I think that once you see some of the stuff on display tonight—the awards ceremony features extensive clips, you know—you'll come around to my viewpoint. Or at least admit that it's a valid basis for further discussion."

"Well, I can't promise anything. But I'm keeping an open mind."

"That's all I ask. Now follow me. We don't have to stand in line here with the fans."

The stage door entrance behind the club, monitored by a chicly scaled Antiquarium employee, granted them exclusive entry into the club. Bash snuffled the funky odor of old spilled beer, drummer sweat and various smokable drugs and experienced a grand moment of disorientation. Where was he? How had he ended up here?

But Dagny's swift maneuvering of Bash across the empty club's main dance floor gave him no time to savor his *jamais vu*.

Crossing the expanse, Bash saw the exhibits that gave the club its name. Dozens of huge aquariums dotted the cavernous space. They hosted creepy-crawly redactors whose appearance was based on the Burgess Shale fossils, but whose actual germ lines derived from common modern fishes and crustaceans. In tank after tank, stubby-winged Anomalocarises crawled over the jutting spikes of Hallucigenias, while slithering Opabinias waggled their long pincered snouts.

Bash felt as if he had entered a particularly bad dream. This whole night, from the tedious argument with Dagny up to this surreal display, was not proceeding as cheerfully as he had hoped.

Workers in STAFF T-shirts were setting up folding chairs in ranks across the dance floor, while others were positioning a lectern onstage and rigging a huge sheet of proteopape behind the podium. As Bash exited the main floor he saw the proteopape come alive:

FIFTH ANNUAL WOODY AWARDS
SPONSORED BY
MUD BUG SPORTS CLOTHES
NASHVILLE SITAR STUDIO
XYLLELLA COSMETICS
AND
THE HUBSTER DUBSTERS

Below these names was a caricature of a familiar bespectacled nebbish, executed by Hirschfeld (well into his second century, the 'borged artist, once revived, was still alive and active in his exoskeleton and SecondSkin).

Now Dagny had dragged Bash into a dressing room of some sort, crowded with people in various states of undress and makeup. They passed through this organized confusion into the club's Green Room. Here, the atmosphere was both less frenetic yet tenser.

"Bash, I want you to meet some special friends. Holland Flanders—"

Bash shook the hand of a well-muscled fellow wearing a wifebeater and cargo shorts, whose bare arms seemed to be slowly exuding miniscule flakes of golden glitter.

"Cricket Licklider—"

The petite woman wore a suit of vaguely Japanese-looking crocodile-skin armor, and blinked reptilian eyes. Contacts or redactions, Bash could not discern.

"Roger Mexicorn—"

This wraithlike, long-haired lad sported banana-yellow skin, and reminded Bash of a certain doomed albino from the literature of the fantastic.

"Lester Schill—"

Bash thought this besuited, bearded guy the most normal, until he clasped Schill's palm and received a distinct erotic tingle from some kind of bioelectrical implant.

"—and Indicia Diddums."

Indicia's broad face cracked in a smile that revealed a set of fangs that any barracuda would have envied.

"These are some of the Hubster Dubsters, Bash. My fellow auteurs. They're all up for one or more Woodies tonight."

Bash tried to make sensible conversation under the slightly oppressive circumstances. "So, I have to confess I had never heard of your special kind of, um, art before Dagny brought me up to speed. You guys, ah, mess with old films. . . ."

Schill frowned. "Crudely put, but accurate enough. Only the dialogue, however."

Diddums chimed in, her speech somewhat distorted by her unnatural teeth. "Thash right. We practish a purer art than thosh lazy chumps who simply fuck with the images. They have their own awards anyway. The Zeligs."

Bash was confused. "Wait a minute. Your awards are named after Woody Allen, correct? Because he altered the soundtrack of that Japanese film over half a century ago—"

"*What's Up, Tiger Lily?*" supplied Dagny, as if coaching a favored but deficient student.

"But didn't Allen also make *Zelig*?"

"Certainly," said Mexicorn in a languid tone. "But just as the magnificent *Tiger Lily* preceded the feeble *Zelig*, so did our ceremony anticipate that of our degenerate rivals. We distinguish, of course, between the Good Woody and the Bad Woody."

"We're *writers*, you see," interjected Flanders, gesturing in a way that left a trail of body glitter through the air. "The *word* is primary with us."

Licklider doffed her angular helmet and scratched the blonde fuzz revealed. "And the artistic challenge arises in fitting our words to the established images, creating a startlingly different film in the process. Any idiot can paste King Kong into *Guess Who's Coming to*

Dinner. But it takes real skill to formulate a new script that hews to the actions of the original film and the mouth movements and gestures of the actors, yet still completely detourns it."

Dagny said, "Well put, Cricket. There's our credo in a nutshell, Bash. Startling novelty born from the boringly familiar. But you'll soon see for yourself. Here, grab a glass of champagne. It's just the cheap stuff made from potatoes, but you'd never know from the taste."

Bash took the drink. Truthfully, it wasn't bad. Dagny left to talk to others backstage, leaving Bash alone.

Cricket Licklider approached Bash. He shifted his stance nervously and drained his glass. A bad mistake, as the potato champagne went straight to his brain.

"So," said the woman, "you're the brainiac who invented proteopape."

"Well, sure," said Bash. "That is, I did, but it didn't seem to require too many brains. After all, others had been messing with e-paper for a while, even if they weren't getting anywhere fast. It's not like I conceptualized the whole thing from scratch. The rest was just solid, if inspired, engineering."

"So why didn't anyone else get there first? No, you deserve all the luster, fizz." Cricket pinned Bash with her alligator eyes. "Tell me, you get much hot tail along with the royalties?"

"Uh, I, that is—"

"Well, believe me, you could walk off tonight with a double armful of proteopape groupies—of any of several genders. So just remember: if your date tonight doesn't come across like she should, there are plenty of other bints in the bleachers. And that includes me."

Cricket grinned broadly, then turned to leave. Bash said, "Wait a minute."

"Yeah?"

"Are you related to—?"

"My great-grandfather. And wouldn't he have sold my grandfather for a single sheet of proteopape?"

Dagny came then to reclaim Bash. "Let's go. We've got seats in the reserved section, but I want to be on the aisle so I can jump up easily when I win."

Bash followed Dagny out of the Green Room, which was emptying rapidly. Out on the main floor, fans were now swarming into chairs. The crush at the various bars was intense, and a palpable excitement filled the club.

Dagny managed to secure more drinks, and she and Bash took

their seats. Before too long, the lights dimmed and the ceremony began.

First came a few live song-and-dance numbers, each one in the spirit of the Woodies. Music and choreography replicated famous routines, but all the lyrics had been altered. The rumble between the Jets and the Sharks from *West Side Story* now limned the current scientipolitical feud between the Viridians and the Dansgaard-Oeschgerites. Gene Kelly's acrobatic leaps from *Singin' in the Rain* now parodied the recent scandal involving Lourdes Ciccone and that prominent EU minister, Randy Rutger.

The audience applauded wildly for every act. Bash found himself bemused by this disproportionate reception to what amounted to some juvenile satire. Was this truly representative of the cultural revolution that proteopape had supposedly engendered? If so, he felt ashamed.

Finally the master of ceremonies appeared, wearing a disposable suit cut along the lines of the famous oversized outfit often worn during shows of the last millennium by singer David Byrne, whose octogenarian career had recently received a boost thanks to a sold-out tour with the Bleeding Latahs. Fashioned entirely from proteopape, the MC's outfit displayed a rapid-fire montage of subliminal images. The flicker rate made Bash's eyes hurt, and he had to avert them.

"Our first category is 'Best Transformation of Tragedy to Comedy.' And the contenders are Faustina Kenny for her *Casablanca*—"

A clip rolled on the big proteopape screen, and on smaller screens scattered throughout the Antiquarium. Bogart leaned over to Dooley Wilson as Sam, seated at the piano, and said, "Are those keys made from redactive ivory or wild ivory?" Sam replied, "Neither, Rick—they're human bone from Chechnya. Can't you see how they glow!"

"Engels Copeland for his *High Noon*—"

A stern Gary Cooper faced an adoring Grace Kelly and said, "Don't worry, Amy, the family jewels won't be damaged. My underwear is redactive armadillo hide!"

"Jim Cupp for his *The Lord of the Rings*—"

Frodo Baggins gazed deeply into Sam Gamgee's eyes as their boat drifted downriver and said, "Admit it, Sam, you ate the last damn antioxidant superchoc bar."

"Lura Giffard for her *Blue Velvet*—"

A dissipated Dennis Hopper, breathing mask clamped to his

face, muttered, "Why the hell did I ever volunteer to beta-test this new crowd-control spray?"

"—and finally, Dagny Winsome for her *Gone with the Wind.*"

Cradling Vivien Leigh in his arms, Clark Gable said, "But Scarlett, if you go in for gender-reassignment, where will that leave me?" "On the bottom," she replied.

"And the winner is—Dagny Winsome for *Gone with the Wind!*"

To a storm of applause, Dagny trotted onstage. Gleefully triumphant, she clutched the offered trophy—a bronze bust of Woody Allen with a blank word-balloon streaming from his lips—and launched into her acceptance speech.

"This was not a lock, folks! I was up against a lot of strong contenders. My thanks to the judges for recognizing that a femplus subtext does not preclude some real yocks. I'd just like to thank the California State Board of the Arts for their continued support, my parents for zygotic foresight, and Alex, my physiotherapist, for those inspirational heated Moon rock treatments. Oh, and let's shed some special luster on Basho Applebrook, the inventor of protcopape, who's with us tonight. Bash, stand up and take a bow!"

Utterly mortified, Bash got out of his seat as a spotlight zeroed in on him. Blinking, he turned to face the audience, essaying a weak smile. After enduring the noise of their clapping for as short a time as politely allowable, he gratefully sat down.

Dagny had returned to his side. She leaned in to kiss his cheek. Bash felt partially recompensed for his forced public exposure. But the rest of the ceremony quickly soured his mood.

"Best Transformation of Comedy to Tragedy" naturally followed the award Dagny had won. Then came "Musical into Nonmusical" and vice versa. "Subtext Foregrounded" and "Mockumentaries" were succeeded by the award for "Bomb Defusing," the object of which category was apparently to rob a suspenseful film of any suspense. "Idiot Plotting" featured all the characters exchanging moronic dialogue and offering the stupidest of motives for their actions. "Comic Book Narration" forced the actors to summarize aloud all their actions, and also to indulge in long-winded speeches during any fight scenes. "Gender Swap" found all the males dubbed with female voices, and contrariwise. "Ethnic Mismatch" covered the introduction of inappropriate foreign accents.

Bash's father had been born in 1970. During Bash's childhood, he had discovered a stash of magazines that York Applebrook had accumulated during his own childhood. Fascinated by the antiques, Bash had devoured the pile of *Mad* magazines, only half-understanding yet still laughing at parodies of movies old before he had been born. At the wise old age of ten, however, Bash had put aside the jejune drolleries of "the usual gang of idiots."

Tonight felt like being trapped in a giant issue of *Mad*. Bash simply could not believe that all these supposedly mature adults felt that such juvenile skewing of classic films constituted a new and exciting art form. And somehow his invention of proteopape had catalyzed this stale quasi-dadaist display. Bash experienced a sense of shame.

He did not of course let Dagny know how he felt. Her pleasure in winning and in the victories of her peers prevented any such honesty. And, selfishly, Bash still thrilled to her kiss. The conversation with Cricket Licklider had made the possibility of post-Woodies sex with Dagny more vivid. No point in sacrificing the first likelihood of unmonied intercourse in two years on the altar of stubborn opinionated speechifying.

Finally the tedious ceremony ended. The assembled auteurs from around the globe split into cliques and adjourned to various other venues to celebrate or weep. Bash found himself accompanying Dagny, the Hubster Dubsters and a pack of hangers-on to a bar called The Weeping Gorilla, whose decorative motif involved the lugubrious anthropoid posed with various celebrities. There Bash consumed rather too much alcohol, rather too little food, and a handful of unidentified drugs.

Somehow Bash found himself naked in a hotel room with Dagny. Sex occurred in lurid kaleidoscopic intervals of consciousness. Afterwards, Bash remembered very little of the perhaps enjoyable experience.

But much to his dismay, he clearly recalled some boastful pillow talk afterwards.

"Hadda put a trapdoor in pro'eopape during testing. Lemme get inna operating system to debug. Still in there! Yup, never took it out, nobody ever found it neither. Every single sheet, still got a secret backdoor!"

Dagny, eyes shuttered, made sleepy noises. But, as evidenced by the subversion of Bash's *Boston Globe* on the morning of June 25, when his newspaper had played a symbolical version of their harsh breakup on the shoals of Bash's eventual honesty during their aborted second date, she had plainly heard every word.

5
The Fugitive

Bash stood up from the breakfast table. His dead newspaper continued slowly to absorb the juices of his abandoned breakfast. The fish-scale wall clock morphed to a new minute. Everything looked hopeless.

Dagny Winsome had hacked the hidden trapdoor in proteopape, the existence of which no one had ever suspected until he blurted it out. Why hadn't he eliminated that feature before releasing his invention? Hubris, sheer hubris. Bash had wanted to feel as if he could reclaim his brainchild from the world's embrace at any time. The operating system trapdoor represented apron strings he couldn't bring himself to cut. And what was the appalling result of his parental vanity?

Now Dagny could commandeer every uniquely identifiable scrap of the ether-driven miracle medium and turn it to her own purposes. For the moment, her only motivation to tamper appeared to consist of expressing her displeasure with Bash. For that small blessing, Bash was grateful. But how long would it take before Dagny's congenital impishness seduced her into broader culture jamming? This was the woman, after all, who had drugged one of MIT's deans as he slept, and brought him to awaken in a scrupulously exact mockup of his entire apartment exactly three-quarters scale.

Bash felt like diving into bed and pulling the covers over his head. But a moment's reflection stiffened his resolve. No one was going to mess with *his* proteopape and get away with it! Too much of the world's economy and culture relied on the medium just to abandon it. He would simply have to track Dagny down and attempt to reason with her.

As his first move, Bash took out his telephone. His telephone was simply a stiffened strip of proteopape. His defunct newspaper would once have served the purpose as well, but most people kept a dedicated phone on their persons, if for nothing else than to receive incoming calls when they were out of reach of other proteopape surfaces, and also to serve as their unique intelligent tag identifying them to I^2 entities.

Bash folded the phone into a little hollow pyramid and stood it on the table. The GlobeSpeak logo appeared instantly: a goofy anthropomorphic chatting globe inked by Robert Crumb, every appearance of which earned the heirs of the artist one milli-cent.

(Given the volume of world communication, Sophie Crumb now owned most of southern France.) Bash ordered the phone to search for Cricket Licklider. Within a few seconds her face replaced the logo, while the cameras in Bash's phone reciprocated with his image.

Cricket grinned. "I knew you'd come looking for some of the good stuff eventually, Bashie-boy."

"No, it's not like that. I appreciate your attention, really I do, but I need to find Dagny."

Frowning, Cricket said, "You lost your girlfriend? Too bad. Why should I help you find her?"

"Because she's going to destroy proteopape if I don't stop her. Where would that leave you and your fellow Dubsters? Where would that leave any of us for that matter?"

This dire news secured Cricket's interest, widening her iguana eyes. "Holy shit! Well, Christ, I don't know what to say. I haven't seen her since the Woodies. She might not even be in town anymore."

"Can you get the rest of your crew together? Maybe one of them knows something useful."

"I'll do my best. Meet us at the clubhouse in an hour."

Cricket cut the transmission, but not before uploading the relevant address to Bash's phone.

Bash decided that a shave and a shower would help settle his nerves.

In the bathroom, Bash lathered up his face in the proteopape mirror: a sheet that digitized his image in real time and displayed it unreversed. The mirror also ran a small window in which a live newscast streamed. As Bash listened intently for any bulletins regarding the public malfunctioning of proteopape, he took his antique Mach3 razor down from the wall cabinet's shelf and then sudsed his face from a spray can. Having been raised in a simple-living household, Bash still retained many old-fashioned habits, such as actually shaving. He drew the first swath through the foam up his neck and under his chin.

Without warning, his mirror suddenly hosted the leering face of Charles Laughton as the Hunchback of Notre Dame.

Bash yelped and cut himself. The Hunchback chortled, then vanished. And now his mirror was as dead as his newspaper.

Cursing Dagny, Bash located a small analogue mirror at the bottom of a closet and finished shaving. He put a proteopape band-aid on the cut, and the band-aid instantly assumed the exact texture and coloration of the skin it covered (with cut edited out), becoming effectively invisible.

Bash's shower curtain was more proteopape, laminated and featuring a loop of the Louisiana rainforest, complete with muted soundtrack. Bash yanked it off its hooks and took a shower without regard to slopping water onto the bathroom floor. Toweling off, he even regarded the roll of toilet paper next to the john suspiciously, but then decided that Dagny wouldn't dare.

Dressed in his usual casual manner—white Wickaway shirt, calf-length tropical-print pants and Supplex sandals—Bash left his house. He took his Segway IX from its recharging slot in the garage, and set out for the nearby commuter-rail node. As he zipped neatly along the wealthy and shady streets of Lincoln, the warm, humid June air laving him, Bash tried to comprehend the full potential dimensions of Dagny's meddling with proteopape. He pictured schools, businesses, transportation and government agencies all brought to a grinding halt as their proteopape systems crashed. Proteopape figured omnipresently in the year 2029. So deeply had it insinuated itself into daily life that even Bash could not keep track of all its uses. If proteopape went down, it would take the global economy with it.

And what of Bash's personal rep in the aftermath? When the facts came out, he would become the biggest idiot and traitor the world had ever tarred and feathered. His name would become synonymous with "fuck up": "You pulled a helluva applebrook that time." "I totally applebrooked my car, but wasn't hurt." "Don't hire him, he's a real applebrook."

The breeze ruffling Bash's hair failed to dry the sweat on his brow as fast as it formed.

At the station, Bash parked and locked his Segway. He bounded up the stairs and the station door hobermanned open automatically for him. He bought his ticket, and after only a ten-minute wait found himself riding east toward the city.

At the end of Bash's car a placard of proteopape mounted on the wall cycled through a set of advertisements. Bash kept a wary eye on the ads, but none betrayed a personal vendetta against him.

Disembarking at South Station, Bash looked around for his personal icon in the nearest piece of public proteopape, and quickly discovered it glowing in the corner of a newsstand's signage: a bright green pear (thoughts of his parents briefly popped up) with the initials BA centered in it.

Every individual in the I^2 society owned such a self-selected icon, its uniqueness assured by a global registry. The icons had many uses, but right now Bash's emblem was going to help him arrive at the Dubsters' club. His pocket phone was handshaking with every piece of proteopape in the immediate vicinity and was laying down a trail of electronic breadcrumbs for him to follow, based on the directions transmitted earlier by Cricket.

A second pear appeared beyond the newsstand, on a plaque identifying the presence of a wall-mounted fire extinguisher, and so Bash walked toward it. Many other travelers were tracking their own icons simultaneous with Bash. As he approached the second iteration of the luminous pear, a third copy glowed from the decorative patch on the backpack of a passing schoolkid. Bash followed until the kid turned right. (Many contemporary dramas and comedies revolved around the chance meetings initiated by one's icon appearing on the personal property of a stranger. An individual could of course deny this kind of access, but surprisingly few did.) The pear icon vanished from the pack, to be replaced by an occurrence at the head of the subway stairs. Thus was Bash led onto a train and to his eventual destination, a building on the Fenway not far from the Isabella Stewart Gardner Museum.

As he ascended the steps of the modest brownstone, Bash's eye was snagged by the passage of a sleek new Europa model car, one of the first to fully incorporate proteopape in place of windshield glass. He marveled at the realism of its "windows," which apparently disclosed the driver—a handsome young executive type —chatting with his passenger—a beautiful woman.

The car windows were in reality all sheets of suitably strengthened proteopape, utterly opaque. The inner surfaces of the "windows" displayed the outside world to the occupants of the car (or anything else, for that matter, although the driver, at least, had better be monitoring reality), while the outer surfaces broadcast the car's interior (the default setting) or any other selected feed. The driver and passenger Bash saw might have been the actual occupants of the Europa, or they might have been canned constructs. The car could in reality hold some schlubby Walter Mitty type, the president-in-exile of the Drowned Archipelagos or the notorious terrorist Mungo Bush Meat. (Suspicious of the latter instance, roving police would get an instant warrant to tap the windows and examine the true interior.)

Returning his attention to the door displaying his icon, Bash phoned Cricket.

"I'm here."

"One second."

The door opened on its old-fashioned hinges and Bash stepped inside, to be met by Cricket.

Today the woman wore an outfit of rose-colored spidersilk street pajamas that revealed an attractive figure concealed the previous night by her formal armor. She smiled and gave Bash a brief spontaneous hug and peck.

"Buck up, Bashie-boy. Things can't be that bad."

"No, they're worse! Dagny is going to bring down civilization if she keeps on messing with proteopape."

"Exactly what is she doing, and how's she doing it?"

"I can't reveal everything, but it's all my fault. I inadvertently gave her the ability to ping and finger every piece of proteopape in existence."

Cricket whistled. "I knew you zillionaires bestowed generous gifts, but this one even beats the time South Africa gave away the AIDS cure."

"I didn't *mean* to pass this ability on to her. In fact, all I did was drop a drunken clue and she ran with it."

"Our Dag is one clever girl, that's for sure."

Bash looked nervously around the dim narrow hallway full of antiques and was relieved to discover only dumb wallcoverings and not a scrap of proteopape in sight. "We should make sure to exclude any proteopape from our meeting with your friends. Otherwise Dagny will surely monitor our discussions."

Following his own advice, Bash took out his phone and placed it on an end table.

"Wait here. I'll run ahead and tell everyone to de-paperize themselves."

Cricket returned after only a minute. "Okay, let's go."

Walking down the long hall, Bash asked, "How did you guys ever end up in a building like this? I pictured your clubhouse as some kind of *xinggan* Koolhaus."

"Well, most of us Dubsters are just amateurs with day jobs, you know. We can't afford to commission special architecture by anyone really catalyzing. But our one rich member is Lester Schill. You met him the other night, right? The Schills have been Brahmins since way back to the 1950s! Big investments in the Worcester bioaxis, Djerassi and that crowd. But Lester's the last of the Schill line, and he owns more properties than he can use. So he leases us this building for our HQ for a dollar a year."

"Isn't he concerned about what'll happen to the family fortune after his death?" This very issue had often plagued the childless Bash himself.

Cricket snickered. "Lester's not a breeder. And believe me, you really don't want to know the details of his special foldings. But I expect he's made provisions."

Their steps had brought them to a closed door. Cricket ushered Bash into a large room whose walls featured built-in shelves full of dumb books. Bash experienced a small shock, having actually forgotten that such antique private libraries still existed.

Close to a dozen Dubsters assembled around a boardroom-sized table greeted Bash with quiet hellos or silent nods. Bash recognized Flanders, Mexicorn, Diddums and the enigmatic Schill himself, but the others were strangers to him.

Cricket conducted Bash to the empty chair at the head of the table and he sat, unsure of what he needed to say to enlist the help of these people. No one offered him any prompting, but he finally came up with a concise introduction to his presence.

"One of your West Coast associates, Dagny Winsome, has stolen something from me. The knowledge of a trapdoor in the operating system of proteopape. She's already begun screwing around with various sheets of my personal protean paper, and if she continues on in this manner, she'll inspire widespread absolute distrust of this medium. That would spell the end of our I^2 infrastructure, impacting your own artistic activities significantly. So I'm hoping that as her friends, you folks will have some insight into where Dagny might be hiding, and also be motivated to help me reach her and convince her to stop."

A blonde fellow whose face and hands were entirely covered in horrific-looking scarlet welts and blisters, which apparently pained him not a whit, said, "You're the brainster, why don't you just lock her out?"

Bash vented a frustrated sigh. "Don't you think that was the very first thing I tried? But she's beaten me to it, changed all my old access codes. She's got the only key to the trapdoor now. But if I could only get in, I could make proteopape safe forever by closing the trapdoor for good. But I need to find Dagny first."

Cricket spoke up. "Roger, tell Bash what you know about Dagny's departure."

The jaundiced ephebe said, "I drove her to the airport a day ago. She said she was heading back to LA."

"Did you actually see her board her flight?" asked Bash.

"No. . . ."

"Well, I think she's still in the Greater Boston Metropolitan region. The time lag between coasts is negligible for most communications. Even international calls ricochet off the GlobeSpeak relays practically instantaneously." Bash was referring to the fleet of thousands of high-flying drone planes—laden with comm gear and perennially refueled in midair—which encircled the planet, providing long-distance links faster than satellites ever could. "But she wouldn't want to risk even millisecond delays if she was trying to pull off certain real-time pranks. Plus, I figure she'll want to finally pop out of hiding to lord it over me in person, once she's finished humiliating me."

The toothy Indicia Diddums spoke. "That raishes a good point. This looksh like a purely pershonal feud between you two. You're the richesht plug in the world, Applebrook. Why don't you just hire some private muschle to nail her assh?"

"I don't want word of this snafu to spread any further than absolutely necessary. I spent a long time vacillating before I even decided to tell you guys."

Lester Schill stroked his long beard meditatively before speaking. "What's in this for us? Just a continuation of the status quo? Where's our profit?"

Bash saw red. He got to his feet, nearly upsetting his chair.

"Profit? What kind of motive for saving the world is that? Was I thinking of profit when I first created proteopape? No! Sure, I'm richer than God now, but that's not why I did it. Money is useless after a certain point. I can't even spend a fraction of one percent of my fortune, it grows so fast. And you, Schill, damn it, are probably in the same position, even if your wealth is several orders of magnitude less than mine. Money is not at the root of this! Proteopape means freedom of information, and the equitable distribution of computing power! Don't any of you remember what life was like before proteopape? Huge electricity-gobbling server farms? Cellphone towers blighting the landscape? Miles of fiber optics cluttering the sewers and the seas and the streets? Endless upgrades of hardware rendered almost instantly obsolescent? Big government databases versus individual privacy? Proteopape did away with all that! Now the server farms are in your pockets and on cereal boxes, in the trash in your wastebasket and signage all around. Now the individual can go head-to-head with any corporation or governmental agency. And I won't just stand helplessly by and let some dingbat artist with a grudge ruin it all! If you people won't help me without bribery, then I'll just solve this problem on my own!"

Nostrils flaring, face flushed, Bash glared at the stubborn Dubsters, who remained unimpressed by his fevered speech.

The stalemate was broken when a segment of the bookshelves seemingly detached itself and stepped forward.

The moving portion of the bookcases possessed a human silhouette. In the next second the silhouette went white, revealing a head-to-toe suit of proteopape. This suit, Bash realized, must represent one of the newest third-generation Parametrics camo outfits. The myriad moletronic cameras in the rear of the suit captured the exact textures and lighting of the background against which the wearer stood, and projected the mappings onto the front of the clothing. The wearer received his visual inputs on the interior of the hood from the forward array of cameras. Gauzy portions of the hood allowed easy breathing, at the spotty sacrifice of some of the disguise's hi-res.

A hand came up to sweep the headgear backward, where it draped like a loose cowl on the individual's back. The face thus revealed belonged to a young Hispanic man with a thin mustache.

"My name is Tito Harnnoy, and I represent the Masqueleros. We will help you, hombre!"

6

The Manchurian Candidate

Tito Harnnoy drove his battered industrial-model two-person Segway down Mass Ave toward Cambridge. Riding behind Harnnoy, Bash experienced a creeping nostalgia, not altogether pleasant, that grew stronger the closer they approached his old alma mater, MIT.

Although Bash, once he became rich, had given generously to his university, endowing entire buildings, scholarship funds, research programs and tenured positions, he had not returned physically to the campus since graduation. The university held too many memories of juvenile sadness and loneliness blended with his culminating triumph. Whenever Bash cast his thoughts back to those years, he became again to some degree the geeky prodigy, a person he felt he had since outgrown. His maturity always a tenuous proposition, Bash felt it wisest not to court such retrogressive feelings. But now, apparently, he had no choice but to confront his past self.

Harnnoy broke Bash's reverie by saying, "Just a few smoots away from help, pard."

Indeed, they were crossing the Charles River into Cambridge.

The scattered structures of MIT loomed ahead, to east and west.

Bash noted extraordinary activity on the water below. "What's happening down there?" he asked Harnnoy.

"Annual Dragon Boat Festival. Big Asian carnival today, pard."

Harnnoy brought the scooter to a gyroscopic stop nearly below the shadow of the Great Dome and they dismounted. Walking into the embrace of the buildings that comprised the Infinite Corridor, they attained grassy Killian Court. The bucolic campus scene reflected the vibrant July day.

Several artists were "painting" the passing parade from various perspectives, employing smart styluses on canvases of proteopape. Depending on the applications the artists used, their strokes translated into digitized pastels or charcoal, acrylics or oils, ink or pencil or watercolor. Some had style filters in place, producing instant Monets or Seurats.

Elsewhere a kite-fighting contest was underway. Made of proteopape with an extra abundance of special MEMS, the kites could flex and flutter their surfaces and achieve dynamic, breeze-assisted flight. Tetherless, they were controlled by their handlers who employed sheets of conventional proteopape on the ground that ran various strategy programs and displayed the kites'-eye view. Curvetting and darting, the lifelike kites sought to batter aerial opponents and knock them from the sky without being disabled in turn.

Elsewhere, sedentary proteopape users read magazines or newspapers or books, watched various videofeeds, mailed correspondents, telefactored tourist autonomes around the globe, or performed any of a hundred other proteopape-mediated functions.

Conducting Bash through the quad and toward the towering Building 54, Harnnoy said, "I'm glad you decided to trust the Masqueleros, Applebrook. We won't let you down. It's a good thing we have our own ways of monitoring interesting emergent shit around town. We keep special feelers out for anything connected with your name, you know."

Bash didn't know. "But why?"

"Are you kidding? You're famous on campus. The biggest kinasehead ever to emerge from these hallowed halls, even considering all the other famous names. And that's no intronic string."

Bash felt weird. Had he really become some kind of emblematic figure to this strange younger generation? The honor sat awkwardly on his shoulders.

"Well, that's a major tribute, I guess. I only hope I can live up to your expectations."

"Even if you never released anything beyond proteopape, you already have. That's why we want to help you now. And it's truly exonic that we managed to get a spy—me—into place for your meeting with the Dubsters. Those sugarbags would never have lifted a pinky finger to aid you."

Despite the worshipful talk, Bash still had his doubts about the utility and motives of the mysterious Masqueleros, but the intransigence of Cricket's friends left him little choice. (Ms. Licklider herself, although expressing genuine sympathy, had had no solid aid of her own to offer.)

"I really appreciate your help, Tito. But I'm still a little unclear on how you guys hope to track Dagny down."

"Cryonize your metabolism, pard. You'll see in a minute."

Descending a few stairs into an access well, they stopped at an innocuous basement door behind Building 54. A small square of proteopape was inset above the door handle. Harnnoy spit upon it.

"Wouldn't the oils on your fingers have served as well?" Bash asked.

"Sure. But spitting is muy narcocorrido."

"Oh."

The invisible lab in the paper performed an instant DNA analysis on Harnnoy's saliva, and the door swung open.

Inside the unlit windowless room, a flock of glowing floating heads awaited.

The faces on the heads were all famous ones: Marilyn Monroe, Stephen Hawking, Britney Spears (the teenage version, not the middle-aged spokesperson for OpiateBusters), President Winfrey, Freeman Dyson, Walt Whitman (the celebrations for his 200th birthday ten years ago had gained him renewed prominence), Woody Woodpecker, SpongeBob SquarePants, Bart Simpson's son Homer Junior.

"Welcome to the lair of the Masqueleros," ominously intoned a parti-faced Terminator.

Bash came to a dead stop, stunned for a moment, before he realized what he was seeing. Then he got angry.

"Okay, everybody off with the masks. We can't have any proteopape around while we talk."

Overhead fluorescents flicked on, and the crowd of conspirators wearing only the cowls of their camo suits stood revealed, the projected faces fading in luminescence to match the ambient light. One by one the Masqueleros doffed their headgear to reveal the grinning motley faces of teenagers of mixed heritage and gender.

One member gathered up the disguises, including Harnnoy's full suit, and stuffed the potentially treacherous proteopape into an insulated cabinet.

Briefly, Bash recapped his problem for the attentive students. They nodded knowingly, and finally one girl said, "So you need to discover this bint's hiding place without alerting her to your presence. And since she effectively controls every piece of proteopape in the I^2-verse, your only avenue of information is seemingly closed. But you haven't reckoned with—the internet!"

"The internet!" fumed Bash. "Why don't I just employ smoke signals or, or—the telegraph? The internet is dead as Xerox."

A red-haired kid chimed in. "No latch, pard. Big swaths of the web are still in place, maintained by volunteers like us. We revere and cherish the kludgy old monster. The web's virtual ecology is different now, true, more of a set of marginal biomes separated by areas of clear-cut devastation. But we still host thousands of webcams. And there's no proteopape in the mix, it's all antique silicon. So here's what we do. We put a few agents out there searching, and I guarantee that in no time at all we spot your girlfriend."

Sighing, Bash said, "She's not my girlfriend. Oh, well, what've I got to lose? Let's give it a try."

The Masqueleros and Bash crowded into an adjacent room full of antique hardware, including decrepit plasma flatscreens and folding PDA peripheral keyboards duct-taped into usability. The trapped heat and smells of the laboring electronics reminded Bash of his student days, seemingly eons removed from the present. Several of the Masqueleros sat down in front of their machines and begin to mouse furiously away. Interior and exterior shots of Greater Boston as seen from innumerable forgotten and dusty webcams swarmed the screens in an impressionistic movie without plot or sound.

Tito Harnnoy handed Bash a can of Glialsqueeze pop and said, "Refresh yourself, pard. This could take a while."

Eventually Bash and Tito fell to discussing the latest spintronics developments, and their potential impact on proteopape.

"Making the circuitry smaller doesn't change the basic proteopape paradigm," maintained Bash. "Each sheet gets faster and boasts more capacity, but the standard functionality remains the same."

"Nuh-*huh*! Spintronics means that all of proteopape's uses can be distributed into the environment itself. Proteopape as a distinct entity will vanish."

Bash had to chew on this disturbing new scenario for a while. Gradually, he began to accept Harmnoy's thesis, at least partially. Why hadn't he seen such an eventuality before? Maybe Dagny had been right when she accused him of losing his edge. . . .

"Got her!"

Bash and the others clustered around one monitor. And there shone Dagny.

She sat in a small comfy nest of cushions and fast-food packaging trash, a large sheet of proteopape in her lap.

"What camera is this feed coming from?" Bash said.

"It's mounted at ceiling level in the mezzanine of the Paramount Theater on Washington Street, down near Chinatown."

When Bash had been born in 1999, the Paramount Theater, one of the grand dames of twentieth-century Hollywood's Golden Age, had already been shuttered for over two decades. Various rehabilitation plans had been tossed about for the next fifteen years, until Bash entered MIT. During that year, renovations finally began. The grand opening of the theater coincided with the churning of the economy occasioned by the release of proteopape and also with a short-lived but scarily virulent outbreak of Megapox. Faced with uncertain financing, fear of contagion in mass gatherings, and the cheapness of superior home-theater systems fashioned of proteopape, the revamped movie house had locked its doors, falling once again into genteel desuetude.

"Can you magnify the view?" Bash asked. "See what she's looking at?"

The webcam zoomed in on the sheet of paper in Dagny's lap.

And Bash saw that she was watching them.

In infinite regress, the monitor showed the proteopape showing the monitor showing the proteopape showing. . . .

Bash howled. "Someone's got proteopape on them!"

Just then a leering Dagny looked backward over her shoulder directly at the webcam, and at the same time Bash's chin spoke.

"It's you, you idiot," said Bash's epidermis in Dagny's stepped-down voice.

Bash ripped off the smart band-aid he had applied while shaving, and the image of the Masqueleros on Dagny's proteopape swung crazily to track the movement.

"Dagny!" Bash yelled into the band-aid. "This has gone far enough! You've had your fun at my expense. Now give me your current password so I can make proteopape secure again."

"Come and get it," taunted Dagny. "I'm not going anywhere."

"I will!"

With that bold avowal, Bash furiously twisted the band-aid, causing the image of the Masqueleros on Dagny's proteopape to shatter. On the monitor screen she appeared unconcerned, lolling back among her cushions like the Queen of Sheba.

Bash turned to Tito. "Lend me a phone and your Segway. I'm going to nail this troublemaker once and for all."

"Some of us'll go with you, pard."

"No, you stay here. Dagny won't react well to intimidation by a bunch of strangers. And besides, I need the Masqueleros to keep on spying on her and feed me any updates on her actions. All I can hope is that she'll listen to me and abandon this insane vendetta. If she doesn't—Well, I'm not sure what I'll do."

"No problemo, fizz."

Someone handed Bash a phone. He downloaded his identity into it, then established an open channel to Harmnoy. After tucking the phone into the neckline of his shirt, allowing him to speak and be spoken to hands-free, Bash darted from the underground room.

7
Phantom of the Opera

Bash made it as far as Killian Court before the first of Dagny's attacks commenced.

On all the canvases of the amateur painters, on all the individual sheets of proteopape held by the idling students, Bash's face appeared, displacing laboriously created artworks, as well as the contents of books, magazines and videos. (Dagny had unearthed a paparazzo's image of Bash that made him look particularly demented.) And from the massed speakers in the proteopape pages boomed this warning in a gruff male voice:

"Attention! This is a nationwide alert from Homeland Security. All citizens should immediately exert extreme vigilance for the individual depicted here. He is wanted for moral turpitude, arrogant ignorance and retrogressive revanchism. Approach him with caution, as he may bite."

This odd yet alarming message immediately caused general consternation to spread throughout the quadrangle. Bash turned up his shirt collar, hunched down his head and hurried toward the street. But he had not reckoned with the kites.

Homing in on his phone, the co-opted kites began to dive-bomb Bash. Several impacted the ground around him, crumpling with a noise like scrunching cellophane, but one scored a direct hit on his head, causing him to yelp. His squeal attracted the eyes of several onlookers, and someone shouted, "There he is!"

Bash ran.

He thought briefly of abandoning his phone, but decided not to. He needed to stay in touch with the Masqueleros. But more crucially, giving up his phone would achieve no invisibility.

Bash was moving through a saturated I^2 environment. There was no escaping proteopape. Every smart surface—from store windows to sunglasses, from taxi rooftop displays to billboards, from employee nametags to vending machines—was a camera that would track him in his dash across town to the Paramount Theater. Illicitly tapping into all these sources, utilizing common yet sophisticated pattern recognition, sampling and extrapolative software, Dagny would never lose sight of her quarry. Bash might as well have had cameras implanted in his eyeballs.

Out on Mass Ave, Bash faced no interception from alarmed citizens. Apparently the false security warning had been broadcast only in Killian Court. But surely Dagny had further tricks up her striped sleeves.

He spoke into his dangling phone. "What's she doing now?"

Harnnoy's voice returned an answer. "Noodling around with her pape. She's got her back to the camera, so we can't see what kind of scripts she's running."

"Okay, thanks. I'm hitting the road now."

Once aboard the Segway, Bash headed back toward downtown Boston.

He came to a halt obediently at the first red light, chafing at the delay. But something odd about the engine noise of the car approaching behind him made Bash look over his shoulder.

The car—a 2029 Vermoulian with proteopape windows—was not slowing down.

In a flash, Bash realized what was happening.

Dagny had edited out both the traffic light and Bash's scooter from the driver's interior display.

Bash veered his Segway to the right, climbing the curb, and the Vermoulian zipped past him with only centimeters to spare. In the middle of the intersection it broadsided another car. Luckily, the crash of the two lightweight urban vehicles, moving at relatively low speeds, resulted in only minor damages, although airbags activated noisily.

Bash drove down the sidewalk, scattering pedestrians, and continued around the accident.

Things were getting serious. No longer was Dagny content merely to harass Bash. Now she was involving innocent bystanders in her mad quest for revenge.

His ire rising, Bash crossed the Charles River. Beneath the bridge, huge jubilant crowds had assembled for the Dragon Boat races.

Bash took several wrong turns. Dagny had changed the street signs, misnaming avenues along his entire route and producing a labyrinth of new one-way streets. After foolishly adhering to the posted regulations for fear of getting stopped by some oblivious rule-bound cop, Bash abandoned all caution and just raced past snarled traffic down whatever avenue he felt would bring him most quickly to Washington Street.

Now Bash began to see his face everywhere, in varying sizes, surmounted or underlined by dire warnings. WANTED FOR CULTURAL ASSASSINATION, GUILTY OF SQUANDERING ARTISTIC CAPITAL, MASTERMIND IN FELONIOUS ASSAULT ON VISIONARIES. . . .

The absurd charges made Bash see red. He swore aloud, and Harmnoy said, "What'd I do, pard?"

"Nothing, nothing. Dagny still at the Paramount?"

"Verdad, compañero."

As he approached the Common, Bash noted growing crowds of gleeful pedestrians. What was going on . . . ?

The Dragon Boat Festival. Chinatown must be hosting parallel celebrations. Well, okay. The confusion would afford Bash cover—

A sheet of proteopape—spontaneously windblown, or aimed like a missile?—sailed up out of nowhere and wrapped Bash's head. He jerked the steering grips before taking his hands entirely off them to deal with the obstruction to his vision, and the Segway continued homeostatically on its new course to crash into a tree.

Bash picked himself up gingerly. The paper had fallen away from his face. Angrily, he crumpled it up and stuffed it into his pocket. He hurt all over, but no important body part seemed broken. The scooter was wrecked. Luckily, he hadn't hit anyone. Concerned bystanders clumped around him, but Bash brusquely managed to convince them to go away.

Harmnoy said, "I caught the smashup on the phone camera, Bash. You okay?"

"Uh, I guess. Sorry about totaling your ride. I'm going on foot now."

As Bash scurried off, he witnessed the arrival of several diligent autonomes converging on the accident. He accelerated his pace, fearful of getting corralled by the authorities before he could deal with Dagny.

Downtown Crossing was thronged, the ambient noise like a slumber party for teenage giants. The windows of Filene's claimed that Bash was a redactive splice between a skunk, a hyena and a jackal. As Dagny's interventions failed to stop him, her taunts grew cruder. She must be getting desperate. Bash was counting on her to screw up somehow. He had no real plan otherwise.

Weaseling his way through the merrymakers, Bash was brought up short a block away from the Paramount by an oncoming parade. Heading the procession was a huge multiperson Chinese dragon. In lieu of dumb paint, its proteopape skin sheathed it in glittery scales and animated smoke-snorting head.

People were pointing to the sky. Bash looked up.

One of the famous TimWarDisVia aerostats cruised serenely overhead, obviously dispatched to provide an overhead view of the parade. Its proteopape skin featured Bash's face larger than God's. Scrolling text reflected poorly on Bash's parentage and morals.

"God *damn!*" Bash turned away from the sight, only to confront the dragon. Its head now mirrored Bash's, but its body was a snake's.

Small strings of firecrackers began to explode, causing shrieks, and Bash utilized the diversion to bull onward toward the shuttered Paramount Theater. He darted down the narrow alley separating the deserted building from its neighbors.

"Tito! Any tips on getting inside?"

"One of our webcams on the first floor shows something funky with one of the windows around the back."

The rear exterior wall of the theater presented a row of weatherdistressed plywood sheets nailed over windows. The only service door was tightly secured. No obvious entrance manifested itself.

But then Bash noticed with his trained eye that one plywood facade failed close-up inspection as he walked slowly past it.

Dagny had stretched an expanse of proteopape across an open frame, then set the pape to display a plywood texture.

Bash set his phone on the ground. "Tito, I'm going in alone. Call the cops if I'm not out in half an hour."

"Uptaken and bound, fizz!"

Rather vengefully, Bash smashed his fist through the disguising pape, then scrambled inside.

Dagny had hotwired electricity from somewhere. The Paramount was well lit, although the illumination did nothing to dispel a moldy atmosphere from years of inoccupancy. Bash moved cautiously from the debris-strewn backstage area out into the general seating.

A flying disc whizzed past his ear like a suicidal mirror-finished bat. It hit a wall and shattered.

Dagny stood above him at the rail of the mezzanine with an armful of antique DVDs. The platters for the digital projectors must have been left behind when the Paramount ceased operations. The writing on a shard at Bash's feet read: *The Silmarillion.*

Dagny frisbee'd another old movie at Bash. He ducked just in time to avoid getting decapitated.

"Quit it, Dagny! Act like an adult, for Christ's sake! We have to talk!"

Dagny pushed her clunky eyeglasses back up her nose. "We've got nothing to talk about! You've proven you're a narrow-minded slave to old hierarchies, without an ounce of imagination left in your shriveled brainpan. And you insulted my art!"

"I'm sorry! I didn't mean to, honest. Jesus, even you said that the Woodies were a big joke."

"Don't try putting words in my mouth! Anyway, that was before I won one."

Bash stepped forward into an aisle. "I'm coming up there, Dagny, and you can't stop me."

A withering fusillade of discs forced Bash to eat his words and run for cover into an alcove.

Frustrated beyond endurance, Bash racked his wits for some means of overcoming the demented auteur.

A decade of neglect had begun to have its effects on the very structure of the theater. The alcove where Bash stood was littered with fragments of concrete. Bash snatched up one as big as his fist. From his pocket he dug the sheet of proteopape that had blinded him, and wrapped it around the heavy chunk. He stepped forward.

"Dagny, let's call a truce. I've got something here you need to read. It puts everything into a new light." Bash came within a few meters of the lower edge of the balcony before Dagny motioned him to stop. He offered the ball of pape on his upturned palm.

"I don't see what could possibly change things—"

"Just take a look, okay?"

"All right. Toss it up here."

Dagny set her ammunition down to free both hands and leaned over the railing to receive the supposedly featherweight pape.

Bash concentrated all his anger and resolve into his right arm.

He made a motion as if to toss underhand. But at the last minute he swiftly wound up and unleashed a mighty overhand pitch.

Dagny did not react swiftly enough to the deceit. The missile conked her on the head and she went over backwards into the mezzanine seats.

Never before had Bash moved so fast. He found Dagny hovering murmurously on the interface between consciousness and oblivion. Reassured that she wasn't seriously injured, Bash arrowed toward her nest of pillows. He snatched up the sheet of proteopape that displayed his familiar toolkit for accessing the trapdoor features of his invention. With a few commands he had long ago memorized as a vital failsafe, he initiated the shutdown of the hidden override aspects of proteopape.

From one interlinked sheet of proteopape to the next the commands raced, propagating exponentially around the globe like history's most efficient cyberworm, a spark that extinguished its very means of propagation as it raced along. Within mere minutes, the world was made safe and secure again for Immanent Information.

Bash returned to Dagny, who was struggling to sit up.

"You—you haven't beaten me. I'll find some way to show you—"

The joyful noises from the continuing parade outside insinuated themselves into Bash's relieved mind. He felt happy and inspired. Looking down at Dagny, he knew just what to say.

"Forget it, Jake. It's Chinatown."

The Time-Travel Heart

Geoffrey A. Landis

YEAH, SO I KILLED HIM. IT REALLY WAS THE THING to do.

When you get down to it, Seth was a geeky little jerk, short and plump and socially clueless. He had an annoying habit of always thinking he was right and never quitting an argument until he made you admit it. That really gets on a guy's nerves. The closest he ever got to exercise was to walk up the stairs to the third-floor apartment we shared, back when neither one of us had any money and we'd split an apartment between us. Even then he'd been annoying and self-righteous. I'd moved out as soon I could borrow enough cash to pay for my own place.

I don't know why I visited him, it wasn't as if he were actually my friend. I guess he was just so pathetic I felt sorry for him. And sometimes it's good to hang out with somebody when you don't give a rat's ass about what they think about you.

So, I was over at the shitty apartment we used to share. "Hey, Davey-baby!" he said. "Check this out!" He was in a phase where he called everybody "baby," his lame attempt to be cool. He didn't actually have any friends, so I was about the only person he could practice on. The place was crammed with textbooks and old computers and piles of empty pizza boxes. I couldn't guess what he needed half a dozen obsolete computers for.

"Just watch this!" he told me.

It was going to be something boring. Last week he'd been chattering about parallel universes. There are ten-to-the-fiftieth parallel universes, he told me, every one of them right next door! And there's no barrier between them; you can slide right from one to another. In fact, people do it all the time.

That seemed reasonable. I can't tell you how many times I put down the keys to my BMW (twelve years old, alas, and in battered condition, but one day I was going to own one new) and then when I looked for them, they were someplace else entirely. I told this to him.

"You are an anencephalic ignoramus, you know that?" He pushed his glasses up his nose to give me a look intended to make me realize exactly how much of an idiot I was. "There is no intercoursing way you would ever be able to tell if you were in a parallel universe. None. Any parallel universes close enough to access are different from each other by the placement of a single atom. Maybe, one atom in the middle of the Earth somewhere. You know how many atoms there are in the Earth? Or did they forget to mention that in the business-major curriculum?"

I didn't have any idea, but I did get the gist of what he was saying. "So, like, if these universes are identical, what difference does it make?"

"What difference?" He pushed his glasses up his nose again. He had a pimple the size of a jellybean on the bridge of his nose, where the glasses rubbed when he pushed them up. It made me wince every time he did it. He seemed about to be outraged by the fact that I didn't think a moved atom made a difference, and then thought about it for a second, and said mildly, "Well, not much, I guess, in your little business-major terms. It's just cool to think about."

"Oh." I didn't have anything to add to this. He was a little geek, and if thinking about moving an atom around pushed his buttons, well, cool for him.

Switching to business major meant that, unlike him, I actually had a chance at getting a job, but it was hardly worth trying to get that point across to him. I had every intention of getting rich and famous and massively laid. He didn't care about getting a job, or impressing chicks, or anything practical.

So when Seth said, take a look at this, I didn't expect to see much.

I looked at it. "What the hell is it? Something you found under your couch?"

He had half a dozen ancient Amiga computers and an even more ancient Osborne—God, where had he scrounged that antique monstrosity from?—wired up to a gadget. It looked like a tangled ball of wire.

"Cool, huh?" He grinned at me. "It's a time machine."

"What?" I looked at him. "You're bullshitting me, dude."

"No way, Davey-baby; it's the genuine thing."

"Sure, Seth. And so's my Aunt Libby, only without the computer."

"Not a joke this time." His grin was bigger than ever. It made him look something like Alfred E. Newman, but not as suave.

"Yeah? What about paradoxes?" I may have been a business major, but that didn't mean I was stupid. In fact, you can tell that I am completely sane and rational: a madman would never ask such a reasonable question.

"No paradoxes."

As he explained it, I almost began to believe he might be serious. Parallel universes, all of them so close to identical that you could never tell one from another, but some of them a little further ahead of us, some a little behind us. So if he just slid into the next universe, and picked one that was, say, an hour ahead—bingo, he's moved ahead in time.

"Shit," I said. "If you're not lying, you've really got something here. You could be rich."

"Lying? You nematode, I've already tried it. In fact, I've already met you—in the future. A bunch of times. Lemme show you." He typed something onto the Osborne, and suddenly he flickered.

There was no other word for it: he flickered. He was hunched over the keyboard, and an instant later he flickered and he was in a slightly different position, his head turned to the side.

"See?"

"Shit," I said. "Where'd you go?"

"Future," he said. "I visited you a couple of times."

"I was in your apartment?"

"Sure."

Well, that was interesting. If he had any sense, the time machine would make him rich and famous, and if I'd been him, once I got famous I'd dump the likes of me like a sack of shit. But, hey, he didn't have any sense. In fact—

"What about lottery tickets?" I said.

"What?"

"The lottery number. If you can go to the future, you can get the lottery number."

"I never play the lottery," he said. "If I wanted to throw money away, I'd burn it. That way I at least get a little heat out of it. Lotteries are a state tax on stupid people."

I sighed dramatically. "Look, dude. If you know the number is going to win, it's not throwing money away."

He thought about it for a second. "Yeah, I guess not. Still, it seems slightly unfair. And, besides," he shrugged. "I don't really need money."

His apartment was furnished in garage-sale rejects. Even the computers were things that other people had thrown out. "Look, it's just taking money from people who can't do math," I told him. "Think of it as an experiment. Get tomorrow's number, let's see if you can do it. I'll buy the ticket."

"Okay." He typed something into the Osborne and flickered again. This time he was facing the opposite direction, and was clutching a pad of paper. I grabbed it from him and examined the number on it.

"What's this one? Is this the Pick 6, or is it the Weekly Millionaire?"

"There's a difference?" he asked.

"Well, sure."

"Hold on, I'll find out." He flickered again, before I could tell him I could just buy a ticket for both.

"It's something called the Six O'Clock Lotto State Number," he said.

"That's the Weekly Millionaire." I laughed, I honestly laughed out loud. "We're going to be rich," I said. "Rich."

"Rich?" he said, as if the idea hadn't occurred to him before. Then he shook his head and said, "Nah, I don't think so. After I publish, you know, they'll cancel the lottery payoff. I mean, the whole thing is distinctly brain-dead if you know the results beforehand, you know? They'll abolish it."

He had a big lamp on his desk, a metal monstrosity that must have weighed ten pounds. I said, "Say, how's the weather next week?"

"I don't know," he said. "I didn't go outside. Hold on, I'll—"

And he flickered again. When he was still blinking, coming back from the flicker, I hit him in the head with the table lamp.

He was tougher than he appeared; the first whack just made him look dazed. Not even an unusual expression for him. I hit him a couple of times, and then when he was on the ground I stepped on his throat and put my weight on it until he stopped moving.

Look, it made sense for me to kill him. Shit, a time machine, and the idiot didn't have any clue what he could do with it. It was really only right for me to kill him, he was so stupid.

I found a big black plastic garbage bag in the kitchen and stuffed the body in and tied it shut, then—after checking that nobody was looking out their windows—lugged it to the dumpster in back. With eighty tons of new garbage sent to the landfill every day, nobody would ever find it. That's the smart way to dispose of a body, let the city do it for you. Only a loser would try to dig some kind of grave.

I'd never doubted him, but I checked the next day, and the ticket I'd bought was a winner. Half a million bucks a year, for twenty years. I stared at it, thinking what to do. I needed to hire a lawyer, that's it, and keep my own identity secret to avoid being besieged by beggars and con men. I headed back to Seth's apartment, working on a plan, and I was just about to put the key I'd grabbed from his jeans into his door when it opened.

I nearly jumped out of my skin. I was eyeball to eyeball with Seth.

"Shit!" I shouted. "You scared the hell out of me!"

"Hey, Davey-baby," he said, just like I hadn't whacked him over the head with a lamp and left his body in the dumpster. "Why so jumpy?" He put his hand on my shoulder, and I'm telling you, I really creeped out at the thought of a dead guy touching me.

"Fuck," I said. "You're dea—" and then I suddenly thought better of telling him he was dead. "You're da man, Seth," I said. "Look at this!"

"That's a lottery ticket?" he said, examining it quizzically and pushing his glasses up on his face to try to read the fine print.

My flesh still felt crawly from where he'd touched my hand taking the ticket. I couldn't believe that he didn't even know what a lottery ticket looked like. "Today's winning ticket, in fact."

"Cool, that's just what I need," he said. He shoved the ticket into the pocket of his button-down shirt. "I'll just bring that and show it to you—"

I reached over and snagged the ticket out of his pocket. "Fuck you, that's mine," I said.

"Hey!" he said. Suddenly I realized he was no ghost, but yesterday's Seth, coming forward to today to answer my question of what the winning lottery ticket was. Of course. He didn't even know he was dead.

And I wasn't about to tell him, either. "Look, dude, just write it down," I told him. I thought about giving him a message to give me in the past, but since I hadn't received a message from me, maybe that wasn't such a good idea.

"Thanks, buddy-boy," he said. He grabbed a pad—the same one he'd brought back yesterday—and turned back into his apartment. I followed along. Yesterday I'd examined the machine after killing him, and wasn't able to figure out the first thing about using it. The computer displayed constantly changing numbers and letters, but there wasn't any sort of help screen to tell me how to get it to work. This time I watched. He looked at the screen, mumbled for a second, typed a series of numbers and letters, almost too fast to follow—"#5F03AE #840C3D #B30A23 #C7F4BB"—and vanished.

Shit. This wasn't going to be easy.

I flopped down on the ratty couch to think, only to jump like a weasel when he suddenly reappeared. "Say, what's that ticket for?" he asked.

"Six O'Clock Lotto State Number," I said. "The weekly mill—"

He didn't even say thanks, just vanished. And, before I could relax, reappeared.

This time he was wearing a laughably out-of-date Hawaiian shirt, one of a dozen that he wore when he wanted to be cool.

"Hey, Davey-baby," he said. "What are you doing here?"

Idiot was so stupid, he deserved to be dead. "Waiting for you, what did you think," I said.

"How did you—" he started, and then laughed. "Oh, guess I must have told you I'd be here. So how's life in the future?" He looked around, puzzled. "Say, where am I, anyway?"

"Right here," I said. "In your—"

"No, I meant, where is my present-time instantiation?" he said, annoyed for no reason I could tell. "Why aren't I waiting for myself?"

"Uh, you went out," I told him. He looked disbelieving, and I realized that I needed to cover fast. "You said, uh, that you, yeah, you didn't want to talk to yourself right now."

"Why—" He stopped for a second, and then said, "No, there can't be a—but then, I'm two days smarter in day-after-tomorrow's instantiation than the me of today, so I've got to take my word for it that I don't want to meet myself."

That was close.

Seth didn't want to do anything, just hang around his apartment, picking things up like he'd never seen them before, and then putting them back. It was creepy, hanging around with a dead guy, trying to think of something to say. I wanted to kick him out, but it was his apartment—or at least he thought it was—and what could I say, really? *So how's life now you're dead?* didn't quite cut it. So I asked him to show me how to work the time machine.

"Say what?" he said.

"You told me that you showed me how to work it already," I told him. "Yeah, you told me in the past, so you have to do it, because you did it."

He looked incredulous. "I told you that? What in the world was I talking about?"

I shrugged.

"Look," he said, and swung the screen over where I could look at it. "Can you do a Feymann integral over multiple possible histories? This—" he pointed to the string of numbers "—that's the contracted Riemann tensor, did your business mathematics—" (his voice dripped sarcasm) "—your *advanced* business mathematics, did it tell you how to read that?"

"Uh—" I said.

"So how could I possibly teach you?" he demanded. "It would take four years of physics before you could even read the notation."

Now I was pissed. "Look, I don't have to understand how it works, you dork," I said. "I just want to run it. You know, set the time and go."

"It doesn't work like that," he said. "What, you think I put in a goocy interface for idiots? You have to input the raw data. If you're too dumb to do a contour integral in your head, you're out of luck."

Shit.

He pushed his glasses up his nose. "I must have been playing some joke on myself, telling you I'd teach you to run this. What an idiot."

When he went back into the machine, I sighed in relief. Time to—

The phone rang, and I picked it up without thinking. It was Seth. "Hey, Davey-baby?"

I dropped the phone, and somebody came up behind me and hung it up. "Hey, Davey-baby," Seth said. "How's life in the future?"

I shoved him away and ran out of the apartment, taking the stairs down to the lobby six at a time. As I hit the lobby door, I nearly slammed the door into Seth, standing with his key extended.

"Hey, Davey—" he started, and I elbowed him off and bolted.

On the street, there was Seth, looking in puzzlement at a newspaper. He looked up at me, opened his mouth, and I screamed and ran.

There's only so much a sane man can take. How many times had he used the damn machine? A dozen? A hundred? How many times would I have to see him again?

How would I keep somebody from renting Seth's supposedly empty apartment and suddenly have the ghost of Seth appear? He's so dumb, he wouldn't even keep the secret, he'd tell everything to the first stranger he saw in his apartment.

What was I to do, keep his apartment like a shrine, old pizza boxes and everything, keep paying the rent and hope nobody noticed that he wasn't there anymore?

I can't take it anymore. He's coming back, I know it. Get me away from here, arrest me, handcuff me, just get me away from me. I'll tell everything.

Can't you hear it? That's him, that's him coming. Can't you hear him?

Can't you hear his voice, saying "Hey, Davey-baby, how's life in the future?"

Takes You Back

George Zebrowski

I LOVED HER. SHE LOVED ME. IT HAD ALWAYS been that way. So deeply that sometimes I imagined that our love had been fixed that way when the universe began, awaiting our coming on the scene.

"It's chemical between you two," her mother liked to say, "some unimaginable sympathy that nothing will break." She said it as if it couldn't be anything else, that it would be impossible otherwise. Heaven and the gods had something to do with it, or it couldn't have happened. People don't just get together on their own.

"You know," I mused as we were watching the evening news, "I really like those French doors of ours." They closed off the foyer and made the front entrance area into a small room by itself. We often used the space for storage. I liked the curtains on the glass panels, and looked forward one of these days to refinishing the doors, stripping the brass hardware and lockset of paint to restore the shine, so that each part would again be as new. The doors were much more interesting than the news.

"You know what I'm up for?" she said. "—some French fries." She gave me a sly guilty smile and rolled her eyes at her segue from French doors to French fries. "Just this one time," she added forgivingly.

It had been a long time. A couple of years, anyway, since we had started watching our weight and nutrition.

"I'll get some," I said, suddenly feeling like taking a brisk walk to the nearby fast food place, rationalizing that I would walk off in advance some of the calories I would bring home. I wondered if the fries would pass the test of nostalgia.

She smiled at me again as I got up and went to the front door, remembering our college days, when she had been sick in bed one day and I had gone out in a snowstorm to get her some cream puffs, feeling as purposeful as a hunter.

I opened the door, then the storm door. I held it while I closed the inside door, then stepped out into a warm summer breeze as the storm door whispered shut behind me. A clear evening sky was bright with stars above the trees around our house.

Memories jabbed at me as I took a deep breath. They cut through me with their regretful, structured beauties, and reminded me again of my ambivalence about moving here. Sarah and I still felt a sense of loss about our abandoned apartment back in our college town, and I still had the feeling that I would get on a bus one day and go "home."

I went down the stone walkway and onto the street—

—and stepped into autumn.

It took a moment for the change to register. I stopped and turned to look at the house. All the lights were off. Around me the trees were losing their leaves as a cool breeze was getting up to speed. Overhead, a few clouds hurried in from the north. I stared up at the glitter of the constellations and saw that they had changed to those of fall. A chill went through me that was not part of the season.

I turned and walked back up to my door. I looked left and right and saw that the other houses were all lit up: Windows flashed from television screens. Motion detector lights blazed in driveways, reminding me of theater lights waiting for the actors to come on stage. But my house was dark. Then I realized that the sensor-lights had failed to go on as I approached the door.

I rang the bell.

"Sarah!" I shouted when I got no answer.

Suddenly the house was quiet and the night was still, as in that Wallace Stevens poem, but I was not even on the right page; I was staring at a closed book, at what seemed a sudden finality, as abrupt as the impending autumn around me.

Something had happened, I told myself, feeling certain that I would have to break into the house to find out what.

I went around to the basement window that I had never fixed. It was on the side of the house facing Mrs. Scheler's driveway. That feisty old woman seemed eternal; she had been ancient even when we had moved here over two years ago. We called the strip of grass and bushes and her asphalt driveway between our houses "The Scheler Neutral Zone." She didn't like the leaves and seeds from our trees covering her driveway every year, but I noticed that her driveway was graded so that our house foundation got all the water draining from her rain gutters. I wasn't going to cut down any trees, but if she pressed the matter I would show her how the water flowed.

I pried out the old wooden storm window. It seemed less decayed than I recalled. The inner window opened easily, since only half the latch was still there. I had not replaced the broken half.

Shaking from fear of what I might find, I climbed in feet first and dropped to the floor. It was only three steps to the light switch. I flicked on the lights, and without looking around went to the stairs, hurrying from fear that there had been some kind of accident and Sarah might need me.

I came upstairs to the kitchen door and found it open. The skeleton key I had bought was not in the lock. I turned off the basement lights out of habit, then crept into the kitchen, tasting the mustiness that followed me from the basement. I found the wall switch, and turned on the lights.

Everything seemed normal.

"Sarah!" I shouted as I went into the dining room. The lights went on, but the room was a shock. The heavy oak table that had gone to Sarah's sister stood in place of our walnut elegance. The upright piano that we had given to charity was here again, up against the left wall. The built-in china closet was empty, as it was when we had moved in.

I hurried into the living room, but it was an alien place, empty of all that we had done to make it our own. Sarah's mother's furniture was all here, as if a giant had taken the roof off the house and put it all back.

"Sarah!" I shouted, hearing my voice break.

I listened for an answer in the silence.

Then I heard a meow.

I turned and saw a black and white cat standing in the doorway to the living room. He gave me the penetrating gaze I had once known, then snarled at me as if at a stranger.

A rush of feeling went through me. "Spencer!" I cried. "You're alive!"

I started toward him, but he turned and fled back to the stairs and down into the basement.

I was breathing hard, wondering by what miracle he could be alive. I had lost my mind, I told myself, struggling to deny it . . .

Spencer had died a few months ago, at the vet's. He was seventeen years old and his kidneys were failing; to have kept him alive would only have prolonged his suffering. Sarah and her mother had held his paws as he drifted away without protest. I remembered how devastated Sarah's mother had been, even though she had allowed us to keep her cat when she had moved out after we took over the house. Long periods of separation from her pet had not cured her of him. "Harvey's allergic to cats," she had told us, meaning her new husband, "and there isn't much room in the townhouse, and we'll be traveling a lot anyway." I supposed she had meant that Spencer would be happier in what he had come to regard as his estate. But when she held his paw, it was as if she had never left him behind. Sarah and I had looked on, our hearts stopped by our uncontrollable denial that Spencer was breathing his last. I had been up with him the night before, hoping his illness was a passing thing as he lay there wrapped in a blanket, trying to rest and shake it off . . .

But my mind was gone, and my knowing it was part of the madness. I was wandering in a nightmare because I had dared venture out for French fries. Something had not wanted me to have them, and that something had been right.

I steadied myself against the old oak table, then sat down in one of the creaky chairs. Spencer was back, looking at me from the doorway again, confused, as he had always been whenever I failed to chase after him into the basement, where we would play hide-and-seek.

But as I gazed into his furry, lost face now restored to me, I knew that we were strangers; somehow, we had not yet met. And that lack of recognition had to be another sign of madness . . .

Finally, I got up and went into the kitchen. The waterfowl calendar displayed October 1996, a full two and a half years before Sarah and I had moved here from our old college town, where we had been living in our second apartment after graduation. Sarah was teaching high school while completing her doctorate, and I was trying to write novels in between monthly stories and handyman work, mostly carpentry and some plumbing.

I stared at the calendar in disbelief. Spencer was at my feet, staring up at me and hissing. I knelt and put out my hand, happy to see him, even if he turned out to be a ghost.

He looked at my hand as if it was an insult, and his eyes said the usual: "Don't you dare say cute kitty things to me." He had never really believed he was a cat, and disliked other cats; they were beneath him. Sarah's mother had always insisted that he thought of himself as a person trapped in a feline's body, and I sometimes believed it.

I stood up, then tried the wall phone. It was dead. I opened the refrigerator. It was empty. I recalled that Sarah's mother had been in Italy in the fall of '96. It had been her first long trip with Harvey, and they had decided to marry not long afterwards. We had moved here in the spring . . .

Something like that, I told myself, hoping to explain this nightmare somehow. I again stared at the calendar, as if it were the great arbiter of time, the one authority I could trust to explain my situation. Who would bother to hang an old calendar?

Lights flashed in the kitchen window, as if a lightning storm was coming. When I heard no thunder, I went to the dining room window, moving as if in a dream. It was the routine police car patrol, and I remembered the night when Spencer had slipped outside and I had gone out in my shorts and sandals looking for him.

"Do you always look for your cat at 3 A.M.?" the cop had asked back then.

"He escapes," I had explained, grinning.

Now I realized, following the logic of my madness, that they had seen the lights and would check the house. Sarah's mother always asked them to keep an eye on things when she was away. These suburban cops would be suspicious of anything in this quiet, parklike neighborhood, where the asphalt ribbons of road, dating back to the 1940s or earlier, were little more than driveways to the houses.

The police car circled the block, and pulled up in front of the house. They would not know me if I opened the door. They had seen lights where there should be no lights. They might even have a key.

I had to turn out the lights and flee before they came in and found me.

But where could I go? It wasn't exactly warm outside. I had only the five bucks in my wallet to buy the fries.

Then I remembered when Sarah had showed me the places in the house where she had hidden as a child. Crawlspaces on the second floor, behind the walls and over the ceilings. Could I fit into any of them?

I turned out the lights and groped my way up the stairs to the second floor bedroom. I opened the closet, turned on the dim light, and saw the panel.

It slid open easily. I turned out the light, then felt my way into the closet. I squeezed into the space, shut the panel, and waited.

The cops moved around on the first floor. One of them came up the stairs, then went back down.

"If there was anyone here," he called to his partner, "he was gone as soon as he saw us coming!"

"Yeah. There's nothing taken down here, not even a TV or radio. Must have been disappointing."

I thought of Sarah's mother hiding silver cups in the back of the old 1940s radio in the basement. Probably helped its reception, I had once imagined.

After a while, I didn't hear the cops. It got cold in the crawlspace, but I didn't come out. I fell asleep, hoping that I'd wake up in front of the television with Sarah, with a bag of warm fries in my lap.

I slept dreamlessly, and awoke with a nose full of dust, startled by the dark unfamiliarity.

Slowly I remembered, but was afraid to move and give myself away. I crouched there, realizing that I was alone in the house, somehow at an earlier time.

Then I began to see the course now open to me. It opened before me like the doors to a prison of time. I would live nearby and wait for the years to run out. Something had set me back two and a half years, subtracting me from my time and adding me here. What cosmic calculator could have made such a thing happen?

As I crawled out of the attic space, the enormity of the implications hit me. Two of me lived in this time. I would have to wait for the night of June 1, 1998, when I had gone out for French fries, and then try to step back into my life. Presumably, I would see myself come out of the house and disappear, leaving me the chance to step back in.

I was assuming that I was not mad, which is what I would assume if I were insane—except that I could also see that much. Who said that sanity was simply consensus madness?

A chill went through me, probably from sleeping in the cold space, as much as from the doubts that played through my mind. I could not be sure that the opportunity to return would ever present itself to me. All I could do was to wait out the time.

I could stay in the house for a while, if I didn't turn on the lights at night. Sarah's mother wouldn't return until November.

I went down into the basement and found a can of tuna among the provisions in the pantry that Sarah and I would later make into a small wine cellar. There was also a package of zwieback. They would go well with the tuna. I wouldn't starve today. There was plenty of bottled water, and canned soups, not to mention bottles of Scotch and a few boxed wines. I could heat the soups on the small camper stove Sarah's mother had bought to deal with power failures and other emergencies. I would not signal my presence by using the kitchen.

As I started upstairs, I heard the back door open and retreated into the basement. Spencer ran past me up the stairs, and I realized that Mrs. Scheler had to be coming in to feed him, groom him, and to clean out his litter box. Sarah and I had relied on her often enough when we were away.

I went into the wine cellar, closed the door, and listened to her moving around in the kitchen. She loved cats, and Spencer in particular. Sometimes she had reproached Sarah's mother for abandoning Spencer. Then I realized that Mrs. Scheler would also be back in the evenings to check on Spencer and the house—every day during the period of her cat-sitting duties. The only protection I had was that Mrs. Scheler was old and a bit dotty, and hence not very observant. With enough care, I could keep out of her way.

I waited. After a while I sat down on the cold floor of the wine cellar and listened through the door. She came down into the basement to refresh Spencer's litter box.

"You dear thing," she said to him softly. "Abandoned and alone here. But you have me. I'll take good care of you."

I imagined Spencer looking at her.

Then he meowed.

I slept in what would later be our bedroom. During the night Spencer joined me, snuggling up against my thigh. But he was gone in the morning. With Spencer it was solidarity through the vulnerable night, pride in the bright daylight.

I spent the day looking around the house, annoyed by all the waiting problems I would fix after we moved in. It was strange seeing the dripping faucets, electrical disrepair, and carpentry, still waiting for me. It had all been done in the future; but not here.

And I was always listening for Mrs. Scheler.

I realized then that I would have to live somewhere else, to get through the two and a half years that would have to pass before I could resume my life. I couldn't stay here; sooner or later I would make a mistake and get caught. I had visions of being identified, of being brought face to face with myself before the situation could right itself—if it ever could be resolved. Some great disaster was waiting for me, and I could not imagine it.

I sat in the shadowy daylight of the living room, thinking that maybe my return might overtake me sooner; maybe at any moment. Why assume that it would happen only at the future moment when I had left the house? I sat in the eternity of that living room, hoping for a miracle. Shapes played at the edges of my vision, memories that had yet to happen in my life with Sarah, my mysterious chemical bondmate.

Finally, aware of my limited funds, I returned to the basement and checked the open back of the enormous standing radio. Yes, there was some silver in the unplugged works, among the dusty old tubes, including Sarah's silver baby cup—quite beat up; but it was silver.

I slipped out that afternoon to hock the silver. On my way back I noticed a "Help Wanted" sign in the local pizzeria. No one would know me here, so I went in and talked to the manager, an aging Pakistani who seemed to like my looks and hired me after about two minutes of conversation. My driver's license was still good, since I had gotten it only two years earlier. No one was going to notice two years off my age. Only my two credit cards were useless.

I would be inconspicuous in the job, since my duties were making deliveries three nights a week and working the store's cash register the rest of the time, opening up, cleaning a bit, and locking up. I would make enough to get by until the appointed time of mysteries, when I would converge with myself. It was a mad hope.

I rented a studio apartment, ten by ten with bath, in one of the old brick apartment buildings some ten blocks away, and went to work at eleven every morning.

It was a dreary life.

Sarah and I were a hundred miles away, in our beloved apartment, not yet aware that we would be moving next spring.

Here now, two and a half years earlier, there was no one I could count on to help me, unless I was ready to call upon people who had not seen me in some time. I would have to impersonate my earlier self in order to talk to them. Living incognito, hiding nothing, would not be difficult, because there was no one who could catch me at it.

I made enough at my job to pay the rent, and I had use of one of the eatery's cars to come and go from work. After six months I was promoted to store manager, when old Karim retired. He had a share of the place, and seemed relieved to keep me in charge. This meant that I no longer had to make deliveries in the area. I now took orders and dispatched other drivers, and continued to do the paperwork, besides opening and closing the store.

I opened the pizzeria by noon, so I had mornings and much of the afternoons to myself, which was not always a good thing, because I had time to twist every complication of my plight into every conceivable outcome. They came into my brain like train wrecks that I saw only as they were happening, never before.

In my first year as a manager, I drove by the house late one spring evening and saw lights. Sarah and I had arrived. I was stunned at the predictability of it; they might have decided otherwise.

I saw a moving van drive away one afternoon, and recalled that it was taking Sarah's mother's furniture away. The garage door was open another day, and I saw Gerard's old beat-up car inside. I thought of myself as him.

One night I received a phone order from that address. I took the order from my *other* self in a kind of bemused state of inevitability. Large deluxe, with a large bottle of Coke. Something in me wanted to make this delivery, but I restrained myself and passed it along, knowing that I would feel as late and incongruous as the storied snail who had been thrown out the door, only to come back three months later to ask, "What was that all about?"

On another evening, I drove by and saw Sarah and Gerard sitting on the enclosed porch, with only a small lamp on, and for a moment I felt a cold knife in my heart. Maybe I would never return. This branching of me would go on as I was now, exiled forever from the rest of my life. I could not take for granted what I wished to happen.

But I had to believe that I was working my way back home. That had to be enough. Keep to the plan. What would happen if I talked to myself? Would the universe blow up? Would I throw variations into the time stream that would forever bar my return?

I made a firm decision to pretty much ignore the world, for my own sanity, and because I feared somehow affecting the future in a way that might make my return impossible. I refused to read newspapers or watch television. After all, I pretty much knew what had happened. I resisted the urge to bet on sports events, even though the chance came my way in the restaurant through the drivers, who sometimes stopped off on their deliveries to place a bet. I remembered an old Ray Bradbury story, in which an expedition of time travellers harms a butterfly in the past and forever loses their own time.

I was a ghost, hoping to return to my own body.

One evening the phone rang .

I answered it. "Say," a woman's voice said. "The pizza was cold!"

"Oh," I said to Sarah. "I'm sorry about that. Would you like a replacement?"

"No, we already reheated."

"Well, next time you get a free one. Just remind me the next time you call in an order."

"Oh—thank you," she said, sounding friendly. "That will be okay." She had always been too kindly, or too cowardly, to carry through a rage.

As I hung up the phone I began to doubt that my waiting would do me any good. They were living there, and would always live there, while I would go on with this life. Did I really think I would be able to step back into the exact right moment? What if it required a fraction of a second of speed beyond my ability, beyond any human ability? As I imagined constructing a strange temporal razor with which to divide the moments, I knew even more clearly that I had no way to be sure that I would have a chance, a year from now or ever. No reason at all to think so.

I grew a beard and wore a hat to avoid being remembered in the neighborhood as anyone except the guy with the beard and hat. I took some care with this, thinking that I must never meet myself or anyone I knew. I had no idea what might happen, but I wasn't taking any chances. At the very least, Gerard would not recognize me.

One evening, Sarah's sister, Gail, came in for a pickup. I had not taken that call, so the first I knew I was handing her the pie. She took the box from my hands and stared at me for a moment.

"Have we met?" she asked in the musical tones I remembered. Sarah had some of that too, but Gail had more.

I shook my head, not daring to speak, even though I was glad to meet someone who knew me, then stared morosely at the floor until she turned and left.

At work I used my own name and social security number, and my area boss even cashed my checks for me. What could he think

if he ran across my name elsewhere—oh, someone else with
Gerry's name. It was a pizza place. What was the worst that could
happen? I wasn't breaking any laws, and lived on a cash basis. All I
had to do was lie low and wait.

One late afternoon, on my way to work, I drove by the house
and saw Sarah and Gerard coming outside. Spencer slipped out just
before Gerard closed the door, and climbed up into a small tree on
Mrs. Scheler's front lawn, gazing at them. He was showing off. I
knew the drill. When they turned away to leave, he hopped down
and loped after them. I knew as I left the scene behind that Spencer
would turn back and go home, after some waving and shouting by
me, to wait by the back door until we returned.

I counted the months toward the coming collision with myself.
That's what I told myself, anyway. Whether it would happen peacefully or not on that distant evening I had no idea.

Today was the day!

I had already given Karim notice that I was leaving my job. I
shaved, then tried to relax in my room. Toward evening I took out
the clean, carefully stored clothes I had worn on the day of my disappearance. I sat in my one big comfy chair and waited until the
evening hour was close before dressing. I had told the building's
manager that I was moving out, and would leave the keys in the
apartment. My rent was paid up for the month; the Gerry who lived
here would simply vanish.

I took my time dressing to be myself again, wondering whether
the coming event would be more like a wedding or a funeral. My
hands shook, and my throat was dry. I felt like a stalker.

I wondered about the path that lay before me. What was it like
up the line? Was there another time, running forward, in which
Sarah wondered what had happened to me when I failed to come
back with the fries? Or would my upcoming return simply cut off
that future? Would it still leave a vague memory in her of something having gone wrong? Would I remember it?

Soft doughlike reasonings twisted in my mind, and baked into
agonized pretzels in the heat of my imaginings. Horizons stood
around me, over which I could not see. I would know the outcome
this evening. Maybe not.

Finally I was again in my brown corduroy pants, black walking
shoes, blue shirt, and a flannel lumberjack overshirt. I had dressed
casually at home, and there had been no reason to dress up to get
some fast food on a warm evening. Yet the exactness of these clothes

was suddenly very crucial to me, as if I had to observe a cosmic dress code. Get one detail wrong, and it would all fall apart.

I walked the ten blocks to my house, checking my watch every few minutes, determined to give myself enough time to be there early in order to observe carefully.

When I reached the Dairy Queen at the edge of the neighborhood, I decided to have a small vanilla cone to settle my stomach. I had the time, since I was now only five minutes away.

I forced myself to eat the soft ice cream as I continued on my way. It was the same evening again, softly blue with starlight and a summer breeze, and memories crowding in on me.

In the house ahead, Sarah and I were talking ourselves into French fries. I scarfed down the rest of the cone and stopped at the corner.

I watched, waiting for the door of the brightly lit house to open.

And I began to feel sick, as if something was terribly wrong; but it was just out of sight over my mental hills. A great beast was coming for me fast out of some dark vastness.

Here I was, at the same moment.

The door opened slightly.

I heard muffled voices arguing as the inner door opened halfway. The words stopped as Gerard opened the storm door and hurried out onto the slate walkway. He paused, then went right back inside.

My mind stopped and was rooted to the moment.

The worst had happened, and could not be undone.

Gerard had not vanished into that sudden autumn I remembered. It was still summer. Somehow my chance to return had passed me by.

I stood there, shaking with fear and nausea. What had gone wrong?

I looked at my watch.

The time was right.

But the date was wrong. The tiny calendar on my watch told me I was a day early! How had that happened? My mind had reached ahead anxiously, yearning to draw me forward to this day.

I thought about all the other small variations that had been creeping into the sequence right from the start. Would some sort of accumulation of unnoticed, small differences keep me from coming home?

I took a deep breath, then thrust my shaking hands into my pockets. My fingers found my key chain; I had forgotten to leave my keys in the apartment. Then I realized why I had messed up on the date. I had paid the next month's rent a day early, making sure that there would be plenty of time for me to disappear into my previous life. Well, at least I would have a place to sleep for one more night.

Feeling miserable, I walked back to my studio apartment. Tomorrow at this time I would be back for another throw of the cosmic dice.

I was back ten minutes early. My clothes were a bit sweatier, but I didn't care. They would be more like they had been when I had first gone outside, two and a half years ago now. I had found a spare set of apartment keys, which I had made some time ago. I brought them with me because I might need to go back again. The fear was a stone in my stomach.

As I watched the door, I began to wonder whether I wanted to go back at all. Was this the same world, the same house, the same Sarah? I asked myself, recalling the shouting of the previous night. Maybe in this world-line I never came back, but lived apart, watching myself, avoiding his mistakes, counting myself lucky to have made the break. If the worlds varied, then there were perhaps an infinite number in which I had not come back. Sarah was forever lost to me.

The inner door opened. I tensed. Gerard pushed at the storm door.

Spencer rushed by him onto the bushy front lawn.

Gerard ran after him.

Spencer scampered across the street toward where I stood in shadows. Gerard was striding after him. It was the French fries, I thought. Without them, Gerard would not disappear.

This was not my world, I realized, because Spencer was still alive.

Gerard stopped and looked up at the sky, and seemed in no hurry to chase the cat. He stood there, and I wondered if he was suddenly seeing the autumn I had walked into.

But I continued to see him. He was still here. Maybe he would always be here, as I had feared, shutting me out.

Spencer padded down the street.

Gerard winked out.

For one second he was there, and in the next he was gone.

"Yes!" I whispered to myself. A shiver of spooky triumph shot up my spine, driving all my doubts out into the starry evening.

Then I looked around at the street, because it seemed to me I had heard an echo of my own voice.

Spencer came up to me and stopped, and I knew with a sinking feeling that it was still not my world. Gerard's disappearance had not been enough. I was not home. It would be wrong for me to go inside this house.

Spencer looked up at me, and the confusion in the eyes of this Einstein among cats seemed to ask, "How the fuck did you get ahead of me?"

Then he sat down and waited.

I reached down and picked him up. He let me hold him. I had always been able to catch him in the house. Outside, he would mock me and amble away, knowing that there was little or no chance that I could catch him; he'd come back when he felt like it. But now I had shown another ability, and this had shaken him up.

I petted his head, scratched him under his chin, and he winked out in my arms. Relief and resignation tore through me. Once again, Spencer had died, even though something in me had hoped that he would remain alive and that I would also have my world back.

It was my world again, I told myself, desperate to believe it. Something had finally made the correction.

I stood there for a moment, empty handed, then approached the house.

I opened the unlocked doors one by one, and stepped back into my living room. Sarah looked up at me and smiled.

"Back so soon?" she asked.

I sat down and stared at the credits on the evening news, realizing that I had been gone maybe twenty minutes.

"How about the French fries?" Sarah asked, tucking her legs under her in the big recliner.

"I can do without," I said. "How about you? I'll go if you still want me to."

"If you can do without," she said smugly, "then so can I."

I looked over at her. She seemed unchanged.

"You look a bit different somehow," she said.

"I washed these clothes yesterday," I said.

"Good for you."

"You won't believe what happened to me," I started to say, again feeling like the snail in the old joke, then felt fearful of saying anything more.

Sarah looked at me strangely and said, "I know exactly what happened to you!"

"How can you know?" I asked, startled. Then, "What do you know?" I said, thinking she was referring to something else.

"I don't know how I know, but suddenly I know—as if something slid it into my mind sideways. I know!" She sounded both awed and very frightened.

I took a deep breath and said, "Tell me."

As she recounted what had happened to me, with uncanny detail, I remembered that a great writer had once written that there is no wall around time. You can have what you want of it, if you remember well enough. But it was worse than that. Suddenly I feared to remember, afraid that I would be thrown somewhere into time again, away from the frontline of my incoming future, back into a flow of varying instants that I could not change.

The past lived as a hunger in all of us, waiting to swallow us when we lost sight of the future. This realization was the most urgent thing I had learned.

"Stop!" I shouted and jumped up from my chair, half expecting Spencer to meow from the kitchen. He had gotten cranky whenever his people argued and made him feel unsafe.

Sarah looked at me in surprise and said. "What is it? What's wrong?"

"Careful. Stop talking. Don't think too much about the past!"

"But why, what's wrong? It's so strange to suddenly know!"

As I looked at her, my hand slipped into my pants pocket and closed around the spare keys. I took the key ring out and looked at it in shock, because this meant that I was still not quite in my own world; my beloved was only some sort of Sarah, but also slightly someone else, and I was something of an intruder.

"What's wrong?" Sarah asked again.

I stared at the keys in my hand—

—and was relieved to see them fade away. A little late. Maybe it had needed a push from me, so the choices among worlds would tend back to my own original. Something was still correcting.

"We have to be careful, not think too much about it. Too much —and you're there!" As I looked at her, I saw my fear in her eyes.

"It—" I started to say, but my voice broke from the strangeness of our helplessness before it. What could I call it—a glitch of some kind? We were at the edge of our world, and something was trying to push us off into the abyss. No, it was trying to pull us in.

But she knew it all, I realized. Somehow it had all piled into her. I didn't have to say it.

"It takes you back," I blurted out.

And sideways.

Twisted sideways.

"Yeah," Sarah said. "You're not the man who went out for French fries, and I'm not the woman you left behind."

"None of us ever are," I said, "even when we are."

"You can't step into the same river twice, Heraclitus said," she added. "Everything flows." She knew her Greek guys. "But I love you anyway," she whispered.

"Same here," I said.

Then she looked at me strangely, and we felt nameless gulfs widening between us. Images from our histories tumbled in that void as we bridged it, along with the figure of Spencer voyaging among the stars with my spare set of keys.

Separate Lives

Ian Watson

A HUNDRED YEARS IN THE FUTURE, BECAUSE OF the affection and admiration which Lawn and Blossom felt for one another and for the sake of excitement too, Lawn illegally bought an antidote to Aunt Aphrodisia. That was the jocular name for the anti-erotic drug in all the piped water supplies of Planet Earth and in many foodstuffs too.

"A contraceptive drug will quickly pollute the environment," had been the winning argument. "Beasts and fish and bees will become sterile. But an anti-erotic drug will be just right for keeping the human population in check and in balance. Beasts will continue to reproduce as before—does a beast feel love and desire, does a fish? Maybe an elephant might, maybe a whale might, but those are already doomed and mostly gone. A beast mates when it's in heat—that's a hormonal matter, not an erotic one."

Feminist voices said, "We will see no more pornography which so demeans woman and man. Men will no longer think the thoughts that pornography caters to."

Some people asked, "What about the erotic content of art? We'll no longer respond to many beautiful things as the creators intended."

Astringent voices of green activists said passionately, "We have indulged our personal desires for too long! We satisfied our greed until the whole world was sick. From now on we must practice self-control like monks and nuns, ones whose focus of adoration is the Earth. The erotic aspect of art is a little thing to lose. What we need is a new puritanism—or else the world perishes."

From eighteen years of age until the age of thirty all suitable gene-carriers would receive the antidote to Aunt Aphrodisia. Youngsters must still be able to desire and to love and to breed to sustain the species. Aunt Aphrodisia was kindly; at age thirty, parents who were by now busy rearing their children would simply lose interest in something which they had once so enjoyed.

Blossom and Lawn were both *far past forty* and possessed a very deviant streak. Maybe they were even immune to Aunt Aphrodisia? Blossom was married to a kindly if somewhat quick-tempered man who could not abide *moods,* and they had a grown-up daughter, Petal. It was decades since parents had started calling their children by names from nature. Recently Lawn's wife had died in a public vehicle accident. She had been childless. The four spouses had known one another socially. Blossom and Lawn were good friends. When he made a certain proposal to her, more than once, she hesitated several times but then she said yes.

You could buy the antidote to Aunt Aphrodisia from a few illegal dealers, expensively so—because the rich (being always with us, in one guise or another) often evade the rules, and because the penalty for dealing in any forbidden drug was to have a cancer implanted in one's body. Dealers are a cancer in the body of society, are they not?

Blossom and Lawn made love a sufficient number of times for love to become, to their surprise, Love, an enduring deepness, a joy which they could not deny themselves. They called one another, "My treasure! My life!" "When you're older," Lawn told Blossom, "you'll be ever so elegant." She was delighted. Their Love was a rekindling of life itself. They were deeply sincere and also deeply irresponsible.

As was inevitable sooner or later, they were discovered. When the Virtue Officers arrived towards the end of their Summer of Love to take Blossom and Lawn into custody, the lovers clung to one another, vowing, "We'll be true to each other forever!"

Lawn and Blossom had known that their punishment would be separation by world-shifting. When their lovemaking had still merely been friendly fun and excitement and had not yet become deep Love, this had not seemed such a terrible prospect. Now in exquisite detail the implications became clear to them.

An infinite number of worlds existed, replicas of Earth which became progressively more and more divergent until no link between near and far was possible. By 2100 it was possible to shift a living person into a replica world, if a replica of that person lived there.

What of the person displaced from his own world by this process? Highly unlikely that he or she would notice any difference. Maybe a door in a distant town would be red instead of blue. Maybe a particular child in China would be a girl instead of a boy. The person whom this person in turn displaced would likewise remain oblivious to his shift. So the process was not unethical.

Of itself this plurality of worlds was no answer to our own world's problems. We ourselves had wounded our own Earth and owed her a duty of care, for this was the era of responsibility not irresponsibility. Also, the worlds closest to us in type, and easiest to shift to, were all similarly wounded.

"We will shift you," one of the judges told Lawn, "to a world where everything is exactly the same—with the one exception that your Blossom died while she was a girl. Blossom, you will remain here in a world without Lawn."

By now the faces of the judges were blurred through a mist of tears, both hers and his, consequently Lawn and Blossom only heard a voice say:

"When sufficient time has passed for this love of yours to fade away entirely, you, Lawn, will be returned to this world—it is not proper that we should burden other worlds with our own woes. However, that will not be for a very long time indeed."

How long? Years, decades, a lifetime?

Lawn lived alone in the same small apartment as before, surrounded by exactly the same belongings. Weekdays, he carried out exactly the same work—of mineral reserves analysis—in exactly the same office amongst exactly the same colleagues. A hundred times by day and night (or was it a thousand?) thoughts came to him of Blossom, triggered by the slightest association, even by a moment of silence which suggested the absence of something, even by the letter "B" in Bauxite.

Previously Lawn had been outgoing, humorous, gregarious. He had not deeply mourned his wife. Over the years she had become somewhat obsessive and sharp-tongued and nursed grievances, although outside the home she was far more exuberant, the way she had once been. Acquaintance with people such as Blossom and her husband had seemed natural and easy.

Now Lawn seemed unaccountably melancholy. Breeze and Dewie insisted he should accompany them to a bar after work, as he used to do before he became preoccupied with Blossom.

"What's wrong with you?" Breeze asked Lawn over beers. "You aren't your old self at all!"

Oh, but Lawn was his old self exactly, in a world not exactly the same. Branch in this world was a bachelor.

"You seem so sad and broody," said Dewie.

How could Lawn confide something which they could not possibly understand, which would seem like despicable madness to those in whom Aunt Aphrodisia resided? Something criminal, anti-social, anti-survival-of-the-world?

"I've been thinking about the way I live alone," Lawn said carefully. The word *alone* pierced his soul like a dagger of ice.

"Why not answer a Lonely Hearts ad?" Breeze suggested. "Or why don't *you* advertise?"

"You don't need to commit yourself in a hurry," said Dewie. "We aren't kids. We're grown-ups—we're beyond all that nonsense. Take your time and choose. Someone to talk to. Someone to share with."

"I know you mean well," said Lawn.

"What are friends for?" asked Breeze. "Though if you're always going to be glum . . ."

Lawn smiled. He would need to pretend.

Back home, Lawn made love to himself, remembering Blossom. He rejoiced in an excellent memory, or might it be truer to say he *suffered* from one? Was this present activity true love, or merely a temporary relief from anguish?

In the other world Blossom would be with Branch, her husband. In time surely Lawn might fade from her memory. From his, she would not fade.

Now he mourned. *This* was true bereavement—not death but endless separation from a living person.

How was Branch treating Blossom? Was he bitter, or forgiving? Did Blossom try to make up to Branch for her error? In what ways? As part of her punishment she had been left eroticised (as had Lawn, for how else could their love decay spontaneously; how else could they atone?), while of course Branch was not erotically alert, so her life with him must involve a uniquely poignant kind of subtle pain.

After a while Lawn's sense of bereavement reminded him that, if Blossom had died in this world while still a girl, a grave might exist.

Nowadays many bodies were buried in fields in lightweight biodegradable containers so as to nourish the earth. A visit to the field at harvest time was an enhancing experience for relatives. Other bodies were burned and the ashes returned to the land. Forty years earlier, how many bodies were still being buried in cemeteries? Was there a chance that young Blossom did lie in a grave which survived to this day? Did a trace of her persist in this world? Just a trace, yet more than nothing.

Blossom's maiden name was an unusual one, Medlicott. This derived from a multicoloured coat, consequently someone who puts on a bit of a show. Blossom (Lawn would whisper her name to himself time and again) had been born in a city half an hour away by maglev train. Quite likely that same city was where she died in girlhood. Her parents might still be alive, though elderly. Surely they had kept pictures of their daughter as a girl. Those would not show her mature self but at least Blossom in bud.

On his infocentre at home Lawn searched and yes, yes, he found where Blossom Medlicott was buried. She had died of mutated meningitis. That particular year saw a nasty outbreak. Next he found full details of her parents.

A year after their daughter's death her parents had emigrated to the other side of the world. Lawn could almost understand this as a way of coping with the grief they must have felt—by distancing themselves. However hard he tried, he could not trace their present whereabouts.

Of a weekend on a Saturday he traveled to the other city, to the wild-hedged old cemetery, neglected and overgrown. As was Blossom's grave, marked by a small black headstone. Her parents may have paid for the grave to be tended or asked relatives to see to this, but that was years ago. Lawn sat by her, remembering the future she had never reached. By now autumn had arrived although many trees remained green.

Leaving the cemetery, Lawn went shopping to buy a small fork and trowel and a vase, a simple stout one of glass unlikely to be stolen, and a bunch of Michaelmas daisies, blue being Blossom's favourite colour, and on afterthought he also bought a bottle of water in case the two taps in the neglected cemetery yielded none.

He worked until the grave was clear, the soil tilled, the vase in place beside the headstone. Tired, he sat for a while longer on the tufty grass.

"Blossom," he said to her, "my delight."

It was time to go back home again; and indeed both taps were dry.

Should he return the very next day, Sunday? Would that be pathological behaviour? This was not really *his* Blossom. He must discipline himself and visit only once a week, no, once a fortnight.

The winter was wet and windy. Once, the vase had blown over. Live flowers did not fare well, but after a fortnight what could one expect? Lawn substituted a pot of rosemary for the vase. *Rosemary, that's for remembrance*—he recalled that saying from somewhere.

Was Blossom sometimes thinking of him at exactly the same times as he thought of her? Since he thought of her so often their thoughts must surely coincide.

Lawn responded to an infonet advertisement promising to train the mind in telepathy. This might be a moneymaking scheme on the part of an ingenious person, though it did *sound* plausible as described. Admittedly telepaths were not a known part of reality —and if telepathy did exist yet was kept a secret, how could one expect to buy the key to it?

Still, he paid and downloaded a fat manual of loose pages, and he studied the mental disciplines and practised the prescribed exercises. He concentrated so hard. Several times he felt that he almost succeeded. Almost.

In dreams he sometimes thought Blossom was truly present, fleetingly or for a little longer, although after he awoke in his half-cool bed he would know that in the dream he and Blossom never understood their true situation, try as Lawn might to prepare himself each night before he fell asleep, sleep rarely fast in coming whenever he thought of her. Once, in the in-between before sleep, he actually felt the physical pressure of her body—and jerked back to full awareness. Briefly the sensation lingered before vanishing.

A year passed, two years, three. Lawn continued to think of Blossom just as often.

Was it quite as often? Surely! Nevertheless, he bought a signet ring inscribed with the letter B so that each time he noticed the ring he would be reminded of her.

Came the time when he paid his fortnightly visit to the cemetery and found it torn up by digging machines which stood around unattended on that Saturday. Blossom's grave had vanished; everything had been erased.

On the Monday he voice-called, to be told that since no burial had occurred during the past thirty years the land had been redesignated for use as an educational urban farm.

"One grave was being tended!" he protested. "One grave was being cared for!"

Alas, this information was not registered.

"It was like a wasteland," he was told. "Soon it will be a lovely place, so good for children to visit."

Ten years passed and still Lawn remembered Blossom's sighs and cries and her turns of phrase and her dark green eyes. Except when he was in his own home, his life was nothing but pretence.

Was ten years enough punishment? Had the Virtue Officers a way of determining whether he had ceased to love Blossom? Surely not, unless they used telepathy! Lawn's own ventures in this area had not succeeded, although he still tried from time to time with an intensity more like prayer, till his head ached and he feared he would harm himself. If he caused himself a stroke, what sort of person would return to Blossom?

He attended fitness classes. He watched his diet. Alcohol was a problem because he oughtn't to imbibe yet he needed to.

Fifteen years passed. Blossom was his identity, yet how could he be *hers* when totally absent from her? She had stayed in the real world. Realism must necessarily rule her days.

If Lawn tried to forget Blossom, if he tried to deprogram himself from his love for her, might this do the trick of returning him to her before it was too late? (Oh how could it ever be too late?) He must concentrate on negative aspects of her such as her irresponsibility, her self-centredness in craving personal gratification in defiance of social codes and common sense. He must think of her as . . . ageing these days, her looks lost or eroding. He must think of her forgetting about him for days on end or weeks on end, tantamount to betrayal as though she had used and discarded him. He must think all these thoughts about her until he quenched that fire in himself.

At the same time somehow he must leave one hot spark hidden within, which later could be fanned and reawakened—whilst all the while pretending, *no, not even knowing*, that the secret spark remained. Just as if he was hypnotised. By this means his return to her would be the sooner. Some trigger would unlock his true feelings which would flare up once more.

Telepathy, no—self-hypnotism, yes.

A terrible decision, this. Through the infonet he bought a manual on self-hypnotism.

Once he mastered the techniques, really he ought to try to dismiss something *different* from his life before he tried to dismiss Blossom, in case he tainted the memory of her all in vain. What could that something else be? What else interested him nearly as much?

In truth, nothing.

Maybe he should not dismiss something, but rather *add* something. A new devotion, a different obsession. Why had he not thought of this years before? If he could have been fascinated by butterflies or by the works of Beethoven this would have served as an oasis in the desert of his heart.

No matter how Lawn tried to hypnotise himself, this failed too.

Years passed by. He had retired. He was old now. Mostly he still felt quite spry but nowadays there were creaks and aches.

One day he noticed a subtly different light in the sky, a different smell to the breeze through his half-open window.

His heart thumped. Oh Blossom, Blossom.

Fearful of yet another disappointment, he seated himself at his infoscreen.

She was listed! Blossom existed. Different address, but same city. This was the original world.

Branch was listed along with Blossom. If Branch still had his wits about him, how could he have forgotten what Lawn had done decades earlier? Would Branch still nurse a grudge? Would he prevent Lawn from speaking to Blossom? Branch might not believe that Lawn could have kept the flame alive.

If Lawn had not remained so sensitised to nuances because of his attempts at telepathy and self-hypnotism, he might have failed to notice that the world-shift had occurred at last! That would have been so terrible, and yet at the same time *unknown*.

Might Lawn already have missed a precious day, a week, a month?

Anxious as much as exultant, Lawn made a call—and it was Blossom herself who appeared on screen. A much older Blossom, a frailer autumnal blossom affected by fogs and frost. Her hair was white.

When he said, "It's Lawn," Blossom uttered such a long sigh as she might have been holding within her for years and years.

"Blossom, can we meet?" He wondered what she thought of his own looks after all these years.

"Oh yes, yes . . . Lawn." She lingered over his name as though it was unfamiliar—or long unspoken, aloud at least. A name internalised, which had become ever so private.

"Can you come here?" he asked. "I'm still at the same place."

"If I do, won't you be sent away again?"

"Don't you think we have been punished enough by now?"

"But the Virtue Officers . . ."

"They can't possibly suppose we have anything more than faded memories. We do have more, don't we? I know I do."

Was her expression pitying, or was she deeply moved?

"I'll find an excuse," she said. "I'll tell Branch something."

She arrived the next evening. She moved more slowly than she used to. Her shoulders stooped. They were alone for the first time since what seemed forever.

"I did wait," she said. For how long had she waited—all the time until the present? Or at some stage did she stop waiting? Lawn could not bear to ask.

"At least," he said, "we can hold each other."

"Dim the light, will you, then?"

After he did so, they both undressed less speedily than once they had. In the faint light her body had aged rather well. She was still slim, or perhaps slimmer.

For the first time in several decades he reached out to touch her. He whispered, "You've ever so elegant."

"My treasure," she said.

For after all, a treasure is often locked away.

After Ildiko
Lucius Shepard

PEDERSON, AN IDLER, A SELF-DECEIVER, AN AMERI-
can fool of no consequence, on vacation from a life of petty
crime and monumental indecision, fell in with Ildiko on the
Caribbean coast of Guatemala, and together they traveled by barge
up the Rio Dulce toward the oil fields at Lake Izabal. Ildiko was
Swiss, a mousy woman in her early thirties, a few years older than
Pederson, pale and slight, with boyishly cut brown hair and a thin
face that generally displayed a withdrawn look. She had spent the
previous fourteen months hiking through the jungles of Central
America, accompanied only by Indian guides. Prior to that, she told
Pederson, she had worked for relief organizations in Africa.

That was all he knew about her after a month of intimacy. It was
not even clear to him why they had hooked up. There had been
some talk, a hint of flirtation, but nothing conclusive, at least not to
his mind, and then one night she had slipped into his hotel room,
offering herself with a casual, rather maternal tenderness, as if sex
were no more significant an act to her than helping him on with his
coat. Her air of vulnerability, at such apparent odds with her history
of self-reliance, intrigued him; yet he found her only marginally
attractive. Perhaps because he had been the pursued in this
instance, he tended to think of her with proprietary disdain, viewing her as an interim solution to the problem of female compan-

ionship. She was damaged goods, he thought. Some old trouble lurked beneath her diffident exterior. Yet despite all of this, their relationship had deepened in ways that left him uneasy, mystified by unaccustomed feelings of affection and tenderness.

The captain of the barge, Joseph Rawley, was a gruff, stocky, sun-darkened man of sixty or thereabouts, with thinning iron-gray hair and a seamed face that might once have been handsome, and a tattoo celebrating his naval service in the Gulf of Tonkin. Under different circumstances Pederson might have enjoyed his company. With his colorful stories of expatriate life, Rawley was just the sort of character whom Pederson relied upon to lend his experiences a Heart-of-Darkness credential when telling his own stories back in New York City; but from the outset it was apparent that Rawley was taken with Ildiko and had no use whatsoever for him. Pederson understood that Ildiko, by contrast to the flashier tourist women to be found along the coast, would seem accessible to an older man, and in this context, Rawley's distaste for him was predictable. Yet his contempt was so pointed, it caused Pederson to revert to a city paranoia, to think that his history of middleman drug scams and yuppie duplicity was an open book to Rawley, and that this horny old swabbie was gazing down at him from some moral Himalaya, taking note of his every perversity and failure.

Early on the second morning of their voyage, Pederson stationed himself on a blanket in the bow, a spot bounded by empty oil drums from which he could see both the jungle and the wheelhouse, and gobbled down the magic mushrooms he had bought from a Guatemalan hippie in Puerto Juarez. He spent the day in queasy, feverish, affrighted communion with old Indian men who stepped forth from the vegetation to offer confusing counsel; and with an indefinable presence whose pronouncements boomed from beneath the water, outvoicing the labored chugging of the barge and the ripping noises made by the motorized canoes that served as river taxis, plying back and forth between Livingston and Reunión. His body seemed to wax and wane—at one moment he was aware of every twinge and tremor, every increment of nausea, and the next he would lose contact with his physical being and find himself immersed in opulent hallucinations, all variations on a single setting: a vast cave floored by a dark blue lake in which he swam, desperately seeking to reach a shore where a radiant white glow bloomed from the rock, passed now and again by galleylike craft with figureheads carved into beasts and serpents, rowed by small men with reddish-brown skins who paid no heed to his cries for help. To Pederson's relief, the mushrooms were not, as had been advertised, a twenty-four-hour trip; after about half that time the hallucinations ceased and he was able to perceive the world more-or-less as it pretended to be.

In late afternoon the barge came to a place where the river widened, the banks lifting into sheer cliffs that shadowed the green water, forming a cup-shaped gorge, and the humid stink of the jungle was overwhelmed by a profound freshness like the smell of an ancient cistern. Birds, their shapes simple as crosses, wheeled in a platinum sky. Propped against an oil drum, enfeebled and slick with a foul sweat, Pederson felt the beginnings of peace. His nerves jumped and his eyes were still afflicted—each leaf, each tree trunk and vine, were shadowed by an orangish aura, and the movements of his fingers trailed ribbony afterimages through the air. When Ildiko emerged from the wheelhouse, wearing only a bikini bottom, her ample breasts quivering, he would have called out if Rawley had not appeared a second later, dressed in sweat-drenched khakis, and pulled her back inside. It was, Pederson soon realized, a game they were playing—Rawley making mock lecherous grabs, Ildiko allowing herself to be caught, then slipping away. The scene grated on him, but he had neither the energy nor the will to express displeasure. He let his thoughts drift up away with the circling birds, their flights level with summits of the vine-enlaced cliffs, and with the palm trees atop the cliffs, spiky crowns swaying like savages in a drunken dance.

Darkness closed down over the barge, seeming to amplify the engine noise, and the jungle, too, grew louder, resonating with the loopy electric cries of frogs. Buttery light chuted from the wheelhouse windows, illuminating a stretch of rivet-studded, orange-painted iron deck. Pederson's joints ached from chemical punishment, and he was tired, grungy. The hot oily smell of metal unpleasantly thick in his nostrils. Moths whirled whitely overhead. Eusebio, Rawley's Indian mate, a squat man with pitted skin, came into view, visible in the upper window of the wheelhouse, and for an instant Pederson assumed him to be a visitation of the drug. Then he spotted Ildiko walking toward him, wearing a green T-shirt over the bikini and carrying a can of Coke. She kneeled beside him, gave him the frosty can, and asked if he was all right. He had forgotten about her fooling around with Rawley until she handed him the can—it was as if the act of kindness had settled the last roiled-up fragments of his personality, restoring his normal reflexes, and he lashed out at her.

"Did you have fun?" he asked, in a harsh, ragged voice. "Did you fuck him?"

She looked at him without expression. "I think it would not be so terrible if I had. He's a nice man . . . He's lonely."

"Not so lonely as he used to be, huh?"

The effervescence of the Coke stung his throat. A white flash zippered his field of vision. Then another. The world coming apart like the print of an old movie, cracks showing the projector beam behind the scenes.

"How are you feeling?" she asked.

"I'm still a little ripped. But I can pass for human." The second swig of Coke didn't sting as much. "You shouldn't lead him on. You know he takes it seriously on some level."

"It makes him feel young," she said. "That's all it is. He knows I'm with you."

A breeze came steadily off the bow, drying Pederson's sweat, and he felt suddenly strong, back in the flesh. He ran a hand along Ildiko's pale thigh and up under the T-shirt. "Are you . . . with me?"

She appeared to be studying him sadly, just as she must have looked at starving refugees from Eritrea, considering their pitiful condition and inevitable fate. He eased a hand beneath the elastic of the bikini, brushed the fringe of her pubic hair with the backs of his fingers, she opened her legs, permitting him to probe more deeply.

"Jesus," he said. "You're ready to go, aren't you?"

"I'm always ready," she said flatly.

He took her by the waist and lifted her astride him; then he wrangled down his shorts and rubbed against her.

"He might see us," she said, alarm in her voice.

"So he sees us."

He fingered the crotch of her bikini to one side and let her sink down onto him. Whatever constraints she felt had been abandoned, and he imagined her in a tent erected on some forlorn, dusty acreage, straddling a doctor, a Red Cross administrator, cultivating an expertise at pleasure to shield herself from the dying, moving with inventive delicacy, employing her body as she employed her compassion, bestowing a kindness, fully rendering the service, investing it with an odd detachment and passivity of mind that made her somehow sexier. His hands roved beneath the T-shirt, sampling her breasts. He thrust vigorously, his desire fueled by a flashback from the mushrooms, a spoonful of delirium that caused him to see her briefly as a creature shaped like a white thighbone with a knobbed head and painted features. Light flared behind his eyes, tiny photic incidents, and when he came the muscles in his chest seized and it seemed everything—heart, guts, juice—was spilling out, leaving him gasping, staring up at stars that bloomed and faded too quickly to be real, while she kneeled at his side, adjusting the bikini, gazing at him mildly.

"Are you happy now?" she asked, her tone so neutral, he could not tell how she intended the question.

"Happier." He caressed her leg, wanting to assure her of his affection. She did not return the gesture and got to her feet.

"Don't go!" He reached out to her.

"I have to wash myself," she said.

He waved, go ahead, and closed his eyes. Thoughts circled in his head like birds above an island, idle and unconsidered. Time flowed sluggishly, adapting itself to the rhythms of the engine, the river, and he was not certain how long he remained in that state, almost empty, registering yet not interpreting the sounds and smells that established his position, his existence. When he opened his eyes he caught sight of Ildiko, now completely naked. She stepped from an area of shadow beside the wheelhouse, and as Pederson watched, thinking he might ask her to fix him some food, she leaped outward from the barge and vanished. It happened so quickly and was so improbable an event, it took him a moment to process, and even after he had done so, he refused to accept the judgment of reason, preferring to believe the whole thing had been another white rip in his vision. He went stumbling across the deck and looked down over the side. The churning darkness beneath made him dizzy. He called out to her, overcome by a confusion of emotion and doubt. Holding onto the rail mounted on the wall of the wheelhouse, he called to her again and again.

"Hell you squawking about?"

Rawley was standing at the wheelhouse door. Khaki shorts and an oil-stained white T-shirt. His unshaven face shaded by the brim of a captain's hat. Holding a glass of rum. A grizzled old salt roused from his solitary joy.

"She jumped!" Pederson said in a bewildered, stricken voice. "She went over the side!"

Rawley made a face of sour disbelief. "Bullshit!"

"I saw her, man! I was sitting back there—" Pederson gestured toward the bow "—and I looked up . . . I saw her!"

"Those goddamn mushrooms, you don't know what you saw." But Rawley looked worried. "Where'd you see her jump?"

"There." Pederson pointed to the spot.

Rawley knocked back his rum, his Adam's apple working in his leathery neck. "I don't want you going over after her. Wait in the wheelhouse. I'll check below."

The light in the wheelhouse was too bright for Pederson. He sat on the deck, knees drawn up, head down, trying to separate out what he felt from how he wanted to feel, but was unable to determine which was which. A few minutes later he heard Rawley ascending the stairs that led below decks.

"Her clothes are gone." Rawley put his hands on his hips and stood watching the water pass beneath them.

Pederson stared at him without comprehension. "Aren't you going to stop? We have to look for her."

"She took her clothes, pal. She didn't get sucked under, and that's a long shot, then she doesn't want us to look for her. She's a smart girl. She'll find a place to wait out the night and catch a river taxi come morning."

"We should do something!" Pederson pushed himself up from the deck.

"What? Report it to the police? Not a chance! She turns up missing, I'll be paying bribes out my ass the next ten years."

Pederson felt like a man in a hurricane trying to hold his hat on, everything flying off around him. "We have to look for her," he said. "We have to fucking look!"

Rawley spat onto the deck. He appeared to have changed in a matter of minutes from a hale man of late middle age to a full-fledged senior citizen.

"C'mon, man!" Pederson said. "You got to do something."

Rawley went chest-to-chest with him, his bitter breath fouling Pederson's air. "Don't put it on me, sonny. I'm not the one she was trying to get away from."

Tears came to Pederson's eyes, produced by an emotion that seemed a marriage of loss and self-pity. "What did she tell you?"

"She told me what a cup of weak tea you are. She told me she wanted to leave your ass, but she was afraid you'd fall apart."

"That's crap! We were just traveling together."

Rawley turned away.

"Only reason we ended up together," Pederson went on, "she begged a ride to Flores with this Guatemalan rancher. This right-wing guy carried a pistol. She got paranoid and asked me to come along. She wanted protection."

"And you were going to protect her?" Rawley snorted. He stuck his head into the wheelhouse and told Eusebio to go below and bring up the gringo's pack.

"What are you doing?" Pederson asked.

"I'm letting you off at Reunión. Till then you can sit on the deck and keep the hell away from me."

"We should look for her," Pederson said feebly as Rawley stepped into the wheelhouse and slammed the door. "We should do something."

Propped against his pack, having reclaimed his spot among the oil drums, Pederson sat, dejected, drinking tepid bottled water. That Ildiko had thrown herself from the barge, risking death in order to escape him—it was unacceptable. He tried once again to persuade himself that he had not seen it. He was still stoned, his eyes playing tricks. But her clothes, the fact that she had taken her clothes . . . What could he have done to make her so desperate? If it *was* desperation that had motivated her. Maybe she had acted independently of any consideration involving him. The damage he had sensed in her. The despondency yielded by years of watching death in Africa. It might have sparked her to want to be alone again, to go back into the jungle where she could avoid the thought of Africa, and to want it so immediately that she had taken drastic measures. Whatever her reasons, the suddenness and finality of her absence hurt him in an unexpected way—it was as if some special organ, heretofore unnecessary, vestigial, like an appendix, had been activated and was producing chemicals that were breaking him down, causing his thoughts to grow so dark and heavy, they tipped his head downward and shuttered his eyes and he saw a white leap into blackness repeated over and over, no longer certain whether it had been Ildiko or merely a flash of female light.

He glanced up to the wheelhouse. Rawley stood in the upper window at the wheel, gazing down on him. Like a funky toy in his captain's hat, an action figure derived from an adventure film. Dissing Rawley enabled him to stop thinking about Ildiko, and he indulged in it, painting him as a failure, a vet who couldn't cut it in the States, so he had scurried on down to Guatemala where he could be the king of Mangoland, boss around the Indians, overcharge the oil workers for the cheap goods he brought from the coast, and screw fourteen-year-old hookers, playing a tough-guy riff on *Lord Jim* to disguise his various inadequacies. But this tactic failed Pederson, and he was cast back upon the moment he wanted to deny. He felt in need of repentance, of absolution, but was not certain which of his sins required expiation.

He was still sitting in the bow, too wired and distressed for sleep, when Rawley came toward him from the wheelhouse, walking unsteadily. He had gone to drinking straight from a labelless bottle that contained a few fingers of pale rum, and he glared at Pederson with distaste.

"I should beat you up," he said.

Anger tightened Pederson's neck. "Leave me alone, man."

"I should beat you up and throw you over the goddamn side!" Rawley appeared to be summoning the will to do this very thing, but instead he slumped to the deck and sat a few feet away, braced on one hand and cradling the bottle to his belly. "You knew that girl's head was screwed up. You had no right treating her like that."

He seemed truly despairing, his turtle mouth drooping, but Pederson, on the defensive, said, "I didn't do a damn thing to her!"

"You fucked her out in the open. Right here." Rawley plunked the bottom of the bottle on the deck for emphasis. "In plain view. You think she felt good about that?"

"I didn't hear any complaints."

With drunken caution, Rawley got to his knees. "You poor dumb shit! You don't have a clue about other people, you're so wrapped up in yourself." He made a gagging noise, wobbled, and had to brace himself again. "She deserved better than you."

"How do you know I fucked her out here?" Pederson asked. "You were watching, right?"

Rawley's expression was slack, febrile, underlying.

"You watched us." Every word Pederson spoke charged his growing sense of outrage. "You hadn't been hitting on her it never would have happened. But you couldn't get it through your head she was being nice to you. She was just being polite."

It looked as if Rawley was having trouble absorbing this. "You knew I was watching? What were you doing? Sending me a message?"

Pederson was not certain this had been his conscious intent, but intent was a banner he wanted to wave. "You weren't getting it. I thought this way it might sink in."

Rawley tilted forward as if he was going to pass out, but then threw a sneaky right hand that caught Pederson flush, twisting his neck and snapping back his head. He heard Rawley talking and realized he was lying on his back; he could feel his left eye beginning to swell.

". . . did it to her," Rawley was saying. "Maybe it was the both of us. But it wasn't me using her like a goddamn whore."

Something exploded into Pederson's ribs, and he understood that he had been kicked.

"That was a sweet girl," Rawley said. "A girl with soul. She did a lotta good in her life. And now she's probably dead . . . 'cause you were trying to teach me a lesson?"

Another kick, this one not so painful, landing on his hip, and Pederson rolled away, cowering behind an oil drum. He peered up at Rawley, trying to bring a smear of khaki and white into sharp focus.

"That's right," said Rawley. "You hide . . . you stay hidden. I don't wanna even see your shadow 'fore we get to Reunión."

There were, Pederson saw, several Rawleys, all opaque and rippling. All enraged, fists clenched and mouths stretched thin. "You think you're such a fucking hotshot!" Rawley said. "Mister World Traveler! Well, this is the real world, hotshot, and a sixty-two-year-old man just kicked your ass. Where's that leave you?"

The river wind came up strong from the north, carrying the scents of smoke, oil, dead fish, the smell of Reunión, and the jungle began to melt up from the blackness, and the sky burned a radiant dark blue. The barge labored against the current, its engine grinding like a portcullis being raised; the light from the wheelhouse grew less sharply defined. Miserable, his eye throbbing, Pederson lay pillowed on his pack, trying to think his way out from beneath the karmic load Rawley had forced him to assume. He had almost convinced himself that Ildiko was alive. Alive and waiting for a river taxi back along the Rio Dulce. He recalled her saying that she felt protected in the jungle, that going there alone with a guide never bothered her. He had not explored this with her—he hadn't been interested in much she said. But he thought now she would have explained it in a way that explained herself, and he wanted an explanation—he wanted to know what security she found there, to fathom all her strangeness. Rawley had been right about one thing: she had deserved better. She did have a soul, a remarkable one, and he, Pederson, had failed to appreciate it. Recognizing this, he determined to find her and settle things between them. At least he would try. She'd head back to Flores, and from there into the deep jungle. If they had no future . . . well, maybe he could change her mind about that. But one way or the other, he had an obligation to fulfill.

That he admitted to this obligation satisfied Pederson's moral concern and he turned his mind to other matters. It was, he figured, another hour to Reunión. Wincing, he sat up and inspected his pack, making certain that nothing had been left in the cabin. In short order he discovered his watch was missing . . . and a gold cross he'd bought for his sister. Rawley's mate. Eusebio. He must have taken them when he fetched the pack from below decks. Pederson rummaged through his clothing, searching for the rolled-up socks in which Ildiko had stashed his cash and traveler's checks that that morning. They were still there. The dumbass could have really made out if he had looked a little harder.

Eusebio and Rawley were visible in the upper window of the wheelhouse, and judging by the flamboyance of Rawley's gestures, Pederson inferred that he was telling the mate about the sucker punch he'd landed. Flimsy notions of vengeance occurred to him. He would report Rawley to the police, the American consulate. But the important thing now was to reclaim his goods, and they were most likely stuffed under Eusebio's pillow or in the stand beside his bunk.

Keeping to the shadows, he went in a crouch toward the wheel-house door. The stair angled downward just inside the door, and Pederson was about to make his move when Eusebio came down the stair from the top of the wheelhouse, swinging on the handrails. He stared at Pederson in surprise and said sternly, "No pase!" See-ing him caused Pederson to recognize how stoned he still was. Instead of being alarmed, he was fascinated by Eusebio's round, dark face, cheeks dented with dozens of pits that resembled the punch marks of a silversmith's hammer, and the jaundiced condi-tion of his left eye, a little yellow cloud occluding a portion of the humor.

"No pase!" Eusebio repeated, and gave Pederson a gentle push.

"The head." Pederson grabbed his crotch. "El baño. Necesito usarlo."

"No pase!" Another, harder push.

"Goddamit!" said Pederson. "Where's my fucking watch? Mi reloj . . . Donde?"

Eusebio's stare became disinterested, impassive.

"Okay, man." Pederson held up a hand and rubbed his thumb and forefinger together to signify cash money. "Puedo pagar. Dame el reloj y le pagaré."

Eusebio shouted up the stairs and shoved Pederson out onto the deck.

"This is bullshit!" Pederson made to reenter the wheelhouse, but Eusebio blocked the door.

When Rawley came down the stair he took one look at Pederson and said to Eusebio, "Tráigame la pistola!"

The mate hurried off downstairs.

Pederson's Spanish was not so good, but he knew the meaning of *la pistola*. "Hey!" he said, backing away. "Fuck are you doing?"

Rawley followed him out onto the deck. He appeared to have sobered some. His eyes were steady, his manner contained and dead serious. "You don't know where you are," he said. "Mister Goddamn World Traveler doesn't have a clue."

Panicking, Pederson said, "Your fucking Indian, man! He stole my watch! What do you want me to do?"

"You better figure it out fast," Rawley said as Eusebio clattered up the stairs.

"Listen," Pederson said, injecting his voice with sincerity, with reason. "All I want's my watch back. Okay?"

Eusebio handed Rawley an automatic with a bronze finish and smiled at Pederson.

"You come on board my vessel acting like King Shit," said Rawley, checking the clip. "You treat a good woman like she's a whore. Drive her to desperation. Now you accuse my friend of stealing. Know what that is?" He cocked an eye toward Pederson and jammed in the clip. "It's what I call justification."

Pederson sprinted for the cover of the oil drums. A gunshot cracked the air behind him. He dived in among the drums, rolling up against his pack. Pain shot through his injured ribs. His heart felt flabby and hot. He wrapped his arms around his pack, as if it could protect him. A second shot. The round *spanged* off one of the drums.

"Want to know where you are?" Rawley shouted. He fired again, and the bullet struck sparks that showered Pederson's head. "You're in the middle of the fucking jungle!"

The implausibility of the situation caused Pederson to flounder in his search for a solution, but when another round notched a rivet close by his hand, he managed to achieve complete acceptance of the fact that Rawley intended to kill him. He hooked the straps of his pack over his elbow and told the One in whom he only believed at times such as these that he was heartily sorry for having offended Him, and ran full tilt for the side of the barge, sped along by yet another shot. He leaped high and wide, tucking his legs into a cannonball. The shock of entry forced air from his lungs; the water gloved him in its slimy fist. Surfacing, he felt the suction of the barge and, bright with fear, he fought for the bank, swimming one-armed, dragging his sodden pack, kicking furiously. In less than a minute he touched mucky bottom. Moments later, he scrambled up onto a thicketed point and collapsed against the muddy incline, breathing hard. He heard a shout. Rawley; the words unintelligible. The barge was passing to the north, a huge shadow, the wheelhouse limned in light. Pederson watched it go, too wasted to feel relief.

Once the barge had vanished around the bend, he tried to establish a comfortable position; but there was no comfort to be had. Mosquitoes started to swarm. Mud oozed into his shorts. He battled the mosquitoes for a while, but they settled in his hair, sheathed his arms, and finally he gave into them, hanging his head and trying to focus on being alive. Sooner or later a river taxi would happen past, and he would hail it, and it would take him to Reunión. He pictured Ildiko waiting somewhere downstream, stoic on her own safe perch. There might be, he told himself, some magical symmetry involved, an illumination to be had for them both, and perhaps a second chance. Sitting alone on the bank, they might come to a strange electric sense of one another, like fireflies trapped in bottles set side by side. He suddenly recalled all her desirable qualities and wondered what had caused him to be so unmindful of them. It might be, he supposed, that her life of sacrifice had made him feel guilty over his own desultory existence. If they got back together, it would be a hell of a story. A redemptive story. He saw himself telling it back in the Chelsea Bar, Ildiko beside him, as living proof. His thoughts sputtered and gazed dully out at the mist forming above the water, rising into the lower boughs, reducing the light of the paling sky and transforming the world into a vague blue-green luminosity hung with vegetable shadows, a limbo created for a single lost soul. Before long, he began to shiver.

He drowsed and was wakened by the trebly grind of an outboard motor. The sun was just up, orange streamers of cloud in the east, and a river taxi with a dark figure at the helm and a slighter, paler figure in the bow was slitting the jade water, passing directly in front of him. He tried to stand, slipped and fell; he called out, but his voice was weak, scratchy, and neither the helmsman nor his passenger gave any sign of notice. He peered after the boat. He could not be sure, but he thought it had been Ildiko in the bow. The longer he considered this, the more certain he became. It gnawed at him that he had missed out on catching the same ride. They could have talked all the way to Reunión, and by the time they arrived, they might have reached an understanding. He got gingerly to his feet and stood with his eyes trained downriver. He could not afford to miss the next ride or he might lose her. Gnats flocked to his swollen eye, almost closed now, and the skin above his injured ribs was feverish. The sun climbed high, and the foetid smell of the bank enveloped him. Parrots screeched, a monkey screamed. Heat lifted from the river; the water slapped against the shore. Pederson's knees trembled, his vision blurred. Sweat trickled down his arms and legs, inflaming the mosquito bites. But he remained at his post, staring into the reflected light glazing the river, listening for salvation.

The boat that eventually came for him was owned by an elderly man with white hair and beard, clad in a ragged shirt and shorts. His features had an East Indian cast, and when asked, he told Pederson his ancestors had been slaves brought over from Peshawar by the British to work on the sugar plantations in Belize. He spoke decent English and seemed eager to reveal more about himself; but Pederson was less interested in stories now that he was living one. He washed in the river before boarding, changed into clean clothes, and sat looking down into the foaming wake all the way to Reunión —a scoured acreage of red dirt set about with shanties and a few buildings of concrete block. He paid the boatman and headed for the bus station along streets rendered nearly impassable by potholes full of stagnant rain. Naked toddlers splashed and built mud structures beside them as if they were at the beach, while their mothers fanned themselves in the doorways and stared listlessly at passers-by. It was an impoverished, desolate place, and would ordinarily have stimulated Pederson, who viewed himself as a connoisseur of such places, of all things desolate, and perhaps, he thought, this was at the core of his attraction to Ildiko, an attraction he now embraced; perhaps her desolation was the charm that had gradually possessed him . . . But at that moment, the rawness of the town was lost on him, and he plodded on with his head down, infected by its stuporous vitality.

The bus station was a one-story building of white stucco with a painted Pepsi logo covering one side, like the flag of a proud nation. The wooden benches within were packed with farmers and old beshawled women; a few teenage boys were goofing in a corner, pushing each other and laughing. Pederson bought a ticket to Flores. On impulse he pulled out a photograph of Ildiko, a Polaroid taken on the first morning of their voyage. It depicted her topless, wearing her bikini bottom. He was too embarrassed to show it to the women; most of the men, however, studied it with polite interest and then shook their heads—they had not seen her. But one, a bleary-eyed *mestizo* with a crust of dried blood at the corner of his mouth, his breath reeking of liquor, mumbled something in response to the picture, and when Pederson asked him to repeat it, he said, "*Que puta! Se fue!*" and gestured loosely toward the door. "*Por el camión . . . a Flores.*" That was proof enough for Pederson. She was on the previous bus to Flores, bound ultimately for the heart of the rain forest, where she would find some counterfeit of peace. He sat at the end of a bench, fingering the photograph as if it were a rosary, an article of faith. He could still catch up with her. It would take her at least a day to secure a guide. He could ask around, follow her trail.

"Very pretty." One of the teenage boys was leaning over his shoulder—he had shoulder-length hair and a rosy brown Mayan complexion; he wore jeans and a T-shirt adorned with a photograph of the youthful Madonna. He grinned at Pederson and said, "She's your girlfren'?"

Pederson did not know how to answer this, but he nodded.

The boy let out a shrill whistle, and in a moment his friends had gathered round, all peering at the Polaroid; one of them pointed at it and said something excitedly in Spanish, speaking too rapidly for Pederson to understand.

"What's he saying?" he asked the first boy.

"*Momentito* . . . wait, wait!" The boy questioned his friend, who replied at some length, accompanying his words with florid gestures. The boy turned a reproving look on Pederson. "He say she's the captain's girlfren'."

"The captain?" At first this struck Pederson as a non sequitur.

"Yes, the old man, the . . ." The boy's brow furrowed. "How you say . . . ? Like a boat, but . . . *mas larga*. Longer."

"A barge?"

"*Sí* . . . barge." The boy repeated the word, perhaps to imprint it on his memory. "My fren' saw this woman with the captain of the barge. This morning in the market."

When Pederson failed to respond, the boys went back to their foolery. The horn of the Flores bus sounded outside; the people on the benches surged to meet it, and Pederson, stunned, obeying a dull communal urge, moved with them. He saw how it could have happened. He might have hallucinated Ildiko's leap, contrived the scene from the visual aftershocks of the mushrooms, and this had presented her with the opportunity to exchange his protection for that of Rawley. But the extent of the duplicity required to substantiate what the boy had told him; the consummate acting ability he would then have to attribute to Rawley; the freakish level of coincidence . . . For the next minute or so, Pederson was involved with forcing his way along the crowded aisle of the bus, pushing past an old woman carrying a cooking pot who was haranguing an even older man with a cane, trying to persuade him to sit. Pederson found a seat at the rear of the bus, next to a farmer wearing a straw cowboy hat, jeans, and a checkered shirt. The farmer tipped his hat and said, "*Buenas dias.*" Half his upper teeth were gold, the other half were missing, and Pederson briefly considered the question of whether the man was replacing his teeth with golden substitutes, or if they had all been gold and were falling out one by one.

Its gears shrieking, the bus lurched forward, and Pederson's knees were compressed painfully against the seat in front of him. This brought him back to the question of real moment. It was not possible, he decided. The boy's witness had been no more reliable than the drunk's. Rawley was incapable of the necessary pretense, and Ildiko incapable of such deceit. He had seen what he had seen. Yet as the bus pulled away from the town, dipping into potholes, setting its passengers bouncing and swaying against one another, following a winding red-dirt road between walls of foliage, the violent, dark green and poison jungle where he and Ildiko had found each other, and would find each other again, Pederson's purity of purpose was assaulted, marred by feelings of anger and betrayal, by the possibility, however slim, that he had misinterpreted everything about Ildiko, and about the world, and the second lie he told himself was that he only wanted to fuck her again.

The Golden Boy

Warren Rochelle

Friday, 20 October 2000

*G*AVIN HADN'T WANTED TO GO TO THE NORTHERN Carolina Provincial Zoo with Cooper Road Elementary's third grade. He had plenty to do in the library: finish up fall book orders, write lesson plans, purge the vertical file. The expected order of his day, the orderly completion of his week, its regularity and normalcy, would be disrupted. Carrie Dunn, the principal, had, on the other hand, waved all his objections aside.

"One of Christina's room mothers can't go; you go and help her with her class. We're short one adult. You know imperial school law as well as I do. It'll be fun, Gav; I promise."

Carrie owes me a pitcher, not just one beer, Gavin thought, as he, twenty-one third graders and their teacher, Christina Phillips, waited in the early morning sunshine at the RJR Nabisco Rocky Coast habitat to see the polar bears, sea lions, and sea birds. His leg still smarted from where the black swan had bit him. Letting water birds wander around loose in a marsh, with the marsh at the entrance, was carrying the natural habitat idea a bit too far. Polar bears all looked the same: big white dirty rugs flopping in and out of ice water. At least they were far enough from Raleigh and the volcanic smoke and ash that he had been able to leave his gas mask in the car. *Wet bears: I bet they smell worse than wet dogs.* And if he had to explain one more time why there were no elephants in the zoo, that they were all in bigger and older zoos, or in Africa on the other side of 30 West, he would explode.

He took some comfort in that he didn't feel as uneasy about the field trip as he had when Carrie talked him into going. Besides, he thought the uneasiness and dread might be a hangover from the rest of his life, and the disruptions to its order and regularity: three phone messages in one week from his mother after ten years' silence (except for the postcard he sent when Grey was born): *call me, it's urgent.* Or the other messages with the shrill voice of his ex, Sophia, whom his mother—God only knew why—had called: *Your mother said she had something urgent to tell me about Grey. You told me your mother was* dead. *What the hell is going on?*

It had taken Gavin a good long while to put things back together, as much as he possibly could, after Sophia had divorced him two years ago, back to the placid life he had built after slamming the door to his mother's house behind him and not looking back. Finish graduate school, job, marry, start a family, jog every day, just live, like any normal. Not like fairies, who got married in fours, with all combinations of gender configurations. *Men lying with men, women with women, are an abomination, fairies are an abomination* had been the theme of more than one church service when Gavin was growing up. Never mind witches and the other First Folk, the so-called paranormals.

Finally realizing that divorce was normal (one in three Columbian marriages ended in divorce, after all) helped, although he had never quite figured out why Sophia wanted out. *I was* not *distant.* Having his three-year-old son, Grey, every other weekend became part of the rhythm of a life. He *was* a normal.

Okay, so the polar bears hadn't been so bad. He loved the otters in the Streamside habitat—if he could choose to be any animal, he'd be an otter. Sleek, dark, free, and at play forever. But when the class came to the next exhibit, the Bestiary of Evil, the uneasiness— now a solid dark fear—returned.

"Gav, you know we have to," Christina said, looking at him a little oddly. "It's imperial law—see the sign? Every Columbian child by the age of eight shall be made aware of the physicality of evil. That's one reason why we do this field trip ever year; you know that. It's our duty and responsibility—I think of it as our privilege. Hey, I liked your gas mask—where'd you get it?" she added.

"A Sears Gash—gas-and-ash—a *gash* mask, get it?" *Why did I let*

Carrie talk me into this? "I know it's the law; I just feel funny about it, that's all."

"Come on—we won't stay long. Peter, stay with the group. Okay, everybody, hold hands with your buddy. Peter, are you paying attention? Janey, eyes forward, look at me. Peter, if I have to call your name one more time, you know what will happen. Now, don't touch the glass—this is the Bestiary of Evil I told you about, remember? Bestiary comes from an old word for beast . . ." Christina went on, giving the required speech and making sure every kid was accounted for. Last in line, Gavin took Latisha's hand, a waiflike towheaded little girl who never had much to say. She clutched his hand as tightly as she could.

Two pegasi with clipped wings, a unicorn. The centaurs' cage was empty. A very unhappy-looking pair of cheshire cats, barely visible. A pair of golden gryphons, also with clipped wings, equally unhappy. Gavin read the signs to Latisha as they walked. The werewolf was next, sitting hunched over on a rock; it hadn't looked up, no matter how loud the others had been or the faces they had made. But it did look up just as Gavin got to the cage and stared at him with bright blue eyes. Gavin froze.

"Mr. Reed?"

He didn't hear the little girl at first. Instead, Gavin watched as the werewolf, shaking its shaggy head, came slowly over to the corner of the cage where they stood. It was an eastern red werewolf, with matted dark yellow-grey fur, and its blue eyes were focused intently on Gavin. It jumped up on its hind legs, its big paws only separated from Gavin's face by the glass.

"Help me, please, fairy, help me," it said in a rough voice. "Get me out of here."

"I'm not a fairy—shut up," Gavin snapped back.

"Mr. Reed? What did it say?"

"Not a fairy? Look at your hands, *fairy*," the werewolf hissed, snarling.

Gavin dropped Latisha's hand and looked. The tips of all his fingers were glowing, a faint, faint yellow, as if he had dipped them in fluorescent paint.

Suppress, suppress, suppress.

"I'm not a fucking fairy," he yelled at the werewolf who only growled in return. "And look at my hands—perfectly fine, see?"

"You aren't supposed to say that word; it's not nice. Mama told me so. What's wrong with your hands? What's it saying?"

"Nothing is wrong with my hands—see? But I—I feel—sick.

Tell Mrs. Phillips I got sick and had to go." Thank God he had driven his own car.

"Fairy, help me—"

Gavin ran, the werewolf howling behind him.

The dream caught him just as he got to his car. *At Long Beach, the family beach trip, I am up before anybody else and I run and run in an early morning rain. Then, from somewhere, there is another boy, standing beside me on the sand. Curly black hair. Eyes greener than mine are blue, and mine are an intense bright electric blue. His age—eleven, maybe twelve. I ask who he is, and where he is from, but the boy says nothing. He only touches me with the palm of his hand on my chest, on my heart. I feel sudden warmth, and a pull, as if my chest is pressing into the boy's hand. My body, and the boy's body, suddenly fill with a glowing yellow-white light—*

"No, no, no—no more. I'm free of that. It's because she called—because Mama called that I am remembering this. That's all."

He sat in his car, hunched over the steering wheel. Not physically ill, no, but definitely sick of heart. He was supposed to be cured—the glowing wasn't supposed to ever come back. Nobody was ever to know, nobody was to ever doubt. Gavin looked at his hands: the glow was gone. He looked in the rearview mirror: nothing different there, blue eyes, straight dark brown hair, a regular forty-year-old guy. Back to school, to Raleigh? Or to Chapel Hill, to the doctor that made sure Gavin got his quarterly supply of little green pills, the doctor his mother had taken him to when he was fourteen, glowing, and having dreams of the golden boy almost every night. His father left, taking the older boys—*they* weren't glowing, *they* didn't have tainted blood. Puberty, the doctor had said. Comes late for fairies and hybrids—didn't matter that Gavin was just quarter-fey. As for the older boys—well, puberty wasn't always the trigger, they would be in for a rude surprise someday.

School. No, then Christina would have way too many questions and Latisha just might—just might what? Had she anything to tell? If she had and did, then the police would be called. Gavin would be arrested and executed—no ghetto option that a full fairy might have. Hybrids were hated even more—a *human* had to participate in their making, had to believe a fairy could be loved, should be loved. The very act of conceiving a hybrid was illegal. No, he would just go home, call in sick from there. Tomorrow, the doctor—if more pills didn't work.

Seventy-odd miles back, from the Zoo, through Asheboro, through Ramseur, Pittsboro, and back to Raleigh. Nothing but pine trees and little white houses, ugly trailers, and more pine trees and big fields. Then, once in town, drive slowly because of earthquake damage. This morning's quake had only messed up out around the Fairgrounds. Dorton Arena had collapsed, as had the Youth Detention Center and the Art Museum. Supposedly the juvies had been rounded up; the Art Museum was a total loss. Put back on the gas mask when he got on the Beltway. Deep breaths, take some more pills when he got home, call in sick, call his mother, his wife—it'd be okay. After circling the Courthouse in Pittsboro, Gavin turned on the radio, his nerves finally calm, his breathing regular, his fingers still their normal color.

Good Morning, this is the CBS Radio News and I am Tom Brokaw, in the Principality of Washington, with the hourly update. The red-rose-and-green-field banner of the Roosevelt-Potomac Dynasty was seen flying this morning over Sagamore Hill, the family estate, con firming reports that the Emperor and his mother have left the capital.

The Prime Minister will meet with the Cabinet and the Regency Council at Mount Vernon tomorrow morning in executive session and it is widely expected that a National State of Emergency will be declared.

In international news, Dom Pedro V, following Washington's lead, is meeting today in Rio de Janeiro with the Brazilian cabinet in closed session to discuss similar measures. New Spain, Nueva Granada, Quebec, and Gran Argentina are expected to follow suit. . . .

And now for Northern Carolina news, this is WRAL FM 101.5, Raleigh:

Governor Easley, following the example of six other provincial governors, declared Northern Carolina to be in a state of emergency. A dawn raid yesterday on the Cherokee Reservation netted authorities a cache of proscribed magical devices. Three Cherokee witches were arrested. This morning Governor Easley ordered the Raleigh, Greensboro, and Charlotte ghettoes sealed and a fifty percent increase in random para and hybrid testing. The bounty paid for identifying paras and hybrids has been doubled.

Gavin punched the station selector and the radio popped, snapped, and a new voice came on the air, a woman, Radio Free Columbia, and the morning news broadcast—*Radio Free Columbia?*

How did they get through? Instead of Brokaw's two-line stories, he got an in-depth story of the Cherokee raid. The reporter cataloged what the hunters had found stashed in one witch's garage: charms, amulets, talismans, crystals—a cornucopia of proscribed artifacts. Illegal herbs, such as St. John's Wort, used in charms to ward off evil—and every word spoken in a very conversational tone. It was as if the reporter was a botanist describing the herbs' use—as if everything was normal. The reporter's description was cut off before she could finish by a series of quick, high beeps: government jamming signals.

Gavin changed channels after that, to an oldie goldie station. No. *Those things aren't normal.* He could relive high school parties until he got back to Raleigh. Stereos cranked as loud as they could go *and I am fifteen, a freshman, and I am supposed to be inside the church, at an all-night Autumn Harvest party, but I have run away, down to the Old Graveyard across the road and it is midnight and the wind rises suddenly as if someone has called it by name. A warm hand touches my shoulder and pulls me around and there he is: the golden boy from the beach, a living candle, a flame in the flesh—*

He had spent the next week at home, on double dosage, before the glowing stopped.

After taking two robin's egg-green pills from the half-gallon jar, Gavin called Cooper Road Elementary first. He ignored the blinking light. He knew it was his mother calling *again* and he wanted to put off talking with her as long as possible. *Damn her: she did this to me. Everything was fine until she called.* He tried to keep his conversation with Carrie brief, but she wanted to talk. Any other day would have been fine—he liked Carrie and they were good friends. She often came by the library early in the morning just to visit with him, carrying her Duke mug with lukewarm coffee, see how he was, tease him about his Carolina mug, and they had had more than one beer together after work. Today, however, it felt like she was dragging things out, and the other calls he had to make were pressing on him, he wanted them done and over. He could just see her: leaning back in her office chair, one hand running through her grey-streaked dirty blond hair, the other thumping the arm of her chair. Finally she let him go, but not before she oh so casually mentioned the Cherokee news, the state of emergency, and to be careful driving.

Is she trying to tell me something? This is crazy. Carrie is my friend; all this other stuff is making me paranoid.

Gavin told Sophia's machine he'd be over tomorrow morning to pick up Grey; they could talk then. Tell Grey he loved him. Then he called his mother. Three rings, four, five, six. He dialed and redialed. Ten, eleven, twelve, thirteen rings. She could just be outside, or taking a walk, or at the public library. Maybe the ringer on the phone was broken. Finally, and with the same sense of dread again in his chest, this time heavier, colder, he hit play on the machine:

Gavin, honey, I didn't want things to ever be this way. But I understand why you did what you did. I love you: always remember that. I left you a letter. The mimosa, remember? When you hear this, I will be dead. I had to protect you and Grey.

His mother's phone wasn't broken; it had burned, along with the house. The ashes were still smoking. Gavin stepped out of his car where he had pulled off the road. Red fire department tape and yellow police tape blocked the driveway, bisected the front yard, lay over the tire tracks of the emergency vehicles, wrapped around dying Lombardy poplars in the side yard, a row of bushes, her clothesline—he remembered household appliances tended to short out around Mama—and then disappeared out of sight. *Of course no one had called him. Eleanora Bennett had burned up, a childless widow, she worked at the public library, real quiet, kept to herself, by the time we saw the fire it was too late, place went up like it was dry as a bone . . .*

Gavin sat down in his car. He could be gone in seconds and no one would know he had been there. It was late morning; the highway was empty. No fire department, no police, nobody. Just start the car and drive away. If anyone asked, he had no idea who had lived here. He had stopped to read a map. *I never want to see you again, do you hear me? Never. You made me this way. You made me a para.* That had only been the beginning of all the ugly things he had said to her. His mother. She had held him the night his father and brothers had left; they had cried together. She had told him old stories of how it had been before the war, when she was a little girl and fairies were still permitted to fly and what it felt like to fly on the wind of a storm. She had told him about his grandmother, a full fairy and . . . His hands were glowing again.

The note.

If anyone found the note in the mimosa—but this wasn't where he grew up, with a mimosa behind the bee-filled bushes in the back. A hole in the trunk; he and his brothers had hidden things there, notes, secret messages for spies. He had only been here once, after she moved, just once to tell her no more. *Has to be another tree, like it, something like it.*

Gavin couldn't make himself walk casually around the house's smoking ruins. He ran as fast as he could to the back of the house, to the small yard where she said she was going to plant roses, and she had, they were everywhere. There. Crape myrtles, a small thicket behind a white fence of climbing roses—and one of them was set slightly apart, a few feet away from the others. Had to be the "mimosa." Finally crying, he felt over the satiny-smooth trunk, up, down—*Mama, I'm sorry, I had to*—there, a knot that felt loose, he pulled it out, there was the note. Holding the paper tight in his hand, Gavin leaned into the trunk and wept.

Eleventh grade and I think I am the last one to take a shower after gym, I planned it that way—safer to be last. But as I step into the hot water, I hear footsteps, someone whistling, and there is another boy, as naked as I am—Jason—who only nods at me, not seeming to care if I am there. Then I start to glow. Just the tips of my ears first, but I know what is happening by the sudden warmth and then my toes, my fingers, the head of my penis. If I don't do something, the golden light will ooze from every orifice. I need more pills—but they are at home. I look up and see Jason watching me and Jason is glowing, too.

Now his hands and his arms were glowing.

Gavin slapped his face, once, twice, to break the memory, stop the tears, and ran even faster back to the car. The glowing winked out. But since I-40 was in such disorder after this morning's quake, it had taken Gavin almost two hours to get to his mother's house just north of Chapel Hill, on 86. He had taken two pills over two hours ago. He shouldn't be glowing at all. The doctor. He had to go see Doctor Deerman, up at Calvander. Was that what she called him about? His mother's note was very short: *The pills don't work anymore for me. The Jacksons turned me in. Zora, the Jacksons' cat, overheard; she told me. I love you, son. Mama.*

He had forgotten that sometimes—she could never count on it—his mother was an animal telepath. *Yeah, Eleanora Bennett burned right up, poor thing. You know, though, I heard she was— well, part-paranormal. She was? Well, the fire was a good thing then.*

Jason hung himself. His family disappeared.

"Do you have an appointment with Dr. Deerman?" the receptionist asked Gavin, frowning.

"No. Just tell him Gavin Paul Reed is here and that I have to see him about my medication."

"You are supposed to make an appointment; that's how we do things at Calvander Internal Medicine," the receptionist said, her frown now a glower.

"I have been Dr. Deerman's patient since I was fourteen. Look on my chart: you will see a note saying if I have to see him about my medication that I should just come."

She read Gavin's folder. She read it again, murmuring the words to herself as if she were translating them from some strange foreign language. Finally she looked up. "Take a seat. Dr. Deerman's nurse will see you when she can work you in. After he gets back from his lunch hour at one o'clock."

From noon to 12:30, Gavin, his stomach growling, wishing he had stopped for lunch at Talbert's Grocery, Grill, and Gas next door, read the two-week-old *Columbian News & World Report*. He stopped when he got to the required-by-imperial-decree advertisement explaining the difference between fairies and witches: *We must always be vigilant, always on guard, always on alert. Magic is of the Devil; Science is of God. Know the difference. No fairy can cast a spell, make a charm, or invoke a curse. No witch can fly or glow or mindtalk with animals. Fairies are magical; witches manipulate and work magic*—He tossed that aside for yesterday's *Columbia Today*, and by 1:15 was polishing off an *Other People* article on the married life of Arnold Schwarzenegger and Lady Maria Shriver when there was a lot of noise at the desk.

Two nurses and the receptionist were huddled, whispering, and ignoring the ringing phone. Finally one of the nurses answered, speaking rapidly in an undertone. The three whispered some more, and a lab tech came out, and the whispering got louder and louder: "He's disappeared? The police are coming here? They think he is a witch, I swear to God. *Nobody* is supposed to leave before they get here . . ."

Gavin slowly laid the magazine down and looked at his hands: no glowing. But, instead, on the tips of his fingers, rust red spots. His iron-sensitivity had come back. The steel door of the car. His finger joints were beginning to ache.

"Bathroom?"

"Down the hall, on the right. Uh, Dr. Deerman will be a little late, Mr. Reed," the receptionist said, smiling this time.

"I don't mind waiting."

There had to be a back door; there was always a back door.

Saturday, 21 October 2000

"You're a quarter-hybrid; your mother—who only *just* died—was a halfer. You made our son one-eighth-hybrid and you expect me to let you in the house? To think I let a paranormal touch me. No, you can't see him. You can never see him again. You're sick, you pervert. Get out, get out, get out, *get out*."

Gavin pleaded and cried and knocked on Sophia's front door for another half-hour. Finally he went home. It took him three hours to drive back cross-town from Glascock Street after the afternoon quake, and going and coming took him right past the central ghetto. He couldn't see much past the chainlink fence. The sky was heavy with ash and smoke. He took two more green pills and sat in the rocking chair in his living room for a long time, the chair he was going to rock Grey in, and rocked and rocked. Gavin's to-do list lay on the kitchen table.

He wasn't normal anymore. Sophia had said so. Why hadn't he told her what Dr. Deerman, a tall, thin witch, had told him once: that witches and fairies and normals—a term Dr. Deerman hated— were all *Homo sapiens*, variations on a theme. Otherwise, how could there be hybrids in the first place? Spaniels and collies and terriers were all dogs, right? If the government had permitted *unbiased* genetic research they might have found out everyone was human, even vampires—not that any were left. Maybe even selkies, mers, wers, pans, and dryads.

Why hadn't he told her? Because he had spent ten years maintaining his constructed normal identity, passing, having a regular life, and believing it. Because even though he hadn't really looked, he had felt a twinge in his hands, his feet, and his groin when he drove past the ghetto. Now that identity had been proven all too fragile. He rocked slowly, hugging himself, holding himself together as much as he could, to be sure nothing else fragile would break.

Monday, 23 October 2000

Gavin called Sophia in the morning from the library office, in the afternoon, and at home. The phone rang and rang and rang. He drove over and knocked and knocked and knocked. There was a message on his machine when he got back: *If you come over here again, I will call the police and turn you in.*

By then, he had tripled his daily dosage.

✿   ✿   ✿

Wednesday, 25 October 2000
This is Dan Rather, with the Evening News. First, the headlines: The Prime Minister, acting under advisement from the Regent, has declared the Columbian Empire under martial law. Imperial troops are being deployed on reservations throughout the Empire in response to increased unrest. The Dineh have lodged a protest with Indigenous Affairs . . . Fey ghettoes across the country have been sealed. Provincial governors have been ordered to call up local militia. House-to-house searches in designated areas are under consideration by the Cabinet and the Regency Council . . . Rogue tornadoes touched ground this morning in downtown Oklahoma City, Spartanburg, Southern Carolina, Tijuana, Lower California . . .

Quadruple the dosage.
Wear latex gloves to handle any metal with iron.
Ibuprofen, 800 mg horse-sized pills, for dull ache in the joints.

Thursday, 26 October 2000
At three A.M. Gavin gave up trying to sleep. He had replayed his last conversation with Sophia and her phone message for the umpteenth time. He had delivered his carefully thought-out counter arguments for the umpteenth-and-first time. He leaned over and turned on the radio, expecting nothing but white noise. Then, faintly, at first, then more loudly:

This is Radio Free Columbia with the headlines: Lower California and Hawaii are in revolt; uprisings have been reported in New Spain . . . Dragon flocks have been sighted over the Northern Rockies for the first time since World War II. Clashes between the Dineh and imperial troops have been verified. Mechanical failures have been reported all over Columbia. Anti-government demonstrations have been reported in New York, Chicago, New Paris . . . Although yet unconfirmed, reliable sources are reporting that the Columbian Empire is arming and targeting its hellmaker missiles—

An explosion of static, beeps, silence, more beeps, then RFC again:

Today's lead story—and that it is the first direct transmission received since the closings of the 179 East and 30 West meridians in 1945 is a story in itself—the British Witch Council has issued denials of any involvement in the seismic, volcanic, and meteorological disturbances in the Northern and Southern Columbian continents. According to

*the Merlin, this is Gaean or Earth magic, repressed chthonic forces
beyond any magician's ability. This is, the Merlin said, but one more
instance of scientists' mistaken belief in the magical powers of the
First Folk. If we couldn't stop the hellmaker missiles fifty-six years
ago, how could we make earthquakes and high wind gusts today six
thousand miles away—?*

Then, a sudden noise, sharp quick pops, of someone falling,
more sharp pops, and the radio went dead.

Friday, 27 October 2000

Gavin got to school a little after seven. A mild tremor woke him up
at five. He got up, paced, showered, tried to forget the dream, ate,
straightened up what had fallen, checked the ash-seals on the windows, the gas filters, paced, tried to forget the dream, and looked
through the photo album he had kept since Grey's birth. Then,
with a Raleigh city map, he figured out a way to Cooper Road
Elementary that avoided the now almost-impassable Beltway and
the old ghetto. When he pulled into the parking lot, there was just
one other car—Carrie's, of course—and her office light was on.
Her house was three blocks up Cooper. Gavin felt sure she practically lived at the school.

No matter, he was here to work, not to talk to Carrie, to not
worry about Grey, not to remember his mother, and to not remember the dream from which he had awakened. He shelved the books
on the carts, unstuck the laminator, unjammed the copier, got set
up for his first class, Christina's, and he finally finished his fall book
order. Gavin was not, however, able to not worry about Grey: he
missed his son and was afraid for him. Would an eighth-hybrid
glow? Could Sophia bear having such a child in her house? He was
not able to not remember his mother; his heart ached all the more.
Gavin was also not able to not remember the dream, especially the
last image: the golden boy, reaching out to him. It kept coming
back, no matter how many cups of coffee. There would be a flickering just outside his peripheral vision, and he would turn and
nothing would be there. A light would fall across Gavin's desk, and
he would look up to see a golden shadow fading.

The worst wasn't that his hands seemed to have decided by
themselves to reach back. The worst was a surge in his groin that he
could stop only by gritting his teeth, and pushing down on his desk
chair as hard as possible, which made his joints hurt all over again.

By nine, when Christina brought her third graders in, things were a little better. The flickerings had stopped, and he could take off his latex gloves, the rust spots covered by makeup. When he had the kids on the floor listening as he read *Ramona Quimby, Age 8,* Gavin felt like he might just make it through all this; he might even get through to Sophia when whatever was going on stopped. Carrie's slow voice on the intercom stopped him after he had read the first page of the chapter.

"Mrs. Capshaw?" she said, speaking first to Christina's aide, "Would you please finish reading to the children? I need to see Mr. Reed. Thank you so much."

Now what?

He nodded and smiled at the secretary, Audrey Greer, who was on the phone. He pantomimed: *What does she want? Is it okay?*

"It's okay, Gavin," Audrey said, cupping the receiver against her shoulder. "Carrie? Gav's here."

Carrie adjusted her gold wire-rim glasses and got up from behind her desk. Gavin noticed for the first time that she had no metal furniture, not even file cabinets, in her office. "Gavin, let's take a walk. Audrey, we're going to go down to the lower field for a bit."

"A walk? Carrie, I have a class; what's up?"

"Just come with me it's all right come on, down the hall," Carrie said and set off, her heels clicking hard on the linoleum. She was nothing if not a fast walker. Gavin paused, and then followed, wondering what the hell was going on. Carrie kept up a relentless chatter down the hall, classroom noises waxing and waning as they walked: book orders done, good thing, she knew he had picked out some good ones, he always did, why had he picked Beverly Cleary to read, she was one of Carrie's favorites, but a bit old-fashioned, no—until they were outside and a good twenty feet from the building.

"Gavin. I'm your friend. You know that, don't you?"

Gavin nodded, ready to bolt, but to where and why he had no idea.

"We have to leave right now—Christina's turned you in; the police are on their way."

"Turned me in? I haven't done anything—"

"Gavin: Latisha told her about your hands at the zoo. There are little rust spots popping up on your neck, and your ears—you're starting to grow points—"

"I checked this morning—" Gavin said, then stopped. He

touched first one ear, then the other: points. "This has just happened."

"I know. This is why you can trust me," Carrie said, taking his arm, and leading him not toward the lower field but the parking lot. She held out her right hand and there, faintly, he saw a yellow glow outlining her fingers. "I'm an eighth-fey; the glowing just started this week. I can still control it," she said, and the glowing winked out. "I've always known you were—but you know how it is—too dangerous. Now come on, we have to get out of here. Here's my car, get in—it has plastic sealant all over it—my dentist is a witch. Let's go."

Gavin got in, too numb to answer, too numb to do more than he was told. He really liked Christina; they had talked, traded jokes. Carrie was passing, too? And now? They were on the run? He could hear, louder and louder, sirens. Carrie gunned the car back in reverse, in a wide arc that had her pointing out the driveway. Down the short hill to the street, right, and she slowed down to the posted speed. One, two, three Raleigh police cars roared past, followed by a WTVD-NEWS Eleven van.

"I'm going to leave you here. It's okay, Audrey will tell them we went to the lower field. She's black and clandestine African Methodist Episcopal Zion; she's on our side. Christina will show them the way—she told me she wanted to spit in your face when they arrested you. I'll tell them you ran for the parking lot, up the street, I followed in the car, you ran into the woods over there. Stay here, okay? You'll be safe here for now. Here's my bedroom, lie down. Yes, I will look for the pills—bottom desk drawer, in the back."

Gavin nodded, not trusting himself to speak. He let her hug him when she left and then he lay down on the neatly made bed, covered by a blue-with-white-stars quilt. He knew then that he, Gavin Paul Reed, was nowhere. He couldn't go to 2550-Q Glenwood Avenue: the police would go there. He could never go there again. All his things, his books, his pictures of Grey: gone. He couldn't go to Sophia, to Grey. He had renounced his mother ten years ago—but, even so, she would have taken him in. *Oh, Mama.* His father, his brothers—he had no idea. He couldn't get up Monday and drive to Cooper Road Elementary, unlock the library door, flip on the lights, check his lesson plans. What had the little house of his lost normal life been made of? Not bricks, not sticks, not even straw. Something finer, more fragile, more insubstantial, that didn't need a strong-winded wolf to break. Just the breath it took to make the sound of one word, maybe two, a phone call. What little had been left after Sophia slammed the door in his face was gone.

He knew if he got up off the bed and looked in the mirror over Carrie's dresser that he would see his face glowing as well. Now he could be shot on sight. *I should have taken more pills this morning. What for? They don't work anymore.* Gavin felt as if he had been in Carrie's house all day; that couldn't be true. He looked at his watch: it had stopped at 9:18. So, that part of him was gone, too. He closed his eyes, even though he knew, that when he fell asleep, he would dream of the golden boy and he knew what he and the boy would do in the dream.

Saturday, 28 October 2000

Gavin ate the last bit of toast Carrie had insisted he eat, and picked up the coffee mug and held it in his hands. The warmth eased the dull ache in his joints. He took a swallow and looked up at Carrie, who sat across the table, reading yesterday's Raleigh *News and Observer*. She had decided, since the governor had closed all provincial schools, that she was going to catch up on *all* her reading. They sat in her kitchen, a friendly little room, with yellow curtains and a red-and-white checkered tablecloth, post-it notes on the refrigerator, and food and water bowls for her cat in one corner. Morning light came in the window.

"Carr, I don't know what to do—other than turn myself in, kill myself—"

"You will not," Carrie said, slapping the table so hard his plate and saucer shook. "You will not let them win. You will just stay here until we figure out what to do next. There is a resistance out there; I'm sure of it—how else could my dentist have gotten enough sealant for me and her other fey patients to cover all their appliances?" she asked, waving her hand at the refrigerator and the stove.

"What's going to happen to me then? What about Grey?"

"You know Sophia will take care of him. I don't know what's going to happen to either one of us, but I am not going to let you die. We've made it this long, didn't we? Hiding one way or another, ever since we were born? Drugs—"

"That don't work anymore. You might as well have left them at school. My witch doctor has disappeared— he may even be ashes by now. And *him*, how do I escape *him*?"

"Him who?"

"The golden boy. He's haunted me since I was eleven and now, since I ran into that werewolf at the zoo, I keep seeing him, dreaming about him. What do I do about him?"

Carrie looked hard at Gavin for a long moment. She held up her hand—*wait*—and got up to get herself a cup of coffee and sat back down, shaking her head.

"Won't be much more coffee—not the way shipping is being disrupted. Better drink up. Don't you know who he is, what he is? Didn't you learn anything about fairies?"

"Not much except what I heard in church and school," he muttered, looking away from her, embarrassed. "Mama only told me a few old stories and to be careful around iron."

"Then all you know are half-truths and lies. You do know a fairy nest has four people in it, right? Earth, air, fire, and water? He's part of your nest, your tetrad. You're supposed to be together, as partners, lovers, mates—plus two others."

"I don't even know his name. Do you see a golden girl?" Gavin said.

"Not yet. In the past day or so, sometimes I think I have. And you do know his name; I bet he's told you. But you are so used to forgetting and pushing away. You know, he's close by; I am sure of it. The old ghetto isn't that far from here, right over between Glascock and Oakwood, up Poole, on North Tarboro—"

"I know where it is. You know what you are saying? That, that I'm—"

"That you are part-fairy; that I am? That's who we are. All the other stuff is wrong; it's hatred and bigotry and fear—"

Gavin wanted to believe her.

Tuesday, 31 October 2000

"Gavin. Gavin: *wake up*. You've got to wake up."

"Huh, what, what is it, Carrie?" Gavin said, his words slurred, as he swam up from sleep.

"The police are just up the street, knocking on doors. You've got to get out of here *now*."

He stared at her, her face in shadow, the light from the hall outlining her head. "Go where?"

"The old ghetto. There's no other place—they're looking for people trying to pass. Here, get dressed, go."

"What about you?"

"I can still dampen the glow. You can't—you're glowing now. If you don't, you'll never see Grey again. They'll kill you."

For Grey, Gavin scrambled into his clothes, hooked on his gas mask, and ran out the back door into the windy night. A low fence, up, over, another backyard, a dog barking, someone yelled—they had seen him, his light, the tiny stars trailing behind him. He ran. More shouting, and a siren. Quick sharp pops, a scream, more pops. Leaves scuttling, rising, spiraling in eddies of air.

Gavin ran. Down one street, up another, and across Poole Road, past cars stalled in the middle of the street, tow trucks stalled, a police car. The drivers yelled, cursed at Gavin, the officer shot at him, the bullets shrieking past. He kept running. Another street, turn left. Another yard and into trees, a park, a green space, thick trees, and he kept running, the branches slapping and cutting his face, blood in his mouth. Gavin ran and ran and ran, his chest burning, gasping. He stopped, leaned into a tree. North Tarboro Street. He was just outside the ghetto. The ghetto of the damned, the godless, reminders, lest we forget. That was how the preacher at NC District 17 Church of the Rational Christ, Scientist, the one he had heard as a boy, had described ghettoes. *People ask me why don't we just drop a hellmaker missile on them all? Cleanse the Earth of the devil's spawn? I tell them: lest we forget.* The periodic pogroms and fairy-killings had been televised for as long as Gavin could remember.

This was St. Augustine, the oldest and smallest fey ghetto, built hurriedly right after the war, on the campus of a small black college that the provincial governor had moved a few miles east. Two bigger ghettoes had been built later, in less visible locations, but St. Augustine wasn't closed: imperial law required every provincial capital have one ghetto in the city center. *Lest we forget.* The college's brick walls had been tripled in size, and enclosed in a doubled chainlink fence, crowned with concertina wire. Dorms and classroom buildings became barracks, new barracks were built, tiny gardens grown in odd patches of earth, fairies born, and buried. It was, Gavin had been told, something between a walled village and a prison camp. The chainlink fence came right up to each of the streets that marked the ghetto boundaries. Not too far from Cooper Road and its middle class neighborhood, but far enough.

Gavin found himself facing the south chainlink fence of the fey ghetto. Or where he knew the fence was supposed to be. One of the quakes had literally pulled the fence and the earth beneath it apart, leaving a deep red gash in between, framed by twisted fence and the broken wall behind it. Gavin felt his bones ache when he walked between the torn metal; he could almost feel the rust blemishes growing. He climbed over the crumbled bricks into a tiny garden behind an L-shaped old dorm. A narrow alley separated the dorm from the newer barracks.

Gavin looked up. For the first time in weeks the sky was clear of smoke and ash and clouds, blown clean by the wind—which was now still. The aurora borealis, like shimmering fireworks on Empire Day, danced in the sky. And the Moon, great and golden. The air felt close and charged, as if he were moving through something sparkly and tingly on his skin. His joints felt a little better.

The ground shook. Gavin tripped, caught himself, walked down the alley, and out into a very narrow street. Barracks on both sides, and in front, and shoehorned between: Stores? Shops? The walls were split, cracked, rubble in several places. He walked right a block and stopped before what had to be a bar. The name was in gold letters on cracked glass: SIDHE'S PLACE. There was a drawn curtain; he could see only a flicker of dim light inside.

The closer to the bar, the greater the compulsion Gavin felt to go in, as if a fine net had dropped and was slowly pulling him to the door. He fought it, knowing if he crossed the threshold that would be it; there would never be a way back to anything resembling his old life. If he just turned and ran—where? Normals didn't enter fey ghettoes except to smash fairy heads. But to enter the bar would be the final admission, the last confession that he was a para, a hybrid, not human, Other.

Gavin shed his gas mask and stood just inside the door for a long moment, blinking against the dark, broken only by the sputtering red light of a handful of wall torches. Breathing hard, he stepped all the way in. Tables, chairs, booths on the wall opposite the bar. Stairs, going up and down, lit by another torch. He could see why there was no one else in the bar except for him and the bartender. The last quake had brought down all the shelves behind the bar, broken the wine rack. The smell made his eyes water.

The bartender, ghostlike in a white shirt, was bent over, sweeping up glass. He stood slowly, and turned to face Gavin.

The same green eyes. The golden boy—who was now a man.

Gavin ran, but he didn't get far, as the ground rolled, shook, throwing him down right at the door, just as the boy caught him, falling with him, covering him. Sounding like crashing waves, first the door, then the entire wall, the glass shattering into a fine sharp rain, fell. A warm, new wind rose into the sudden silence, low, close, whispering to the dust.

"Are you all right?" the boy said, close to his ear. "Gavin?" The boy pushed the door off and rolled back, taking Gavin with him until they lay on their sides, facing each other, surrounded by broken bricks and wood, glass glinting in their hair. "You're bleeding, and you're going to have a goose egg pretty soon right there," he said, and touched Gavin's right temple. Slowly, he brushed the glass out of Gavin's hair.

"Come on, we have to get downstairs. Everybody else has taken cover," the boy said. He pulled Gavin up and into a hug, and at the touch of that body to his, all over his, Gavin felt something give, break loose, let go. And his body glowed—shone—the brightest he could remember. He, too, was a flame in the flesh, as the boy was again.

"There's nowhere else to run, Gav. You're here. Let's go. It's going to be pretty bad up here in a few minutes; we'll be safe down below," the boy said, his voice both insistent, and to Gavin, oddly glad.

"You know my name. You've chased me since I was eleven and I don't know yours. And you're bleeding, too," Gavin said slowly, feeling both terror and wonder, and timidly touched a wet cut on the boy's forehead.

"I told you when we were eleven; you've forgotten. Torin. We have to go quickly, before it's too late: this is no ordinary wind, it's coming out of the Earth." The wind keened and moaned, picked up a broken board, dropped, pushed stones, gathered up more dust. No longer at their feet, they felt it circling around and up their legs.

Gavin, the terror now bewilderment, the wonder now joined with hope, let Torin take his hand and lead him through the bar's wreckage and down the stairs, as the wind blew out the torch behind them.

"Is everything ending?" Gavin whispered.

"No, magic is rising out of the Earth, and the balance is restoring itself," Torin said confidently over his shoulder. The stairs went down, down, until the walls were no longer brick and mortar, but chiseled stone. Their bodies' glowing was the only light. At the bottom, they stepped into a tunnel and Torin led Gavin straight ahead past one, two doors, and then he opened the third into a tiny room, with barely enough space for a bed and a table and an oil lamp. Torin lit it, and looked at Gavin who still stood in the door. Torin's eyes were green fires.

"What's going to happen to us, to everybody? My little boy, my friend Carrie, you and me? Are we safe here?" Gavin's voice shook.

"I don't know, for sure, what is going to happen—just that the balancing will take a long, long time," Torin said softly. "I can't tell you if we'll be able to find your friend or your little boy. There's only one thing I am sure of: you're earth and I'm fire and we bonded when we were eleven. How else could we be in each other's dreams since then? Yes, there are supposed to be four—but I don't know if we will ever find water and air. Since the war, a lot of tetrads only partially form. We're safe from the wind; the quakes, I think, are over. The tunnel comes out in an open place—we won't be able to go back up through the debris. Now come here."

Gavin took the last step inside.

Samhain morning

Gavin woke first. For a while he just lay there in the close darkness, listening to Torin breathe, wondering what world waited above them. *Different* was too small for the world, Gavin thought, but it worked for how he felt: *different*. It wasn't a feeling he could name or trust, but still, he *could* feel it: warm, yellow, soft, like cat fur. Torin stirred, mumbled something in his sleep, and Gavin turned and murmured his name. Torin muttered and turned on his back, a hand flung back over his head, the sheet falling away. The light from the lamp washed over his naked chest as it rose and fell. Slowly and carefully, Gavin rolled over onto one side, and with his free hand, touched Torin's hair, and then, even more slowly and carefully, Gavin placed his fingertips, now faintly glowing, on Torin's face and he let Torin's breath warm the palm of his hand.

Cowboy Grace

Kristine Kathryn Rusch

"**E**VERY WOMAN TOLERATES MISOGYNY," ALEX said. She slid her empty beer glass across the bar, and tucked a strand of her auburn hair behind her ear. "How much depends on how old she is. The older she is the less she notices it. The more she expects it."

"Bullshit." Carole took a drag on her Virginia Slim, crossed her legs, and adjusted her skirt. "I don't tolerate misogyny."

"Maybe we should define the word," Grace said, moving to the other side of Carole. She wished her friend would realize how much the smoking irritated her. In fact, the entire night was beginning to irritate her. They were all avoiding the topic *du jour*: the tiny wound on Grace's left breast, stitches gone now, but the skin still raw and sore.

"Mis-ah-jenny," Carole said, as if Grace were stupid. "Hatred of women."

"From the Greek," Alex said. "*Misos* or hatred and *gyne* or women."

"Not," Carole said, waving her cigarette as if it were a baton, "misogamy, which is also from the Greek. Hatred of marriage. Hmm. Two male *misos* wrapped in one."

The bartender, a diminutive woman wearing a red and white

cowgirl outfit, complete with fringe and gold buttons, snickered. She set down a napkin in front of Alex and gave her another beer.

"Compliments," she said, "of the men at the booth near the phone."

Alex looked. She always looked. She was tall, busty, and leggy, with a crooked nose thanks to an errant pitch Grace had thrown in the ninth grade, a long chin, and eyes the color of wine. Men couldn't get enough of her. When Alex rebuffed them, they slept with Carole and then talked to Grace.

The men in the booth near the phone looked like corporate types on a junket. Matching gray suits, different ties—all in a complimentary shade of pink, red, or cranberry—matching haircuts (long on top, styled on the sides), and differing goofy grins.

"This is a girl bar," Alex said, shoving the glass back at the bartender. "We come here to diss men, not to meet them."

"Good call," Carole said, exhaling smoke into Grace's face. Grace agreed, not with the smoke or the rejection, but because she wanted time with her friends. Without male intervention of any kind.

"Maybe we should take a table," Grace said.

"Maybe." Carole crossed her legs again. Her mini was leather, which meant she felt like being on display that night. "Or maybe we should send drinks to the cutest men we see."

They scanned the bar. Happy Hour at the Oh Kaye Corral didn't change much from Friday to Friday. A jukebox in the corner, playing Patty Loveless. Cocktail waitresses in short skirts and ankle boots with big heels. Tin stars and Wild West art on the walls, unstained wood and checkered tablecloths adding to the effect. One day, when Grace had Alex's courage and Carole's gravely voice, she wanted to walk in, belly up to the bar, slap her hand on its polished surface, and order whiskey straight up. She wanted someone to challenge her. She wanted to pull her six-gun and have a stare-down, then and there. Cowboy Grace, fastest gun in the West. Or at least in Racine on a rainy Friday night.

"I don't see cute," Alex said. "I see married, married, divorced, desperate, single, single, never-been-laid, and married."

Grace watched her make her assessment. Alex's expression never changed. Carole was looking at the men, apparently seeing whether or not she agreed.

Typically, she didn't.

"I dunno," she said, pulling on her cigarette. "Never-Been-Laid's kinda cute."

"So try him," Alex said. "But you'll have your own faithful puppy dog by this time next week, and a proposal of marriage within the month."

Carole grinned and slid off the stool. "Proposal of marriage in two weeks," she said. "I'm that good."

She stubbed out her cigarette, grabbed the tiny leather purse that matched the skirt, adjusted her silk blouse, and sashayed her way toward a table in the middle.

Grace finally saw Never-Been-Laid. He had soft brown eyes, and hair that needed trimming. He wore a shirt that accented his narrow shoulders, and he had a laptop open on the round table. He was alone. He had his feet tucked under the chair, crossed at the ankles. He wore dirty tennis shoes with his Gap khakis.

"Cute?" Grace said.

"Shhh," Alex said. "It's a door into the mind of Carole."

"One that should remain closed." Grace moved to Carole's stool. It was still warm. Grace shoved Carole's drink out of her way, grabbed her glass of wine, and coughed. The air still smelled of cigarette smoke.

Carole was leaning over the extra chair, giving Never-Been-Laid a view of her cleavage, and the guys at the booth by the phone a nice look at her ass, which they seemed to appreciate.

"Where the hell did that misogyny comment come from?" Grace asked.

Alex looked at her. "You want to get a booth?"

"Sure. Think Carole can find us?"

"I think Carole's going to be deflowering a computer geek and not caring what we're doing." Alex grabbed her drink, stood, and walked to a booth on the other side of the Corral. Dirty glasses from the last occupants were piled in the center, and the red-and-white-checked vinyl tablecloth was sticky.

They moved the glasses to the edge of the table and didn't touch the dollar tip, which had been pressed into a puddle of beer.

Grace set her wine down and slid into the booth. Alex did the same on the other side. Somehow they managed not to touch the tabletop at all.

"You remember my boss?" Alex asked as she adjusted the tiny fake gaslamp that hung on the wall beside the booth.

"Beanie Boy?"

She grinned. "Yeah."

"Never met him."

"Aren't you lucky."

Grace already knew that. She'd heard stories about Beanie Boy for the last year. They had started shortly after he was hired. Alex went to the company Halloween party and was startled to find her boss dressed as one of the Lollipop Kids from *The Wizard of Oz*, complete with striped shirt, oversized lollipop, and propeller beanie.

"Now what did he do?" Grace asked.

"Called me honey."

"Yeah?" Grace asked.

"And sweetie, and doll-face, and sugar."

"Hasn't he been doing that for the last year?"

Alex glared at Grace. "It's getting worse."

"What's he doing, patting you on the butt?"

"If he did, I'd get him for harassment, and he knows it."

She had lowered her voice. Grace could barely hear her over Shania Twain.

"This morning one of our clients came in praising the last report. I wrote it."

"Didn't Beanie Boy give you credit?"

"Of course he did. He said, 'Our little Miss Rogers wrote it. Isn't she a doll?' "

Grace clutched her drink tighter. This didn't matter to her. Her biopsy was benign. She had called Alex and Carole and told them. They'd suggested coming here. So why weren't they offering a toast to her life? Why weren't they celebrating, really celebrating, instead of rerunning the same old conversation in the same old bar in the same old way? "What did the client do?"

"He agreed, of course."

"And?"

"And what?"

"Is that it? Didn't you speak up?"

"How could I? He was praising me, for godsake."

Grace sighed and sipped her beer. Shania Twain's comment was that it didn't impress her much. It didn't impress Grace much either, but she knew better than to say anything to Alex.

Grace looked toward the middle of the restaurant. Carole was standing behind Never-Been-Laid, her breasts pressed against his back, her ass on view to the world, her head over his shoulder peering at his computer screen.

Alex didn't follow her gaze like Grace had hoped. "If I were ten years younger, I'd tell Beanie Boy to shove it."

"If you were ten years younger, you wouldn't have a mortgage and a Mazda."

"Dignity shouldn't be cheaper than a paycheck," she said.

"So confront him."

"He doesn't think he's doing anything wrong. He treats all the women like that."

Grace sighed. They'd walked this road before. Job after job, boyfriend after boyfriend. Alex, for all her looks, was like Joe McCarthy protecting the world from the Red Menace: she saw anti-female everywhere, and most of it, she was convinced, was directed at her.

"You don't seem very sympathetic," Alex said.

She wasn't. She never had been. And with all she had been through in the last month, *alone* because her two best friends couldn't bear to talk about the Big C, the lock that was usually on Grace's mouth wasn't working.

"I'm not sympathetic," Grace said. "I'm beginning to think you're a victim in search of a victimizer."

"That's not fair, Grace," Alex said. "We tolerate this stuff because we were raised in an anti-woman society. It's gotten better, but it's not perfect. You tell those Xers stuff like this and they shake their heads. Or the new ones. What're they calling themselves now? Generation Y? They were raised on Title IX. Hell, they pull off their shirts after winning soccer games. Imagine us doing that."

"My cousin got arrested in 1977 in Milwaukee on the day Elvis Presley died for playing volleyball," Grace said. Carole was actually rubbing herself on Never-Been-Laid. His face was the color of the red checks in the tablecloth.

"What?"

Grace turned to Alex. "My cousin. You know, Barbie? She got arrested playing volleyball."

"They didn't let girls play volleyball in Milwaukee?"

"It was ninety degrees, and she was playing with a group of guys. They pulled off their shirts because they were hot and sweating, so she did the same. She got arrested for indecent exposure."

"God," Alex said. "Did she go to jail?"

"Didn't even get her day in court."

"Everyone gets a day in court."

Grace shook her head. "The judge took one look at Barbie, who was really butch in those days, and said, 'I'm sick of you girls coming in here and arguing that you should have equal treatment for things that are clearly unequal. I do not establish public decency laws. You may show a bit of breast if you're feeding a child, otherwise you are in violation of—some damn code.' Barbie used to quote the thing chapter and verse."

"Then what?" Alex asked.

"Then she got married, had a kid, and started wearing nail polish. She said it wasn't as much fun to show her breasts legally."

"See?" Alex said. "Misogyny."

Grace shrugged. "Society, Alex. Get used to it."

"That's the point of your story? We've been oppressed for a thousand years and you say, 'Get used to it'?"

"I say Brandi Chastain pulls off her shirt in front of millions—"

"Showing a sports bra."

"—and she doesn't get arrested. I say women head companies all the time. I say things are better now than they were when I was growing up, and I say the only ones who oppress us are ourselves."

"I say you're drunk."

Grace pointed at Carole, who was wet-kissing Never-Been-Laid, her arms wrapped around his neck and her legs wrapped around his waist. "She's drunk. I'm just speaking out."

"You never speak out."

Grace sighed. No one had picked up the glasses and she was tired of looking at that poor drowning dollar bill. There wasn't going to be any celebration. Everything was the same as it always was—at least to Alex and Carole. But Grace wanted something different.

She got up, threw a five next to the dollar, and picked up her purse.

"Tell me if Carole gets laid," Grace said, and left.

Outside Grace stopped and took a deep breath of the humid, exhaust-filled air. She could hear the clang of glasses even in the parking lot and the rhythm of Mary Chapin Carpenter praising passionate kisses. Grace had had only one glass of wine and a lousy time, and she wondered why people said old friends were the best friends. They were supposed to raise toasts to her future, now restored. She'd even said the "b" word and Alex hadn't noticed. It was as if the cancer scare had happened to someone they didn't even know.

Grace was going to be forty years old in three weeks. Her two best friends were probably planning a version of the same party they had held for her when she turned thirty. A male stripper whose sweaty body repulsed her more than aroused her, too many black balloons, and aging jokes that hadn't been original the first time around.

Forty years old, an accountant with her own firm, no close family, no boyfriend, and a resident of the same town her whole life. The only time she left was to visit cousins out east, and for what? Obligation?

There was no joy left, if there'd ever been any joy at all.

She got into her sensible Ford Taurus, bought at a used car lot for well under Blue Book, and drove west.

It wasn't until she reached Janesville that she started to call herself crazy, and it wasn't until she drove into Dubuque that she realized how little tied her to her hometown.

An apartment without even a cat to cozy up to, a business no more successful than a dozen others, and people who still saw her as a teenager wearing granny glasses, braces, and hair too long for her face. Grace, who was always there. Grace the steady, Grace the smart. Grace, who helped her friends out of their financial binds, who gave them a shoulder to cry on, and a degree of comfort because their lives weren't as empty as her own.

When she had told Alex and Carole that her mammogram had come back suspicious, they had looked away. When she told them that she had found a lump, they had looked frightened.

I can't imagine life without you, Gracie, Carole had whispered.

Imagine it now, Grace thought.

The dawn was breaking when she reached Cedar Rapids, and she wasn't really tired. But she was practical, had always been practical, and habits of a lifetime didn't change just because she had run away from home at the age of thirty-nine.

She got a hotel room and slept for eight hours, had dinner in a nice steak place, went back to the room and slept some more. When she woke up Sunday morning to bells from the Presbyterian Church across the street, she lay on her back and listened for a good minute before she realized they were playing "What a Friend We Have in Jesus." And she smiled then, because Jesus had been a better friend to her in recent years than Alex and Carole ever had.

At least Jesus didn't tell her his problems when she was praying about hers. If Jesus was self-absorbed he wasn't obvious about it. And he didn't seem to care that she hadn't been inside a church since August of 1978.

The room was chintz, the wallpaper and the bedspread matched, and the painting on the wall was chosen for its color not for its technique. Grace sat up and wondered what she was doing here, and thought about going home.

To nothing.

So she got in her car and followed the Interstate, through Des

Moines, and Lincoln, and Cheyenne, places she had only read about, places she had never seen. How could a woman live for forty years and not see the country of her birth? How could a woman do nothing except what she was supposed to from the day she was born until the day she died?

In Salt Lake City, she stared at the Mormon Tabernacle, all white against an azure sky. She sat in her car and watched a groundskeeper maintain the flowers, and remembered how it felt to take her doctor's call.

A lot of women have irregular mammograms, particularly at your age. The breast tissue is thicker, and often we get clouds.

Clouds.

There were fluffy clouds in the dry desert sky, but they were white and benign. Just like her lump had turned out to be. But for a hellish month, she had thought about that lump, feeling it when she woke out of a sound sleep, wondering if it presaged the beginning of the end. She had never felt her mortality like this before, not even when her mother had died. Not even when she realized there was no one remaining of the generation that had once stood between her and death.

No one talked about these things. No one let her talk about them either. Not just Alex and Carole, but Michael, her second in command at work, or even her doctor, who kept assuring her that she was young and the odds were in her favor.

Young didn't matter if the cancer had spread through the lymph nodes. When she went in for the lumpectomy almost two weeks ago now, she had felt a curious kind of relief, as if the doctor had removed a tick that had burrowed under her skin. When he had called with the news that the lump was benign, she had thanked him calmly and continued with her day, filing corporate tax returns for a consulting firm.

No one had known the way she felt. Not relieved. No. It was more like she had received a reprieve.

The clouds above the Tabernacle helped calm her. She plugged in her cell phone for the first time in days and listened to the voice mail messages, most of them from Michael, growing increasingly worried about where she was.

Have you forgotten the meeting with Boyd's? he'd asked on Monday.

Do you want me to file Charlie's extension? he'd demanded on Tuesday.

Where the hell are you? he cried on Wednesday and she knew, then, that it was okay to call him, that not even the business could bring her home.

Amazing how her training had prepared her for moments like these and she hadn't even known it. She had savings, lots of them, because she hadn't bought a house even though it had been prudent to do so. She had been waiting, apparently, for Mr. Right, or the family her mother had always wanted for her, the family that would never come. Her money was invested properly, and she could live off the interest if she so chose. She had just never chosen to before.

And if she didn't want to be found, she didn't have to be. She knew how to have the interest paid through off-shore accounts so that no one could track it. She even knew a quick and almost legal way to change her name. Traceable, but she hadn't committed a crime. She didn't need to hide well, just well enough that a casual search wouldn't produce her.

Not that anyone would start a casual search. Once she sold the business, Michael would forget her, and Alex and Carole, even though they would gossip about her at Oh Kaye's every Friday night for the rest of their lives, wouldn't summon the energy to search.

She could almost hear them now: *She met some guy*, Carole would say. *And he killed her*, Alex would add, and then they would argue until last call, unless Carole found some man to entertain her, and Alex someone else to complain to. They would miss Grace only when they screwed up, when they needed a shoulder, when they couldn't stand being on their own. And even then, they probably wouldn't realize what it was they had lost.

Because it amused her, she had driven north to Boise, land of the white collar, to make her cell phone call to Michael. Her offer to him was simple: cash her out of the business and call it his own. She named a price, he dickered half-heartedly, she refused to negotiate. Within two days, he had wired the money to a blind money market account that she had often stored cash in for the firm.

She let the money sit there while she decided what to do with it. Then she went to Reno to change her name.

Reno had been a surprise. A beautiful city set between mountains like none she had ever seen. The air was dry, the downtown tacky, the people friendly. There were bookstores and slot machines and good restaurants. There were cheap houses and all-night casinos and lots of strange places. There was even history, of the Wild West kind.

For the first time in her life, Grace fell in love.

And to celebrate the occasion, she snuck into a quickie wedding chapel, found the marriage licenses, took one, copied down the name of the chapel, its permit number, and all the other pertinent information, and then returned to her car. There she checked the boxes, saying she had seen the driver's licenses and birth certificates of the people involved, including a fictitious man named Nathan Reinhart, and *viola!* she was married. She had a new name, a document the credit card companies would accept, and a new beginning all at the same time.

Using some of her personal savings, she bought a house with lots of windows and a view of the Sierras. In the mornings, light bathed her kitchen, and in the evenings, it caressed her living room. She had never seen light like this—clean and pure and crisp. She was beginning to understand why artists moved west to paint, why people used to exclaim about the way light changed everything.

The lack of humidity, of dense air pollution, made the air clearer. The elevation brought her closer to the sun.

She felt as if she were seeing everything for the very first time.

And hearing it, too. The house was silent, much more silent than an apartment, and the silence soothed her. She could listen to her television without worrying about the people in the apartment below, or play her stereo full blast without concern about a visit from the super.

There was a freedom to having her own space that she hadn't realized before, a freedom to living the way she wanted to live, without the rules of the past or the expectations she had grown up with.

And among those expectations was the idea that she had to be the strong one, the good one, the one on whose shoulder everyone else cried. She had no friends here, no one who needed her shoulder, and she had no one who expected her to be good.

Only herself.

Of course, in some things she was good. Habits of a lifetime died hard. She began researching the best way to invest Michael's lump-sum payment—and while she researched, she left the money alone. She kept her house clean and her lawn, such as it was in this high desert, immaculate. She bought a new car and made sure it was spotless.

No one would find fault with her appearances, inside or out.

Not that she had anyone who was looking. She didn't have a

boyfriend or a job or a hobby. She didn't have anything except herself.

She found herself drawn to the casinos, with their clinking slot machines, musical come-ons, and bright lights. No matter how high tech the places had become, no matter how clean, how "family-oriented," they still had a shady feel.

Or perhaps that was her upbringing, in a state where gambling had been illegal until she was twenty-five, a state where her father used to play a friendly game of poker—even with his friends—with the curtains drawn.

Sin—no matter how sanitized—still had appeal in the brand-new century.

Still, she was too sensible to gamble away her savings. The slots lost their appeal quickly, and when she sat down at the blackjack tables, she couldn't get past the feeling that she was frittering her money away for nothing.

But she liked the way the cards fell and how people concentrated—as if their very lives depended on this place—and she was good with numbers. One of the pit bosses mentioned that they were always short of poker dealers, so she took a class offered by one of the casinos. Within two months, she was snapping cards, raking pots, and wearing a uniform that made her feel like Carole on a bad night.

It only took a few weeks for her bosses to realize that Grace was a natural poker dealer. They gave her the busy shifts—Thursday through Sunday nights—and she spent her evenings playing the game of cowboys, fancy men, and whores. Finally, there was a bit of an Old West feel to her life, a bit of excitement, a sense of purpose.

When she got off at midnight, she would be too keyed up to go home. She started bringing a change of clothes to work and, after her shift, she would go to the casino next door. It had a great bar upstairs—filled with brass, Victorian furnishings, and a real hardwood floor. She could get a sandwich and a beer. Finally, she felt like she was becoming the woman she wanted to be.

One night, a year after she had run away from home, a man sidled up next to her. He had long blond hair that curled against his shoulders. His face was tanned and lined, a bit too thin. He looked road-hardened—like a man who'd been outside too much, seen too much, worked in the sun too much. His hands were long, slender, and callused. He wore no rings, and his shirt cuffs were frayed at the edges.

He sat beside her in companionable silence for nearly an hour, while they both stared at CNN on the big screen over the bar, and then he said, "Just once I'd like to go someplace authentic."

His voice was cigarette growly, even though he didn't smoke, and he had a Southern accent that was soft as butter. She guessed Louisiana, but it might have been Tennessee or even Northern Florida. She wasn't good at distinguishing Southern accents yet. She figured she would after another year or so of dealing cards.

"You should go up to Virginia City. There's a bar or two that looks real enough."

He snorted through his nose. "Tourist trap."

She shrugged. She'd thought it interesting—an entire historic city, preserved just like it had been when Mark Twain lived there. "Seems to me if you weren't a tourist there wouldn't be any other reason to go."

He shrugged and picked up a toothpick, rolling it in his fingers. She smiled to herself. A former smoker then, and a fidgeter.

"Reno's better than Vegas, at least," he said. "Casinos aren't family friendly yet."

"Except Circus Circus."

"Always been that way. But the rest. You get a sense that maybe it ain't all legal here."

She looked at him sideways. He was at least her age, his blue eyes sharp in his leathery face. "You like things that aren't legal?"

"Gambling's not something that should be made pretty, you know? It's about money, and money can either make you or destroy you."

She felt herself smile, remembering what it was like to paw through receipts and tax returns, to make neat rows of figures about other people's money. "What's the saying?" she asked. "Money is like sex—"

"It doesn't matter unless you don't have any." To her surprise, he laughed. The sound was rich and warm, not at all like she had expected. The smile transformed his face into something almost handsome.

He tapped the toothpick on the polished bar, and asked, "You think that's true?"

She shrugged. "I suppose. Everyone's idea of what's enough differs, though."

"What's yours?" He turned toward her, smile gone now, eyes even sharper than they had been a moment ago. She suddenly felt as if she were on trial.

"My idea of what's enough?" she asked.

He nodded.

"I suppose enough that I can live off the interest in the manner in which I've become accustomed. What's yours?"

A shadow crossed his eyes and he looked away from her. "Long as I've got a roof over my head, clothes on my back, and food in my mouth, I figure I'm rich enough."

"Sounds distinctly un-American to me," she said.

He looked at her sideways again. "I guess it does, don't it? Women figure a man should have some sort of ambition."

"Do you?"

"Have ambition?" He bent the toothpick between his index and middle fingers. "Of course I do. It just ain't tied in with money, is all."

"I thought money and ambition went together."

"In most men's minds."

"But not yours?"

The toothpick broke. "Not anymore," he said.

Three nights later, he sat down at her table. He was wearing a denim shirt with silver snaps and jeans so faded that they looked as if they might shred around him. That, his hair, and his lean look reminded Grace of a movie gunslinger, the kind that cleaned a town up because it had to be done.

"Guess you don't make enough to live off the interest," he said to her as he sat down.

She raised her eyebrows. "Maybe I like people."

"Maybe you like games."

She smiled and dealt the cards. The table was full. She was dealing 3-6 Texas Hold 'Em and most of the players were locals. It was Monday night and they all looked pleased to have an unfamiliar face at the table.

If she had known him better she might have tipped him off. Instead she wanted to see how long his money would last.

He bought in for $100, although she had seen at least five hundred in his wallet. He took the chips, and studied them for a moment.

He had three tells. He fidgeted with his chips when his cards were mediocre and he was thinking of bluffing. He bit his lower lip when he had nothing, and his eyes went dead flat when he had a winning hand.

He lost the first hundred in forty-five minutes, bought back in for another hundred and managed to hold onto it until her shift ended shortly after midnight. He sat through dealer changes and the floating fortunes of his cards. When she returned from her last break, she found herself wondering if his tells were subconscious after all. They seemed deliberately calculated to let the professional poker players around him think that he was a rookie.

She said nothing. She couldn't, really—at least not overtly. The casino got a rake and they didn't allow her to do anything except deal the game. She had no stake in it anyway. She hadn't lied to him that first night. She loved watching people, the way they played their hands, the way the money flowed.

It was like being an accountant, only in real time. She got to see the furrowed brows as the decisions were made, hear the curses as someone pushed back a chair and tossed in that last hand of cards, watch the desperation that often led to the exact wrong play. Only as a poker dealer, she wasn't required to clean up the mess. She didn't have to offer advice or refuse it; she didn't have to worry about tax consequences, about sitting across from someone else's auditor, justifying choices she had no part in making.

When she got off, she changed into her tightest jeans and a summer sweater and went to her favorite bar.

Casino bars were always busy after midnight, even on a Monday. The crowd wasn't there to have a good time but to wind down from one—or to prepare itself for another. She sat at the bar, as she had since she started this routine, and was about to leave when he sat next to her.

"Lose your stake?" she asked.

"I'm up $400."

She looked at him sideways. He didn't seem pleased with the way the night had gone—not the way a casual player would have been. Her gut instinct was right. He was someone who was used to gambling—and winning.

"Buy you another?" he asked.

She shook her head. "One's enough."

He smiled. It made him look less fierce and gave him a rugged sort of appeal. "Everything in moderation?"

"Not always," she said. "At least, not anymore."

Somehow they ended up in bed—her bed—and he was better than she imagined his kind of man could be. He had knowledgeable fingers and endless patience. He didn't seem to mind the scar on her breast. Instead he lingered over it, focussing on it as if it were an erogenous zone. His pleasure at the result enhanced hers and when she finally fell asleep, somewhere around dawn, she was more sated than she had ever been.

She awoke to the smell of frying bacon and fresh coffee. Her eyes were filled with sand, but her body had a healthy lethargy. *At least,* she thought, *he hadn't left before she awoke.*

At least he hadn't stolen everything in sight.

She still didn't know his name, and wasn't sure she cared. She slipped on a robe and combed her hair with her fingers and walked into her kitchen—the kitchen no one had cooked in but her.

He had on his denims and his hair was tied back with a leather thong. He had found not only her cast-iron skillet but also the grease cover that she always used when making bacon. A bowl of scrambled eggs steamed on the counter, and a plate of heavily buttered toast sat beside it.

"Sit down, darlin'," he said. "Let me bring it all to you."

She flushed. That was what it felt like he had done the night before, but she said nothing. Her juice glasses were out, and so was her everyday ware, and yet somehow the table looked like it had been set for a *Gourmet* photo spread.

"I certainly didn't expect this," she said.

"It's the least I can do." He put the eggs and toast on the table, then poured her a cup of coffee. Cream and sugar were already out, and in their special containers.

She was slightly uncomfortable that he had figured out her kitchen that quickly and well.

He put the bacon on a paper-towel-covered plate, then set that on the table. She hadn't moved, so he beckoned with his hand.

"Go ahead," he said. "It's getting cold."

He sat across from her and helped himself to bacon while she served herself eggs. They were fluffy and light, just like they would have been in a restaurant. She had no idea how he got that consistency. Her home-scrambled eggs were always runny and undercooked.

The morning light bathed the table, giving everything a bright glow. His hair seemed even blonder in the sunlight and his skin darker. He had laugh lines around his mouth, and a bit of blond stubble on his chin.

She watched him eat, those nimble fingers scooping up the remaining egg with a slice of toast, and found herself remembering how those fingers had felt on her skin.

Then she felt his gaze on her, and looked up. His eyes were dead flat for just an instant, and she felt herself grow cold.

"Awful nice house," he said slowly, "for a woman who makes a living dealing cards."

Her first reaction was defense—she wanted to tell him she had other income, and what did he care about a woman who dealt cards, anyway? – but instead, she smiled. "Thank you."

He measured her, as if he expected a different response, then he said, "You're awfully calm considering that you don't even know my name. You don't strike me as the kind of woman who does this often."

His words startled her, but she made sure that the surprise didn't show. She had learned a lot about her own tells while dealing poker, and the experience was coming in handy now.

"You flatter yourself," she said softly.

"Well," he said, reaching into his back pocket, "if there's one thing my job's taught me, it's that people hide information they don't want anyone else to know."

He pulled out his wallet, opened it, and with two fingers removed a business card. He dropped it on the table.

She didn't want to pick up the card. She knew things had already changed between them in a way she didn't entirely understand, but she had a sense from the fleeting expression she had seen on his face that once she picked up the card she could never go back.

She set down her coffee cup and used two fingers to slide the card toward her. It identified him as Travis Delamore, a skip tracer and bail bondsman. Below his name was a phone number with a 414 exchange.

Milwaukee, Wisconsin, and the surrounding areas. Precisely the place someone from Racine might call if they wanted to hire a professional.

She slipped the card into the pocket of her robe. "Is sleeping around part of your job?"

"Is embezzling part of yours?" All the warmth had left his face. His expression was unreadable except for the flatness in his eyes. What did he think he knew?

She made herself smile. "Mr. Delamore, if I stole a dime from the casino, I'd be instantly fired. There are cameras everywhere."

"I mean your former job, Ms. Mackie. A lot of money is missing from your office."

"I don't have an office." His use of her former name made her hands clammy. What had Michael done?

"Do you deny that you're Grace Mackie?"

"I don't acknowledge or deny anything. When did this become an inquisition, Mr. Delamore? I thought men liked their sex uncomplicated. You seem to be a unique member of your species."

This time he smiled. "Of course we like our sex uncomplicated. That's why we're having this discussion this morning."

"If we'd had it last night, there wouldn't be a this morning."

"That's my point." He downed the last of his orange juice. "And thank you for the acknowledgement, Ms. Mackie."

"It wasn't an acknowledgement," she said. "I don't like to sleep with men who think me guilty of something."

"Embezzlement," he said gently, using the same tone he had used in bed. This time, it made her bristle.

"I haven't stolen anything."

"New house, new name, new town, mysterious disappearance."

The chill she had felt earlier grew. She stood and wrapped her robe tightly around her waist. "I don't know what you think you know, Mr. Delamore, but I believe it's time for you to leave."

He didn't move. "We're not done."

"Oh, yes, we are."

"It would be a lot easier if you told me where the money was, Grace."

"Do you always get paid for sex, Mr. Delamore?" she asked.

He studied her for a moment. "Don't play games with me, honey."

"Why not?" she asked. "You seem to enjoy them."

He shoved his plate away as if it had offended him. Apparently this morning wasn't going the way he wanted it to either. "I'm just telling you what I know."

"And I'm just asking you to leave. It was fun, Travis. But it certainly wasn't worth this."

He stood and slipped his wallet back into his pocket. "You'll hear from me again."

"This isn't high school," she said, following him to the door. "I won't be offended if you fail to call."

"No," he said as he stepped into the dry desert air. "You probably won't be offended. But you will be curious. This is just the beginning, Grace."

"One person's beginning is another person's ending," she said, as she closed and locked the door behind him.

The worst thing she could do, she knew, was panic. So she made herself clean the kitchen as if she didn't have a care in the world, and she left the curtains open so that he could see if he wanted to. Then she went to the shower, making it long and hot. She tried to scrub all the traces of him off her.

For the first time in her life, she felt cheap.

Embezzlement. Something had happened, something Michael was blaming on her. It would be easy enough, she supposed. She had disappeared. That looked suspicious enough. The new name, the new car, the new town, all of that added to the suspicion.

What had Michael done? And why?

She got out of the shower and toweled herself off. She was tempted to call Michael, but she certainly couldn't do it from the house. If she used her cell, the call would be traceable too. And if she went to a pay phone, she would attract even more suspicion. She had to consider that Travis Delamore was following her, spying on her.

In fact, she had to consider that he had been doing that for some time.

She went over all of their conversation, looking for clues, mistakes she might have made. She had told him very little, but he had asked a lot. Strangely—or perhaps not so strangely anymore—all of their conversations had been about money.

Carole would have been proud of her. Grace had finally let her libido get the better of her. Alex would have been disgusted, reminding her that men couldn't be trusted.

What could he do to her besides cast suspicion? He was right. Without the money, he had nothing. And she had a job, no criminal record, and no suspicious investments.

But if he continued to follow her, she could go after him. The bartender had seen them leave her favorite bar together. She had an innocent face, she'd been living here for a year, got promoted, was well-liked by her employer. Delamore had obviously flirted with her while he played poker the night before, and the casino had cameras.

They probably had records of all the times he had watched her before she noticed him.

It wouldn't take much to make a stalking charge. That would get her an injunction in the least, and it might scare him off.

Then she could find out why he was so sure he had something on her. Then she could find out what it was Michael had done.

The newly remodeled ladies room on the third floor of the casino had twenty stalls and a lounge complete with smoking room. It had once been a small restroom, but the reconstruction had taken out the nearby men's room and replaced it with more stalls. The row of pay phones in the middle stayed, as a convenience to the customers.

Delamore wouldn't know that she called from those pay phones. No one would know.

She started using the third floor ladies room on her break and more than once had picked up the receiver on the third phone and dialed most of her old office number. She'd always stop before she hit the last digit, though. Her intuition told her that calling Michael would be wrong.

What if Delamore had a trace on Michael's line? What if the police did?

A week after her encounter with Delamore, a week in which she used the third floor ladies room more times than she could count, she suddenly realized what was wrong. Delamore didn't have anything on her except suspicion. He had clearly found her—that hadn't been hard, since she really hadn't been hiding from anyone —and he had probably checked her bank records for the money he assumed she had embezzled from her former clients. But the money she had gotten from the sale of the business was still in that hidden numbered account—and would stay there.

Her native caution had served her well once again.

She had nothing to hide. It didn't matter what some good-looking skip trace thought. Her life in Racine was in the past. A part of her past that she couldn't avoid, any more than she could avoid the scar on her breast—the scar that Delamore had clearly used to identify her, the bastard. But past was past, and until it hurt her present, she wasn't going to worry about it.

So she stopped making pilgrimages to the third floor women's room, and gradually, her worries over Delamore faded. She didn't see him for a week, and she assumed—wrongly—that it was all over.

He sat next to her at the bar as if he had been doing it every day for years. He ordered a whiskey neat, and another "for the lady," just like men in her fantasies used to do. When he looked at her and smiled, she realized that the look didn't reach his eyes.

Maybe it never had.

"Miss me, darlin'?" he asked.

She picked up her purse, took out a five to cover her drink, and started to leave. He grabbed her wrist. His fingers were warm and dry, their touch no longer gentle. A shiver started in her back, but she willed the feeling away.

"Let go of me," she said.

"Now, Gracie, I think you should listen to what I have to say."

"Let go of me," she said in that same measured tone, "or I will scream so loud that everyone in the place will hear."

"Screams don't frighten me, doll."

"Maybe the police do. Believe me, *hon*, I will press charges."

His smile was slow and wide, but that flat look was in his eyes again, the one that told her he had all the cards. "I'm sure they'll be impressed," he said, reaching into his breast pocket with his free hand. "But I do believe a warrant trumps a tight grip on the arm."

He set a piece of paper down on the bar itself. The bartender, wiping away the remains of another customer's mess, glanced her way as if he were keeping an eye on her.

She didn't touch the paper, but she didn't shake Delamore's hand off her arm, either. She wasn't quite sure what to do.

He picked up the paper, shook it open, and she saw the strange bold-faced print of a legal document, her former name in the middle. "Tell you what, Gracie. How about we finish the talk we started the other morning in one of those dark, quiet booths over there?"

She was still staring at the paper, trying to comprehend it. It looked official enough. But then, she'd never seen a warrant for anyone's arrest before. She had only heard of them.

She had never imagined she'd see her own name on one.

She let Delamore lead her to a booth at the far end of the bar. He slid across the plastic, trying to pull her in beside him, but this time, she shook him off. She sat across from him, perched on the seat with her feet in the aisle, purse clutched on her lap. Flee position, Alex used to call it. You Might Be a Loser and I Reserve the Right to Find Someone Else, was Carole's name for it.

"If I bring you back to Wisconsin," he said, "I get a few thousand bucks. What it don't say on my card is that I'm a bounty hunter."

"What an exciting life you must lead," Grace said dryly.

He smiled. The look chilled her. She was beginning to wonder how she had ever found him attractive. "It's got its perks."

It was at that moment she decided she hated him. He would forever refer to her as a perk of the job, not as someone who had given herself to him freely, someone who had enjoyed the moment as much as he had.

All that gentleness in his fingers, all those murmured endearments. Lies.

She hated lies.

"But," he was saying, "I see a way to make a little more money here. I don't think you're a real threat to society. And you're a lot of fun, more fun than I would've expected, given how you lived before you moved here."

The bartender came over, his bar towel over his arm. "Want anything?"

He was speaking to her. He hadn't even looked at Delamore. The bartender was making sure she was all right.

"I don't know yet," she said. "Can you check back in five minutes?"

"Sure thing." This time he did look at Delamore, who grinned at him. The bartender shot him a warning glare.

"Wow," Delamore said as the bartender moved out of earshot. "You have a defender."

"You keep getting off track," Grace said.

Delamore shrugged. "I like talking to you."

"Well, I find talking with you rather dull."

He raised his eyebrows. "You didn't think so a few days ago."

"As I recall," she said, "we didn't do a lot talking."

His smile softened. "That's my memory too."

She clutched her purse tighter. It always looked so glamorous in the movies, finding the right person, having a night of great sex. And even if he rode off into the sunset never to be seen again, everything still had a glow of perfection to it.

Not the bits of sleaze, the hardness in his expression, the sense that what he wanted from her was something she couldn't give.

"You know, the papers said that Michael Holden went into your old office, and put a gun in his mouth and pulled the trigger. Then the police, after finding the body, discovered that most of the money your clients had entrusted to your firm had disappeared."

She couldn't suppress the small whimper of shock that rose in her throat.

Delamore noted it and his eyes brightened. "Now, you tell me what happened."

She had no idea. She had none at all. But she couldn't tell Delamore that. She didn't even know if the story was true.

It sounded true. But Delamore had lied before. For all she knew he was some kind of con man, out to get her because he smelled money.

He was watching her, his eyes glittering. She could barely control her expression. She needed to get away.

She stood, still clutching her purse like a school girl.

"Planning to leave? I wouldn't do that if I were you." His voice had turned cold. A shiver ran down her spine, but she didn't move, just stared down at him unable to turn away.

"One call," he said softly, "and you'll get picked up by the Nevada police. You should sit down and hear what I have to say."

Her hands were shaking. She sat, feeling trapped. He had finally hooked her, even though she hadn't said a word.

He leaned forward. "Now listen to me, darling. I know you got the money. I been working this one a long time, and I dug up the records. Michael closed all those accounts right after you disappeared. That's not a coincidence."

Her mouth was dry. She wanted to swallow, but couldn't.

" 'Member our talk about money? One of those first nights, here in this bar?"

She was staring at him, her eyes wide and dry as if she'd been driving and staring at the road for hours. It felt like she had forgotten to blink.

"I told you I don't need much, and that's true. But I'm getting tired of dragging people back to their parole officers or for their court dates, or finding husbands who'd skipped out on their families, and then getting paid five grand or two grand. Then people question your expenses, like you don't got a right to spend a night in a motel or eat three squares. Or they demand to know why you took so danged long to find someone who'd been hiding so good no cop could find them."

His voice was so soft she had to strain to hear it. In spite of herself, she leaned forward.

"I'm forty-five years old, doll," he said. "And I'm getting tired. You got one pretty little scar. Did you notice all the ones I got? On the job. Yours is the first case in a while where I didn't get a beating." Then he grinned. "At least, not a painful one."

She flushed, and her fingers tightened on the purse. Her hands were beginning to hurt. Part of her, a part she'd never heard from before, wanted to take that purse and club him in the face. But she didn't move. If she moved, she would lose any control she had.

"So," he said, "here's the deal. I like you. I didn't expect to, but I do. You're a pretty little thing, and smart as a whip, and this is probably going to be the only crime you'll ever commit, because you're one of those girls who just knows better, aren't you?"

She held her head rigidly, careful so that he wouldn't take the subtlest movement for a nod.

"And I think you got a damn fine deal here. The house is nice—lots of light—and the town obviously suits you. I met those friends of yours, the ball-buster and the one who thinks she's God's Gift to Men, and I gotta say it's clear why you left."

Her nails dug into the leather. Pain shot through the tender skin at the top of her fingers.

"I really don't wanna ruin your life. It's time I make a change in mine. You give me fifty grand, and I'll bury everything I found about you."

"Fifty thousand dollars?" Her voice was raspy with tension. "For the first payment?"

His eyes sparkled. "One-time deal."

She snorted. She knew better. Blackmailers never worked like that.

"And maybe I'll stick around. Get to know you a little better. I could fall in love with that house myself."

"Could you?" she asked, amazed at the dry tone she'd managed to maintain.

"Sure." He grinned. That had been the look that had made her go weak less than a week ago. Now it sent a chill through her. "You and me, we had something."

"Yeah," she said. "A one-night stand."

He laughed. "It could be more than that, darlin'. It took you long enough, but you might've just found Mr. Right."

"Seems to me you were the one who was searching." She stood. He didn't protest, and she was glad. She had to leave. If she stayed any longer, she'd say something she would regret.

She tucked her purse under her arm. "I assume the drink's on you," she said, and then she walked away.

He didn't follow her—at least not right away. And she drove in circles before going home, watching for his car behind hers, thinking about everything he had said. Thinking about her break, her freedom, the things she had done to create a new life.

The things that now made her look guilty of a crime she hadn't committed.

She didn't sleep, of course. She couldn't. Her mind was too full—and her bed was no longer a private place. He'd been there, and some of him remained, a shadow, a laugh. After an hour of tossing and turning, she moved to the guest room and sat on the edge of the brand new unused mattress, clutching a blanket and thinking.

It was time to find out what had happened. Delamore knew who she was. She couldn't pretend anymore. But he wasn't ready to turn her in. That gave her a little time.

She took a shower, made herself a pot of coffee, and a sandwich that she ate slowly. Then she went to her upstairs office, sat down in front of her computer and hesitated. The moment she logged on was the moment that all her movements could be traced. The moment she couldn't turn back from.

But she could testify to the conversation she'd had with Delamore, and the bartender would back her up. She wouldn't be able to hide her own identity should the police come for her, and so there was no reason to lie. She would simply say that she was concerned about her former business partner. She wanted to know if any of what Delamore told her was true.

It wouldn't seem like a confession to anyone but him.

She logged on, and used a search engine to find the news.

It didn't take her long. Amazing how many newspapers were online. Michael's death created quite a scandal in Racine, and the pictures of her office—the bloody mess still visible inside—were enough to make the ham on rye that she'd had a few moments ago turn in her stomach.

Michael. He'd been a good accountant. Thorough, exacting. Nervous. Always so nervous, afraid of making any kind of mistake.

Embezzlement? Why would he do that?

But that was what the papers had said. She dug farther, found the follow-up pieces. He'd raised cash, using clients' accounts, to bilk the company of a small fortune.

And Delamore was right. The dates matched up. Michael had stolen from her own clients to pay her for her own business. He had bought the business with stolen money.

She bowed her head, listening to the computer hum, counting her own breaths. She had never once questioned where he had gotten the money. She had figured he'd gotten a loan, had thought that maybe he'd finally learned the value of savings.

Michael. The man who took an advance on his paycheck once every six months. Michael, who had once told her he was too scared to invest on his own.

I wouldn't trust my own judgement, he had said.

Oh, the poor man. He had been right.

The trail did lead to her. The only reason Delamore couldn't point at her exactly was because she had stashed the cash in a blind account. And she hadn't touched it.

Not yet.

She'd been living entirely off her own savings, letting the money from the sale of her business draw interest. The nest egg for the future she hadn't planned yet.

Delamore wanted fifty thousand dollars from her. To give that to him, she'd have to tap the nest egg.

How many times would he make her tap it again? And again? Until it was gone, of course. Into his pocket. And then he'd turn her in.

She wiped her hand on her jeans. It was a nervous movement, meant to calm herself down. She had to think.

If the cops could trace her, they would have. They either didn't have enough on her or hadn't made the leap that Delamore had. And then she had confirmed his leap with the conversation tonight.

She got up and walked away from the computer. She wouldn't let him intrude. He had already taken over her bedroom. She needed to have a space here, in her office, without him.

There was no mention of her in the papers, nothing that suggested she was involved. The police would have contacted the Reno police if they had known where she was. Even if they had hired Delamore to track her, they might still not have been informed of her whereabouts. Delamore wanted money more than he wanted to inform the authorities about where she was.

Grace sat down in the chair near the window. The shade was drawn, but the spot was soothing nonetheless.

The police weren't her problem. Delamore was.

She already knew that he wouldn't be satisfied with one payment. She had to find a way to get rid of him.

She bowed her head. Even though she had done nothing criminal she was thinking like one. How did a woman get rid of a man she didn't want? She could get a court order, she supposed, forcing him to stay away from her. She could refuse to pay him and let the cards fall where they might. Years of legal hassle, maybe even an arrest. She would certainly lose her job. No casino would hire her, and she couldn't fall back on her CPA skills, not after being arrested for embezzlement.

Ignoring him wasn't an option either.

Then, there was the act of desperation. She could kill him. Somehow. She had always thought that murderers weren't methodical enough. Take an intelligent person, have her kill someone in a thoughtful way, and she would be able to get away with the crime.

Everywhere but in her own mind. No matter how hard she tried, no matter how much he threatened her, she couldn't kill Delamore.

There had to be another option. She had to do something. She just wasn't sure what it was.

She went back to the computer and looked at the last article she had downloaded. Michael had stolen from people she had known for years. People who had trusted her, believed in her and her word. People who had thought she had integrity.

She frowned. What must they think of her now? That she was an embezzler too? After all those years of work, did she want that behind her name?

Then again, why should she care about people she would never see again?

But she would see them every time she closed her eyes. Elderly Mrs. Vezzetti and her poodle, trusting Grace to handle her account because her husband, God rest his soul, had convinced her that numbers were too much for her pretty little head. Mr. Heitzkey who couldn't balance a checkbook if his life depended on it. Ms. Andersen, who had taken Grace's advice on ways to legally hide money from the IRS—and who had seemed so excited when it worked.

Grace sighed.

There was only one way to make this right. Only one way to clear her conscience and to clear Delamore out of her life.

She had to turn herself in.

She did some more surfing as she ate breakfast and found discount tickets to Chicago. She had to buy them roundtrip from Chicago to Reno (God bless the casinos for their cheap airfare deals) and fly only the Reno to Chicago leg. Later she would buy another set, and not use part of it. Both of those tickets were cheaper than buying a single roundtrip ticket out of Reno to Racine.

Grace made the reservation, hoping that Delamore wasn't tracking roundtrips that started somewhere else, and then she went to work. She claimed a family emergency, got a leave of absence, and hoped it would be enough.

She liked the world she built here. She didn't want to lose it because she hadn't been watching her back.

Twenty-four hours later, she and the car she rented in O'Hare were in Racine. The town hadn't changed. More churches than she saw out west, a few timid billboards for Native American casinos, a factory outlet mall, and bars everywhere. The streets were grimy with the last of the sand laid down during the winter snow and ice. The trees were just beginning to bud, and the flowers were poking through the rich black dirt.

It felt as if she had gone back in time.

She wondered if she should call Alex and Carole, and then decided against it. What would she say to them, anyway? Instead, she checked into a hotel, unpacked, ate a mediocre room-service meal, and slept as if she were dead.

Maybe in this city, she was.

The district attorney's office was smaller than Grace's bathroom. There were four chairs, not enough for her, her lawyer, the three assistant district attorneys, and the DA himself. She and her lawyer were allowed to sit, but the assistant DAs hovered around the bookshelves and desk like children who were waiting for their father to finish business. The DA sat behind a massive oak desk that dwarfed the tiny room.

Grace's lawyer, Maxine Jones, was from Milwaukee. Grace had done her research before she arrived and found the best defense attorney in Wisconsin. Grace knew that Maxine's services would cost her a lot—but Grace was gambling that she wouldn't need Maxine for more than a few days.

Maxine was a tall, robust woman who favored bright colors. In contrast she wore debutante jewelry—a simple gold chain, tiny diamond earrings—that accented her toffee-colored skin. The entire look made her seem both flamboyant and powerful, combinations that Grace was certain helped Maxine in court.

"My client," Maxine was saying, "came here on her own. You'll have to remember that, Mr. Lindstrom."

Harold Lindstrom, the district attorney, was in his fifties, with thinning gray hair and a runner's thinness. His gaze held no compassion as it fell on Grace.

"Only because a bounty hunter hired by the police department found her," Lindstrom said.

"Yes," Maxine said. "We'll concede that the bounty hunter was the one who informed her of the charges. But that's all. This man hounded her, harassed her, and tried to extort money out of her, money she did not have."

"Then she should have gone to the Reno police," Lindstrom said.

An assistant DA crossed her arms as if this discussion was making her uncomfortable. It was making Grace uncomfortable. Never before had she been discussed as if she weren't there.

"It was easier to come here," Maxine said. "My client has a hunch, which if it's true, will negate the charges you have against her and against Michael Holden."

"Mr. Holden embezzled from his clients with the assistance of Ms. Reinhart."

"No. Mr. Holden followed standard procedure for the accounting firm."

"Embezzlement is standard procedure?" Lindstrom was looking directly at Grace.

Maxine put her manicured hand on Grace's knee, a reminder to remain quiet.

"No. But Mr. Holden, for reasons we don't know, decided to end his life, and since he now worked alone, no one knew where he was keeping the clients' funds. My client," Maxine added, as if she expected Grace to speak, "would like you to drop all charges against her and to charge Mr. Delamore with extortion. In exchange, she will testify against him, and she will also show you where the money is."

"Where she hid it, huh?" Lindstrom said. "No deal."

Maxine leaned forward. "You don't have a crime here. If you don't bargain with us, I'll go straight to the press, and you'll look like a fool. It seems to me that there's an election coming up."

Lindstrom's eyes narrowed. Grace held her breath. Maxine stared at him as if they were all playing a game of chicken. Maybe they were.

"Here's the deal," he said, "if her information checks out, then we'll drop the charges. We can't file against Delamore because the alleged crimes were committed in Nevada."

Maxine's hand left Grace's knee. Maxine templed her fingers and rested their painted tips against her chin. "Then, Harold, we'll simply have to file a suit against the city and the county for siccing him on my client. A multimillion-dollar suit. We'll win, too. Because she came forward the moment she learned of a problem. She hasn't been in touch with anyone from here. Her family is dead, and her friends were never close. She had no way of knowing what was happening a thousand miles away until a man you people sent started harassing her."

"You said he's been harassing you for a month," Lindstrom said to Grace. "Why didn't you come forward before now?"

Grace looked at Maxine who nodded.

"Because," Grace said, "he didn't show me any proof of his claims until the night before I flew out. You can ask the bartender at the Silver Dollar. He saw the entire thing."

Lindstrom frowned at Maxine. "We want names and dates."

"You'll get them," Maxine said.

Lindstrom sighed. "All right. Let's hear it."

Grace's heart was pounding. Here was her moment. She suddenly found herself hoping they would all believe her. She had never lied with so much at stake before.

"Go ahead, Grace," Maxine said softly.

Grace nodded. "We had run into some trouble with our escrow service. Minor stuff, mostly rudeness on the part of the company. It was all irritating Michael. Many things were irritating him at that time, but we weren't close, so I didn't attribute it to anything except work."

The entire room had become quiet. She felt slightly lightheaded. She was forgetting to breathe. She forced herself to take a deep breath before continuing.

"In the week that I was leaving, Michael asked me how he could go about transferring everything from one escrow company to another. It required a lot of paperwork, and he didn't trust the company we were with. I thought he should have let them and the new company handle it, but he didn't want to."

She squeezed her hands together, reminded herself not to embellish too much. A simple lie was always best.

"We had accounts we had initially set up for clients in discreet banks. I told Michael to go to one of those banks, place the money in accounts there, and then when the new escrow accounts were established, to transfer the money to them. I warned him not to take longer than a day in the intermediate account."

"We have no record of such an account," the third district attorney said.

Grace nodded. "That's what I figured when I heard that he was being charged with embezzlement. I can give you the names of all the banks and the numbers of the accounts we were assigned. If the money's in one of them, then my name is clear."

"Depending on when the deposit was made," Lindstrom said. "And if the money's all there."

Grace's lightheadedness was growing. She hadn't realized how much effort bluffing took. But she did know she was covered on those details at least.

"You may go through my client's financial records," Maxine said. "All of her money is accounted for."

"Why wouldn't he have transferred the money to the new escrow accounts quickly, like you told him to?" Lindstrom asked.

"I don't know," Grace said.

"Depression is a confusing thing, Harold," Maxine said. "If he's like other people who've gotten very depressed, I'm sure things slipped. I'm sure this wasn't the only thing he failed to do. And you can bet I'd argue that in court."

"Why did you leave Racine so suddenly?" Lindstrom asked. "Your friends say you just vanished one night."

Grace let out a small breath. On this one she could be completely honest. "I had a scare. I thought I had breast cancer. The lumpectomy results came in the day I left. You can check with my doctor. I was planning to go after that—maybe a month or more—but I felt so free, that I just couldn't go back to my work. Something like that changes you, Mr. Lindstrom."

He grunted as if he didn't believe her. For the first time in the entire discussion, she felt herself get angry. She clenched her fingers so hard that her nails dug into her palms. She wouldn't say any more, just like Maxine had told her to.

"The banks?" Lindstrom asked.

Grace slipped a small leather-bound ledger toward him. She had spent a lot of time drawing that up by hand in different pens. She hoped it would be enough.

"The accounts are identified by numbers only. That's one of the reasons we liked the banks. If he started a new account, I won't know its number."

"If they're in the U.S., then we can get a court order to open them," Lindstrom said.

"Check these numbers first. Most of the accounts were inactive." She had to clutch her fingers together to keep them from trembling.

"All right," Lindstrom said and stood. Maxine and Grace stood as well. "If we discover that you're wrong—about anything—we'll arrest you, Ms. Reinhart. Do you understand?"

Grace nodded.

Maxine smiled. "We're sure you'll see it our way, Harold. But remember your promise. Get that creep away from Grace."

"Right now, your client's the one we're concerned with, Maxine." Lindstrom's cold gaze met Grace's. "I'm sure we'll be in touch."

Grace thought the eight o'clock knock on her hotel room door was room service. She'd ordered another meal from them, unable to face old haunts and old friends. Until she had come back, she had never even been in a hotel in Racine, so she felt as if she wasn't anywhere near her old home. Now if she could only get the different local channels on the television set, her own delusion would be complete.

She undid the locks, opened the door, and stepped away so that the waiter could wheel his cart inside.

Instead, Delamore pushed open the door farther. She was so surprised to see him that she didn't try to close him out. She scuttled away from him toward the nightstand, and fumbled behind her back for the phone.

His cheeks were red, and his eyes sparkling with fury. His anger was so palpable, she could feel it across the room.

"What kind of game are you playing?" he snapped, slamming the door closed.

She got the phone off the hook without turning around. "No game."

"It is a game. You got away from me, and then you come here, telling them that I've been threatening you."

"You have been threatening me." Her fingers found the bottom button on the phone—which she hoped was "O." If the hotel operator heard this, she'd have to call security.

"Of course I'd been threatening you! It's my job. You didn't want to come back here and I needed to drag you back. Any criminal would see that as a threat."

"Here's what you don't understand," Grace said as calmly as she could. "I'm not a criminal."

"Bullshit." Delamore took a step toward her. She backed up farther and the end table hit her thighs. Behind her she thought she heard a tinny voice ask a muted question. The operator, she hoped.

Grace held up a hand. "Come any closer and I'll scream."

"I haven't done anything to you. I've been trying to catch you."

She frowned. What was he talking about? And then she knew. The police had put a wire on him. The conversation was being taped. And they—he—was hoping that she'd incriminate herself.

"You're threatening me now," she said. "I haven't done anything. I talked to the DA today. I explained my situation and what I think Michael did. He's checking my story now."

"Your lies."

"No," Grace said. "You're the one who's lying, and I have no idea why."

"You bitch." He lowered his voice the angrier he got. Somehow she found that even more threatening.

"Stay away from me."

"Stop the act, Grace," he said. "It's just you and me. And we both know you're not afraid of anything."

Then the door burst open and two hotel security guards came in. Delamore turned and as he did, Grace said, "Oh, thank God. This man came into my room and he's threatening me."

The guards grabbed him. Delamore struggled, but the guards held him tightly. He glared at her. "You're lying again, Grace."

"No," she said, and stepped away from the phone. He glanced down at the receiver, on its side on the table, and cursed. Even if he hadn't been wired, she had a witness.

The guards dragged him out of the room, and Grace sank onto the bed, placing her head in her hands. She waited until the shaking stopped before she called Maxine.

Grace had been right. Delamore had been wearing a wire, and her ability to stay cool while he attacked had preserved her story. That incident, plus the fact that the DA's office had found the money exactly where she had said it would be, in the exact amount that they had been looking for, went a long way toward preserving her credibility. When detectives interviewed Michael's friends one final time, they all agreed he was agitated and depressed, but he would tell no one why. Without the embezzlement explanation, it simply sounded as if he were a miserable man driven to the brink by personal problems.

She had won, at least on that score. Her old clients would get their money back, and they would be off her conscience. And nothing, not even Delamore, would take their place.

Delamore was under arrest, charged with extortion, harassment, and attempting to tamper with a witness. Apparently, he'd faced similar complaints before, but they had never stuck. This time, it looked as if they would.

Grace would have to return to Racine to testify against him. But not for several months. And maybe, Maxine said, not even then. The DA hoped that Delamore would plea and save everyone the expense of a trial.

So, on her last night in Racine, perhaps forever, Grace worked up enough courage to call Alex and Carole. She didn't reach either of them; instead she had to leave a message on their voice mail, asking them to meet her at Oh Kaye's one final time.

Grace got there first. The place hadn't changed at all. There was still a jukebox in the corner and cocktail waitresses in short skirts and ankle boots with big heels. Tin stars and Wild West art on the walls, unstained wood and checkered tablecloths adding to the effect. High bar stools and a lot of lonely people.

Grace ignored them. She sashayed to the bar, slapped her hand on it, and ordered whiskey neat. A group of suits at a nearby table ogled her and she turned away.

She was there to diss men not to meet them.

Carole arrived first, black miniskirt, tight crop top, and cigarette in hand. She looked no different. She hugged Grace so hard that Grace thought her ribs would crack.

"Alex had me convinced you were dead."

Grace shook her head. "I was just sleeping around."

Carole grinned. "Fun, huh?"

Grace thought. The night had been fun. The aftermath hadn't been. But her life was certainly more exciting. She didn't know if the tradeoff was worth it.

Alex arrived a moment later. Her auburn hair had grown, and she was wearing boots beneath a long dress. The boots made her look even taller.

She didn't hug Grace.

"What the hell's the idea?" Alex snapped. "You vanished— kapoof! What kind of friend does that?"

In the past, Grace would have stammered something, then told Alex she was exactly right and Grace was wrong. This time, Grace set her whiskey down.

"I told you about my lumpectomy," Grace said. "You didn't care. I was scared. I told you that, and you didn't care. When I found out I didn't have cancer, I called you to celebrate, and you didn't care. Seems to me you vanished first."

Alex's cheeks were red. Carole stubbed her cigarette in an ashtray on the bar's wooden rail.

"Not fair," Alex said.

"That's what I thought," Grace said.

Carole looked from one to the other. Finally, she said, very softly, "I really missed you, Gracie."

"I thought some misogynistic asshole picked you up and killed you," Alex said.

"Could have happened," Grace said. "Maybe it nearly did."

"Here?" Carole asked. "At Oh Kaye's?"

Grace shook her head. "It's a long story. Are you both finally ready to listen to me?"

Carole tugged her miniskirt as if she could make it longer. "I want to hear it."

Alex picked up Grace's whiskey and tossed it back. Then she wiped off her mouth. "What did I tell you, Grace? Women always tolerate misogyny. You should have fought him off."

"I did," Grace said.

Alex's eyes widened. Carole laughed. "Our Gracie has grown up."

"No," Grace said. "I've always been grown-up. You're just noticing now."

"There's a story here," Alex said, slipping her arm through Grace's, "and I think I need to hear it."

"Me, too." Carole put her arm around Grace's shoulder. "Tell us about your adventures. I promise we'll listen."

Grace sighed. She'd love to tell them everything, but if she did, she'd screw up the case against Delamore. "Naw," Grace said. "Let's just have some drinks and talk about girl things."

"You gotta promise to tell us," Alex said.

"Okay," Grace said. "I promise. Now how about some whiskey?"

"Beer," Alex said.

"You see that cute guy over there?" Carole asked, pointing at the suits.

Grace grinned. Already, her adventure was forgotten. Nothing changed here at Oh Kaye's. Nothing except Cowboy Grace, who'd finally bellied up to the bar.

Tropical Nights at the Natatorium

Richard Paul Russo

$\mathcal{T}$HEY CAME AS THE SUN DISAPPEARED AND THE SKY turned from blood red to deep violet-blue and the stars came to life with a hard and shiny light. They arrived in gyro-pods, drop-flyers, and humjets, and some even in armored ground vehicles (adding an extra edge of excitement to the evening), emerging from the nearby ruins with headlights marking the way along roads no longer maintained, entering the heavily manned security station, then finally passing with a shimmer through the encrypted energy barrier to park on the cleared lot of crushed shells just outside the transparent walls of the natatorium.

The Samarra Natatorium stood at the edge of the sea, surrounded by the ruins of a once thriving neighborhood that had been forsaken some decades earlier. A quarter mile to the north, a muddy river flowed into the sea. The natatorium was an extensive complex of interconnected swimming pools, spas, and rejuvenation ponds fed by thermal mineral springs, all enclosed in a structure built of faceted steelglass. Eight hundred people could comfortably take their pleasure in the natatorium, bathe in the warm waters believed to have antiaging and aphrodisiac properties, or simply indulge in alcohol and narcotics and socialize with their peers throughout the long and sweltering nights. During the week, three or four hundred would come each evening, but on Friday and

Saturday nights more than a thousand men and women would crowd in and stay until dawn. It was the place to make one's appearance that summer—it was the place to renew acquaintances, the place to meet new people, the place to eat and drink too much, the place to indulge appetites of all sorts. That summer, it was the place to *be*.

McDermott approached the natatorium on foot, alone and unarmed. Night had fallen, but the bioluminescent glow from the structure's interior spread throughout the nearby ruins, casting unnatural shadows but providing enough illumination for him to make his way among the wreckage of deserted buildings, abandoned streets and alleys, derelict cars, and mounds of stinking garbage. An electric buzz of insects saturated the hot and humid air, nearly drowning out the occasional animal yowl or piercing caw from birds in the upper reaches of the run-down buildings around him.

Stinking garbage? McDermott nodded to himself. Perhaps the ruins weren't quite as abandoned as they appeared. When he stopped and looked away from the natatorium and intently studied the buildings, he could make out faint gleams of light in some of the windows, and when he breathed slowly and deeply he could smell hints of cooking food cloaked by the stench of the garbage.

From the edge of the ruins, he watched the stragglers arriving by air and land, and studied the wide sterile buffer zone surrounding the natatorium grounds, the energy barrier, and the security drones hovering in the airspace above. He moved from building to building, keeping to the harsh shadows, coming around from south to north so he could view the resort from all angles. Through the semitransparent steelglass he could see the blurred images of people moving in an insectlike mass, and the large globes of bioluminescence suspended from the ceilings, giving everything a radiant cast. He learned nothing new.

As the moon rose, he discerned in the distance a lean figure sitting by the riverbank, fishing. McDermott watched the figure for a time, then emerged from the shadows and walked across an open stretch of sand and grasses toward the river. As he neared the river, the figure turned.

It was an old man, dark skinned with short white curly hair and a sparse white beard; he sat on a wooden stool and held a homemade fishing pole in both hands. The man seemed unconcerned, and calmly watched McDermott approach. McDermott stopped a few feet away and greeted him.

"Good evening," the old man said.

"Any luck?" McDermott asked.

The old man leaned forward, picked up a chain staked to the ground beside him and raised it out of the water. One tiny silver-streaked brown fish hung limply by its mouth from a closed loop of wire. "Oh, yes," the old man said with a smile. "Poor." He dropped chain and fish back into the water with a quiet splash.

McDermott stepped closer and they shook hands and introduced themselves. The man's name was Samuel Latu and he'd been fishing since dusk and would probably be there all night. It was too hot during the day for the fish, which apparently napped while the sun beat down on the water. So he fished at night.

"A man has to eat, yes?" Samuel said.

McDermott nodded toward the glowing natatorium in the distance. "*They* eat just fine."

"Yes," Samuel replied. "I am not one of them, however, so I'll just stay here for a while. And you?" he asked. "Are you one of them?"

"Do I look like one of them?"

"Yes and no," the old man said. He cocked his head, studying McDermott. "I think you *were* one of them once—a man of prestige and power. But now you've chosen to go your own way."

"That's an interesting notion."

He shrugged. "It's just a guess."

"Do you watch them much?" McDermott asked, nodding toward the natatorium.

"I watch them come and I watch them go. There is a kind of beauty to their vehicles in the air. What they do inside, however, is ridiculous and of no interest to me." He rested the fishing pole in a makeshift holder driven into the ground beside him, and took a single cigarette from his shirt pocket. "This is the last, or I would offer you one."

"I don't smoke," McDermott said.

"Ah, better for both of us." He lit the cigarette and smoked in silence for a time. "Why are you out here?" he asked with a raised eyebrow. "Taking the air?"

McDermott chuckled. "I haven't heard that expression in a long time. In fact, I'm not sure I've ever actually heard it. Read it, more likely." He nodded. "Yes, just out for a stroll."

Samuel turned and jerked his fishing pole, then waited several moments before shaking his head. "Nothing."

"I'll leave you to your fishing, then," McDermott said. "Good night."

"Good night," the old man replied.

McDermott turned and walked back toward the ruins.

Two nights later, well after midnight, he returned carrying a rucksack with two packs of cigarettes, sandwiches, and coffee. The natatorium was aglow, its light reflecting from the listless waves that washed up the gentle slope of beach. He spotted the old man on his stool at the same bend in the river, and walked out to join him.

"Luck any better tonight?" McDermott asked.

"Worse," Samuel answered.

McDermott opened the rucksack, took out the cigarettes and handed them to Samuel.

Samuel examined the cigarettes, then looked up at McDermott. "What do you want from me?"

"Nothing."

Samuel regarded him thoughtfully, then said, "Why do I believe you?"

"Because it's true."

"That must be it."

McDermott dragged over a driftwood log from nearby and sat on it beside the old man. He brought out the sandwiches and they shared them as they watched the river and the tip of the fishing pole, which never moved. When he brought out the coffee, Samuel nodded appreciatively.

Samuel sipped at his and murmured, "This is very good."

They drank coffee, and Samuel smoked cigarettes and talked while McDermott listened. Samuel was eighty-three years old and lived on the second floor of a derelict townhouse just on the other side of the low dunes, with a view of the ocean and the natatorium. Three other families and a few other singles like himself lived in the townhouse complex, and they each had their own place. Plenty for everyone. No electricity, sewage, or running water, of course, but otherwise more than adequate. He had lived there for thirteen years, ever since his wife had died. They'd had no children. There was family on the East Coast he hadn't seen in twenty years, and family back in the Sudan that he had *never* seen, or couldn't remember—he had come to the United States when he was fourteen.

"And you?" he asked McDermott. "Where do you live?"

"Nowhere for very long."

"Family?"

McDermott just shook his head. He didn't want to talk about

family, he didn't want to talk about himself at all. Samuel seemed to sense and accept that, and asked no more personal questions.

Sometime later, Samuel caught a large rainbow trout with several cauliflower-like growths near its tail.

"Is it safe to eat?" McDermott asked.

Samuel coughed out a laugh. "I'd guess nothing I catch in this river is safe to eat. But I'm an old man, so it can't matter much. I'll eat it."

Near dawn, he caught another fish, smaller but completely normal in appearance. "You've brought me luck," Samuel said.

McDermott stood and shouldered the rucksack. "I need to go."

"Thanks for the cigarettes and the company," Samuel said. "Both are appreciated."

A dropflyer flew overhead, continued out over the ocean, then swung around, headed back in toward the natatorium to pick up passengers it had presumably dropped off early in the evening.

"Entertainment's over," McDermott said.

"It's never over for them," Samuel replied.

Watching the dropflyer land, and figures emerging from the bright lights of the natatorium to stagger toward it, McDermott said, "We'll see."

Posing as a management recruiter from out-of-town, McDermott frequented Financial District restaurants and cafés during the lunch hours, and bars and lounges in the early evenings. It took most of the week, but he finally managed an invitation to join a small party of corporate attorneys who were going to the Samarra Natatorium that weekend. At nine o'clock Saturday evening, as darkness fell, he was on a rooftop pad with a young, handsome, and single intellectual property attorney, waiting to be picked up by the party's hired dropflyer. The man's name was Myricks, and he stood silently swaying, wearing a sleepy-eyed smile.

The dropflyer landed and they boarded, greeting the others and strapping themselves into the two remaining seats. The Financial District skyscrapers fell away from them as the dropflyer lifted off, pressing McDermott into his thickly cushioned seat; the buildings blazed with lights, the brightest pocket of radiance in the city that revealed itself to them as they rose and then accelerated forward, arcing out toward the ocean. Below them, the city was a patterned network of lights broken by large areas of near darkness. Within the dark areas, flickering lights appeared, the flames of drum fires and clustered candlelight and camp lanterns.

The dropflyer flew out over the ocean, bobbing up and down in the air like a carnival ride, then turned sharply and headed in toward the natatorium. The pilot called in the access codes while the waves were still below them, then they were flying over wet sand, dry sand, then decelerating sharply into a shaky hover before finally descending and settling on one of the landing pads. At the door their IDs were checked, they walked through a series of scanners, and finally McDermott was inside.

It wasn't much different from what he'd imagined, but it was far larger. The rooms were vast, the ceilings thirty or forty feet above the floor, and each housed an enormous swimming pool as well as several rejuvenation ponds and numerous small spas for groups of five or six people at a time. Dozens of tables surrounded the pools, occupied by a mix of people in a bizarre array of swimsuits, eveningwear, or the current rage of fluorescent body suits. Spheres of bioluminescent fluids, suspended from the ceiling, emitted a bright and silvery iridescent light almost imperceptibly tinged with pink. Flocks of colorful macaws flew among the spheres, or perched on artificial tree limbs, a flagrant violation of the law.

Attendants moved among the tables and pools and the mingling crowds, carrying trays of champagne in fluted glasses and cocktails of a seemingly endless variety, or pushing carts loaded with smoked salmon and oysters, stuffed crab canapés, caramelized tropical fruits, enormous prawns with caviar cream, seared duck livers, and much more, all with elegant, calligraphic labels.

After the members of his party withdrew to dressing rooms to change into swimwear, McDermott wandered from one room to the next, still surprised at the number of people—the pools were full, few chairs were available at the tables, and he had to fight through dense crowds to move from one place to the next.

A string quartet performed in one room, a jazz ensemble in another, a slash-and-burn band in a third, while other rooms were filled only with the overload of dozens of simultaneous conversations and the constant background splashing of bathers; a miracle of acoustics kept the music and other noises isolated within the individual rooms. Private booths were available for rent in some of the rooms, and most of these, too, were occupied, their curtains drawn tightly shut.

In one room was a tiered balcony high above the floor, with tables and lounge chairs and booths overlooking the pools. McDermott climbed a spiral staircase and there he finally found a small unoccupied table and took a seat. Next to him, a group of men lounged on a sofa and discussed the dearth of premium items that would be available at an upcoming art auction. A woman in a sharkskin dress stopped by McDermott's table and asked if she could join him. Unable to say no, he invited her to sit; her dress slithered as she moved a chair closer to him and sat. It was going to be an interminable night.

By dawn, McDermott was exhausted even though he hadn't indulged in anything but mineral water, a few hors d'oeuvres, and mindless conversations too numerous to count. His pager chirped, alerting him that the hired dropflyer was on its way in to pick them up. He moved among the pools and spas and ponds, all of them nearly empty as people left or prepared to leave, the warm waters now pallid and cloudy.

Outside, the air was fresh, heavy with the smell of salt as a warm morning breeze came in from the ocean. The sun was just rising in the east, peeking above the surrounding ruins, reflecting from the natatorium windows in bright fiery colors. McDermott looked toward the river, but there was no sign of Samuel. He walked out toward the landing pads and joined his haggard party to wait for their ride home.

When he went to the river that night he brought two cartons of cigarettes and a pound of ground coffee. Samuel wasn't there. McDermott sat on the driftwood log and waited. He watched the murky river flowing past, and the air vehicles flying in and out of the natatorium, listened to the rustle of animals moving through the grass and kicking up sand; he walked up and down the river, then followed it out to where it widened and flowed into the ocean, meeting the waves and creating thick ropes of foam in a constantly moving backwash. The moon rose, but Samuel didn't appear. At midnight, McDermott left.

The next night, Samuel was on his stool with his line in the water when McDermott arrived. McDermott gave him the coffee and cigarettes, and Samuel smiled, saying, "I don't smoke *that* much. Mind if I share them? They're scarce around here."

"They're yours," McDermott answered. "You can do what you want with them."

"Thanks."

McDermott sat on the log, facing the natatorium rather than the river, and poured coffee for them both. It was Monday night and the air traffic had been light; only two or three ground vehicles sat in the lot.

"You have something on your mind," Samuel said. "Something you want to ask me?"

McDermott drank from his cup then turned to Samuel. "Yes, but I don't want you to misunderstand. The second time we met, you asked me what I wanted, and I said I wanted nothing."

"I remember."

"I meant it. I still mean it."

"But now you want something from me."

McDermott shook his head. "Not exactly. I'm expecting delivery of some specialized maps sometime tomorrow night. The maps are old, and things have changed around here since then, and I don't know this place at all." He nodded at the water. "From what I understand, that river isn't even on the maps."

"That river didn't exist ten years ago." He lit a cigarette without taking his eyes from McDermott. "You want me to help you find something on your maps."

"Yes, but I don't want you to—"

Samuel cut him off with a wave of the cigarette. "It's all right. What are you looking for?"

McDermott shook his head, saying nothing.

Samuel smiled. "I see, trust only goes so far. Well, that's understandable, we don't really know each other." He nodded. "I'll help you find it, whatever it is. Something new and different. That doesn't come along very often for me anymore."

They were to meet two days later, at ten in the morning in the lobby of the deserted Sunset Beach Motel. McDermott drove a small, rusted and dented truck, the enclosed bed filled with a variety of tools. He saw a few people on the streets as he wound his way among potholes and old appliances and bounced over cracked curbs, but by mutual agreement they passed one another with nothing more than nods. He parked in front of the motel and entered the sand-filled lobby, where Samuel waited for him.

They raised the blinds in the manager's office, cleared off the desk, and McDermott laid out his maps—an old city street map, a topographic map, and a Water Department survey map. On the Water Department map, two tiny blue squares were circled in pencil.

"That's what I need to find," McDermott said, pointing at the circled squares. "Either one. Don't have to find both."

Samuel studied the map, then looked up and stared at McDermott. "I know who you are," he said.

McDermott held his breath, wondering if it was true, and wondering what, if anything, Samuel would do if he *did* know.

"Who am I?" he asked.

Samuel just shrugged as if McDermott's identity was of little concern. "There's a substantial reward for turning you in," Samuel said. "And a severe penalty for aiding you." He turned his attention back to the maps and said, "Let's see if we can't determine where these are."

Everything appeared different in the daylight. The buildings, though dilapidated and run-down, did not have the appearance of ruins, but rather of a neighborhood that had fallen on hard times, sorely in need of basic repairs and maintenance but with the potential to be restored. Of course, McDermott thought to himself, the economics were never going to turn around for any of the people living here, and the place would continue to deteriorate. As they slowly drove through the streets, they met a few people on foot who called to Samuel by name, as he did to them. He had McDermott stop the truck while he talked for a few minutes with a young woman and her small child, asking how they were doing, and promising to stop by later in the day to check on their propane stove.

On the westernmost block, at the edge of the half-mile of buffer zone, they parked the truck and Samuel asked to look at the maps again. He looked back and forth between the maps and their surroundings, then nodded once. They got out and Samuel attached a green flag to the broken side mirror. "This'll keep it from getting stolen or stripped," he said.

They walked around the corner of a two-story building that had once been a restaurant, and looked out at the natatorium. At this distance and in the bright light of midday, it appeared small and somehow lifeless, like a big greenhouse that had gone to seed.

Samuel led the way to a small cluster of tiny, shabby cabins at the end of a long, curving gravel drive. The cabins were ramshackle, with broken windows and doors, and rotten, sagging roofs; what little paint remained on the siding was faded, cracked and peeling. Each cabin had a small porch and a weathered rocking chair.

"Between the cabins, I think," Samuel said.

He was right. They found the round metal lid at ground level between the third and fourth cabins, half-buried by sand and dirt, hidden by overgrown weeds. The lid was about two feet across and rusted shut. McDermott returned to the truck and brought back a crowbar, hammer and chisel, a can of rust solvent, and a flashlight.

In less than half an hour they had the lid pried open. McDermott, on hands and knees, could hear the bubbling of water and feel the damp warmth of the thermal springs. He aimed the flashlight beam down the concrete pipe, and could just make out flashing reflections of water far below. He switched off the flashlight and lowered the lid.

They sat in a narrow strip of shade on the north side of the cabin. They drank coffee McDermott had brought, and Samuel smoked.

"What do you plan on dumping into the springs?" Samuel asked.

McDermott hesitated, then decided it didn't matter. Samuel wasn't going to turn him in. Or if he was, then it truly didn't make any difference what he told him.

"Two things," he finally said. "First, several drums of a concentrated chemical that slowly reacts with human skin over a period of an hour or so, staining the skin of anyone in the water a dark bright red. It will take days, if not weeks, to get rid of the color. It's completely colorless, so no one should notice it until it's spread throughout the pools. After that, a couple of drums of an extremely noxious compound that should permanently foul the waters, the pipes, the pools, everything inside the natatorium with an unbearable stench. I know someone who was able to calculate water volumes and dispersion rates, so I'm pretty sure the quantities I've got will be sufficient." He nodded once to himself. "That should put an end to their nights at the natatorium."

"When will you do this?"

"Saturday night. When it's the most crowded."

They sat in silence for a time. McDermott poured more coffee for both of them, and Samuel smoked another cigarette.

"I've been smoking more since I've met you," Samuel said. "You've made cigarettes too readily available."

"You haven't asked why I'm doing this," McDermott said.

"I know why you're doing it," Samuel replied. "I know why you sabotaged the cloud-sculpting festival in New Mexico, and created the snowmelt in Aspen during the Winter holidays, and sank that luxury casino riverboat in New Orleans, and all the other things you've done over the years."

"It's not some personal revenge or anything like that," McDermott said.

"Oh, I didn't think it was. You're trying to change things. You're trying to wake up the wealthy and privileged. You're trying to make them realize that there's a price *they'll* have to pay, too, for the growing economic disparities, for their indifference to the ever-increasing numbers of the poor, for . . . well, for being such miserable and uncaring human beings."

McDermott had to smile in his surprise. "Something like that, yeah. You've thought a lot about it."

"Thinking about things like that was what I did for a living. For a while, anyway."

"Really? What did you do?"

"I was an economist. I worked as an economics analyst for the State Department. For Saharan Africa."

"I'm impressed."

Samuel shook his head. "I was completely ineffective at changing policy or helping anyone in those countries. I was just as ineffective at changing the way anything was done in the State Department. I finally gave up, and resigned."

"And after that?"

"I taught economics at MIT until they decided not to renew my contract because my politics were too disruptive. That was years ago. Now I have a simple life, I sit by the river at night, and I have more time to think than I've ever had."

"And what do you think about what I've been doing?" McDermott asked.

This time it was Samuel's turn not to answer. "Are we done here?" he asked. "I promised Consuela I would stop by her place."

McDermott got to his feet and glanced once more at the natatorium. "Yes, we're done here. For now."

Saturday night he drove his truck through the streets with the windows open and the lights off, creeping along by the light of the stars and the distant glow of the natatorium. As he headed up the winding drive to the cabins, he could hear the loud crunch of gravel beneath the tires. He backed the truck into position, got out, and was not surprised to see Samuel step out of the shadows. McDermott remained motionless, waiting to see if anyone else would appear, which *would* have surprised him greatly, but Samuel was alone. The old man approached and they shook hands.

"So it is tonight," Samuel said.

"Yes."

"You should poison them, you know," Samuel said calmly.

"What?" The words took him by surprise, so that he felt unsure of what he'd heard.

"You should poison them," Samuel repeated. "Take away those barrels you have in the truck, find sufficient quantities of poison, and then return here some other Saturday. Do it properly."

"Kill them?"

"Yes. Kill them."

McDermott shook his head, feeling a growing sense of discomfort. "Then I would be no better than they are."

Samuel shrugged. "That's irrelevant. You want to change the status quo. What you plan to do tonight will be nothing more than an irritation to them. Like some annoying pest. Like everything else you have done. If you want to change anything, you must do much more. You must hurt them badly or they will go on as before. They will just find another place to amuse themselves, and nothing will change." When McDermott didn't reply, Samuel went on.

"Nothing you've ever done has changed anything. Even more violent and destructive events brought about by others have had no effect on these people. Look at the water riots in Southern California last year. The citywide public services strikes in New York three years ago. The nightclub bombings in Chicago, and the flooding of the subways in Boston after the transit workers strike, and all of the other smaller localized disturbances, the lootings and arson outbreaks, more and more every year. Those with money always find ways to insulate and protect themselves while at the same time completely denying the possibility that any of this is a consequence of their greed and indifference. Not until they are more directly and severely harmed will they ever believe they need to do anything differently."

"You would kill them?" McDermott said.

"I?" Samuel smiled and shook his head. "Oh, no, not at all. I'm not trying to change anything. You are." He sighed. "Now I try to accept things as they are, and live with them as best I can. Change is far too difficult and costly."

"The way things are now is too difficult and costly," McDermott said fiercely.

"I would not argue that with you," Samuel replied. "Both things are true."

McDermott looked out at the natatorium, which gleamed like some fantastic and immense living jewel out on the sands. *Both things are true.* He felt a nascent fear rising in his chest and gut, fear of the reality of Samuel's words, fear of the implications. Fear of blood.

"There must be some middle ground, some way to effect change without resorting to killing and destruction."

"I think not," Samuel said sadly. "Not anymore. If there was such a time when that was possible, it has been gone for years. For decades."

McDermott shook his head, fighting the fear, struggling to crush it and eliminate it. He felt as though Samuel had excavated a truth McDermott had long known but had managed to suppress, and now he was trying to suppress it once again. "I'm not ready to accept that," he said. "Not yet."

"I understand. Someday, however, you will realize you have no choice. I suspect that day is coming soon. Then . . . well, I wonder what path you will choose."

Distressed but determined, McDermott went to the back of the truck and unlocked the shell cover and tailgate, revealing the large barrels, carefully packed to prevent them from rolling or crashing into each other.

"Let me help you with those," Samuel offered.

"Why? I thought you didn't see any point to it."

"That doesn't matter. I am here, and I am helping a friend with a difficult task. *That* is worth doing."

McDermott rigged up the makeshift ramp he'd prepared, then together they rolled the three large metal barrels down the ramp and along the ground to the edge of the hole. They carried the other two smaller drums between them, and set them back against the cabin wall. McDermott retrieved two respirators and two pair of neoprene gloves from the truck seat and handed one of each to Samuel.

"I brought extras in case you were here."

They fitted the respirators over their faces, pulled on the gloves, then McDermott raised the round metal lid, exposing the concrete-lined hole. With Samuel's help, he positioned the first barrel over the edge of the hole, propping up the bottom end on a concrete block so the barrel was tilted toward the hole, then unscrewed the wide cap.

The liquid emerged fitfully from the barrel until McDermott popped open the vent at the other end of the lid, then it flowed smoothly and quickly, a steady stream pouring down the hole and into the thermal springs. It took several minutes for the barrel to empty, then McDermott and Samuel repeated the process with the other two barrels. They waited fifteen minutes, then McDermott motioned for Samuel to keep back, and took care of the two smaller drums himself. The compound was thick but nearly clear, so that it seemed he was pouring pure water into the springs.

When both drums were empty, McDermott dropped the lid back over the hole, and the two of them moved back toward the truck, removing the respirators.

"Now what?" Samuel asked. "What about the barrels?"

"I'm going to leave them. I don't care if they find them. I *want* them to know it was deliberate. But we need to get away from here. I'm not sure how long it will take for this stuff to reach the natatorium, but it won't be *that* long."

They climbed into the truck and pulled away from the cabins. McDermott still drove without the headlights, but he drove more quickly now, and they bounced and banged over potholes and unidentifiable chunks of rubble.

"Where do you want me to take you?" McDermott asked.

"I know a place you can hide the truck," Samuel answered. "Then you can come to my place and watch the results of your work, if you like."

McDermott glanced at Samuel, thought about it for a moment, then nodded.

Samuel directed him down one street, then another, then eventually pointed the way to an underground parking garage beneath what had once been a supermarket. They parked the truck in the back corner, behind two concrete pillars, then walked back up the ramp and onto the street.

Samuel grabbed McDermott's arm and pulled him back into the shadows up against the supermarket wall. Moments later McDermott heard the thumping of a police dragoncopter, and almost immediately afterward they saw the flashing blue and white lights of the copter pass overhead, waves of heat distortion in its wake.

"It's started," Samuel said quietly. "We'll have to be careful."

They moved cautiously from building to building and street to street, sticking to the shadows whenever possible, listening intently for sirens and the sound of dragoncopters, holing up whenever one passed. Four more flew overhead as they made their way to Samuel's townhouse, and once they had to press themselves into a thicket of dense shrubs as an armored police cruiser rolled past with headlights blazing and rooftop searchlight beam sweeping the street.

They climbed the stairs to the second floor of the townhouse. In the darkness, McDermott couldn't see much, but he noticed there was no carpeting and guessed that it had all been torn out years ago. Samuel led the way to the front room with its large picture windows and sliding glass doors that opened onto a large balcony. The picture windows were cracked but still intact; the air coming in through the open doors was warm and humid, but refreshing as it broke up the still air inside the rooms.

Samuel had been right about the view. They were high enough to see over the top of the low, grass-topped dunes, with an unobstructed view of the natatorium aglow on the edge of the sea. Right now it was chaos, with dragoncopters circling the area, vying for airspace with dozens of private aircraft arriving and trying to land to pick up panicked clients who had called them back early. A few of the copters were on the ground, along with ground cruisers, ambulances, and haz-mat vans, while hundreds of people scrambled around outside the natatorium, swarming over the pads and making landing even more difficult. From this distance, the noise was a roaring confusion of shouts and high-pitched cries, thumping from the copters and whining from the pods and flyers, garbled orders barked out over speakers, and shattering glass and banging metal. He thought many of the people were still in swimsuits, but at this distance and with the crazed mix of lights and shadow and frantic motion everywhere, it was difficult to tell anything for sure.

McDermott felt surprisingly empty and uneasy. Samuel was right, there was something absurd and ridiculous about what was happening out there right now. It had the surface appearance of some kind of disaster, but in a few weeks it would all be forgotten except for the occasional ribbing of those who still bore traces of red stain on their skin, jokes told about the panic and the stench, and fond reminiscences of tropical nights at the natatorium. The natatorium would be closed down, but there would be some new place for the privileged to amuse themselves at night, some new source of indulgent pleasures, some new mode of excess.

He stepped out onto the balcony and leaned against the rail, unafraid of being seen—no one was searching this area, no one was doing anything right now except out at the natatorium itself, and it would be hours before things were under control there. Samuel joined him, bringing out two folding chairs. "No sense being uncomfortable," he said.

They set up the chairs and sat in them and watched the events playing out at the natatorium. Samuel put a cigarette in his mouth but didn't light it.

"There's some good in seeing all of those people scared and out of control for a while," Samuel said. "Too bad it won't last."

McDermott breathed in long and deep, held it for a few moments, then slowly let it out. "It's not enough, is it?" he said.

"No, it's not enough." Samuel took the cigarette from his mouth and looked at it, then turned to McDermott. "How old are you?"

"Forty-seven."

"Then you've been alive long enough to see many changes, but I've seen even more, and almost none of them have been for the better." He turned back toward the ocean. "This is the kind of weather we had in the Sudan when I was growing up, hot and humid like this, but it was never like this here when my family first came to this city, not even in the hottest of summers. Now, this is considered mild. Remember last summer?"

McDermott nodded. The death toll across the country had been astonishing.

Samuel gestured at the natatorium with his cigarette. "Those people don't understand what that means. Or if they do understand, they don't care, and they don't care that it'll just get worse. That's just one example, and there are plenty of others. They don't care that everything is getting worse, because they think it's not getting worse for them, that their money and their influence and their power will protect them. What they don't understand is how wrong they are, and they won't understand that until it's too late, until it's too late for everyone." He sighed. "I think it's already too late, and they still don't understand."

McDermott felt the fear growing in his gut once more, stronger now. "You're a disturbingly wise man, Samuel."

"No. I've seen a lot in my life, that's all. As I said to you before, I've had a lot of time to think about things." He put the cigarette back between his lips and shook his head. "It does no one any good."

They remained on the balcony watching the spastic dance of air vehicles and the kaleidoscope of lights, the sliver of moon moving slowly overhead, the waves curling up against the sand, and the river flowing through the night and into the dark, vast ocean like blood from riots and clashes and other struggles to come. Neither of them spoke again, for there was nothing more to be said.

McDermott returned a week later and found Samuel by the river, this time without his fishing pole. He sat on his stool, but facing away from the river, looking out toward the natatorium, which was now little more than a hulking lifeless shadow against the beach and the ocean, the steelglass only dimly reflecting bits of light.

"I'm sick of fish," Samuel explained with a smile.

McDermott sat on the driftwood log and handed a key to Samuel. "This is for the truck. It's under the supermarket, where we parked it that night. I'm leaving, and I won't need it."

Samuel pocketed the key. "Thanks. It might come in handy."

"It's got a full tank of fuel. You should look at it soon, there are a few things in the back end you might be able to use." In fact, the back of the truck was filled with canned food, bags of rice, cigarettes, coffee, and first aid supplies, as much as McDermott could pack into it.

"Where are you going now?" Samuel asked.

"I don't know. I'll decide when I get to the train station. I like riding trains, and I'm not sure how much longer they'll be around."

"And when you arrive wherever you're going, what will you do then?"

"I don't know that, either. I'm afraid now, Samuel. I wasn't afraid before, but I am now." He stood. "Thanks for everything."

Samuel shook his head. "I don't think I did you any good."

"You were a friend. That was worth a lot." They shook hands. "Good-bye, Samuel. Take care of yourself."

"You too."

McDermott took one last look at the abandoned natatorium, then turned and headed toward the city, toward a future now more frightening and uncertain than before.

Night of Time

Robert Reed

*A*SH DRANK A BITTER TEA WHILE SITTING IN THE
shade outside his shop, comfortable on a little seat that he
had carved for himself in the trunk of a massive, immortal bristlecone pine. The wind was tireless, dense and dry and pleasantly
warm. The sun was a convincing illusion—a K-class star per-
petually locked at an early-morning angle, the false sky narrow and
pink, a haze of artful dust pretending to have been blown from
some faraway hell. At his feet lay a narrow and phenomenally
deep canyon, glass roads anchored to the granite walls, with hundreds of narrow glass bridges stretched from one side to the other,
making the air below him glisten and glitter. Busier shops and
markets were set beside the important roads, and scattered between
them were the hivelike mansions and mating halls, and elaborate
fractal statues, and the vertical groves of cling-trees that lifted
water from the distant river: The basics of life for the local species,
the 31-3s.

For Ash, business was presently slow, and it had been for some
years. But he was a patient man and a pragmatist, and when you
had a narrow skill and a well-earned reputation, it was only a matter of time before the desperate or those with too much money
came searching for you.

"This will be the year," he said with a practiced, confident tone. "And maybe, this will be the day."

Any coincidence was minimal. It was his little habit to say those words and then lean forward in his seat, looking ahead and to his right, watching the only road that happened to lead past his shop. If someone were coming, Ash would see him now. And as it happened, he spotted two figures ascending the long glass ribbon, one leading the other, both fighting the steep grade as well as the thick and endless wind.

The leader was large and simply shaped—a cylindrical body, black and smooth, held off the ground by six jointed limbs. Ash instantly recognized the species. While the other entity was human, he decided—a creature like himself, and at this distance, entirely familiar.

They weren't going to be his clients, of course. Most likely, they were sightseers. Perhaps they didn't even know one another. They were just two entities that happened to be marching in the same direction. But as always, Ash allowed himself a seductive premonition. He finished his tea, and listened, and after a little while, despite the heavy wind, he heard the quick dense voice of the alien—an endless blur of words and old stories and lofty abstract concepts born from one of the galaxy's great natural intellects.

When the speaker was close, Ash called out, "Wisdom passes!" A Vozzen couldn't resist such a compliment.

The road had finally flattened out. Jointed legs turned the long body, allowing every eye to focus on the tall, rust-colored human sitting inside the craggy tree. The Vozzen continued walking sideways, but with a fatigued slowness. His only garment was a fabric tube, black like his carapace and with the same slick texture. "Wisdom shall not pass," a thin, somewhat shrill voice called out. Then the alien's translator made adjustments, and the voice softened. "If you are a man named Ash," said the Vozzen, "this Wisdom intends to linger."

"I am Ash," he replied, immediately dropping to his knees. The ground beneath the tree was rocky, but acting like a supplicant would impress the species. "May I serve your Wisdom in some tiny way, sir?"

"Ash," the creature repeated. "The name is Old English. Is that correct?"

The surprise was genuine. With a half-laugh, Ash said, "Honestly, I'm not quite sure—"

"English," it said again. The translator was extremely adept, creating a voice that was unnervingly human—male and mature, and pleasantly arrogant. "There was a tiny nation-state, and an island, and as I recall my studies, England and its confederate tribes acquired a rather considerable empire that briefly covered the face of your cradle world."

"Fascinating," said Ash, looking back down the road. The second figure was climbing the last long grade, pulling an enormous float-pack, and despite his initial verdict, Ash realized that the creature wasn't human at all.

"But you were not born on the Earth," the Vozzen continued. "In your flesh and your narrow build, I can see some very old augmentations—"

"Mars," Ash allowed. "I was born on—"

"Mars," the voice repeated. That simple word triggered a cascade of memories, facts and telling stories. From that flood, the Vozzen selected his next offering. "Old Mars was home to some fascinating political experiments. From the earliest terraforming societies to the Night of the Dust—"

"I remember," Ash interrupted, trying to gain control over the conversation. "Are you a historian, sir? Like many of your kind—?"

"I am conversant in the past, yes."

"Then perhaps I shouldn't be too impressed. You seem to have been looking for me, and for all I know, you've thoroughly researched whatever little history is wrapped around my life."

"It would be impolite not to study your existence," said the Vozzen.

"Granted." With another deep bow, Ash asked, "What can this old Martian do for a wise Vozzen?"

The alien fell silent.

For a moment, Ash studied the second creature. Its skeleton and muscle were much like a man's, and the head wore a cap of what could have been dense brown hair. There was one mouth and two eyes, but no visible nose and the mouth was full of heavy pink teeth. Of course many humans had novel genetics, and there were remoras on the Ship's hull—men and women who wore every intriguing, creative mutation. But this creature was not human. Ash sensed it, and using a private nexus, he asked his shop for a list of likely candidates.

"Ash," the Vozzen said. "Yes, I have made a comprehensive study of your considerable life."

Ash dipped his head, driving his knees into the rough ground. "I am honored, sir. Thank you."

"I understand that you possess some rather exotic machinery."

"Quite novel. Yes, sir."

"And talents. You wield talents even rarer than your machinery."

"Unique talents," Ash replied with an effortless confidence. He lifted his eyes, and smiled, and wanting the advantage in his court, he rose to his feet, brushing the grit from his slightly bloodied knees as he told his potential client, "I help those whom I can help."

"You help them for a fee," the alien remarked, a clear disdain in the voice.

Ash approached the Vozzen, remarking, "My fee is a fair wage. A wage determined by the amoral marketplace."

"I am a poor historian," the Vozzen complained.

Ash gazed into the bright black eyes. Then with a voice tinged with a careful menace, he said, "It must seem awful, I would think. Being a historian, and being Vozzen, and feeling your precious memories slowly and inexorably leaking away . . ."

The Ship was an enormous derelict—a world-sized starship discovered by humans, and repaired by humans, and sent by its new owners on a great voyage around the most thickly settled regions of the galaxy. It was Ash's good fortune to be one of the early passengers, and for several centuries, he remained a simple tourist. But he had odd skills leftover from his former life, and as different aliens boarded the Ship, he made friends with new ideas and fresh technologies. His shop was the natural outgrowth of all that learning. "Sir," he said to the Vozzen. "Would you like to see what your money would buy?"

"Of course."

"And your companion—?"

"My aide will remain outside. Thank you."

The human-shaped creature seemed to expect that response. He walked under the bristlecone, tethering his pack to a whitened branch, and with an unreadable expression, stood at the canyon's edge, staring into the glittering depths, watching for the invisible river, perhaps, or perhaps watching his own private thoughts.

"By what name do I call you?"

"Master is adequate."

Every Vozzen was named Master, in one fashion or another. With a nod, Ash began walking toward the shop's doorway. "And your aide—"

"Shadow."

"His name is?"

"Shadow is an adequate translation." Several jointed arms emerged from beneath his long body, complex hands tickling the edges of the door, a tiny sensor slipped from a pocket and pointed at the darkness inside. "Are you curious, Ash?"

"About what, Master?"

"My companion's identity. It is a little mystery to you, I think."

"It is. Yes."

"Have you heard of the Aabacks?"

"But I've never seen one." Then after a silence, he mentioned, "They're a rare species. With a narrow intelligence and a fierce loyalty, as I understand these things."

"They are rather simple souls," Master replied. "But whatever their limits, or because of them, they make wonderful servants."

The tunnel grew darker, and then the walls fell away. With a silent command, Ash triggered the lights to awaken. In an instant, a great chamber was revealed, the floor tiled simply and the pine-faced ceiling arching high overhead, while the distant walls lay behind banks upon banks of machines that were barely awake, spelling themselves for those rare times when they were needed.

"Are you curious, Master?"

"Intensely and about many subjects," said the Vozzen. "What particular subject are you asking about?"

"How this magic works," Ash replied, gesturing with an ancient, comfortable pride. "Not even the Ship's captains can wield this technology. Within the confines of our galaxy, I doubt if there are three other facilities equally equipped."

"For memory retrieval," Master added. "I know the theory at play here. You manipulate the electrons inside a client's mind, increasing their various effects. And you manipulate the quantum nature of the universe, reaching into a trillion alternate but very similar realities. Then you combine these two quite subtle tricks, temporarily enlarging one mind's ability to reminisce."

Ash nodded, stepping up to the main control panel.

"I deplore that particular theory," his client professed.

"I'm not surprised."

"That many-world image of the universe is obscene. To me, it is simply grotesque and relentlessly ridiculous, and I have never approved of it."

"Many feel that way," Ash allowed.

A genuine anger surged. "This concept of each electron exist-ing in countless realities, swimming through an endless ocean of potential, with every possible outcome achieved to what resembles an infinite number of outcomes—"

"We belong to one branch of reality," Ash interrupted. "One minor branch in a great tree standing in an endless canopy in the multiverse forest—"

"We are not," Master growled.

The controls awoke. Every glow-button and thousand-layer display had a theatrical purpose. Ash could just as easily manipulate the machinery through nexuses buried in his own body. But his clients normally appreciated this visible, traditional show of structured light and important sounds.

"We are not a lonely reality lost among endless possibility." In Vozzen fashion, the hind legs slapped each other in disgust. "I am a historian and a scholar of some well-earned notoriety. My long, long life has been spent in the acquisition of the past, and its interpretation, and I refuse to believe that what I have studied—this great pageant of time and story—is nothing more than some obscure twig shaking on the end of an impossible-to-measure shrub."

"I'm tempted to agree with you," Ash replied.

"Tempted?"

"There are moments when I believe . . ." Ash paused, as if selecting his next words. "I see us as the one true reality. The universe is exactly as it seems to be. As it should be. And what I employ here is just a trick, a means of interacting with the ghost realities. With mathematical whispers and unborn potentials. In other words, we are the trunk of a great and ancient tree, and the dreamlike branches have no purpose but to feed our magnificent souls. . . !"

The alien regarded Ash with a new respect. The respect showed in the silence, and then, with the hands opening, delicate spider-web fingers presenting themselves to what was, for at least this moment, their equal.

"Is that what you believe now?" Master asked.

"For the moment." Ash laughed quietly. Two nexuses and one display showed the same information: The historian had enough capital to hire him and his machinery. "And I'll keep believing it for a full day, if necessary."

Then he turned, bowing just enough. "What exactly is it that you wish to remember, Master?"

The alien eyes lost their brightness.

"I am not entirely sure," the voice confessed with a simple

horror. "I have forgotten something very important . . . something essential, I fear . . . but I can't even recall what that something might be . . ."

Hours had passed, but the projected sun hadn't moved. The wind was unchanged, and the heat only seemed worse, as Ash stepped from the cool depths of his shop, his body momentarily forgetting to perspire. He had left his client alone, standing inside a cylindrical reader with a thousand flavors of sensors fixed to his carapace and floating free inside the ancient body and mind. Ash kept a close watch over the Vozzen. His nexuses showed him telemetry, and a mind's eye let him watch the scene. If necessary, he could offer words of encouragement or warning. But for the moment, his client was obeying the strict instructions, standing as motionless as possible while the machines made intricate maps of his brain—a body-long array of superconducting proteins and light-baths and quantum artesians. The alien's one slight cheat was his voice, kept soft as possible, but always busy, delivering an endless lecture about an arcane, mostly forgotten epoch.

The mapping phase was essential, and quite boring.

From a tiny slot in the pink granite wall, Ash plucked free a new cup of freshly brewed, deliciously bitter tea.

"A pleasant view," a nearby voice declared.

"I like it." Ash sipped his drink. As a rule, Aabacks appreciated liquid gifts, but he made no offer, strolling under the bristlecone, out of the wind and sun. "Do you know anything about the 31-3s?"

"I know very little," Shadow confessed. The voice was his own, his larynx able to produce clear if somewhat slow human words.

"Their home is tidally locked and rather distant from its sun," Ash explained. "Their atmosphere is rich in carbon dioxide, which my Martian lungs prefer." He tapped his own chest. "Water vapor and carbon dioxide warm the day hemisphere, and the winds carry the excess heat and moisture to the cold nightside glaciers, which grow and push into the dawn, and melt, completing the cycle." With an appreciative nod, he said, "The Ship's engineers have done a magnificent job of replicating the 31-3 environment."

Shadow's eyes were large and bright, colored a bluish gray. The pink teeth were heavy and flat-headed, suitable for a diet of rough vegetation. Powerful jaw muscles ballooned outwards when the mouth closed. A simple robe and rope belt were his only clothes. Four fingers and a thumb were on each hand, but nothing like a fingernail showed. Ash watched the hands, and then the bare, almost human feet. Reading the dirt, he felt certain that Shadow hadn't moved since he had arrived. He was standing in the sun, in the wind, and like any scrupulously obedient servant, he seemed ready to remain on that patch of ground for another day, or twenty.

"The 31-3s don't believe in time," Ash continued.

A meaningful expression passed across the face. Curiosity? Disdain? Then with a brief glance toward Ash, he asked, "Is it the absence of days and nights?"

"Partly. But only partly."

Shadow leaned forward slightly. On the bright road below, a pack of 31-3s was dancing along. Voices like brass chimes rose through the wind. Ash recognized his neighbors. He threw a little stone at them, to be polite. Then with a steady voice, he explained, "The endless day is a factor, sure. But they've always been a long-lived species. On their world, with its changeless climate and some extremely durable genetics, every species has a nearly immortal constitution. Where humans and Vozzens and Aabacks had to use modern bioengineering to conquer aging, the 31-3s evolved in a world where everything can live pretty much forever. That's why time was never an important concept to them. And that's why their native physics is so odd, and lovely—they formulated a vision of a universe that is almost, almost free of time."

The alien listened carefully. Then he quietly admitted, "Master has explained some of the same things to me, I think."

"You're a good loyal audience," Ash said.

"It is my hope to be."

"What else do you do for Master?"

"I help with all that is routine," Shadow explained. "In every capacity, I give him aid and free his mind for great undertakings."

"But mostly, you listen to him."

"Yes."

"Vozzens are compulsive explainers."

"Aabacks are natural listeners," said Shadow, with a hint of pride.

"Do you remember what he tells you?"

"Very little." For an instant, the face seemed human. An embarrassed smile and a shy blinking of the blue-gray eyes preceded the quiet admission, "I do not have a Vozzen's mind. And Master is an exceptional example of his species."

"You're right," said Ash. "On both accounts."

The alien shifted his feet, and again stared down at the 31-3s. "Come with me."

"He wants me here," Shadow replied. Nothing in the voice was defiant, or even a little stubborn. He intended to obey the last orders given to him, and with his gentle indifference, he warned that he couldn't be swayed.

Sternly, Ash asked, "What does the Master want from this day?"

The question brought a contemplative silence.

"More than anything," said Ash, "he wants to recover what's most precious to him. And that is—"

"His memory."

Again, Ash said, "Come with me."

"For what good?"

"He talks to you. And yes, you've likely forgotten what he can't remember." Ash finished his tea in one long sip. "But likely and surely are two different words. So if you truly wish to help your friend, come with me. Come now."

"I do not deserve solitude," the Vozzen reported. "If you intend to abandon me, warn me. You must."

"I will."

Then, "Do you feel that?"

"Do I . . . what. . . ?"

"Anything. Do you sense anything unusual?"

The alien was tethered to a new array of sensors, plus devices infinitely more intrusive. Here and in a hundred trillion alternate realities, Master stood in the same position, legs locked and arms folded against his belly, his voice slightly puzzled, admitting, "I seem to be remembering my cradle nest."

"Is that unusual?"

"It is unlikely," the Vozzen admitted. "I don't often—"

"And now?"

"My first mate," he began. "In the nest, overlooking a fungal garden—"

"What about now?"

He paused, and then admitted, "Your ship. I am seeing the Great Ship from space, our taxi making its final approach." With a warm laugh, he offered, "It is a historian's dream, riding in a vessel such as this—"

"And now?" Ash prompted.

Silence.

"Where are you—?"

"Inside a lecture hall," Master replied.

"When?"

"Eleven months in the past. I am giving a public lecture." He paused, and then explained, "I make a modest living, speaking to interested parties."

"What do you remember about that day's lecture?"

"Everything," Master began to say. But the voice faltered, and with a doubting tone, he said, "A woman?"

"What woman?"

"A human woman."

"What about her?" Ash pressed.

"She was attending . . . sitting in a seat to my right. . . ? No, my left. How odd. I usually know where to place every face—"

"What was the topic?"

"Topic?"

"Of your lecture. The topic."

"A general history of the Great Wheel of Smoke—"

"The Milky Way," Ash interrupted.

"Your name for everyone's galaxy, yes." With a weblike hand, the alien reached in front of his own face. "I was sharing a very shallow overview of our shared history, naming the most important species of the last three billion years." The hand closed on nothing, and retreated. "For many reasons, there have been few genuinely important species. They have been modestly abundant, and some rather wealthy. But I was making the point . . . the critical line of reasoning . . . that since the metal-rich worlds began spawning intelligence, no single species, or related cluster of sentient organisms, have been able to dominate more than a small puff of the Smoke."

"Why is that?"

The simple question unleashed a flood of thoughts, recollections, and abstract ideas, filling the displays with wild flashes of color and elaborate, highly organized shapes.

"There are many reasons," Master warned.

"Name three."

"Why? Do you wish to learn?"

"I want to pass the time pleasantly," said Ash, studying the data with a blank, almost impassive face. "Three reasons why no species can dominate. Give them to me, in brief."

"Distance. Divergence. And divine wisdom."

"The distance between stars . . . is that what you mean. . . ?"

"Naturally," the historian replied. "Star-flight remains slow and expensive and potentially dangerous. Many species find those reasons compelling enough to remain at home, safe and comfortable, reengineering the spacious confines of their own solar system."

"Divergence?"

"A single species can evolve in many fashions. New organic forms. Joining with machines. Becoming machines. Sweeping cultural experiments. Even the total obliteration of physical bodies. No species can dominate any portion of space if what it becomes is many, many new and oftentimes competing species."

Ash blinked slowly. "What about divine wisdom?"

"That is the single most important factor," said Master. "Ruling the heavens is a child's desire."

"True enough."

"The galaxy is not a world, or even a hundred thousand worlds. It is too vast and chaotic to embrace, and with maturity comes the wisdom to accept that simple impossibility."

"What about the woman?"

"Which woman?" Master was surprised by his own question, as if another voice had asked it. "That human female. Yes. Frankly, I don't think she's important in the smallest way. I don't even know why I am thinking about her."

"Because I'm forcing you to think about her."

"Why? Does she interest you?"

"Not particularly." Ash looked up abruptly, staring at the oval black eyes. "She asked you a question. Didn't she?"

"I remember. Yes."

"What question?"

"She asked about human beings, of course." With a gentle disdain, the historian warned, "You are a young species. And yes, you have been fortunate. Your brief story is fat with luck as well as fortuitous decisions. The Great Ship, as an example. Large and ancient, and empty, and you happened to be the species that found it and took possession. And now you are interacting with a wealth of older, wiser species, gaining knowledge at a rate rarely if ever experienced in the last three billion years—"

"What did she ask you?"

"Pardon me. Did you just ask a question?"

"Exactly. What did this woman say?"

"I think . . . I know . . . she asked, 'Will humanity be the first species to dominate the Milky Way?' "

"What was the woman's name?"

A pause.

Ash feathered a hundred separate controls.

"She did not offer any name," the historian reported.

"What did she look like?"

Again, with a puzzled air, the great mind had to admit, "I didn't notice her appearance, or I am losing my mind."

Ash waited for a moment. "What was your reply?"

"I told her, and the rest of my audience, 'Milk is a child's food. If humans had named the galaxy after smoke, they wouldn't bother with this nonsense of trying to consume the Milky Way.' "

For a long while, Ash said nothing.

Then, quietly, the historian inquired, "Where is my assistant? Where is Shadow?"

"Waiting where you told him to wait," Ash lied. And in the next breath, "Let's talk about Shadow for a moment. Shall we?"

"What do you remember . . . now. . . . ?"

"A crunch cake, and sweet water." Shadow and Ash were standing in a separate, smaller chamber. Opening his mouth, he tasted the cake again. "Then a pudding of succulents and bark from the Gi-Ti tree—"

"Now?"

"Another crunch cake. In a small restaurant beside the Alpha Sea."

With a mild amusement, Ash reported, "This is what you remember best. Meals. I can see your dinners stacked up for fifty thousand years."

"I enjoy eating," the alien replied.

"A good Aaback attitude."

Silence.

And then the alien turned, soft cords dragged along the floor. Perhaps he had felt something—a touch, a sudden chill—or maybe the expression on his face was born from his own thoughts. Either way, he suddenly asked, "How did you learn this work, Ash?"

"I was taught," he offered. "And when I was better than my teachers, I learned on my own. Through experiment and hard practice."

"Master claims you are very good, if not the best."

"I'll thank him for that assessment. But he is right: No one is better at this game than me."

The alien seemed to consider his next words. Then, "He mentioned that you are from a little world. Mars, was it? I remember something . . . something that happened in your youth. The Night of the Dust, was it?"

"Many things happened back then."

"Was it a war?" Shadow pressed. "Master often lectures about human history, and you seem to have a fondness for war."

"I'm glad he finds us interesting."

"Your species fascinates him." Shadow tried to move and discovered that he couldn't. Save for his twin hearts and mouth, every muscle of his body was fused in place. "I don't quite understand why he feels this interest—"

"You attend his lectures, don't you?"

"Always."

"He makes most of his income from public talks."

"Many souls are interested in his words."

"Do you recall a lecture from last year?" Ash gave details, and he appeared disappointed when Shadow said:

"I don't remember, no." An Aaback laugh ended with the thought, "There must not have been any food in that lecture hall."

"Let's try something new," said Ash. "Think back, back as far as possible. Tell me about the very first meal you remember."

A long, long pause ended with, "A little crunch cake. I was a child, and it was my first adult meal."

"I used to be an interrogator," Ash said abruptly.

The eyes were gray and watchful.

"During that old war, I interrogated people, and on certain days, I tortured them." He nodded calmly, adding, "Memory is a real thing, Shadow. It's a dense little nest made, like everything, from electrons—where the electrons are and where they are not— and you would be appalled, just appalled, by all the ways that something real can be hacked out of the surrounding bullshit."

"Quee Lee."

"Pardon?"

"The human woman. Her name was, and is, Quee Lee." Ash began disconnecting his devices, leaving only the minimal few to keep shepherding the Vozzen's mind. "It was easy enough to learn her name. A lecture attended by humans, and when I found one woman, she told me about another. Who mentioned another friend who might have gone to listen to you. But while that friend hadn't heard of you, she mentioned an acquaintance of hers who had a fondness for the past, and her name is Quee Lee. She happened to be there, and she asked the question."

Relief filled Master, and with a thrilled voice, he said, "I remember her now, yes. Yes. She asked about human dominance in the galaxy—"

"Not quite, no."

Suspicion flowered, and curiosity followed. "She didn't ask that about human dominance?"

"It was her second question, and strictly speaking, it wasn't hers." Ash smiled and nodded, explaining, "The woman sitting next to her asked it. Quee Lee simply repeated the question, since she had won your attention."

A brief pause ended with the wary question:

"What then did the woman ask me?"

Ash stared at the remaining displays, and with a quiet firm voice said, "I've spoken with Quee Lee. At length. She remembers asking you, 'What was the earliest sentient life to arise in the galaxy?'"

The simple question generated a sophisticated response. An ocean of learning was tapped, and from that enormity a single turquoise thread was pulled free, and offered. Five candidates were named in a rush. Then the historian rapidly and thoroughly described each species, their home worlds, and eventual fates.

"None survived into the modern age," he said sadly. "Except as rumor and unsubstantiated sightings, the earliest generation of intelligence has died away."

Ash nodded, and waited.

"How could I forget such a very small thing?"

"Because it is so small," Ash replied. "The honest, sad truth is that your age is showing. I'm an old man for my species, but that's nothing compared to you. The Vozzen journeyed out among the stars during my Permian. You have an enormous and dense and extraordinarily quick mind. But it is a mind. No matter how vast and how adept, it suffers from what is called bounded rationality. You don't know everything, no matter how much you wish otherwise. You're living in an enriched environment, full of opportunities to learn. And as long as you wish to understand new wonders, you're going to have to allow, on occasion, little pieces of your past to fade away."

"But why did such a trivial matter bother me so?" asked Master.

And then in the next instant, he answered his own question. "Because it was trivial, and lost. Is that why? I'm not accustomed to forgetting. The sensation is novel . . . it preyed upon my equilibrium . . . and wore a wound in my mind. . . !"

"Exactly, exactly," lied Ash. "Exactly, and exactly."

*　　*　　*

After giving him fair warning, Ash left the historian. "The final probes still need to disengage themselves," he explained. Then with a careful tone, he asked, "Should I bring your assistant to you? Would you like to see him now?"

"Please."

"Very well." Ash pretended to step outside, turning in the darkened hallway, centuries of practice telling him where to step. Then he was inside the secondary chamber, using a deceptively casual voice, mentioning to Shadow, "By the way, I think I know what you are."

"What I am?"

With a sudden fierceness, Ash asked, "Did you really believe you could fool me?"

The alien said nothing, and by every physical means, he acted puzzled but unworried.

Ash knew better.

"Your body is mostly Aaback, but there's something else. If I hadn't suspected it, I wouldn't have found it. But what seems to be your brain is an elaborate camouflage for a quiet, nearly invisible neural network."

The alien reached with both hands, yanking one of the cables free from his forehead. Then a long tongue reached high, wiping the gray blood from the wound. A halfway choked voice asked, "What did you see inside me?"

"Dinners," Ash reported. "Dinners reaching back for billions of years."

Silence.

"Do you belong to one of the first five species?"

The alien kept yanking cables free, but he was powerless to void the drifters inside his double-mind.

"No," said Ash, "I don't think you're any of those five." With a sly smile, he reported, "I can tell. You're even older than that, aren't you?"

The tongue retreated into the mouth. A clear, sorry voice reported, "I am not sure, no."

"And that's why," said Ash.

"Why?"

"The woman asked that question about the old species, and you picked that moment because of it." He laughed, nodded. "What did you use? How did you cut a few minutes out of a Vozzen's perfect memory. . . ?"

"With a small disruptive device—"

"I want to see it."

"No."

Ash kept laughing. "Oh, yes. You are going to show it to me!" Silence.

"Master doesn't even suspect," Ash continued. "You were the one who wanted to visit me. You simply gave the Vozzen a good excuse. You heard about me somewhere, and you decided that you wanted me to peer inside his soul, and yours. You were hoping that I would piece together the clues and tell you what I was seeing in your mind—"

"What do you see?" Shadow blurted.

"Basically, two things." With a thought, he caused every link with Shadow to be severed, and with a professional poise, he explained, "Your soul might be ten or twelve years old. I don't know how that could be, but I can imagine: In the earliest days of the universe, when the stars were young and metal-poor, life found some other way to evolve. A completely separate route. Structured plasmas, maybe. Maybe. Whatever the route, your ancestors evolved and spread, and then died away as the universe grew cold and empty. Or they adapted, on occasion. They used organic bodies as hosts, maybe."

"I am the only survivor," Shadow muttered. "Whatever the reason, I cannot remember anyone else like me."

"You are genuinely ancient," Ash said, "and I think you're smarter than you pretend to be. But this ghost mind of yours isn't that sophisticated. Vozzens are smarter, and most humans, too. But when I was watching you thinking, looking at something simple— when I saw dinners reaching back for a billion years—well, that kind of vista begs for an explanation."

Ash took a deep breath, and then said, "Your memory has help. Quantum help. And this isn't on any scale that I've ever seen, or imagined possible. I can pull in the collective conscience of a few trillion Masters from the adjacent realities . . . but with you, I can't even pick a number that looks sane . . ."

The alien showed his pink teeth, saying nothing.

"Are you pleased?" Ash asked.

"Pleased by what?"

"You are probably the most common entity in Creation," said Ash. "I have never seen such a signal as yours. This clear. This deep, and dramatic. You exist, in one form or another, in a fat, astonishing portion of all the possible realities."

Shadow said, "Yes."

"Yes what?"

"Yes," he said with the tiniest nod, "I am pleased."

*   *   *

Always, the sun held its position in the fictional sky. And always, the same wind blew with calm relentlessness. In such a world, it was easy to believe that there was no such monster as time, and the day would never end, and a man with old and exceptionally sad memories could convince himself, on occasion, that there would never be another night.

Ash was last to leave the shop.

"Again," the historian called out, "thank you for your considerable help."

"Thank you for your generous gift." Ash found another cup of tea waiting for him, and he sipped down a full mouthful, watching as Shadow untethered the floating pack. "Where next?"

"I have more lectures to give," Master replied.

"Good."

"And I will interview the newest passengers onboard the Ship."

"As research?"

"And as a pleasure, yes."

Shadow was placing a tiny object beside one of the bristlecone's roots. "If you don't give that disruptor to me," Ash had threatened, "I'll explain a few deep secrets to the Vozzen."

Of course, Shadow had relented.

Ash sipped his tea, and quietly said, "Master. What can you tell me about the future?"

"About what is to come—?" the alien began.

"I never met a historian who didn't have opinions on that subject," Ash professed. "My species, for instance. What will happen to us in the next ten or twenty million years?"

Master launched himself into an abbreviated but dense lecture, explaining to his tiny audience what was possible about predicting the future and what was unknowable, and how every bridge between the two was an illusion.

His audience wasn't listening.

In a whisper, Ash said to Shadow, "But why live this way? With him, in this kind of role?"

In an Aaback fashion, the creature grinned. Then Shadow peered over the edge of the canyon, and speaking to no one in particular, he explained, "He needs me so much. This is why."

"As a servant?"

"And as a friend, and a confidant." With a very human shrug, he asked Ash, "How could anyone survive even a single day, if they didn't feel as if they were, in some little great way, needed?"

The Haw River Trolley

Andy Duncan

CHARLIE POOLE AND HIS FRIENDS WENT INTO GIB-
sonville one Sunday to see a pirate movie, and there he took
another step toward his ruination and glory.

"Boys," Charlie barked as they emerged into the sunlight, blinking, and greasy with popcorn. As he spoke he looked at none of
them but at the sky and the buildings all around, as if by "Boys" he
meant not just the pockmarked, lint-eared mill hands he currently
happened to stand among, but anyone in earshot in the heavens
and the earth who had the sense to listen. "Boys, that Mr. Jean
Lafitte, he done it up right, now, I tell you what. Fan out, men.
Must be something we can sail off with in this dink-ass tank town."

Ding came the reply, and then again: Ding. Ding. Ding. It was
the Haw River trolley creeping down the middle of the street, old
Whitesell flailing away at the bell to warn away traffic and doing so
fine a job there were no wagons, no horses, no automobiles in sight.
The street was deserted, except for a blue-tick hound astraddle the
tracks, riveted by the oncoming trolley that nosed to a stop two
inches from the hound's left hind leg. The traveler's first rule is to
piss when you can, so the well-traveled hound lifted his leg and
mustered some piddle onto the bumper as old Whitesell called out:

"Capri Theater, all out for the Capri Theater, next stop First
Baptist."

No one got off, because there was no one on in the first place. The trolley sagged sideways as Charlie stepped aboard. As many a juke-joint tough had learned, Charlie looked like a little banty-weight man, but he carried a lot of weight. He won bets whenever there was a scale nearby, and after turning out his pockets looking for sinkers but finding only picks and garters and a bottle opener, the losers would pay up and ask where a little man could hide one hundred and ninety pounds. "I my ownself weigh only one hundred and forty," Charlie would reply. "All the rest is dick and talent."

No jailhouse built in Gibsonville could hold Charlie Poole, for there was no jailhouse built in Gibsonville. Boys who ran shine or fought in the streets or fired their guns on payday were fined on the spot and taken home to be shamed by their mothers and whaled by their fathers and emulated by their siblings. By seventeen, Charlie Poole knew the police on a first-name basis, both of them, and their wives and parents and children and pets, too, and he was always good to remember their birthdays and slip them a little extra along with the fine, because—he reasoned—they didn't hardly make nothing and, being public servants, made all sorts of sacrifices, such as staying sober each day for hours at a time.

"You ain't a bad sort, Charlie Poole," the police chief said to him one evening, amid yet another drunk and disorderly. "Why you want to cut up any such a way, and pay out everything you make at the mill?"

"Aw, Chief, if I didn't spend it on gals and liquor," Charlie replied, "you know I'd probably just waste it."

Other than devilment, the only thing to which Charlie applied himself was playing the banjo, which was devilment enough for some in the town. On fine sunny days he sent a youngun down to the mill to report that Charlie Poole was sick today and couldn't come, and then the invalid proceeded to sit in the sun on the Haw River bridge, in plain sight of the mill, picking and singing "Baltimore Fire" and "Falling by the Wayside" and "Jealous Mary." The giggling worker girls crowded into the big arched windows on the top floor to clap and sing along and holler requests. The ones who had been to Greensboro whistled. When the foreman eventually came out and told Charlie Poole he was fired and banished and done, Charlie just laughed at him, slung his banjo over his shoulder, went on up to the mill and took his place in the line, big as houses, and collected notes from the gals the rest of the day.

This was Charlie Poole, and old Whitesell knew him well, so he squinted at his new passenger, suspicious.

"This here's one fine hardworking hound," Charlie told old Whitesell, leaning out and down to scratch the dog's head one-handed. "Yessiree Bob. When he's on the case, I hardly have to pee on a thing. Come up out of there, Mr. Whitesell, my turn now."

Old Whitesell looked at Charlie, at the trolley's empty benches, at the no-account boys on the sidewalk. "Huh?" he said, and meant it.

"I said, come up out of there," Charlie repeated, and the next thing old Whitesell knew, the two men had switched places: old Whitesell in the street, Charlie at the tiller ringing the bell and wearing old Whitesell's little red cap. Until that moment, old Whitesell always thought the cap made him look rakish and sophisticated, but it made the wide-toothed, bristly-haired Charlie Poole look like a grinder's monkey, and old Whitesell resolved never to wear it again.

Ding, ding. "All aboard!" Charlie yelled, pulling away. Everyone watched the trolley gather speed, there being nothing else to watch, and rather than brake at the curve, Charlie seemed to step it up a little, so that it went into the bend at something approaching a brisk walk. Old Whitesell closed his eyes and clenched his jaw and waited for a crash that didn't happen. He opened his eyes to see only the empty track vanishing around the corner of Schlosser's general store.

Forgetting, in his excitement, to shuffle, old Whitesell scampered with the hound and the wastrel youth to the corner. From there a person could look until his eyes gave out down the track's longest single stretch, five miles straight as a, well, straight as a rail through the loblolly pines toward the town of Haw River. They reached this corner and stopped dead, mouths open. Far away, past First Baptist and the next stop and the next and the edge of town, tracks and pines converged in a gray-green blur, but between that blur and the gawkers, the trolley was nowhere to be seen. The Haw River trolley, like Haw River itself from this vantage point, had been rendered purely theoretical.

"Damn," said one wastrel. "Charlie must be flying in that thing."

"Charlie don't waste no time, that's for sure," said another.

Old Whitesell knew there was no way in creation any part of that trolley could go five miles a minute even if you blew it up and clocked the fragments, but like most people who know the impossible to be true, or the truth to be impossible, he kept his mouth shut.

By now, a veteran crime victim who knew his obligations would

have hollered for the police, and he would not have had to holler
long. The police chief was only a few yards away, relaxing over a
cocaine-and-soda in Schlosser's back room with Schlosser himself,
who was relating yet again the story of the Danville man of his
thirdhand acquaintance who died of a brain full of earwigs, a brain
now on display by appointment at the Mutter Museum in Phila-
delphia. But old Whitesell had no such police experience, no such
understanding of the many demands society makes on a crime
victim—no understanding, really, that he *was* a crime victim,
merely that he had witnessed a marvel, like a hoop snake or a
murder light.

The Lottie Moon ladies were beginning to file out of First Baptist and look for the trolley. Old Whitesell didn't know what to tell
them. A man who flouted the maximum possible electric-trolley
speeds ordained by Thomas Edison and God wasn't likely to put a
crick in his back bowing to the printed schedule of the Graham-
Haw River-Burlington Transit Co. The fine print at the bottom of
that document said: "All times approx. owing to the unforeseen."
Old Whitesell sat with a sigh on the curb, where the hound ropily
nuzzled him. This was definitely one of those approx. days.

Years later, people across six counties, from Yadkinville to Hills-
borough, claimed to have seen Charlie Poole clanging past on his
trolley that lazy afternoon.

The scabby-kneed children running along behind in Belews
Creek and Cornatzer and Tyro and Stony Knoll had never seen a
trolley before, and they didn't know it was customarily preceded
into town by tracks. They skipped and waved and whooped at the
grinning, towheaded man at the tiller who slowed just long enough
to let them scramble aboard and then sped off again. Later, safely
returned to dusty yards and splintered porches, they couldn't
remember how they got back, exactly.

One who remembered quite vividly not climbing aboard in the
first place was sixteen-year-old Maude Gibson of Haw River, out on
a rare stroll without her folks. A fresh young man paced her in his
trolley for blocks, begging and wheedling and promising the moon
and the stars and the Haw River itself coursing backward for her
pleasure, if only she would take a "little spin." The trolley teemed
with soapless ragamuffins who egged him on, and Maude had the
odd notion that were she to climb aboard, she too would become
dirty-faced and ten. She walked faster, then trotted, then ran, then
cut across yards and vaulted fences, and still there were the masher
and his trolley, each clang of his bell reverberating inside her.

Finally home, minus her hat and one heel, she slammed and locked the front door and stumbled squalling into the arms of her parents, who over her sobs exchanged grave looks that said they knew this day would come the day the rails were laid, for Satan is packed and ready to ride, yes Lord.

More than a year later, as Maude, a grown woman now, stood before a nightshirted J. P., straining both to hear his mumbled recitation and to prop up a drunken Charlie Poole at her side, the *dings* of the wind chimes dancing in tornado weather outside the parlor window made her think of the masher on the trolley and realize, for the first time, that he had been none other than this self-same Charlie Poole. This belated realization suddenly made their union look like fate. Well, hell, then, she told herself, relaxing the leg muscles she had tensed to spring, I reckon I'll go through with it—a decision she would alternately regret and revel in for the next fifty years. Not an hour after the ceremony, Maude wept in the bathroom, Charlie in the bed picked "You Ain't Talkin' to Me," and the J. P.'s new chickenhouse was carried away in the storm.

Far Barbary

R. Garcia y Robertson

"From the fury of the Tartars, Oh Lord deliver us."
—Pope Gregory IX

Khwarezm

SIR GARETH DOUGLAS HAD DARK TOUSLED HAIR, gray eyes, a ready grin, and deft fingers, but never acquired the knack for chopsticks, not in nearly two years with the Tartars. Reduced to eating rice with his fingers, Sir Gareth sat in full armor, the bowl in his steel lap, on the forward pagoda tower of the Cathayan warship *Hwang Hai*, feeling the stroke as banks of galley slaves brought him ever closer to the fortress palace on the promontory ahead. Vultures circled above, drawing wild rocs as well, looking forward to lunching on human carrion.

Not that hungry himself, Gareth ate compulsively to numb his fear, wanting something bland in his stomach before going into battle. On the far side of sparkling Khwarezm Bay, the landward wall of the Shah's palace was under assault by an army of Tartars, using siege towers, Greek fire, and war kites—much to the delight of the circling scavengers. Arrows flew and men died, comfortably far away at the moment, but getting closer with each pull of the oar. Sir Gareth studied the opposite bulkhead, noting how the *Hwang Hai*'s pagoda forecastle was put together like a carved Chinese puzzle box, without a single nail or peg.

"Ready to go round-eyes?" asked his *minghan* commander, a thin-faced Tartar with a sharp chin and scared cheeks.

Gareth had heard enough Tartar to know he had been insulted, but he gave the commander his best dumb Scots barbarian grin, licking rice grains off his fingers. Tartars liked you to go happy into battle, otherwise why go to war? As the Tartars saw it, they were totally in the right. Khwarezm had massacred a peaceful embassy, killing merchants and diplomats, along with some number of Tartar spies—which Tartars did not take lightly.

Already the Tartar Khan had taken Bokhara and Samarkand, stabling his horses in the Golden Mosque, and telling the aghast mullahs, "You must have greatly angered your God, for I am who he has sent." Being in the right did not make the Tartars any less terrible, instead it made them insanely ferocious, coldly determined to crush their enemy into dust.

And they wanted Gareth to do the crushing. Pulling on his steel gauntlets, he lowered his visor, picking up the big two-handed claymore leaning against the polished bulkhead. So far the Shah's fortress palace had turned back every Tartar attack, but spies had found a weak spot on the seaward side, a stretch of seawall north of the Harem Tower defended solely by steep cliffs and harem eunuchs. Regular troops were not allowed on the wall walk overlooking the harem gardens, to keep offending eyes off the Shah's women. Tartars thought it ludicrous to put modesty above military necessity, never cutting corners when it came to war; employing Cathayan engineers, Hindu courtesans, and Western knights, as occasion demanded. Right now they needed someone in heavy plate armor to be first out of the puzzle box when the bow's upper gangplank came down on the water gate's battlements—that someone was Gareth.

Grinning Tartars in leather and iron patted his armored back as he made his way to the front, where the big ironbound drawbridge stood ready to drop. "Very good, round-eyes. Being white-faced does not make you a coward."

Sir Gareth cheerfully gave them the armored finger. Tartars disdained foolhardy courage, witness their willingness to let him lead the charge. Gareth had the armor, so he should go first. Tartars fought to win, not to impress the enemy with heroics.

Hefting his heavy claymore, Gareth also had small use for heroics. He was going to fight—because he dared not say no to the Tartars—but he would not like it. He hated fighting people he did not even know. Tartars might despise the Muslims for massacring their embassy, but the Shah of Khwarezm had done nothing to Gareth. He far preferred fighting someone he really had a hate for —like the English, who had taken his lands and driven him into exile. He would have happily fought the English.

With a thud, the *Hwang Hai* hit the wall and the pagoda tower swayed alarmingly. Bugles blew, and firecrackers banged, sounding the attack. Down came the drawbridge with a crash, and Sir Gareth charged forward swinging his claymore, giving the clan battle cry, "A Douglas, A Douglas—"

—running straight into a wall of flames. Eunuchs with flame-throwers were waiting for him, crouched behind brass tubes full of Greek fire, attached to hand bellows, pumping flaming naphtha onto Sir Gareth's face and chest.

But that was why he had armor. Searing heat shot through his visor slits, shutting Gareth's eyes and singeing his lashes. His surcoat caught fire as he surged forward, a mass of flames, blindly swinging his huge claymore. Gareth did not hit anyone, but he cleared a spot on the battlements, driving back the flamethrowers, as arrows clanged off his armor. Nothing Khwarezm could throw at him would get through tempered German steel.

When he could see again the eunuchs had vanished, and Tartar shock troops were pouring past, dodging his sword and shouting, "Dumb barbarian, be careful with that cleaver."

Grounding the claymore, he tried to put himself out, ripping off the last of his surcoat and beating at the flames. Two Tartars stopped to help, swatting at parts he could not reach. None of the naphtha had gotten through the armor, much less the padded arming coat underneath.

Scorched and shaken, Gareth opened his visor to gulp air, and glance about. Tartars had taken the wall walk and were lowering themselves on lassos into the inner court. Not practical in plate armor, so Gareth headed for a plank laid across the gap separating the battlements from the harem wall—at the far end was a scaling ladder leading down into the harem gardens. Crossing the plank and descending the ladder, he entered a world of sunlight and silken luxury, ringed by tall green cypresses. Pebbled paths led between perfumed fountains and ponds dotted with water lilies. Alas there were no harem damsels bathing by the fountains, just dead eunuchs face down amid the golden carp, and merciless Tartar assault troops scurrying about armed with fire maces and rapid-fire bows.

Never having been in a harem before, Gareth could not resist sightseeing. Having no interest in how the battle might be going, he tucked his steel helmet under his arm and strolled through light airy rooms divided by white arabesque screens. Colorful birds sang in ivory cages. Clanking past tiled baths and cushioned alcoves of aromatic wood, he pictured them filled with young women in various states of undress, eyes downcast, set to do their master's bidding. The place even smelled of women, a clean musky odor tinged with soap and perfume, totally different from an attack tower jammed with sweaty farting Tartars. Women were such different creatures —just seeing their things and smelling their odors put him in another world—soft, clean, and exciting. How fitting that a place inhabited solely by females should be so beautiful.

Gareth was jerked out of his reverie by the first female body. Slumped on some cushions, long dark hair veiling her face, she seemed peacefully asleep until he bent down to look closer. Her skin had the color and delicacy of a fawn's, but unseeing eyes looked back through the strands of hair with an astonished death stare. Sir Gareth had seen dead bodies aplenty, even women's bodies, but this was not a battlefield, nor some diseased camp. Someone came into this woman's tasteful bedroom, not to rob or rape, but to casually put an end to her, then go on about his business.

Sickened, Gareth wanted to do something for her, but the woman was dead, and a foreigner to boot, so he could not even say the right words. What a senseless Godless waste. Taking off his steel gauntlets, he closed her eyes with his bare hand, thinking whoever you are, you are dearly missed.

Sir Gareth rose to retrace his steps, but quickly came upon another body, this one in a white head-to-ankle gown, soaked with red blood. At the same time he heard screams and the slap of bare feet on marble. Stepping out into a sunlit court, he saw several women run past, one unveiled and wide-eyed. Seeing his bared sword they cried in terror, and dashed off down a vine-covered arcade, frantic to escape him.

Hard to blame them. He meant to get out of the harem himself, cutting across the garden, heading for the plank that led back to the battlements. More veiled women ran past. He wanted somehow to help them but could not even speak their language, and they wanted nothing to do with him. Another woman came pattering up the path he was on, completely veiled, and nearly colliding with him. Suddenly confronted by a strapping Scot in scorched armor holding a huge shining claymore, she came to a dead stop, shrieking, "Holy shit!"

Hardly believing his ears, Gareth grabbed the veiled woman's arm to keep her from getting away, asking, "Did you say 'shit'?"

Again English issued from beneath the veil, more guarded this time, "May Allah forgive, I did not mean to, sir."

Still holding her silken arm, Sir Gareth lifted the veil from the woman's face, and found scared blue eyes looking back at him. She was young and blonde with Cupid's bow lips and tear-stained mascara—beautiful, not the face he expected to find under a harem veil. He asked, "Who are you?"

"Lynette," she replied softly, looking directly back at him. "Lynette Hedley."

He knew some Redesdale Hedleys on the English side of the Borders—not the sorts you want to meet on a dark moor. "Lynette Hedley? From where? Reidswire? Otterburn?"

"London." She thought for a moment, then added, "White Chapel really, though mother moved to Bankside when I was but a girl . . ."

He should have known from the hard-clipped accent that Lynette was a true southron, London-born, with no trace of the Borders left in her. And a Muslim renegade as well from the sound of it. Sir Gareth could not shake the feeling that he was hallucinating all this. "How in hell did you ever get here?"

Lynette looked unsure how to answer. "Praise be to Allah, 'tis a terrible long story, but when I was just a girl . . ."

Before she could even get started, a couple out-of-breath Tartars arrived, plainly disappointed to see Lynette caught by an overarmed Scot. One bowman told him in curt Tartar, "Kill her when you are through, Noyan's orders."

"Naturally," Gareth replied pleasantly, trying not to alarm Lynette, "but we could use a bit of privacy first."

Nodding in terse agreement, the two Tartars dashed off, looking for their own women to ravage. Lynette asked suspiciously, "What did they say?"

"You really and truly do not wish to know." Sir Gareth was scared, more than Lynette in some ways, who obviously thought she had a protector. Gareth knew how tenuous his standing was with the Tartars: They valued his plate armor in an assault, but thought him just another dumb barbarian underneath. And they were right. Tartars were fiendishly smart, making the fierce Scots aristocracy look like fey posers in plaid skirts, gay bonnets, and French hose. His only hope was to get Lynette out of the harem and onto the *Hwang Hai*, then cut a deal with his superiors, who owed him something for being first out of the box—with luck, Lynette could be that something. Turning toward the battlements, he commanded, "Come with me."

"Of course, Sir Knight." Lynette happily let him drag her down the garden path, saying, "It is so terribly good to see an Englishman after so many years abroad . . ."

"In truth, I have the honor to be Scots," Gareth told her, hoisting Lynette up onto the harem wall, setting her next to the plank bridge that led to the battlements.

"That explains the dreadful accent," Lynette laughed from her perch atop the wall.

"Learned it in prison to pass the time," Gareth explained.

Coyly Lynette extended a small white hand to help him up the scaling ladder. "Any fellow Briton is always roundly welcome."

Taking the cool slim hand in his, he scrambled up to stand beside her, no small trick in full armor. "We were at war when I left Scotland."

"Seems like we still are," Lynette sniffed, getting up and walking the narrow plank to the battlements. From there they could see Tartars pouring through the harem bridgehead into the heart of the Shah's fortress, cutting the palace off from the sea gate, trapping the doomed defenders on the landward wall, which was already under heavy assault. So much for the Shah of Khwarezm, who only this spring had ruled an empire stretching from the Indian Ocean to the great sea of grass.

And Gareth had been the first man across, a point he made in some force to Kaidu, his foxy *minghan* commander, when they met on the tower drawbridge. Tartars were notoriously just—witness their total trashing of Khwarezm to rectify robbery and murder—so traditionally the first man to enter an enemy fortress, and live, got his pick of the loot. Ushering Lynette modestly forward, Gareth announced happily, "Here is my pick."

Kaidu laughed courteously. "She is indeed a gem, with her sapphire eyes, ivory skin, and spun gold hair. But how like a barbarian to chose a girl. This is a Shah's palace, you could have a real sapphire worth ten-score women."

Gareth admitted he was a big dumb barbarian easily led about by his prick, but he was happy with what he had. Lynette beamed cheerfully, not understanding Tartar, but knowing they were complimenting her. Kaidu grimaced, hating to take away a child's bauble. "Alas, all women in the harem must be killed."

"She is not in the harem," Gareth pointed out brightly, hoping Kaidu would stretch the point.

Kaidu rubbed his sharp chin, easily spotting the flaw in this argument. "But she came from the harem, did she not?"

"Then let me speak to the Noyan," Gareth demanded, knowing

his recent heroism guaranteed an audience—prompt, successful obedience being the prime Tartar virtue. So with Gareth and Lynette looking on, Kaidu courteously made his case to the Noyan in the forward pagoda tower, saying this big ironclad Scot led the attack, entitling him to his pick of the spoils—but the dumb barbarian was stuck on this one woman, even refusing a small fortune, which made Gareth sound ridiculously choosy. Would the Noyan grant an exception and let the woman live?

One-eyed and battle-scarred, the black-armored Noyan politely indulged his victorious subordinates, but told them, "Our Khan's orders are that all the Shah's women must die." He smiled at Lynette to show he had no hard feelings, and Lynette beamed back, not knowing she was hearing her death sentence. Apologizing to Gareth, the Noyan added, "I know this is hard on you, seeing she is of your people."

"No, she is actually English," Gareth explained, "our rude neighbors to the south, who continually invade and harass us." Being taken for English in distant parts was a cross Scots had to bear. "They are in fact the reason I am in exile."

"Splendid." The Noyan smiled broadly. "There is no problem. Revenge yourself for the wrongs done your people by ravishing and killing her, then take your reward from among the wives and daughters of the garrison."

Of course, how stupid of him not to see it. Giving his best dumb barbarian smile, Gareth backed out of the audience, leading Lynette across the drawbridge to the wall walk. Sensing something wrong, she asked, "Why are you taking me back?"

"This is bad, very bad," he told Lynette, terribly worried for her. "They say you must die."

"Are you sure?" Lynette did not look convinced. "They were so awfully nice to me. How well do you know the language?"

Too well. "Oh, they liked you well enough—they just want you dead. Nothing personal, all the Shah's women have to die." That shut Lynette up, leaving her with nothing to say for the first time today, shocked by the enormity of the crime. "But it is not a total loss," he told her, "they promised me first pick of any lasses left alive."

"What will you do?" Lynette asked meekly, losing her easy air of English superiority, horrified by such senseless slaughter and desperately needing his aid. What was happening here was no worse than what the English had done in Scotland—like massacring the women of Berwick when they took it from the Douglases—but he found it hard to blame that on Lynette.

"Astounding as it sounds, I would save you if I could. Save both of us in fact." He had no real alternative given a direct order by his Noyan—except to kill her, which he would not do. So he was about to commit arrant disobedience in battle, a flaying offense. "But we must find a way out of here, and you know the palace far better than I."

Lynette nodded, suddenly all brisk business, lifting her skirt and crossing the plank, telling her knight, "Follow me."

He did, back through the ghastly harem gardens to a little door half-hidden by a rose arbor. Lynette tried the door and found it locked. Stepping back, she told him, "This door leads to the quarters of the black eunuchs, and the Mews Gate."

Using his claymore as a lock pick, Gareth bought it down in an overhand blow that shattered the bolt and door. His steel boot finished the job, and they were in, dodging through dark deserted rooms smelling of ambergris, heading deeper into the palace labyrinth. Lynette halted when they came to a tiled chamber lit by an airshaft, with a silk divan, a giant parrot cage, and a prettily painted wooden cabinet on the wall. "This is the chamber of the chief of the black eunuchs," she explained, "and that locked cabinet holds the gate keys."

His claymore demolished the pretty little painted cabinet, and Lynette scooped up the big iron keys, leading him to another locked gate, thicker and stronger than the one in the rose arbor. Glad he did not have to hack his way through, Gareth asked what was on the other side. "This is the Mews Gate," Lynette replied, as she tried the keys, finding one that turned the lock. "It leads to the Mews Tower and the eunuchs' baths, so nobody uses it but eunuchs and mews boys."

And Tartar bowmen. Waiting on the far side of the door was a grim-faced sentry who informed Gareth, "Noyan's orders, no women may leave the harem alive—take her back or kill her here."

Damning Tartar efficiency, Gareth took a swipe at the fellow with his claymore, driving the startled guard away from the door. His bow useless, the astonished Tartar fell back, parrying with his short scimitar and blowing furiously on an alarm whistle hanging from his neck. Knowing the man could not get through his plate armor, Gareth pressed the whistling Tartar back into the courtyard beyond, not wanting to kill the fellow if he could help it—having displeased his Noyan enough already.

Ducking daintily past the grunting, slashing men, her veil held demurely in place, Lynette went straight to the door at the base of the Mews Tower and started frantically trying keys. Boot steps echoed through the eunuchs' quarters as Tartars rushed to answer the guard's frantic whistle—in seconds they would swarm into the courtyard, too many to deal with at once. Gareth slammed the Mews Gate closed with his heel, making sure it locked, hoping it held the Tartars. They immediately started beating on the Mews Gate, but Gareth kept his attention on the man in front who was still hopping about, blowing his whistle.

"I have the door," Lynette called to him, straightening up and turning the lock, swinging the tower door open. "Please, finish up your fight."

"Just get in," he shouted between swings, "I'll be there." Seeing the woman getting away, the Tartar redoubled his efforts, weaving in and out, but Gareth backed into the Mews Tower, and Lynette slammed the door shut, shooting the bolt. "Well done," he wheezed, pleased he did not fight Tartars every day. "What now?"

"Up," Lynette pointed to winding wooden stairs decorated with bird droppings, leading up into the mews. Stair climbing was the second hardest thing to do in armor, but Gareth threw himself into it, grabbing the dung-spattered rail and hauling himself up after Lynette.

She had to pick the tallest tower in the keep, with the steepest, most rickety stairs, not to mention the bird shit. Huffing and clanking up the steps, he heard the door splintering behind him, knowing the Tartars would soon have it down, being frighteningly adept at such things. Lynette beckoned cheerfully from the top of the steps, holding open the trapdoor like an angel atop the stairway to Heaven. What did Saint Augustine say about the English?—"Not Angles, but Angels." For once the old Roman was right—though being clergy, he meant the boys.

As Lynette helped hoist him into the mews, the tower door went flying off its hinges below, and Tartars poured in, starting up the wooden steps two at a time. An arrow came shooting through the open trap, followed by another. Lynette dropped the trap shut behind Gareth, thanking Allah as she slammed home the bolt. Two more arrows thudded into the door from below.

Sitting on the straw floor gasping for breath, Gareth looked about, amazed by the big quiet barnlike mews, lit by dusty gold shafts of light falling from bright chinks of blue sky beneath the high eves. Hawks and even eagles sat on wall roosts reached by long ladders. Pigeons cooed in cages and among the rafters. Most surprising were the rocs, huge twelve-foot-tall raptors, silent and hooded, sitting on perches spaced along the floor, their razor-sharp beaks able to sever a head or a hand. Gareth had seen wild ones aloft, at a distance where size was difficult to judge—up close they made the eagles seem like sparrows.

"Here, help me with this," Lynette called out, tugging on what looked like an oversized doll's house, or a very tiny cottage made from wood and paper, about shoulder tall, with a large bird's perch on top. He helped her haul it over to the tallest roc, a fifteen-foot giantess with red-brown plumage. Lynette clamped a manacle to the huge raptor's leg, chaining it to the roof of the tiny house, saying, "This is not made for a man in armor."

He looked up at the tremendous bird. "I thought rocs could carry off baby elephants?"

"Poetic exaggeration," Lynette explained, as Tartars began beating on the trapdoor.

Seeing he had no choice, he stripped off the fine tempered German steel that made him virtually invulnerable, and had been his livelihood—keeping only his dagger and claymore. While he stripped, Lynette threw open the great wooden downwind doors, letting blue limitless space into the mews. Then she went around opening the pigeon cages, and then loosing the smaller hawks, which chased after the fleeing pigeons into the blue sky beyond.

With a bang, the trap flew open, and a Tartar head popped up. Taking a swipe with his sword, Gareth made the nomad duck back down. Lynette returned with two pigeons in a bamboo cage, which she placed inside the little house, saying, "Now the rocs."

Gareth grunted in agreement, still stabbing through the open trap, dodging arrows fired from below, while Lynette ran from roc to roc, freeing the huge birds, untying the traces and stripping off their hoods. When only the giantess remained, she called to Gareth, holding open the door to the little house, "Come, Sir Knight, your castle awaits."

Slamming the trap shut, he dashed for the door to the little house. As he dived through, Lynette pulled the line releasing the roc's hood, then tumbled in herself, closing the door. Inside was a single room with a rattan floor, wood and paper walls, sliding windows, and bedding folded neatly in one corner. An arrow ripped through the paper wall, passing between them.

With a lurch the roc took off, seizing the perch atop the house with her talons, lifting them easily, and flying down the length of the mews and out the wide-open downwind door. The top of the

Mews Tower was set on a windmill turntable, keeping it always oriented for take-off, and the roc's huge long wings did the rest, catching the wind and carrying them away. Tartar arrows arched after the rising raptor. Looking out a window Gareth saw the Shah of Khwarezm's doomed fortress palace fall away behind them, already on fire and crawling with Tartars. Blue water spread out beyond the besieged palace, the flat sparkling Inland Sea, warm and calm beneath the noontide sun. Birds flew alongside them, hawks and doves fanning out into the sky, soaring in all directions, free as the wind.

And so were they. Three Tartar flying boats took off in fast pursuit—light boat hulls suspended from big gas-filled parasails, propelled by the wind and lifting vapors. By dropping ballast and tilting their parasails they rapidly gained on the roc. But the bird was headed upwind, and as soon as the flying boats hit their pressure height they lost headway and swiftly fell behind—nothing the Tartars had could touch them.

Sir Gareth looked over at Lynette lying within easy reach and grinning at him—everything in the little room was within reach. Next to her sat the two caged pigeons, the only ones not freed. He asked her, "What did they do?"

"Nothing," Lynette admitted, "but we may need them."

"Why did you loose the others?" Gareth asked, watching the flock around them slowly dissipate as he stripped off his boots and baldric, leaving only his hose and arming doublet.

"Have you never wanted to set caged birds free?" Lynette had a wild look that Gareth had not seen in the harem—but which he liked. "Sometimes you just have to set things free," she told him, "to feel the sheer joy of liberation. His Highness the Shah used to bring me caged birds just to see my glee at setting them free. Besides," Lynette added prosaically, "I knew if I let the others go, our roc would follow."

Right now their roc was lagging well behind the others who had nothing to carry. All the huge raptors were headed west, away from the Shah's palace, farther out over the Inland Sea, leaving Khwarezm and the Black Sands Desert behind. To the south lay Hyrcania and beyond that Persia, to the west Georgia and the White Salt steppe. Loosening the ties on his doublet, Gareth wondered idly, "Where are we going?"

"*Inshallah*," Lynette shrugged, "wherever the bird decides." She seemed fairly carefree about it, curled up on a cushion and smiling over at him, clearly enjoying setting herself free as well. "Rocs are trained to carry these traveling rooms, but usually they have a boy on their back to guide them."

"So we will go where she wills?" Gareth noted how comely Lynette looked, veil gone and gown askew, gold hair cascading over perfumed curves of harem-white skin—too bad Tartars meant to kill her. But thank goodness Englishwomen were notoriously loose and forward, having the morals of a mink in heat.

"Does it really matter so much?" Lynette smiled, innocently acknowledging the tension between them.

"Not at all." He reached out and pulled Lynette to him, kissing her hard on the lips—knowing you must take a firm line with the English or they never respected you. His hand slid inside her robe, feeling smooth firm curves that showed the late Shah well knew how to stock a harem. Taking eager advantage of Turkish diligence, he seized hold of her breast . . .

"Wait, wait, Sir Knight," Lynette whispered, catching his hand with hers. "You must tell me one thing first."

"What is that?" he asked, wondering what more he must do for this woman? He had saved her life and freed her from the harem. Giving up his job, his armor, the trust of the Tartars, and four very good horses—all to get her safely away. Surely he deserved a knight's reward. What more was there?

"Your name, Sir Knight." Lynette giggled coyly, guiding his hand down between her thighs. "Mother taught me as a child, 'Knowing the man's name is what separates a romantic from a whore.' So unless it absolutely cannot be helped . . ."

"Sir Gareth Douglas, at your service." His fingers found the fold they were seeking and Lynette gasped with pleasure.

"Gareth, what a sweet name," she whispered, as he pushed up her chemise, baring her white perfumed body, which the Turks kept cleanly shaved, hating to see hair on their women. It made her seem strangely childlike. "Just like King Arthur's knight."

"My mother was Welsh, and romantic," he explained, stripping off his wool and mail arming doublet.

"As opposed to Scots and practical?" Lynette asked, coolly confident even while submitting. Having escaped death and the harem, Lynette talked like she feared nothing, least of all him. "You must learn to be impractical," she warned, "otherwise you will get nowhere with me."

To prove Lynette wrong, Gareth spread her legs with a knee and slid inside her, at the same time kissing her soft acquiescent mouth, taking total possession of her. His Noyan was right, having Lynette made him feel incredibly better, and Gareth freely forgave every English atrocity committed against the Scots in their many centuries as neighbors.

As he pressed to the point of orgasm, Lynette wrapped her bare legs enthusiastically about him, drawing him in deeper, whispering, "Good knight, do not hold back in the least." Nor did he. Gareth drove harder, savoring the pleasure of possessing her, not stopping until he was totally spent, lying with Lynette curled close against him. "That was lovely," she sighed sleepily. "And worry not, dear knight. Thanks be to Allah, I am already with child."

Roc Island

Damn the English. Sir Gareth did not doubt Lynette, though she was small and hardly showed. Nor was there any doubt about the father—His Highness the late great Shah of Khwarezm, the only intact male organ allowed in the harem. Gareth had not just saved a blonde harem slave, but a potential heir to Khwarezm as well—if the baby was a boy. Under Turkish law, any royal son could succeed to the Peacock Throne making inheritance a bloody free-for-all. Boy or not, if word got out about Lynette's condition, everyone would want this baby. Tartars meant to kill it sight unseen, rooting out any remnant of the Shah who murdered their ambassadors; while survivors among the Shah's family would want the child to crown, kill, or marry off, as occasion required. Gareth asked, "Who knows this?"

"Knows what?" Lynette asked sleepily.

"That you are with child?"

"You do," she pointed out, "and my lord the Shah. Plus anyone he told, and whoever they have told, and whoever . . ." Lynette drifted peacefully off to sleep.

Wonderful. Anyone might know, even the Tartars, who had excellent spies including several in the royal household. His only consolation was that none of them knew where he and Lynette were headed—that was up to the roc. Out the windows he saw only sparkling wave tops, and tall billowing anvilheads towering over the Inland Sea. Lying back, Gareth closed his eyes, keeping a hand on Lynette's sleeping rump, well knowing she would be passing hard to hold onto—more so even than most women. Slowly the roc's long wing-beats rocked him to sleep alongside his pregnant prize.

Landfall came as a loud unexpected impact. Gareth was jerked awake by a bang and crash that threw him against one wall, with

Lynette on top of him. As he struggled to rise the little room bounced, slid, then slammed to a halt. Gulls cried, and sunlight streamed through a rent in the paper wall. They were down, but where?

Lynette sat up, leaning on him to look out the rip in the wall. "Allah be thanked, this is Roc Island. I thought she might head here."

"Roc Island?" Peering through the torn paper he saw the sea, and enormous boulders spattered with bird droppings.

"I will show you." Lynette got off him, reaching up the tilted floor to open the door, now on the ceiling. Gareth hoisted himself through the doorway, claymore in hand, finding that they had landed alongside a roc's nest made from uprooted saplings, interwoven with driftwood and jungle vines. Standing calmly beside the huge bird's nest was the feathered giantess who brought them there, still shackled to the broken house.

"This is an island rookery," Lynette told him, handing up the pigeon cage. Standing guard at the door, Gareth surveyed the jumble of bird-spattered boulders, ending in cliffs overlooking a great circle of sea. Most of the giant nests were empty—for it was past the mating season—but he saw several still occupied by late-nesting pairs. Lynette stood in the doorway, writing in Persian on tiny slips of paper with a slim brush. When he asked where she had ever learned Persian, Lynette laughed. "In a harem there is time to learn a dozen languages. I speak Turkic too."

Finishing with a flourish, she tucked the brush and ink back into her sleeve, tied the tiny slips to the pigeons' legs, then released the birds, sending them winging off to the west.

"We might have eaten those," Gareth pointed out. Roc Island looked remarkably bare. "Where are they headed?"

"Baku," she replied, with a dimpled smile. "I have friends in Baku." Lynette scrambled up to unchain the roc, releasing the giant raptor from the house, adding proudly, "Important friends."

No doubt, but food and water were more important. Telling Lynette to stay safe in the little house, he set out with sword in hand trying hard not to look like a meal; finding rainwater in natural rock pools, and stealing a mangled cow haunch from some squawking six-foot nestlings, giving new meaning to "aged beef." He returned to find Lynette engaged in afternoon prayer, on her knees and turned toward Mecca, giving industrious thanks to Allah. Making a fire, he roasted tidbits, which Lynette greedily devoured, admitting, "I am eating much more of late."

Like a mare in foal. Putting more meat on the fire, he asked,
"How came you to Khwarezm?"

Smiling, she lifted a gold strand of hair. "I was sold to Dutch
traders when I was ten. The Shah has a tremendous passion for
blondes, and his agents scour Europe for pretty blonde virgins. I
fetched a very fancy price."

More than Gareth would have brought for sure. "I never knew
the international trade in blondes was that bad."

"Hideously awful," she assured him, taking another tidbit.

"How did you become a Muslim?" Gareth thought that strange,
even for an Englishwoman.

"*La Allah il Allah,*" Lynette replied, "there is no God but God.
Actually it is a very rational religion, far more than the Gospels. I
mean if Jesus was God, how come he ate, drank, and died like a
man? How could men even kill God? After awhile I ran out of
arguments and admitted they were right. Praise be to Allah. God is
God, and Jesus and Mohammed are but his prophets."

"Enough." Gareth raised a hand. "You will not convert me."

She smiled, saying, "Just so long as you do not mind sleeping
with an infidel."

"Why should I?" Gareth had found so many biblical passages
favoring fornication with enemy women he practically considered
it a commandment. "Do you?"

Lynette laughed, "If we women could be trusted there would be
no need for harems." That night, snug in their tiny house, she told
him gravely how wonderful it felt to be safe and free—"And I fear I
have not been properly thankful to my knight and hero." Gareth
laughed, and kissed her, saying that showed she knew little of men.
"That is the whole purpose of a harem," she reminded him. "You
are only the second man I have spoken to since turning twelve."
And she was naive enough to trust him completely.

Two days later a triangle sail showed on the noontide horizon,
Arab rigged. Gareth asked, "Are your friends Arabs?"

Lynette shook her head. "These could be anyone, egg stealers,
lost mariners, fishermen seeking fresh water . . ."

"At least they are not Tartars." Gareth watched the ship anchor
in a small cove, sending boats rowing toward shore, while worried
rocs called and circled above. Men were the only beings daft
enough to raid a roc's nest. Close up, these men proved to be Turks
in armor and tufted helmets, turbaned Arab mariners, and an
incongruous quartet of Persian eunuchs in gay flowing gowns.

"These are my husband's men," Lynette declared confidently,

insisting they meet the boats at the beach. "See, they are bringing eunuchs, which means they have come for me."

Why else bring eunuchs to sea? Slinging his sword over his shoulder, he escorted Lynette down to the beach creating an incredible commotion. Eunuchs wailed and tried to hide Lynette from the men, who fell to arguing over their fate. Gareth knew enough Turkic to follow the debate—all were scandalized that he passed unchaperoned nights with one of the Shah's favored wives, and being born Godless Christians, they surely took the chance to couple like wanton dogs. Arabs among them wanted him castrated on the spot, and her stoned to death. Turks scoffed at that, saying only the Shah could stone his wives, "And gelding does little good once the mare's mounted." Persians suggested a compromise, stone him, and take her alive to the Shah.

Lynette silenced them all, calmly announcing that she carried His Highness's child, and Sir Gareth had been her chaste guardian. "We must both be safely conveyed to His Majesty's palace at Baku, or wherever it might be."

None believed her feigned modesty but all bowed to the child in her womb, hastening to obey. Arabs, Turks, and Persians all revere their mothers. And if the baby was a boy, Lynette might one day be the most revered mother of all, the Shah's mother, the Valide Sultana, mother of all mothers, with the power to put anyone who displeased her to death in cruel and amusing ways. Should Allah let that day come, none wanted to be remembered badly, for women's memories are notoriously long.

Eunuchs closed around Lynette, and hustled her into the aft cabin as soon as they were aboard ship. Gareth suddenly realized he would probably never see Lynette again, naked or otherwise.

In fact, Gareth found himself shunned aboard ship, not for being a Godless infidel, but because no one wanted to strike up a friendship with a guy about to be gelded and impaled—the usual punishment for passing a night with the Shah's wife. Bad as that was, missing Lynette was far worse. Lynette had got him hated by the Tartars, and slated for gruesome execution by the Turks—about the reward to expect for befriending the English—but all Sir Gareth could think of was her dimpled smile, and the warm weight of her body lying beside him at night. How terrible to never see her again. His own impending execution hardly seemed more final.

Sitting alone at dusk he saw the Shah's floating palace ahead, anchored off the port of Baku, which belonged to the Christian King of Georgia. The palace was saved from infidel ways by being completely self-contained, built on a huge trimaran hull, with its own gardens, bakeries, kitchens, sheep pens, and potted fruit trees. Born a nomad, the Shah of Khwarezm had devised a floating palace so he could tour his Inland Sea domains, or visit Georgia and the wild Cumans amid the comforts of home. On calm days the gleaming four-story palace could indeed be towed from one port to the next across the shallow Inland Sea. Floating above the palace was a big Cathayan balloon made of silk lined with gold-beater's skin and filled by light vapors, tethered to the top floor by a stout cable, with a small pretty two-story pavilion hanging below it. Supposedly the whole topmost floor of the palace was a harem, reserved for women and eunuchs, and roofed with gardens and walkways, splashed by freshwater fountains. That was where Lynette was headed.

Gareth got a tiny windowless room atop the palace bilges, dank, below water level, and lately used by livestock, with just a narrow cot and an oil lamp. Late that night, lying on the cot, listening to the rhythmic creak of the sea-going palace, he thought of Lynette four stories above him, lounging in some perfumed alcove or moonlit garden. Lynette must have thought of him as well because there was a knock on the door, which opened to reveal a cute young eunuch in palace colors, with a veiled woman in tow. Salaaming elaborately, the boy introduced his veiled companion. "Here is my lord's reward for his chaste defense of His Highness's honor."

How like Lynette to think of him and to cling hopelessly to their silly fairy tale of a chaste stay on Roc Island. Too bad his heart was so set on Lynette—though Gareth had heard harem courtesans diligently practiced the Karma Sutra on each other to perfect all the positions. Hastily inviting the young woman in, he shooed the eunuch off and shut the door. Then Gareth slowly lifted the veil to look at his Turkish delight.

Make that Persian, with great doelike eyes, long black lashes, and skin like pale honey. Unbelievably beautiful. Dark shining hair fell in jasmine-scented curls onto her soft cleavage. Moist rose-red lips moved, saying in Turkic, "My name is Yasmi. Does my lord like what he sees?"

Gareth just gaped at dainty little Yasmi. What was not to like? Lynette was so thoughtful to send him a woman this lovely.

"Does my lord perhaps prefer blondes?" inquired the comely young Persian.

"Blondes?" Gareth thought maybe he misheard.

"Yes, blondes," Yasmi nodded eagerly, "with blue eyes and

smooth-flowing curves?" Slim hands traced twin curves in midair.
"Perhaps," Gareth admitted, though he was certainly no fanatic.
Yasmi's light honey coloring was exquisite.

"Do not be embarrassed," Yasmi told him, "I do too."

"Really?" It had not occurred to Gareth that Yasmi had any
preference besides pleasing him. "I am sorry to be so dark."

"Oh, no, not blonde men," Yasmi laughed, "blonde women,
with round white breasts and dimples when they smile. I have never
liked men, who are all hard and hairy and do not bathe nearly as
often as they should—luckily we see little of them in a harem."

Gareth had to admit, men never much appealed to him either.

Yasmi beamed, happy they agreed, adding, "And if my lord will
permit me, many men are oafish embarrassments in bed."

"I am sorry." Gareth sincerely apologized, ashamed that his sex
had fallen short just where it tried the hardest.

"Did you know we courtesans practice the Karma Sutra
together, so we can inflame you with novel positions?" Gareth
admitted he had heard as much. "What two men would do that for
a woman?" Yasmi demanded triumphantly.

None that Gareth knew. How like Lynette to send him an
utterly lovely lesbian. Gareth asked, "Exactly why has my lady
come here?"

Yasmi smiled, "To show you something special, even magical."

"What is that?" By now Gareth guessed that special magical
something was not beneath Yasmi's silk skirts.

"Come with me, my lord." Yasmi unlatched the cabin door.
"What I must show you is without. That absurd tale of making
impassioned love in the palace bilges was just for the boy's ears."
Yasmi wrinkled her pretty nose at the stink of brine and sheep, daintily replacing her veil. "You know how eunuchs love to talk. Luckily they believe anything."

Just like dumb Scots barbarians. Slinging his claymore across
his back, Gareth followed Yasmi into the night. She led him along
a dark passage below decks that led past stinking sheep pens, store-
rooms full of lentils, and silent kitchens smelling of baking bread.
At the far end of the passage a stairway led up to the main deck.
Yasmi said a few curt words to a Persian guard, who laughed and
passed them up. Emerging on the main deck Yasmi chuckled,
telling him in Turkic, "Happily, my lord is clean shaven, so I said
you were my eunuch bodyguard, adding that your tongue was
ripped out too. Which he found most funny."

Hilarious. Gareth found himself on the palace's broad dark

fantail; with crew and servants asleep below decks and royalty disporting themselves in salons and gardens above, the aft deck was deserted, aside from sailors sleeping in the skiffs and boats moored alongside. Raising a finger for silence, Yasmi produced a pipe from her robe, lifted her veil and began to play. Into the pitch-dark night drifted the high melodious piping, which Gareth found pretty enough, but not especially magical—

—until the rope descended. In a neat reversal of the Indian rope trick, a thick knotted rope dropped out of the darkness above to hang in midair a few feet away, its frayed end just brushing the deck. Yasmi stopped piping and tucked the instrument back into her robe. "The rope is for you."

"Where does it go?" Gareth asked warily.

"My lord must answer that himself." Yasmi rose on her toes to give him a long lingering kiss good-bye, showing Gareth what he was missing, then adding slyly, "More awaits my lord above."

Or he could go back to the bilges to await execution. Gareth seized the rope, finding it gave, as though not firmly attached at the top—wherever that was. Great. Bad enough to be climbing into nowhere, he must do it on a shaky rope. Planting his foot on the bottom knot he hoisted himself onto the swaying rope, scrambling past the first few knots until his feet finally left the deck. Free of the fantail, he begin a steady ascent into darkness, climbing hand-over-hand past the upper decks, able to see into silk-curtained salons and to look down upon torchlit gardens. Luckily they could not see him. Slowly he left the lights behind, climbing higher into the warm summer night, with blackness above and blackness behind.

Something dark and solid loomed above him, turning into the wicker floor of the pretty little pavilion he had seen hanging from the Cathayan balloon. His knotted rope was tied to the first floor rail, and Gareth hauled himself onto the balcony that ran around the floating pavilion. The whole first floor was a curtained bedroom, lit warmly from within; he parted the curtains and found Lynette waiting, lying in a perfumed bed wearing silk pajamas. Lynette smiled archly at him, saying, "Bet you never thought to see me again."

"Not like this," Gareth admitted, completely thrilled by this latest turn of fortune. Slipping his sword off his shoulder he sat down beside Lynette, nuzzling her neck.

"So I was worth passing up your pick of the spoils?" Lynette asked, pleased by his enthusiasm for her.

"Well, I would have liked at least a look at the others first," Gareth admitted, starting to untie her pajamas.

Lynette giggled, stopping him with her hand. "I told you I had friends in Baku. Highly placed friends."

"Like Yasmi?" The lovely Persian that preferred blondes—too bad she could not be here too.

"Yes, Yasmi is utterly devoted. So much, I sometimes think she is sweet on me," Lynette added, coyly keeping his hands at bay. "Yasmi is but a harem slave. I have far higher friends. Come, I will show you." Lynette slid out of his grasp, leading him to stairs spiraling up behind the perfumed bed.

Disappointed they would not dally, he picked up his sword and followed Lynette upstairs to a still more sumptuous bedroom—this one jammed with women, an old white-haired grande dame seated on the bed, attended by handmaids, lute girls, and a pair of cute Cathayan manicurists. Lynette introduced Gareth to the old lady, who was Khanum Sofia, the Valide Sultana, mother to the Shah, Queen Mother of Khwarezm. Gareth bowed low, and the old lady sniffed. "He appears to be armed? And an infidel?"

"That could not be helped," Lynette explained.

"At least he is a eunuch," the Queen Mother sighed happily.

Lynette signed Gareth to silence, responding, "Which makes him perfect for our needs, able to join Yasmi without suspicion."

Looking him over minutely, the Queen Mother asked, "What does he know?"

"Nothing, thank Allah," Lynette replied brightly, as if his ignorance were a sterling recommendation. "I can tell him all he needs to know." Getting a nod from the Queen Mother, Lynette turned to Gareth. "You must understand that Her Majesty opposed plundering the Tartar embassy, and her son's war policy, which she fears has killed him."

Gareth nodded. Reasonable assumption. Plundering the Tartars was a catastrophic stupidity that had cost thousands of innocent lives—like trying to steal lunch from a lion pride. And the Tartars would keep killing until they had destroyed everyone responsible.

"Crown Prince Bayazid is gathering Kipchaks, Kazaks, and Cumans to face the Tartars," Lynette told him, though neither saw much hope there. Bayazid's father led four hundred thousand riders against the Tartars, and ten score returned. Kazaks and Cumans would do no better. "Worse yet," Lynette added, "Prince Bayazid's immoral mother is a bitter foe of the Queen Mother and schemes to replace her as Valide Sultana." So if by some miracle

Bayazid beat the Tartars, the best the Queen Mother could expect from her victorious daughter-in-law was a visit by the three mutes-of-the-bowstring. Whereas the Tartars would sew her in a sack and throw her in the sea as punishment for her son's crimes—being firm believers in parental responsibility. No wonder the old Sultana was for peace; if one side won she would be strangled, if the other side won she would drown.

Lynette went on, saying, "Her Majesty has stood for peace, and now with the support of the Caliph of Baghdad and the King of Georgia, she hopes that . . ."

Gareth never heard what the Queen Mother hoped. High piping came from below and Lynette stopped, cocking her head to listen.

"Someone is coming up the cable," cried a handmaid. Baskets and counterweights allowed people to travel up and down the balloon cable, between the pavilion and the palace's harem deck.

Grasping Gareth's hand, Lynette led him downstairs to her room, but it was too late—a basket had docked below. If Gareth tried to go back down the knotted rope, whoever was in the basket would have a clear shot at him. Instead Lynette hustled both of them into her curtained *garde robe*, setting him down on the *chaise precée*, while she watched through a chink in the curtain.

Sitting on the *chaise precée*, sword in hand, Gareth heard a trapdoor open in the bedroom floor, then armed men climbed into the room, weapons clanking. Lynette whispered to him, "It is Inaljuk, former governor of Otrar, with four bowmen."

Inaljuk was the viceroy who massacred the Tartar embassy and pocketed the plunder, a murderous felon sure to fight to the death since the Tartars had a huge reward on his head. Two bowmen stayed to guard the trap while Inaljuk and the others ascended the stairs. Shrieks and angry words came down from above. Gareth heard Inaljuk grimly announce that the Shah was dead, and the "former" Valide Sultana must vacate her quarters, turning over the slave girl Lynette. To which the Queen Mother frostily replied, "My son is no more dead than I. What proof have you?"

Good point. Inaljuk had no way of knowing whether the Shah lived. Only the Tartars knew for sure, and they were not telling —preferring to keep their enemy guessing.

But not good enough. Inaljuk won by brute force, hustling the Queen Mother and her women down the stairs to the waiting basket, rudely lifting veils, looking for the blonde one. When they did not find her, they would search the pavilion, then it would be his sword against five men in armor—not pleasant odds. He looked at Lynette, knowing she faced the same fate as the Queen Mother; Tartars already wanted her dead, while Prince Bayazid would have her strangled to kill the child in her womb. Dire circumstances had made the two women natural allies.

Hearing the basket with the Queen Mother and her women start to descend, Gareth rose from his seat. Lynette backed away from the curtain, whispering, "Bowman, coming this way."

Lynette seized his hand again and steered him around the *chaise precée*, thrusting him bodily through the curtained rear of the *garde robe*. Gareth stumbled out onto the outer balcony; the slit in the curtain was used to discreetly dump the chamber pot. Lynette backed out behind him, and he whispered to her, "I can hold them if you can make it down the knotted rope."

Spinning about, she shushed him. "No, you must find Yasmi now. Allah willing, she will know what to do."

"Yasmi?" Gareth had totally forgotten the Persian below.

"Yes, Yasmi." Lynette told him. "I will be safe enough here, until they are sure the Shah is dead and Bayazid is the new Shah. So find Yasmi as fast as you can."

"Why? How?" None of this made any sense to Gareth.

"Yasmi will know," Lynette insisted. "Now go!"

Gareth refused. "No, I will not go, not without you . . ."

Lynette silenced his protests with a long reckless kiss, then whispered, "Allah be with you, my love. Hurry back." Before Gareth could object further she gave him a hearty shove that sent him tumbling backwards over the balcony rail.

Taken by surprise, Gareth was in the air before he realized what had happened. Damn the English! His dear sweet love had shoved him over the balcony rail sending him flying into empty space— and not for the first time either. The flight from the Mews Tower had cost him his armor, and this one cost him his sword, which flipped from his grasp as he cartwheeled through the night.

Down he tumbled, picking up speed. With Scots practicality, Gareth made the best of things, twisting in midair to straighten himself out, then putting his feet together. Plunging into blackness, he prayed he would cleave the water cleanly—and not hit the palace fantail.

Missing the fantail, he slammed into the black water of the Inland Sea, shooting straight down, almost to the shallow bottom, pressure stabbing at his ears. Kicking fiercely with his feet he forced himself back to the surface, lungs bursting. His head broke the black water and he looked about, gasping for air, seeing the lights of the palace shining overhead. Lynette had aimed right, but not by much. "Sir Gareth," a soft voice called down to him from the fantail. "Is that you? It is me, Yasmi."

"It is me," he sputtered, shaking his head sourly.

"Stay there," Yasmi called down. "I will come get you."

Wondering what the slave girl meant by that, Gareth treaded water, glad the Inland Sea was shallow and warm, so friendly that storms off the desert seemed to come from nowhere. He heard splashing headed his way and presently Yasmi appeared, paddling a single-masted skiff taken from the boats moored to the fantail. Yasmi brought the skiff neatly alongside him, a boat so small that Gareth almost swamped it getting in. While he lay wet and exhausted in the bow, Yasmi broke out the sail and dropped the rudder, steering them away from the palace—off into the night. Gareth asked, "Where are we going?"

"Away from the palace," Yasmi replied, "it is not safe."

"Without Lynette?" Despite having been dropped and dunked Gareth was still worried for her, left to face Inaljuk alone.

"Inaljuk had four bowmen with him in that basket. Could you really climb the rope and cut through them to her?"

Not without his sword, now resting on the muddy sea bottom. What a witless business! Yet short of storming the floating palace barehanded he had no choice but to trust Yasmi—after all, Lynette did. Huddled under a cloak provided by the pretty Persian, Gareth asked a second time, "Where are we going?"

"Hush," Yasmi told him, "we are almost there."

Without warning a dark vessel loomed ahead of them, nearly invisible and showing no lights. Yasmi hurriedly took in sail, and Gareth made out a boat hull with a hugely oversized rig. Paddling nimbly alongside, Yasmi called out a cheery Tartar greeting. Gareth sat bolt upright cursing in surprise, seeing it was indeed a Tartar flying-boat sitting hull down on the water, keeping silent watch on the floating palace.

Gareth was grabbed and taken aboard, then bound to a wooden yoke in the flying-boat's tiny cabin. Sitting roped to the wicker deck, unable to use his hands, he felt the craft take off—first the splash of ballast bags, then the light giddy feeling of lift-off. Airborne again. Headed east this time, straight downwind toward Tartar territory and a painful interview with his former Noyan. When Yasmi came to feed him, Gareth demanded angrily, "How could you betray us so?"

"Betray who?" Yasmi looked prettily perplexed, spooning some yogurt for him since Gareth could not use his hands.

"Me. Khwarezm. Your Queen . . ." The list went on and on.

"Tush." Yasmi shook her head. "Have some yogurt, it is honeyed. I betrayed no one—no one that mattered at least."

Tartars were infamous poisoners but he took the yogurt anyway. "What about Lynette? You claimed to love her . . ."

"I do," Yasmi protested, wiping his face, then spooning more yogurt. "But you heard who they spoke of, the Caliph in Baghdad, the King of Georgia. Are they going to free Lynette?" Not likely. The Caliph and the King of Georgia were a pair of weak sisters who feared Khwarezm more than the Tartars—showing how little they knew the Tartars.

Yasmi fed him more yogurt, asking, "Are Kipchaks, Kazaks, and Cumans going to stop your Noyan?" Gareth admitted they would not. Yasmi grinned, and wiped his lips. "Then logically we must take our case to the Tartars."

Who knew harem slaves were schooled in logic? Yasmi planned this perfectly, having something immediate to offer the Tartars—him. Plus she knew who in the harem opposed Prince Bayazid, and how to get hold of Inaljuk, the Turk who had hurt them the most; things the Tartars would pay well to know. The boat came down in the Black Sands Desert east of Khwarezm, and by dawn the next day Gareth was back in the Tartar camp, still bound to his yoke, kneeling before the Noyan he had betrayed—having lost Lynette, and feeling like he would be flayed for nothing. Nor did his one-eyed Noyan make him feel any better, wearing that same sad indulgent look as when he condemned Lynette. Gareth listened to Yasmi offer to trade Inaljuk for him, saying, "Spare this poor hapless barbarian, and I seek no other reward."

"Extremely generous terms," the Noyan declared, as if that made them particularly suspicious. "What about the woman this barbarian left with? We have heard that one of the Shah's yellow-haired wives is pregnant."

"Not this one," Yasmi lied blandly. "Trust me, a woman would know."

"Yes, a woman would," the Noyan agreed significantly, not the least fooled. Whoever brought in Inaljuk would greatly please the Tartar Khan, and the loss of Lynette could well be overlooked. What did another knocked-up blonde more or less really matter? "Whether this wife is pregnant or not, we want Inaljuk most of all."

"Before he joins Bayazid," Yasmi suggested amiably. The Noyan nodded, not ashamed to discuss strategy with harem girls and half-wit barbarians—being far too concerned with winning to care for appearances. Yasmi claimed that Inaljuk would soon be taking the floating palace north to join Bayazid, concluding that, "With an *arban* of flying-boats we can intercept him."

We can? Gareth dared not object, trying to look happy and confident, no easy task with a wooden yoke about his neck. Luckily he was a witless barbarian, barely able to carry out orders correctly and seldom consulted in a crisis.

His Noyan nodded. "Give us Inaljuk and you get your freedom. We will melt down the reward, and pour it into his eyes and ears, should we be lucky enough to take him alive."

Keeping that jovial reminder of Tartar justice in mind, they set out. *Arban* means "troop" in Tartar and consisted of three flying-boats, which were towed by galleys across the Inland Sea, from the Black Sands Desert to a cove north of Baku, where the White Salt steppe merged with the marshy shore of the Inland Sea—a secluded region inhabited by pagan Turks and Christian nomads, who did their best to ignore the trio of Tartar flying-boats. Wind permitting, one boat was always tethered aloft like a huge kite, watching for sign of the moving palace.

When the palace was spotted, headed north for Cuman country, winds were light at sea level and westerly aloft—perfect for maneuvering the lumbering palace. And for what Yasmi had planned. Gareth departed with Yasmi in the lead boat, which dropped ballast and rose aerostatically, flying swiftly eastward until it reached pressure height, where they could look down upon the palace gardens and see the big balloon towed aloft. Yasmi studied the balloon through a Cathayan tube with glass at both ends, announcing, "There are four streamers flying from the bottom of the pavilion—one gold, one black, and two blue. That means Lynette, Inaljuk, and two guards. And the basket is up."

Lowering the spyglass Yasmi told him, "You and I are the only ones I can trust for this." Gareth nodded; no Tartar could be trusted not to kill Lynette. Useless with a bow, he armed himself with a Tartar scimitar, and thrust a pair of fire maces through his belt. Yasmi took nothing but the spyglass; both were dressed in tumbler's pants and tight jackets, the safest clothes for working aloft. By releasing gas, the sky boat was able to bear down on the big balloon. Yasmi's plan leaned heavily on surprise since no one in the pavilion below could see them coming, and Inaljuk would not be expecting an attack from above.

Adept at midair maneuvers, the Tartar crew set down directly atop the balloon. As soon as Gareth and Yasmi leaped down onto the gasbag, the lightened flying-boat shot away to windward, leaving them alone, clinging to the balloon netting. Crawling hand-over-hand, Gareth followed Yasmi to a rope ladder that led down to the pavilion. From there on he went first, warily watching where he put each foot. At first all he saw was the broad silk balloon and the blue water below, but gradually the pavilion roof came into view. Thankfully it was empty.

When operated as a free balloon, the roof doubled as a control deck, but right now it was deserted. Descending past the line of ballast bags, Gareth drew level with the top floor of the pavilion, but found the curtains closed—no telling who was inside. Signaling to Yasmi he decided to drop down to the lower balcony, doubting they would keep Lynette next to the control deck and gas-release lines. He was right, and as soon as his feet hit the lower balcony he saw a surprised and happy Lynette lounging in her pajamas. Jumping up she cried, "My knight!"

Gareth signed for silence. Too late; the trap in the floor opened and a helmeted guard emerged, directly between them, crouched behind a wicker shield and clutching a scimitar.

Knowing he must act quickly, Gareth stepped into the room, drawing a fire mace from his belt and breaking it against the man's upraised shield. The mace's glass head shattered, allowing naphtha and an igniter to come together, bursting into flames. Horrified, the guard leaped about, trying desperately to rid himself of the flaming shield, finally managing to fling it from the balcony. Gareth was right behind him, giving the man a shove, sending him tumbling after the burning shield.

Spinning about, Gareth saw Lynette and Yasmi stamping out bits of burning naphtha with their slippers. He took over, telling them, "Down, into the basket."

For once, both obeyed, but just as he finished smothering the last sparks, Inaljuk and another guard appeared on the stairs, alarmed by the fiery commotion below them. Gareth drew his second mace, a deadly threat aboard a balloon filled with explosive vapor. His opponents froze in abject horror.

As they did, Gareth felt the balloon give a lurch. Lynette and Yasmi had released the cable to the palace, so now the pavilion was hanging from a free balloon, drifting slowly downwind—the signal Gareth was waiting for. He tossed the fire mace to Inaljuk, who hastened to catch it, while Gareth dropped down into the basket, closing the trap behind him.

Yasmi already had her hand on the basket release, pulling it as soon as he closed the trap—attached to it was a brake line that allowed the basket to be lowered in flight. They dropped like a stone until Gareth threw his weight on the brake lever, helping Yasmi hold it down. At the last moment they both let go and the line slipped free, dropping them into the sea. Caulked and weighted to float upright, the basket bobbed like a cork in the warm waters. They were down and safe, thank Allah.

Looking up, Gareth saw the big balloon drifting slowly eastward toward the Black Sands Desert, watched over by the three flying-boats. More flying-boats were waiting in Tartar territory to bring down the balloon and take Inaljuk home to the Great Khan, which should satisfy the Tartars for the time being—at least until they disposed of Bayazid. Delighted to have his most dangerous enemies rending each other, Gareth slid the scimitar into his scabbard.

Lynette laughed uproariously, throwing her arms around his neck. "You were magnificent. Her Majesty the Queen Mother will be grateful when she hears, and will lavish rewards on my brave and brilliant champion."

Gareth smiled down at her, saying, "Brave, maybe." Yasmi had planned everything; he was just the big barbarian muscle.

"Brilliant beyond belief," she insisted. "You chose me over every other woman in Khwarezm, sight unseen." Lynette knelt down in the bottom of the basket and thanked Allah first hand for sending her such a knight, when she was so desperately in need.

Kwantum Babes

Neal Barrett, Jr.

"**W**OWEEE!" SAID BOBBY LEE SPOCK, WHICH IS what Spock said whenever he was stunned, staggered, stupefied by long-legged girls, girls with belly buttons, girls with good knees, girls with painted toes, girls in high-stepping heels that could squash a bug or two. The goodies he could see, and all the stuff he couldn't, stuff that whirled about like NGC one-five-one-two, which had once brought Spock to self-abuse as a NASA drunkie in Old Mexico.

Spock, who had a weakness for Dos Equis beer, barred spiral galaxies, and women who were under twenty-two, knew, with a glance from the lobby, this seminar was likely a bust except for the broad array of babes and a well-stocked bar. One good clue was the city itself, which was Cincinnati, and not Las Vegas, Miami, or even Buffalo. Clue number two was the hotel's dim marquee that read

WELCOME SCIENSE GUYS

Not a good start, but a beer might help, a beer and one of the lovelies who scampered like wide-eyed does about the room . . .

"Hey, attention, Spock on the bridge!" said Dickie Vernal, before Spock could veer off to the bar. Everyone had a good laugh, a good haw-haw, Eddie Mass and Lew Bender and Max von Vorhaut who smelled like cheese, and Jackie B. Quick who was seven feet tall.

"Dickie," Spock said, going right for the kill, "put on a little, have you? Fifty, sixty pounds or so?"

"Haw!" said Bender and Mass, Jackie and Max.

"You bring your lovely wife, Bobby Lee," said Dickie, coming back fast, you had to give the asshole that, "how's my favorite Louisiana gal?"

"In Cedar Rapids, with a gentleman who's heavy into wheat, soy, and illegal enterprise. How's the Vernal bunch, Dicko? Darryl out of high school yet?"

"Darryl's a real good boy," Dickie said, peering at his glass like it didn't look right, like a bird maybe dropped by, left him a surprise.

"Hey, sure he is. Can't everyone be of the cranial persuasion. Someone's got to make those fries."

Nobody but Eddie Mass laughed. Dickie went red. He wanted to go for Bobby Lee, but went for a drink instead.

"That was somewhat unkind," said Lew.

"Downright mean," Jackie said.

"Fuck him," Bobby Lee said. "He knows Aileene took off, he didn't have to ask."

"I'm feeling a real high energy emission from that redhead over there," Eddie said.

"You're feeling something in your pocket," Bobby Lee said. "Say, where's our Nobel farter, the distinguished Dr. Ziggit? His name was on the list."

"Phil's dead," Lew said, "can't make it this year."

"Oh, man."

"Fell off ze big dome at Mount Vilson," said Max. "Very sad t'ing."

"What the hell was he doing up there?"

"Looking at ze stars."

"You look at the stars from the *inside*, Max."

"I knew zat."

"Good man," Bender said, "gave a lot to the field."

Eddie emptied his glass. "I won't ever look at a gas giant again without thinking of Phil."

"Damn right."

"No shit."

"Amen to that."

Bobby Lee went right to her, as any man would, for she was unique, the brightest star about, a singularity, a doll, a gravity well of lust and sweet desire.

"Hi, I'm Bobby Lee Spock," he told her, "sorry about the name, daddy came from the Doc Spock branch, not the one with ears. Got to *tell* everyone before they do the other thing."

The girl blinked china-blue eyes. "What other thing is that?"

"Well, bless you, love. Bobby Lee's the name, astrophysics is my game. And you'd be whom—I mean, besides the most knocked-out honey I have ever had the pleasure to gaze upon in Cincinnati or anywhere else. Hope you don't think I'm forward, miss, but life is shorter than we think, and time, though relative at best, and, if you get down to it, isn't really there at all, appears to be fleeting to beings such as you and I."

"You and me."

"Right. Show me a science nerd, I'll show you a guy flunked third grade twice."

"I'm Celeste," she said. "Celeste duSpheer."

"Woweee. You're something else, Celeste. I mean that, I'm totally sincere."

He was, too. For this was a fox without a blemish or a freckle or a mole or a mark. All the right stuff, all the lovely parts just where they ought to be. The golden hair and the honeybee tan, the wide-wide lips and tilty nose. Everything was perfect, everything that ought to curve did.

Bobby Lee didn't know where to look. Latch onto one place —*bam!* Your eyes wander off to something else.

"You are flat staring at me, Bobby Lee," Celeste said. "I think I ought to blush."

"Say, if I'm out of line, I do apologize. I'm simply stricken by your charms, Celeste duSpheer, I mean that in a most respectful way."

"I don't think you're out of line at all. I do think you lack a little polish, that you're kinda short of cool, that *crude* might be a step up on a scale from one to two. But I'll overlook that, Bobby Lee Spock, for I am simply nuts about stuff from outer space."

She touched his chin with a cherry-pink nail, a gesture that chilled him, thrilled him, nearly dashed him to the floor.

"I'm not going to let you get away until you tell me everything. I want to know *all* about the stars."

"Oh, well, everything, right?" Bobby Lee badly wanted a drink, but didn't dare quit, didn't want to stop the flow.

"First, there's a whole lot of stars. Billions and billions, and many we can't even see. There's red stars and blue stars, and yellow stars too. The nebulae, now, that's the birthplace of stars. You're a lady, I can see, I won't go into that.

"Then you got your galaxies, which are lots of stars at once. There's your roundies and your tilties and whirlies of every sort. I guess my favorite's old NGC one-five-one-two, a really pretty sight. Some of 'em, now, aren't attractive at all. One good example is your excremental galaxy which is giving off gas all the time. No offense, that's what they've got to do.

"There's urinal energy everywhere you look. You maybe can't see it, but it's there. See, that's the mystery of space. You're in the trade, you learn to live with it, okay? Now and then you get a break. We had a bunch of hydrogen missing but we found a lot of that . . ."

Bobby Lee paused to get his breath. Celeste was so close he could inhale the fumes from her basically animal self.

"I didn't know *any* of that, Bobby Lee. It all makes you feel so— small."

"Astronomy's not as hard as your average person might suspect. I mean, it's not like being a doctor, or a guy that fixes cars."

"Oh, I think it's much more important than that."

"No, really, I'm sincere about this. It's not like on *Discovery,* Cele, if I may call you that. I'm just a man like anybody else, a man with hopes, dreams, a man who can experience sadness and joy, a man who has *needs,* you know? You, I think, and I'm kind of sensing this, might understand those needs. You know what I'm saying, you with me on this?"

If she was, it was only for an instant, and when the spell was broken, she was gone, leaving him with wants, desires, needs unfulfilled, and the musky, haunting scent of her presence, steamy flesh and whiskey, hair spray and Joy. Bar peanuts and a subtle hint of dip.

Eddie Mass was going for the bar with Lew Bender, the gaunt, wasted form of Max von Vorhaut trailing along in the rear.

"That now, that is some chickie, man, that is a sweetie, that is a dish. That is a babe old Dr. Eddie could give up tenure for."

"Her name is Celeste duSpheer. She wants to know all about the stars."

Eddie rolled his eyes. "You tell her about the great, cosmic orgasm at the beginning of time? You tell her how it got all hot and big and there was this incredible explosion and the universe came into being, and if we really care for each other, we can share that moment, too?"

"Damn," said Jackie.

"I was getting to that," Bobby said. "She wandered off somewhere."

"Zat one, now," said Max, "ze vun with the hair like witchy moss. I am feeling ze deviation, I am feeling ze acts unspoken here."

Lew Bender said, "Witchy moss. What the fuck is that?"

"Where you figure they come from?" Bobby said, feeling unsteady, slightly off center, ready for another beer that might bring the world into focus once again. "The room's full of lookers, man. I'm getting a totally new concept of Ohio."

"Hotel," Eddie said. "Guy at the desk told me. They've got this list. Hire 'em for the big conventions everywhere. Not hookers or anything, totally respectable girls. Secretaries, models, ladies like that."

"Yeah, right." The room was beginning to waver for Bobby, another dimension creeping in. "I've got a secretary, looks like my Aunt Auderbeck."

"The one in the fire engine dress?" Bender nodded toward the bar. "Look at those binaries, pal."

"I'm looking, I'm looking."

"I talked to Stuart, he iss here," von Vorhaut said. "He vas at Columbia, two veeks back. Berthold Zeck iss dead."

"Berthold?" Bobby Lee had to grab at the bar. "I went to the MIT with Zeck. God, he isn't any older than I am."

"He iss dead."

"I *heard* you, Max. Oh, hell, Bertie? I can't believe that."

"He gave us a great deal," Bender said. "He was a man before his time."

"He left a shitload of knowledge in his wake," Eddie said. "They can't take that away, we'll always have that."

"I won't ever look at dark matter again, I don't think about him," Bobby Lee said.

"Never be another."

"No lie, man."

"I vill drink to zat."

She was dark, dusky, delicate, and fine, a product, likely, of a Delhi maiden and a tourist from Milan, a teacher of French and a pom-pon girl from Tahiti Junior High. She of the orchid lips and teaky eyes, a startling contrast to the blonde, blatantly naughty Celeste.

Yet, this sweet as a mango honey with breasts like new tennis balls right out of the can, reeked with the smoldering sexuality that, in centuries past, had driven a thousand British sailor lads mad.

"Hi," Bobby Lee said, "don't think we've met. Bobby Lee Spock from the Doc Spock clan, not the one with ears. Woweee, you smell like bougainvillea on a hot steamy night. I bet you're a knock-out in a sarong, something with a kinda hibiscus motif, maybe a *H. tiliaeus*, something like that. My ex used to grow 'em, that's how I know the names. I hope I'm not imposing, okay? Can I get you a drink, one of those weenies they cram inside of dough? My God, who thinks up that stuff? Sorry, I didn't get your name."

"How do you do, Bobby Lee Spock. I am Betty Sue Hilo-kawani."

"Oh, man. Know what that sounds like to me, your voice, the way you do your name? Sounds like wind through the palms, dawn, coming up in the islands, I love that, what island you from?"

"Depew. That's on Highway 44 between Oke City and Tulsa. Legend has it, though, my people came from Dallas long ago."

"You are cute, you know? You are just cute as you can be. I'm with the astro bunch, I bet you guessed that. You met anyone else? God, I hope not."

"Him," said Betty Sue, shifting almond eyes across the room. "Dr. Dickie Vernal. I believe he's in the particle physics game."

"Dandruff's a particle, and Dickie's into that." Bobby Lee blinked, for there seemed to be two Dickies now, and, as a matter of fact, two of everyone else. How come you never know before you've had one too many, instead of the two after that?

"I am real excited 'bout the facts of science," said Betty Sue from Depew, in a sweet, Oahu/Oklahoma kind of twang. "There's a lot I'd like to know."

"I'll—try and remember something," Bobby Lee said, making every effort to continue standing up. He tried not to think about the awesome speed of light, about quarks, quirks, quacks, and the like. Space was a sobering thought, but not quite enough.

"Okay, first there's creation, you heard about that. Big Bang, lot of nucleosynthesis going on. Made a lot of hydrogen, helium and lithium, too."

"I was on that for a while. I'm not anymore."

"Right. Aileene was too. Didn't help a bit. You got a real healthy conical mass there, you know? No offense, Mary Lou."

"Betty Sue."

"Another thing you got is your runaway neutron star. It's runaway, see, because you wouldn't even *know* it was there if it wasn't just bare-ass naked, all alone, zipping around without a friend of any sort."

"How awful for it."

"How do you know? How do you know it has feelings, needs, any comprehension of fast food, credit, Madonna, and the Pips?"

Bobby Lee laughed. There was something funny there, but he couldn't think what.

"Truth is, everything matters, Annie Lou. Even matter matters. Just think of something, it matters. Twitch your little finger, whamo —you got a red shift out past the Dogs, out past the Crux."

"I had a black shift once. Wore it to a dance in Muskogee, they made me go home. Listen, you okay?"

"Some enchanted *eve*-ning . . ."

"What?"

"I tell you Aileene used to grow hibuscus? Hibiscii? I liked the yellow ones best. Didn't like the reds. I think I'd like to sit down."

"You're already sittin' down, Bobby Lee."

"Say, you sure look real good up there. Did I introduce myself? Bobby Lee Spock. Dr. Spock, as a fact. Berkeley, NASA, the MIT, not the other guy, don't get me started on that . . ."

"What happens, is, there's a whole bunch of stars. Billions and zillions, and seven we can't even see. There's red stars an' blue stars and—"

"—yellow stars, too. You told me, you don't have to tell me again."

"I did?" Bobby Lee blinked. Something pounded in his head. "Did I mention quarks at all?"

"Not to me. I expect that was somebody else."

He noted, then, that her hair was gold, and her eyes were blue. Wide lips. Good tan. Tilty-type nose.

"You're the other one. Celeste. What happened to Betty Sue?"

"It's just you and me, pal. Everybody's gone."

"Huh?" Bobby peered around the big ballroom. She was right. There was no one there. No babes, no science guys, no one at all. Two sleepy waiters cleaning up. Plastic cups and cigarette butts. Canapés on the floor.

"Party's over," said Celeste, helping him to his feet, somewhat stronger, for sure, than she appeared. "Let's step outside, get a little air."

Outside was the parking lot behind the hotel. The air was Cincinnati, burger parts, auto farts, waste of every sort. Dog-do, effusions, Midwest delusions.

"We need to talk," Celeste said. "There's something I want to say, Bobby Lee."

"We could do this upstairs. Have a little drink, do a little talking and stuff up there."

"That's where everyone is. Upstairs. Every astrophysical guy has taken a girl up to his room. Their purpose is to remove the girl's clothing and engage in copulation. This is why you wish to take *me* upstairs, Dr. Bobby Lee Spock. You would like to touch my secret places and enter every orifice you can.

"This will not happen. However, in the morning, every man of the science persuasion will awaken with a feeling of satiated parts. He will believe he has reached the orgasmic state many times, with a female consumed with unbridled passion and lust."

"Hold it a minute, I've had a lot to drink, babe, you're not coming through . . ."

"You will *not* call me a babe!" Celeste gave him a look that nearly brought him to his knees. "I am not a babe, I am not a cutie or a honey or a broad. I am not a doll or a sweetie or a hump. I am not a human, I am not from your world, science guy, I am from the galaxy you call ESO one-five-zero dash six-one-three."

"Woweee, no kidding?" Bobby Lee was understandably taken aback. "Cripes, that's the warpie, the frisbee, I love it—looks like God tossing pizza dough about in the cold and perilous realm of outer space. It's my favorite, really, I mean, next to NGC one-five-one-two. Say, how do you people get around the problem of Light? Don't tell me, it's a quantum thing, right?"

Celeste glanced up at the sky, at the stars, which were very far away, as a dense, oppressive layer of smog had settled in over down-town Cincinnati.

"I must tell you that we utterly detest your planet, Bobby Lee. Many of your females are weak, useless vessels for your seed, though much has been accomplished through Janet Reno and Cher.

"Your males are crude, insufferable oafs. Vile, offensive, and odorous creatures with nothing on their minds but football, nookie, and beer."

"I don't think that's entirely true—"

"Members of our race are gathering at astrophysical conventions all over the world. There, we will implant our messages in science guys as they dream of corrupting our parts.

"You have been looking at galactic spheres long enough, Bobby Lee. You will all go forth and destroy your observatories and other methods of seeing. You will remove the despicable Hubble device at once. You will help carry this message to other astronomical persons as well."

Bobby Lee was as sober as he ever intended to be. "I can't believe any of this is true, Celeste. It couldn't be. You're—lovely, desirable. Your dimensions are perfect and you certainly are tall. I think we could mean something to each other. I'm thinking in more than a physical way, though we'd want to do that too . . ."

"No. We would not. I am lovely and desirable because I am able to reach your weakness that way. When I leave you in a moment, you will not remember me at all."

"Oh, I will, Celeste. We may come from different worlds but—"

Celeste kicked off her high heels. Kicked off her high heels and kicked off—*kicked off her feet as well, stood there in nothing but her bare and dirty hooves* . . .

"Oh, man. . . !" Bobby Lee felt his stomach turn over, felt as if he'd surely throw up. "You're an ungulate, right? Jesus, Cele, I can't handle this."

"We are of the Kow people. Our race is old and wise. Yours is young and foolish. I doubt you will survive."

"Does the—rest of you look like that?"

Celeste, for only an instant, let one shoulder strap fall free. "Trust me, repulsive human male, you don't want to know . . ."

A hot breeze reached him on the dense night air. Bobby Lee heard laughter from the hotel kitchen. Someone said something in Spanish, or possibly Sudanese. A stunning, very tall blonde caught his eye.

"Pardon me," Bobby Lee said, "I'm Bobby Lee Spock, from the Doc Spock clan, not the ones with ears. I can tell from here you've got stars in your eyes, and stars are old Bobby Lee's game . . ."

For Scott Cupp

Fire Dog

Joe R. Lansdale

$\mathcal{W}$HEN JIM APPLIED FOR THE DISPATCHER JOB the fire department turned him down, but the Fire Chief offered him something else.

"Our fire dog, Rex, is retiring. You might want that job. Pays good and the retirement is great."

"Fire dog?" Jim said.

"That's right."

"Well, I don't know . . ."

"Suit yourself."

Jim considered. "I suppose I could give it a try—"

"Actually, we prefer greater dedication than that. We don't just want someone to give it a try. Being fire dog is an important job."

"Very well," Jim said. "I'll take it."

"Good."

The Chief opened a drawer, pulled out a spotted suit with tail and ears, pushed it across the desk.

"I have to wear this?"

"How the hell you gonna be the fire dog, you don't wear the suit?"

"Of course."

Jim examined the suit. It had a hole for his face, his bottom, and what his mother had called his pee-pee.

324

"Good grief," Jim said. "I can't go around with my . . . well, you know, my stuff hanging out."

"How many dogs you see wearing pants?"

"Well, Goofy comes to mind."

"Those are cartoons. I haven't got time to screw around here. You either want the job, or you don't."

"I want it."

"By the way. You sure Goofy's a dog?"

"Well, he looks like a dog. And he has that dog, Pluto."

"Pluto, by the way, doesn't wear pants."

"You got me there."

"Try on the suit, let's see if it needs tailoring."

The suit fit perfectly, though Jim did feel a bit exposed. Still, he had to admit there was something refreshing about the exposure. He wore the suit into the break room, following the Chief.

Rex, the current fire dog, was sprawled on the couch watching a cop show. His suit looked worn, even a bit smoke stained. He was tired around the eyes. His jowls drooped.

"This is our new fire dog," the Chief said.

Rex turned and looked at Jim, said, "I'm not out the door, already you got a guy in the suit?"

"Rex, no hard feelings. You got what, two, three days? We got to be ready. You know that."

Rex sat up on the couch, adjusted some pillows and leaned into them. "Yeah, I know. But, I've had this job nine years."

"And in dog years that's a lot."

"I don't know why I can't just keep being the fire dog. I think I've done a good job."

"You're our best fire dog yet. Jim here has a lot to live up to."

"I only get to work nine years?" Jim said.

"In dog years you'd be pretty old, and it's a decent retirement."

"Is he gonna take my name too?" Rex said.

"No," the Chief said, "of course not. We'll call him Spot."

"Oh, that's rich," said Rex. "You really worked on that one."

"It's no worse than Rex."

"Hey, Rex is a good name."

"I don't like Spot," Jim said. "Can't I come up with something else?"

"Dogs don't name themselves," the Chief said. "Your name is Spot."

"Spot," Rex said, "don't you think you ought to get started by coming over here and sniffing my butt?"

The first few days at work Spot found riding on the truck to be uncomfortable. He was always given a tool box to sit on so that he could be seen, as this was the fire department's way. They liked the idea of the fire dog in full view, his ears flapping in the wind. It was very promotional for the mascot to be seen.

Spot's exposed butt was cold on the tool box, and the wind not only blew his ears around, it moved another part of his anatomy about. That was annoying.

He did, however, enjoy the little motorized tail-wagging device he activated with a touch of a finger. He found that got him a lot of snacks from the fire men. He was especially fond of the liver snacks.

After three weeks on the job, Spot found his wife Shella to be very friendly. After dinner one evening, when he went to the bedroom to remove his dog suit, he discovered Shella lying on their bed wearing a negligee and a pair of dog ears attached to a hair band.

"Feel frisky, Spot?"

"Jim."

"Whatever. Feel frisky?"

"Well, yeah. Let me shed the suit, take a shower . . ."

"You don't need a shower . . . And baby, leave the suit on, will you?"

They went at it.

"You know how I want it," she said.

"Yeah. Doggie style."

"Good boy."

After sex, Shella liked to scratch his belly and behind his ears. He used the tail-wagging device to show how much he appreciated it. This wasn't so bad, he thought. He got less when he was a man.

Though his sex life had improved, Spot found himself being put outside a lot, having to relieve himself in a corner of the yard while his wife looked in the other direction, her hand in a plastic bag, ready to use to pick up his deposits.

He only removed his dog suit now when Shella wasn't around. She liked it on him at all times. At first he was insulted, but the sex was so good, and his life was so good, he relented. He even let her call him Spot all the time.

When she wasn't around, he washed and dried his suit carefully, ironed it. But he never wore anything else. When he rode the bus to work, everyone wanted to pet him. One woman even asked if he liked poodles because she had one.

At work he was well respected, and enjoyed being taken to schools with the Fire Chief. The Chief talked about fire prevention. Spot wagged his tail, sat up, barked, looked cute by turning his head from side to side.

He was even taken to his daughter's class once. He heard her say proudly to a kid sitting next to her, "That's my Daddy. He's the fire dog."

His chest swelled with pride. He made his tail wag enthusiastically.

The job really was the pip. You didn't have fires every day, so Spot laid around all day most days, on the couch sometimes, though some of the fireman would run him off and make him lie on the floor when they came in. But the floor had rugs on it and the television was always on, though he was not allowed to change the channels. Some kind of rule, a union thing. The fire dog can not and will not change channels.

He did hate having to take worm medicine, and the annual required trips to the vet were no picnic either. Especially the thermometer up the ass part.

But, hell, it was a living, and not a bad one. Another plus was after several months of trying, he was able to lick his balls.

At night, when everyone was in their bunks and there were no fires, Spot would read from *Call of the Wild*, *White Fang*, *Dog Digest*, or such, or lie on his back with all four feet in the air, trying to look cute.

He loved it when the firemen came in and caught him that way and ooohheeed and ahhhhhed and scratched his belly or patted his head.

This went on for just short of nine years. Then, one day, while he was lying on the couch, licking his ass—something he cultivated after three years on the job—the Fire Chief and a guy in a dog suit came in.

"This is your replacement, Spot," the Chief said.

"What?"

"Well, it has been nine years."

"You didn't tell me. Has it been? You're sure? Aren't you supposed to warn me? Rex knew his time was up. Remember?"

"Not exactly. But if you say so. Spot, meet Hal."

"Hal? What kind of dog's name is that? Hal?"

But it was no use. By the end of the day he had his personal dog biscuits, pinups from Dog Digest, and his worm-away medicine packed. There was also a spray can the firemen used to mist on his poop to keep him from eating it. The can of spray didn't really belong to him, but he took it anyway.

He picked up his old clothes, went into the changing room. He hadn't worn anything but the fire dog suit in years, and it felt odd to try his old clothes on. He could hardly remember ever wearing them. He found they were a bit moth-eaten, and he had gotten a little too plump for them. The shoes fit, but he couldn't tolerate them.

He kept the dog suit on.

He caught the bus and went home.

"What? You lost your job?" his wife said.

"I didn't lose anything. They retired me."

"You're not the fire dog?"

"No. Hal is the fire dog."

"I can't believe it. I give you nine great years—"

"We've been married eleven."

"I only count the dog years. Those were the good ones, you know."

"Well, I don't have to quit being a dog. Hell, I am a dog."

"You're not the fire dog. You've lost your position, Spot. Oh, I can't even stand to think about it. Outside. Go on. Git. Outside."

Spot went.

After a while he scratched on the door, but his wife didn't let him in. He went around back and tried there. That didn't work either. He looked in the windows, but couldn't see her.

He laid down in the yard.

That night it rained, and he slept under the car, awakened just in time to keep his wife from backing over him on her way to work.

That afternoon he waited, but his wife did not return at the usual time. Five o'clock was when he came home from the fire house, and she was always waiting, and he had a feeling it was at least five o'clock, and finally the sun went down and he knew it was late.

Still, no wife.

Finally, he saw headlights and a car pulled into the drive. Shella got out. He ran to meet her. To show he was interested, he hunched her leg.

She kicked him loose. He noticed she was holding a leash. Out of the car came Hal.

"Look who I got. A real dog."

Spot was dumbfounded.

"I met him today at the fire house, and well, we hit it off."

"You went by the fire house?"

"Of course."

"What about me?" Spot asked.

"Well, Spot, you are a little old. Sometimes, things change. New blood is necessary."

"Me and Hal, we're going to share the house?"

"I didn't say that."

She took Hal inside. Just before they closed the door, Hal slipped a paw behind Shella's back and shot Spot the finger.

When they were inside, Spot scratched on the door in a half-hearted way. No soap.

Next morning Shella hustled him out of the shrubbery by calling his name. She didn't have Hal with her.

Great! She had missed him. He bounded out, his tongue dangling like a wet sock. "Come here, Spot."

He went. That's what dogs did. When the master called, you went to them. He was still her dog. Yes sirree, Bob.

"Come on, boy." She hustled him to the car.

As he climbed inside on the back seat and she shut the door, he saw Hal come out of the house stretching. He looked pretty happy. He walked over to the car and slapped Shella on the butt.

"See you later, baby."

"You bet, you dog you."

Hal walked down the street to the bus stop. Spot watched him by turning first to the back glass, then rushing over to the side view glass.

Shella got in the car.

"Where are we going?" Spot asked.

"It's a surprise," she said.

"Can you roll down the window back here a bit?"

"Sure."

Spot stuck his head out as they drove along, his ears flapping, his tongue hanging.

They drove down a side street, turned and tooled up an alley. Spot thought he recognized the place.

Why yes, the vet. They had come from another direction and he hadn't spotted it right off, but that's where he was.

He unhooked the little tag that dangled from his collar. Checked the dates of his last shots.

No. Nothing was overdue.

They stopped and Shella smiled. She opened the back door and took hold of the leash. "Come on, Spot."

Spot climbed out of the car, though carefully. He wasn't as spry as he once was.

Two men were at the back door. One of them was the doctor. The other an assistant.

"Here's Spot," she said.

"He looks pretty good," said the doctor.

"I know. But . . . Well, he's old and has his problems. And I have too many dogs."

She left him there.

The vet checked him over and called the animal shelter. "There's nothing really wrong with him," he told the attendant that came for him. "He's just old, and well, the woman doesn't want to care for him. He'd be great with children."

"You know how it is, Doc," said the attendant. "Dogs all over the place."

Later, at the animal shelter he stood on the cold concrete and smelled the other dogs. He barked at the cats he could smell. Fact was, he found himself barking anytime anyone came into the corridor of pens.

Sometimes men and woman and children came and looked at him.

None of them chose him. The device in his tail didn't work right, so he couldn't wag as ferociously as he liked. His ears were pretty droopy and his jowls hung way too low.

"He looks like his spots are fading," said one woman whose little girl had stuck her fingers through the grating so Spot could lick her hand.

"His breath stinks," she said.

As the days went by, Spot tried to look perky all the time. Hoping for adoption.

But one day, they came for him, wearing white coats and grim faces, brandishing a leash and a muzzle and a hypodermic needle.

Three thousand copies of this book have been printed by the Maple-Vail Book Manufacturing Group, Binghamton, NY, for Golden Gryphon Press, Urbana, IL. The typeset is Electra, printed on 55# Sebago. Typesetting by The Composing Room, Inc., Kimberly, WI.

Water damage noted 2/25/05